# "Do you *know* any games?"

It was such an extraordinary question that it threw Indigo completely and, as she floundered, another child piped, "We have seen you. We know you are the foreign healer. Will you heal us?"

Indigo had no warning but, as the child spoke, intuition suddenly and shockingly displaced logic, and the shock was redoubled as, at the same moment, she realized that she could see the contours of the drab hall not only behind the children, but *through* them. Their bodies were translucent.

She only had time to say, "Sweet Mother, I—"

The three children vanished. . . .

"A master of fantasy. . . . If Ms. Cooper can sustain this vibrant intensity, it will turn into a real classic."

—*Rave Reviews*

# REVENANT
## BOOK · SEVEN · OF · INDIGO

# LOUISE · COOPER

A TOM DOHERTY ASSOCIATES BOOK
NEW YORK

This is a work of fiction. All the characters and events portrayed in this book are fictitious, and any resemblance to real people or events is purely coincidental.

REVENANT

Copyright © 1993 by Louise Cooper

Cover art by Robert Gould

A Tor Book
Published by Tom Doherty Associates, Inc.
175 Fifth Avenue
New York, N.Y. 10010

Tor ® is a registered trademark of Tom Doherty Associates, Inc.

ISBN: 0-812-50807-6

First edition: September 1993

Printed in the United States of America

0 9 8 7 6 5 4 3 2 1

O Lord, if there is a Lord
Save my soul, if I have a soul

—*Ernest J. Renan: "A Sceptic's Prayer"*


For Shân,
who has been not only a great agent
but also a great friend

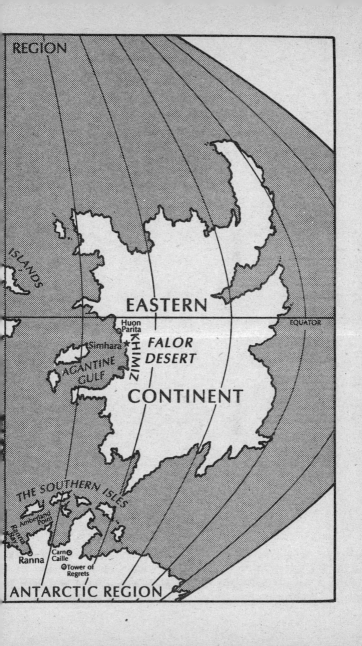

# ·PROLOGUE·

The seasons change slowly and gently in the land that, in the tongue of its inhabitants, is called the Nation of Prosperity. Winters are rarely severe, and the hot months that follow winter meld into autumns so mellow that it seems summer is always reluctant to depart. This is a bare country of hills and valleys and mountains, primitive in many ways. There are few roads linking the isolated and stubbornly independent settlements, and most of the roads that do exist make hard going for the traveler. But travelers are few and far between; each town has little contact with its neighbors, and foreign visitors, though tolerated, are not encouraged to cross the country's borders.

Yet some foreigners do come, for despite its name the Nation of Prosperity is not self-sufficient. The nature of the land has made farmers of its people, but even they cannot thrive on the fruits of their fertile soil alone, and though they may dislike the notion of strangers in their midst, they have an avid desire for the benefits that strangers bring. So the foreigners come; some simply to trade and leave, others to settle and to establish more lasting enterprises. And a few—a very few—simply to seek a place where they can be sure of anonymity; a land where they are neither accepted nor rejected; a land where they may feel, and be, alone.

Indigo is one such traveler. She came to this country for three reasons, or at least that is what she tells herself. Her first desire was to find relief from the sweltering, humid forests of the Dark Isle, where disease and superstition stalk hand in hand, and where she was caught up in a living nightmare whose horrors she wants only to forget. Her second desire was to find a country where no old memories will haunt her, a place where her name and her face will arouse no interest: a place where she can find the space, both physical and mental, to take stock of her life. And the third reason for her sojourn here is to prove that, after more than fifty years of following a path ordained for her by other powers, she has defied her destiny and is at last her own mistress.

Though in fifty years she has met countless people, Indigo's story has been told only to a very few, and by far the majority of those old friends are dead now. Some died because of her—some even at her hand—but most simply aged and faded and went to their natural rest. Had her life been different, had she not taken one small step into folly, Indigo would be an old woman now, nearing the end of her days. But since that calamitous day, half a century ago, when she opened the door of the Tower of Regrets, Indigo has been caught in the limbo of immortality. She does not age, she does not change; she cannot die. And until the seven demons that she released from the Tower are confronted and destroyed, that is how her existence will continue.

Five times Indigo has faced one of those demons. She has triumphed over each one, though more often than not her victories have brought her little comfort, and two more trials still await her. But on the Dark Isle, she learned some new lessons. She learned that deities and demons are not always what they seem, and she learned the extent—and perhaps something of the nature—of her own, human power. And she found the courage—as she sees it—to put aside the duty imposed on her by others and follow her own heart.

For fifty years she carried a lodestone that guided her steps unerringly to her next encounter and her next obligation. Now that lodestone lies at the bottom of the deep, still lake into which Indigo cast it as an ironic offering to an unlikely mentor. Without it, she has felt naked . . . but she has also felt free. And with freedom has come a single desire and a single determination. Indigo has embarked on a new quest. A quest to find the lover she lost fifty years ago— Fenran, her betrothed, caught like herself in a timeless limbo from which he cannot escape. For a long, long time Indigo believed that only when the last demon was conquered could she hope to find him again. Now, though, that belief has been overturned. And neither demons nor gods nor any other power, good or evil or any of the myriad shades between, will sway her from her search. Nothing else matters to her. *Nothing*.

So Indigo travels through the Nation of Prosperity, and while she travels, she makes her plans. Her daily existence is no burden to her; she is long used to living by her wits, and her skills, from herbalism to hunting to the making of music and telling of stories, ensure that she will not starve. And she is not lonely, for by her side, day and night, is the one friend who has shared with her the trials of half a century's wandering. Not a human friend, but Grimya, the brindled she-wolf, cursed at birth by the gift of speech and cast out of her pack as a mutant. The circumstances of their meeting are an ancient joke between them now, but Indigo will never forget the day when Grimya chose to share her burden of immortality, and she knows that, in love and loyalty, the she-wolf has no rival.

Indigo doesn't yet know where her journeyings will take her. With no lodestone to guide her she must rely on instinct alone; but her instinct, she believes, is sure. Fenran is waiting for her. She can find him. She *will* find him. And until she succeeds, there will be no more demons.

Or so she believes . . .

# ·CHAPTER·I·

Although strangers weren't unheard of in the Nation of Prosperity, they were enough of a rarity for the workers toiling in the terraced fields to pause in their labors and watch, shielding their gazes against the slanting sun, as the newcomers went by on the dusty road. Assessing eyes in weather-browned faces followed the progress of the tall young woman riding one sturdy pony and leading another laden with baggage, and the minds behind the eyes each speculated privately on the function and usefulness of the rangy gray dog that padded at the woman's heels. But no one called out to her, either in greeting or in challenge, and a small child who pointed and made a loud remark to his mother was sternly reprimanded and set back to work.

The young woman herself was aware of the scrutiny, but two months in this moist, cool, mountainous country of neat and carefully tended farms and well-organized townships had taught her that it was considered bad form to offer any greeting of her own, or even to acknowledge the laborers'

presence. From the rough map she'd bought at the Foreigners' Duty House at the last sizable town on her route she
had surmised that her next destination was now only a mile
or two ahead, and she calculated that she should reach its
boundaries with an hour or more to spare before sunset.

She hoped that this new settlement would yield more than
the last had done. While she hadn't exactly been driven out
of the town, it had been made emphatically clear to her that
her departure would be welcomed, and only one person—
the middle-aged woman with whom she'd conducted her
business at the Duty House—had unbent sufficiently to add
that the town of Joyful Travail, some thirty miles to the east,
was well known to prosper less diligently than their own
fine settlement and might therefore have need of her skills.
So for three more days she had taken to the road, sleeping
by the trackside (thankful that the chills of autumn didn't
yet have the country in their grip), meeting no one, and
trusting that the woman had been right.

The neat rows of greenstuffs were giving way to terraces
of other crops now: tall beans carefully staked by posts with
hemp twine strung between them, low, shrubby fruit bushes
heavy with dark blue berries, and the exuberant summer
growths of root vegetables that wouldn't be harvested until
the winter. The road was beginning to wind as it turned
down the mountains' gentle flanks, and a few hundred yards
ahead she saw one of the ubiquitous watering-places, a well
shielded by a small stone turret with a thatched roof. The
customary guard stood outside the well-house, but in addition to the now-familiar rigid and silent figure there were
also several others grouped around the entrance. The quality
of their clothes marked them as people of some rank; one,
the young woman noticed as she approached, also wore the
colored sash of a town official.

She would have passed them by without a word or a
look, having learned that this was the correct procedure, but
just before she drew level with them the figure in the sash

stepped from the group and held up his hand, palm outward, signaling her to halt. She reined in, and dismounted two paces from where he stood.

"This is a fine day, and allows for diligence in the fields." The official inclined his head as he spoke, with the precise level of courtesy offered to a foreigner toward whom—as yet—there was no cause for hostility. The young woman made a slightly deeper bow in return and replied to the formal greeting.

"The fields are a great pleasure to the stranger's eye." She had a facility for languages and had learned the tongue of this land quickly, together with its many and varied modes of proper address. "To witness their bounty is an up-lifting experience."

The official was clearly pleased with her answer, for he addressed her directly now. "You are traveling to the town of Joyful Travail?"

"With hope and optimism, sir, yes."

"I see." His eyes, which were unusually pale, raked over her small entourage, then he walked slowly to her ponies and examined them more closely, running an expert hand across their flanks and down their hind legs. One laid its ears back and stamped; the official straightened up.

"These are animals of good quality. Is that what you do? Are you a seller of livestock?"

She shook her head, passing one hand across her face in the sign of self-effacement. "That is not my value. My worth lies elsewhere." She smiled at him. "I am a physician."

"A physician?" The man's expression animated a little. "A useful and worthy profession. Do you hope for employment in Joyful Travail?"

The young woman made another bow. "That is my desire, if there is a requirement for my service."

This was considered for some moments. Then: "It may be so." The official thrust one hand into a pocket set into his sash, and after a moment brought out a short, carved wooden stick with a scrap of orange ribbon tied to it. He held the stick out to her.

"You may take this to the Foreigners' Duty House. Accommodation will be given to you at a fair price, and you may remain in the strangers' enclave until an estimation of your usefulness has been made." He inclined his head and allowed his mouth to curve in a faint, patronizing smile. Realizing this to be a signal that their conversation was concluded, the young woman bowed yet again.

"I thank you for your generosity, and wish you good day."

She remounted, tugged at the pack-pony's leading rope, and moved on. Unlike the field laborers the official didn't trouble to watch after her departing back but turned immediately to resume his discussion with his companions; the low murmur of their voices carried faintly on the breeze as the travelers moved away along the rough road.

For a few minutes all was quiet but for the dull clop of the ponies' hooves and the softer pad of paws in the dust. Then, when there could be no doubt that they were out of earshot of the group by the well-house, the brindled, doglike animal looked back over her shoulder and then up at the young woman's face. Her jaws parted, and a husky, guttural voice issued from her throat.

"I did not l . . . like that man, Indigo. He is not very important, but he thh-inks much of himself."

The young woman's serious face lightened suddenly and her mouth relaxed into a broad smile. These were the first words that Grimya had spoken since the terraces of cultivated fields had come in sight—she had been too afraid to use her voice lest someone should overhear and uncover her secret, which only she and her human friend had shared for more years than either cared to count. Grimya was no dog, but a wolf, born in the forests of the great western continent and cast out from her pack because she was a mutant with the ability to speak in the way of humans. The bond between Grimya and Indigo was unwavering and indissoluble—and that bond was more than fifty years old, for Indigo and Grimya shared another secret, deeper and stranger even than the wolf's mutation. For half a century, since they had embarked together on their long and eventful journeyings, neither had aged by a single day. They were gifted—or cursed—with immortality.

Indigo tried not to dwell on the distant memory of how, through her own folly, she had brought the burden of unaging, unchanging and eternal life upon her own shoulders; but even now she still asked herself why Grimya, who owed her nothing, should have chosen of her own free will to share her burden. Grimya would have given her a simple answer to the question—she was an uncomplicated creature, and her loyalty had no caveats or boundaries—but still, sometimes, Indigo woke in the night and gave silent, bewildered thanks for the wolf's love and companionship, which had been the saving of her on many occasions.

She smiled now at Grimya's words, which were prosaic, blunt, and to the point. In her customary way she had assessed the official and made a judgment; Indigo suspected that, as usual, her judgment was right.

"He was at least willing to be helpful, which is more than we can say for the last people we encountered. And he's given us this token." Gently but emphatically she shook the small stick with its bright ribbon, trying to recall what she'd learned about the extraordinary complexity of rank-colors employed by officials in this land. Orange . . . the shade of a minor official, she thought, but even minor officials carried a good deal of weight in this country where outsiders were looked on with suspicion at best and outright hostility at worst. "If nothing else, it'll guarantee us a few days' respite at the Foreigners' Enclave." She glanced down at Grimya with sympathy. "And a chance to rest your feet!".

They continued on their way, passing more well-kempt

fields, more silently and busily toiling workers. Indigo counted two more of the half-mile posts that had been set at intervals all along this road; then another curve, sharper and steeper than those before it, brought them round the mountain's flank, and they saw the town of Joyful Travail before and below them.

There was little to distinguish it from the last settlement. Rows of neat buildings of one or at most two stories, with roofs of reddish-brown clay tiles, were set about a system of straight, tidy streets of hard-trodden earth. A wooden paling fence surrounded the entire town, with an arched gate set into it that straddled the road.

Indigo slowed and stopped, holding back the ponies as they tried to snatch at the grass growing by the roadside.

"At least the gate's open and there are no guards." She had acid memories of their previous welcome: the officious little bully at the town gate with a cudgel at his belt and a sheaf of rule-papers in his hand; the suspicious escort to see that she didn't deviate from the route that led her to the Foreigners' Duty House; the sense that her status among the townsfolk was somewhat lower than that of a crippled dog. Joyful Travail at least appeared to be open to strangers—and, contrary to what she had been told, it also looked considerably larger and more prosperous than its westerly neighbor. She could see the Foreigners' Duty House, a taller building than most, identifiable by the white pennant that flew from a pole raised on its roof. White, Indigo had learned, denoted the lowest status of all, and it was reserved exclusively for foreigners.

She smiled thinly and tapped her heels against her mount's flanks. But they'd only gone three paces when she realized that Grimya hadn't followed but was hanging back, her posture suddenly tense, her head raised and her ears pricked alertly.

"Grimya, what is it?" Indigo stopped again.

The she-wolf looked at her, her eyes troubled. "D-didn't you hear?"

"Hear what?"

"It was . . ." Grimya hesitated, then suddenly switched into telepathic speech, her words coming silently into Indigo's mind. *I heard the voices again.*

"The voices . . .?" Indigo felt a strange, queasy little sensation assail her.

*Listen,* Grimya said. *Listen hard. They are here again. They have come back.*

Indigo listened. The wind was nothing more than a breeze, making no sound; any noise from the people toiling in the fields didn't carry as far as the road. Her mount jingled its bit, bored and restless—and then, in the wake of the metallic noise, she heard it. A faint murmuring, as though several children were whispering eagerly together a short way off. But there were no children to be seen. No one within earshot, nowhere for the whisperers to conceal themselves. Only the voices, faint and indistinguishable and disembodied.

Grimya looked at Indigo with huge, dark eyes. "I th-*ought* it was over," she said very quietly. "I thought it was just some strrrangeness and it wouldn't happen again. I was wrong, Indigo. They are back."

Whoever and whatever *they* were . . . "Can you see anything, Grimya?" Indigo asked softly. "Can you feel a presence, the way you did last time?"

"N-no." The wolf shook her head emphatically. "Nothing l . . . ike that. But this was how it started before, don't you rr-remember? Just voices."

She was right. It must have been, Indigo calculated, nine or ten days ago that they had had their first eerie encounter. They'd been walking on the stone-paved highway known as the Splendid Progress Road, which ran through the backbone of the mountain range, when Grimya had begun to insist that she could hear, as she put it, "the wind speaking."

Then Indigo, too, had started to hear the strange whisperings, and it soon became clear that the sounds were following them, as though some invisible presence dogged their footsteps. No words were discernible, but Indigo felt with unpleasant, irrational certainty that the voices were human. The sounds had continued all through the night while they sat wakeful and fearful by the side of the road. Once, briefly, Indigo's nerve had snapped and she called out in challenge, but her words only echoed hollowly away into the hills and the voices hadn't responded.

Then the next day Grimya had become convinced that they were being followed, and though there was no trace of anyone to be seen, nothing could persuade her that she was mistaken. She sensed them, she said. Human or animal or something else, she didn't know, but they were *there*. And once, though briefly, she glimpsed a ghostly face, which hovered in the air behind them for a few moments before vanishing.

The eerie sounds had followed them for three days, and by the third day they were both deeply uneasy. Grimya speculated nervously about ghosts and ghouls—in a land like this, she said, such things might easily haunt the roads, looking for unwary travelers. Indigo was reluctant to dwell on that thought; she was more reluctant still to consider the other possibility that had crept into her mind and now lodged there, dormant but only waiting to be allowed to flower. She said nothing of that to Grimya, though, and tried to ignore the nagging goad of it within her.

Then, on the night following the third day, the voices and the invisible presence suddenly vanished. Sheer exhaustion had finally overcome Indigo's fears, and when they made camp at sunset she fell asleep, only to be woken under the cold, bright light of a full moon by Grimya, who told her that, moments ago, the whisperings had abruptly ceased and the sense of being watched was gone. Their followers, whatever they might be, were simply no longer there. And since that moment they'd not returned . . . until now.

Grimya said uneasily. "Wh-at should we do, do you thh . . . ink?"

Indigo stared speculatively back along the road. It all looked so ordered and peaceful, without the smallest hint of anything untoward. This just didn't make sense. Unless that nagging suspicion of a few days ago had some foundation after all . . .?

Abruptly she made a decision. She didn't want to think about suspicions and possibilities, didn't want to speculate, not now. What she wanted now was a bath, a meal, and a bed soft enough and warm enough to give her the chance of an uninterrupted night's sleep. If there was a mystery here, it could wait until morning.

"We'll do nothing," she told the wolf firmly. "Ignore it, behave as though nothing's happened, and go on into Joyful Travail." Her blue-violet eyes narrowed. "If there's anything afoot, I don't want to know what it is."

The woman who answered Indigo's knock at the door of the Foreigners' Duty House was inclined at first to treat the auburn-haired stranger with cold suspicion, but when Indigo produced the stick the official had presented to her, there was a sudden and marked thawing.

"Ah." The woman inclined her head politely, though still with a slight hint of her people's distaste for outsiders. "You carry the token of a Councillor: this, then, means that you are most welcome." She cast a glance over one shoulder, her short, dark hair bobbing and glinting in the meager light of the rushlight she carried. "Sianu! Who in the Enclave has sleeping-space to spare? Quickly, now!"

A younger voice murmured from within the bowels of the building, and the woman turned back to Indigo with a broad smile.

"You will be conducted to the residence of the foreigner

Hollend, and there you will be comfortably housed until the Councillor sends word for you. The charge to you will be six tokens." One hand was extended, palm upward. "To be proffered in advance, please."

The sum was just short of extortionate, but Indigo kept her thoughts to herself and paid over the six wooden pieces without quibble. The woman put five in a drawer, pocketed the sixth herself, then made a formal bow. "Please to await someone who will conduct you to the proper place. I wish you good rest and nutritious victualing."

Indigo returned the bow, then waited for several minutes—waiting, she had learned, was an art among these people—until a blank-faced youth of fifteen or so arrived to escort her and her small entourage to their quarters. The sun was close to setting, and long shadows stretched across the compound, giving a peculiar, dreamlike quality to the low but highly ornamented buildings set in a seemingly random fashion around the bare-earth streets of the Foreigners' Enclave. Unspeaking, head down as though to avert any attempt the stranger might have made at conversation, the boy led them at an awkward jog past one after another lit house until they reached a building larger than its neighbors, where lamplight poured from an open door and spilled across a broad wooden veranda. Shadowed in the doorway a slim yet motherly looking woman, her rich, fair hair bound up in complicated braids, stood watching out for them. The boy ran to her and there was a whispered exchange; then, bowing, he backed down from the veranda, turned, and ran as though fleeing from a plague.

Indigo and the woman looked at one another. Then, cutting through the silence that had fallen as the boy's footfalls died away, a warm voice spoke in a tongue that shocked Indigo to the marrow with its familiarity.

"I don't know your name, stranger, but you're welcome to our hospitality, such as it is—and doubly welcome to sanctuary in this forsaken corner of the world!"

\* \* \*

"We aren't offered a choice in matters such as these."
Calpurna reached across the table and, ignoring Indigo's
protest that she had already eaten more than her share,
heaped her plate with a second helping of diced and shred-
ded vegetables. "No, no, stop arguing and eat it; we've
enough status to ensure that our household never goes short.
And I mean no slight on you, Indigo—far from it. But as
foreigners, and therefore the lowest of the low, we're
obliged to take in anyone the Committee chooses to billet
on us, and I mean *anyone*." She raised an expressive eyebrow.

Hollend, Calpurna's husband, swallowed the piece of
roasted fowl he was chewing and waved his fork. "Remember those two brothers from the Western Continent? Sullen as
a pair of kicked dogs, couldn't speak a word of any language
known to the civilized world, and everywhere they went they
left a powerful odor of the swine-barn in their wake!"

Their two children, a boy and girl who Indigo had surmised were respectively about eight and ten years old, giggled immoderately at that. Calpurna admonished them with
a look and a sharp rap on the table, and as their mirth subsided she turned to Indigo again.

"That, my dear, is why we're doubly glad that *you* were
sent to us. To have intelligent and civilized company in this
benighted place is a boon. So whether you like it or whether
you don't, you must resign yourself to being fussed and
feted and royally treated; and I sincerely hope that your stay
with us will be a long one!"

Hollend raised his glass—a fine glass, cut and faceted to
reflect the color of the excellent wine. "I'll second that. To
Indigo—and Grimya, too. And our heartfelt thanks to them
for coming to our door!"

Their words, and the undoubted sincerity behind them,
drove out the last of Indigo's doubts, and she felt herself re-
lax in a way that she hadn't known since she and Grimya

had crossed the borders into this peculiar country. In her most illogical fancies she'd never dreamed that she would find such people as Hollend and Calpurna in Joyful Travail. People with whom she felt an instant rapport; people who called her back to ancient ties and ancient loyalties. For this kindly, hospitable, and entertaining couple were Agantians, born in the small but prosperous kingdom from which the Agantine Gulf, far to the south in this great Eastern Continent, took its name. Agantia shared a common tongue, heritage, and culture with its many small neighboring states along the Gulf's shores—and among those neighbors was Khimiz, where Indigo's own mother had been born, and where Indigo and Grimya had spent a thirteen-year sojourn during their long travels. Many of Indigo's memories of Khimiz were far from happy; yet in meeting Hollend and Calpurna she felt a peculiar—disturbing, yes, but at the same time comforting—sense of having come home.

Hollend and Calpurna, she had learned, had lived in Joyful Travail for the past seven years. Hollend had the misfortune, as he dryly termed it, to have been born the second son of a wealthy and influential Agantian merchant whose especial interest lay in metals, and when their father died his elder brother had taken control of the family trade at home, while it fell to Hollend to become an emissary, seeking and opening up new sources of raw mineral. This northern country was rich in ores of iron, copper, silver, and nickel, and had never been properly exploited, Hollend said; so his task was to trade with the land's ruling Committees, draw up agreements, and see to it that the bargains thus made were kept on both sides. It was, as he freely admitted, an uphill struggle. Despite their relative proximity—"we are, at least, on the same continent!"—the way of life here in the north was as far removed from the luxury, sophistication, and easy facility of the Agantine Gulf as it was possible to be.

"The greatest problem with these people," he said, helping first Indigo, then Calpurna, then himself to more wine, "is that they have no idea of how to appreciate any of the finer things in life. They like wealth—no, I'll rephrase that: they covet and *crave* wealth above anything else—and take delight in showing off every last artifact they own, but they don't possess a shred of discernment." He sipped the wine. "Or taste."

Indigo smiled at him. "You seem to have done a lot to counter the influence in your own home, Hollend."

"Well ..." Returning the smile, Hollend looked about him at the good-quality furnishings, the rugs, the table with its array of fine dishes and cutlery. "We've brought as many of our own possessions from home as is practical, and we do a little bartering on the side with our fellow sufferers in the Enclave. We get by well enough, I suppose."

Calpurna's mouth pursed with faint amusement. "My husband is, as ever, playing the pessimist," she said. "In truth, we get by very well indeed by local standards. We're respected ... or as respected as any foreigners can be here, which means that people are at least polite to us—"

"They have to be," Hollend interrupted. "However much they may dislike the principle, they know full well that they have to trade with the outside world, and they need our wealth. As I've already said, they covet wealth above all else. But that doesn't stop them from looking on us as dirt beneath their feet."

"Yes, yes," Calpurna agreed peaceably, "but they *are* at least polite. Outwardly, anyway. That, Indigo, is a major concession, I assure you!"

Indigo recalled the manner of the man in the orange sash whom she'd met on the road. "I encountered one of the town officials on my way here today," she said. "He was courteous enough, in his way. He even gave me a token to present at the Duty House, and I think that without it I'd have been a good deal less welcome."

From her pouch she produced the small stick with its orange pennant and showed it to her hosts. Calpurna raised her eyebrows again, and Hollend laughed.

"Well, well! Old Choai's token—you *are* the favored one!"

"Is he a high-ranking official? I don't yet know the system of colors."

"Uncle Choai—and yes, that *is* the title they give themselves—doesn't have a particularly high rank. Orange counts for more than red or brown but it's a lesser color than the yellows and greens and blues and so on. But he has influence; and more to the point, he's very hard to please. You must have some skill that the town sorely needs." Hollend's gray eyes grew mischievous. "Have you?"

Calpurna said, *"Hollend!"* but he waved her protest away.

"I know it's not considered civil where we come from to pry into another person's business, but I'm sure that Indigo doesn't mind," he insisted. "Besides, I'm curious to know what possible motive an intelligent young woman could have for wanting to come to a place like Joyful Travail." He looked up. "Well, Indigo? What *does* bring you here?"

She'd anticipated the question and had an answer prepared. "It's quite simple," she told him. "Like anyone else, I'm seeking a living to keep body and soul together."

Hollend nodded, understanding. "And what do you do that makes Uncle Choai so ready to sponsor you?"

She smiled dryly. "I have some herbalist's skills, but the only word I knew to describe them in the local tongue was 'physician.' "

Hollend grinned broadly. "No wonder the old busybody was impressed! Joyful Travail's one and only physician died of old age ten days ago, and he'd trained no apprentice to follow him. Oh, you'll be welcome here, Indigo, welcome a hundredfold."

"Will I?" She was surprised. "If they look on foreigners as 'dirt beneath their feet' as you phrased it, I can't imagine them tolerating a foreign physician in their midst, let alone making me welcome."

"Ah," Hollend said, "but that's the contrariness of these people. If there was a native physician ready to step into old Huni's shoes they'd march you out of town as though you were a bad smell under their noses. But there is no local replacement, so they'll put their bigoted principles aside and happily use you."

" 'Use' is the word," Calpurna interjected. "Don't fear that the locals will feel any respect toward you; there's no danger of that even if they pretend otherwise. And you can be sure that as soon as they *do* find another healer from among their own kind, they'll cast you aside without so much as a word of thanks."

"In the meantime, though," Hollend said, "at least you'll be paid for your services. And whether anyone likes it or not, you'll be in a position of power. The elders won't dare cross you for fear of what you might do to them if they fall ill and find themselves helpless in your hands!"

Indigo joined in his laughter, but inwardly she felt discomforted as she wondered what the townsfolk—and Uncle Choai in particular—would expect of her. In truth her skills extended only to the little training she'd had long ago at the knee of her old nurse, Imyssa, supplemented by some rough-and-ready experience during her years of traveling, when necessity had made its own demands. She was no physician in the true sense, and if she was expected to practice in Joyful Travail, it couldn't be long before her shortcomings were found out.

Hollend seemed to understand her dilemma and said kindly, "Seriously, Indigo, I shouldn't let the misunderstanding worry you. For all their pretenses the people here are very simple and their standards primitive. If you can only mix febrifuges and bind sprained ankles, you'll impress them, for with Huni gone that's more than anyone else can do."

"I'm relieved to hear it," Indigo said with feeling. "If I'd thought when Choai asked me—" She stopped, overcome by a sudden vast yawn. "Oh—forgive me; I didn't mean—"

"My dear child, there's nothing to forgive." Calpurna rose quickly from her chair. "We're the ones at fault, for sitting here prating half the night when you must be exhausted!" She scanned the table and her eyes lit on her son and daughter. "And you children should have been asleep long ago. Ellani," she said gesturing to the girl, "you may help me show Indigo to her room and then it's bed immediately for you and Koru." The boy started to protest, but she silenced him with a stern look and warning finger. "No argument, please! I'm sure we all have a lot more to say, but it can be said tomorrow."

The soporific effects of the best meal she'd eaten and the only wine she'd drunk in more than a month had taken their toll on Indigo, and as weariness washed over her she allowed herself to be swept along on the tide of Calpurna's brisk mothering. A little bemusedly she said her good nights to Hollend and young Koru, then followed Calpurna and Ellani up the ladderlike stairs to the house's upper story and a small but comfortable room under the eaves, with a south-facing window and a ceiling that sloped almost to the floor. To lie in a comfortable bed again and to know that nothing need disturb her until she had slept the exhaustion from her bones was a boon that Indigo had all but forgotten. When Calpurna wished her good night and left her, with Grimya curled on a rug by the window, she climbed under the warm blankets, stretching luxuriously on the fleece-filled palliasse and feeling the sheer softness of the pillow beneath her head. She whispered to Grimya, *"Good night, love. Sleep well,"* but Grimya's only reply was a soft grunt. Indigo smiled. Her own eyes closed, and her mind rallied just long enough to give silent thanks to her generous hosts, and to the Earth Mother for leading her to them, before she, too, was soundly asleep.

# ·CHAPTER·II·

Ironically, the bed in which Indigo lay that night, and for which she'd given such heartfelt thanks, was so soft and comfortable that she couldn't sleep soundly. Accustomed to moss or heather for her mattress at best and hard-packed earth at worst, she tossed and turned restlessly, sometimes waking to see the dim, silver-gray light of moon and stars shining in her window.

At her third awakening, she heard muffled voices on the far side of the wall.

For several minutes Indigo lay somnolent, aware of the soft, distant sounds but not consciously listening to them. She was still suspended between sleep and wakefulness, and everything in the still night seemed a little unreal to her drowsy mind. Moonshadows played across the room's unfamiliar furnishings, and a light breeze stealing through the part-open window stirred the curtains gently. Turning her head she looked toward the rug where Grimya lay, expecting to see the hummock of her sleeping form—but instead the silhouette of the she-wolf's head showed sharply outlined against the window, her ears pricked and her muzzle at a tense angle.

"Grimya?" Still not fully awake Indigo spoke aloud, and immediately Grimya's head turned.

*Hush!* Her telepathic voice sounded an urgent warning in Indigo's mind. *Listen! Do you hear them?*

With an effort Indigo thrust away the mental fog of sleep. The vague, distant murmurings had stopped when she spoke Grimya's name, but now they began again, fading in slowly as though borne toward the house on a gentle breeze. Too tired to think with any real clarity she struggled to find some rational explanation.

*Hollend and Calpurna must still be awake,* she projected.

*No.* Grimya was emphatic. *These are children's voices.*

*Ellani and Koru, then.* Illogically, Indigo was beginning to feel annoyed. The whispering disturbance irritated her, and Grimya's disquiet was making matters worse. But before she could tetchily tell the wolf to go back to sleep, Grimya said,

*It is not them. Listen, Indigo. Listen closely.*

Indigo sighed, realizing that she'd have no peace until her friend was placated. She struggled upright, pushing back the blankets, and shook strands of hair from her eyes as, reluctantly, she set herself to listen.

Then she understood what Grimya had meant. The voices *did* sound young, but they had an odd, slightly artificial timbre, as though the whispered words were being spoken by adults who were trying to imitate children's tones and almost—but not quite—succeeding. And as she listened harder she realized that, as the wolf had said, these weren't the voices of Hollend or Calpurna or their son and daughter, for they murmured and chattered and giggled together not in the familiar language of Agantia but in the clipped, husky tongue of the local people.

Their mysterious followers had returned again.

Grimya turned her head and her eyes glowed dim amber as they focused on Indigo's face in the gloom. She didn't speak as Indigo climbed out of bed and padded across the floor, but her gaze followed as Indigo reached the window, lifted back the curtain, and looked out. The moon rode high in the sky among a few thin streaks of cloud, and its light was strong enough to illuminate the Foreigners' Enclave, the hard-packed roadway, the wooden picket fences, the crouched shapes of the other houses nearby. There were no lights in the compound and not a living soul to be seen.

*I know,* Grimya said somberly as her friend turned away from the window at last. *I looked, too. There's no one out there.*

Indigo sat down on the bed, pulling one of the blankets round her shoulders and suppressing a shiver. She didn't need to project her feelings or utter them aloud; Grimya was well aware of what she was thinking.

*Why have they come back?* She tried unsuccessfully to shake off some none-too-pleasant images of the manner of beings that might be haunting the dead of this still, untroubled night. *What can they want?*

*I can hear something of what they are saying this time,* Grimya told her. She rose, came to the bed, and jumped up beside Indigo as though anxious for comfort. *But it makes no sense to me. They have been talking of "us" and "them," and saying that there is something "they" do not know. And they laugh. It's foolish laughter, yet very sad at the same time. They sound . . . lonely.*

"Lonely?" Taken aback, Indigo spoke aloud again. Instantly the murmuring voices ceased, and she started as she realized that the voices' owners could hear them. Wildly, she looked round the room as though expecting to see faces and forms materializing out of the dark. *Where were they?*

"I don't know." Catching the unguarded thought, Grimya spoke softly against her ear. "But I thh . . . ink they are not *here*. Not in this room or this house. Per-haps not even in this world."

Not in this world; yet they had the power and, it seemed, the desire, to make their presence known. "I think," Indigo told the wolf softly, "that when morning comes I should speak with Hollend and Calpurna. They may be able to shed some light on this . . . or if they can't, they may know others who will."

"I'm not so sure," Grimya said. "Remember, they are ff . . . *oreigners*, too."

"Nonetheless, they know this country. This may have happened to others before us. If it has, Hollend and Calpurna will have heard about it."

Grimya blinked and tilted her head to one side. "You have a th . . . theo . . . what is the word?"

"A theory? No, I haven't, not yet. But there's something stirring in my bones, Grimya. Call it an inkling; I wouldn't put it any more strongly than that." Indigo paused, listening to the silence, wondering if the voices in their turn were listening to her. She could sense nothing untoward now, but she still couldn't shake off the feeling that she and Grimya weren't alone in the room. She'd been mistaken, she thought. Back there on the road she'd feared that those small, insidious whispers in the night were ghosts of her own, creeping softly but surely out of the past to haunt her. Now, though, she believed she knew better. Something else was speaking to her. Something whose nature she didn't yet comprehend, but whose source lay not in her own mind but in the bones of this strange, fertile yet bleak country.

She reached out and grasped the blankets, pulling them up over her body while her other arm slipped over the she-wolf's muscular, dense-furred flank.

"Stay here with me tonight, Grimya," she said, and Grimya knew that somewhere in the depths of her mind a small, ambiguous, yet undeniable worm of fear was stirring.

The she-wolf wriggled closer and fondly licked Indigo's face.

"I will guard you," she said huskily. "Don't fear, Indigo, don't fear. I shall keep you warm!"

Whether it was Grimya's comfort or her own sheer exhaustion that made the difference Indigo would never know, but when she closed her eyes again she slept soundly and tranquilly through the rest of that night. She was finally woken by a tentative knocking at her door, and opened her eyes to find daylight filling the attic room and the wolf stirring and yawning beside her. As she struggled into a sitting position, the door opened and Ellani's face appeared.

"Indigo?" The girl's unbound, honey-fair hair swung over her shoulder, glinting in the bright light. "Are you awake? I've brought you a hot brew." Without waiting for an answer she came in and set a small brass tray containing two pottery mugs down on the bedside table.

Indigo rubbed at her eyes and stifled a yawn as wide as Grimya's. "Ellani . . . what's the hour? Have I overslept? I'm so sorry—"

"No, no. Mother said you were to sleep yourself out; but we have a visitor." Expressively she rolled her eyes toward the ladderlike staircase and mouthed, "Uncle Choai has called."

Indigo picked up her mug, hiding a smile behind the rim as she sipped at the brew, which was strong and unsweetened just as she liked it best. "Am I required?"

Ellani made a deferential gesture. "When you're ready, Mother says. But if . . ." Her voice trailed off.

"If I can hurry myself, your mother will appreciate it. Don't worry, Ellani; I've encountered the likes of Uncle Choai many times before."

Ellani was a pretty child, and when she smiled unreservedly her face showed the beauty she would inherit when she grew to adulthood. She sat down on the edge of Indigo's bed, reaching out to ruffle the fur on Grimya's head as she did so, a natural and fearless gesture that greatly pleased the wolf. "May I drink my brew with you, Indigo? Mother and Father are entertaining their visitor and I'd much rather not sit with them unless I must. Uncle Choai always makes me think of frogs."

Calpurna wouldn't have approved, but Indigo couldn't resist a soft chuckle. "Of course; you're welcome." She took a sip of the brew, burned her tongue, and set it down again to cool while she began to dress. She would greatly have liked a bath—there'd been time only for a quick wash before the meal last night—but it wouldn't do to keep Uncle Choai waiting too long, so she took some garments cleaner than her traveling clothes from her pack and pulled them on, hoping that she'd pass muster.

"Did you sleep well?" Ellani asked solicitously.

Indigo and Grimya exchanged a look, and the wolf's voice spoke in Indigo's mind. *Ask her,* Grimya said. *There's no harm in it.*

Indigo nodded acknowledgment, the movement of her head barely perceptible. Aloud, her tone quite casual, she said, "I slept very well ... Oh, but for one thing." She turned to face the girl, smiling. "I think some late revelers must have returned to the Enclave. Their voices woke me."

"Revelers?" Ellani looked blank.

"I assume they must have been. They were whispering and laughing together outside; they seemed to be directly below my window." Indigo paused. "You heard nothing?"

"No." Was she mistaken, or was there suddenly a furtive glimmer in Ellani's eyes? Indigo glanced at Grimya again, and the wolf said silently, *I know. I see it, too. Something has unsettled her, but she doesn't want you to know what it is.*

Ellani had turned her face away now, hiding her expression behind the rim of her mug as she gulped hastily at her brew. "If you're nearly ready," she said indistinctly, between scalding mouthfuls, "perhaps we should go downstairs . . ."

She was clearly very disconcerted, and Indigo surmised that any attempt to probe would only make her withdraw further into her shell. Reluctantly she decided that it would be more prudent to go down, put on a pleasant face for Uncle Choai, and forget the matter of last night's mystery, at least for the present. Later, though, if the opportunity arose, she would certainly speak to Calpurna.

There was no looking glass in the room, but Indigo could make out a fair approximation of her own reflection in the window. Her clothes were tidy enough; her hair would do. She took a quick sip from her mug, then smiled reassuringly at Ellani.

"I'm ready," she said.

Hollend, Calpurna, and their visitor were sitting in three of four chairs that had been placed at precisely calculated distances from one another in the house's reception room. As Indigo entered through the curtain that separated the room from the stairwell, Calpurna gave her a welcoming smile and Hollend rose and bowed, belying the formal gesture with a wink that Choai couldn't see.

The Uncle himself—whose chair was noticeably larger than the others'—acknowledged Indigo with a precise nod of his head, then addressed Calpurna. "It is gratifying for a hostess to know that a visitor has spent a comfortable and revitalizing night under her roof."

Indigo wasn't yet at home with the finer nuances of protocol and didn't know what to say, but Hollend came to her rescue. Signaling her to seat herself on the fourth and smallest chair, he beamed at Choai. "Our guest is well rested, Uncle, and my wife and I are pleased to have been of useful service. We thank you again for your generosity in sending Indigo to us."

The old man looked pleased. "I have no doubt that your

guest will be as useful to you as you have been to her. She has told you that she is a physician?"

Hollend and Calpurna exchanged a conspiratorial glance and then both dissembled, pretending that they'd known nothing of Indigo's talents. This seemed to please Choai even more, and he turned to face Indigo directly. "I am happy to convey the news that a temporary place of work has been found for you, so that you may begin to practice your healing skills without any unproductive delays. Your first patient will present himself at noon today, and the last at sunset. There will be thirty patients in all, and a juvenile will be assigned to you to carry out all menial tasks."

Indigo was dumbfounded. She found it impossible to credit that Choai could have worked so fast or so efficiently, and swiftly began to reassess her early impressions of him as no more than a self-important bumbler. Hastily she expressed thanks and admiration, hoping that her words didn't betray the panic that was threatening to take hold of her at the thought of being hurled headlong into a role for which she knew she wasn't qualified. However carelessly her hosts might dismiss the abilities of Joyful Travail's previous physician, Indigo didn't know whether she could cope with such a responsibility. Or rather, if she was to be strictly honest with herself, whether she could get away with it.

Uncle Choai, however, seemed to have no doubts about her skills. He was obviously ready to take her entirely on trust, and Indigo suspected that to bring a new healer into their midst would earn him a good deal of kudos among his fellow elders on Joyful Travail's ruling committees; so much so that the minor question of the healer's competence could be swept aside and ignored. Her suspicion was soon confirmed when the conversation began to turn, by slow and subtle degrees, to a new topic, as Hollend and Calpurna insisted that Choai must accept some small token of their esteem. Choai argued vehemently, putting up both hands palms outward before his face in a self-deprecating gesture, and insisting that the honor and the pleasure were his alone. Hollend brushed this politely aside, proclaiming that the gifts—plural now—were merely an inadequate expression of the regard and affection that his entire family felt for their kindly mentor and friend of such long-standing, and to decline these slight offerings would be to bring the greatest disappointment to himself, his wife, and his children. It was a ritual, Indigo realized, practiced and perfected with the exactitude of a solemn ceremonial dance; the argument would sway back and forth until the desired point of balance was reached, then at last Choai would make a show of capitulating to Hollend's will, and the fee—for that, stripped of its trappings, was what the Agantian was offering and the elder greedy to receive—would be paid.

Hollend and Calpurna gave Choai three gifts. The first was for himself: a knife of Agantian manufacture, with a blade of tempered steel and a hilt carved from a single piece of amethyst quartz. This was clearly intended to be displayed to friends and colleagues as a valuably useful artifact. The second gift, a set of fine china drinking cups, was, as Hollend deftly implied, to be passed on to whichever official of a higher color had sanctioned the arrangements Choai had made for Indigo; pure bribery, and very thinly disguised. And the third gift set the seal on the bargain. It was a pen, but no ordinary writing instrument. Indigo had seen something similar many years ago in Khimiz—within the body of the pen was a flexible sac made from animal gut, and this sac fed ink in a steady flow to a metal nib, allowing the user to dispense with the tedious necessity of ink pots and sharpened quills. When the ink in the sac ran out, a new and full sac could be inserted in its place, and the whole instrument was decorated in delicate silver filigree. No other man or woman in Joyful Travail owned such a pen, and no one but Hollend could supply the replacement sacs. It was a gesture that stated, more clearly than any words, the mutual dependence between Choai and the Agantian family he had chosen to take under his wing.

Indigo was surprised and gratified to learn how much she herself would be paid for her services. The sum seemed very generous—but she soon discovered that by no means would all of it end up in her hands. A large deduction was made for "administrative expense"—little more than a blatant gratuity for the elders—and further payments were exacted for rental of the physician's room, accommodation for her ponies in the town's communal stables, and her own board and lodging under Hollend and Calpurna's roof. What proportion of this last payment would ever reach her hosts Indigo didn't care to speculate, but by the time the deductions were added together, more than half of her stipend had been accounted for.

There was a little more stilted conversation, a ritualistic proffering and declining of refreshment, then Uncle Choai took his leave, telling Indigo that the juvenile allocated to her would arrive to escort her to her workplace in good time. As his dumpy, brisk figure trotted away in the direction of the Enclave gates, Hollend closed the door and turned to Indigo with a helpless look.

"I'm sorry, Indigo," he said. "We had no idea that he'd arrange anything so rapidly; normally these matters take days." He paused, his eyes scanning her face. "Can you cope?"

"I'll manage." Indigo made a wry face. "I don't seem to have much choice."

Calpurna, who in the wake of Choai's departure had gone in search of Ellani and Koru, returned, shepherding the children before her. "It's quite monstrous," she said indignantly. "Indigo hasn't been in this town for half a day; she's barely had time for a night's sleep, let alone to prepare herself for work!"

Hollend shrugged expressively. "She's in no position to

argue with the Uncles, my dear. Neither, for that matter, are we."

Calpurna made a scornful noise. "That wretched little man, strutting and preening like a cockerel . . . and as for the gifts, Hollend, you were *far* too generous! I know these things must be done, but to give him the pen as well as the knife—"

"Calpurna, my love, the gifts were nothing to us, as you well know. These people are primitive and ignorant as well as greedy, and we can supply enough new toys to go on buying their cooperation until the end of our days!" He patted her shoulder. "Don't agitate yourself. It isn't worth it."

Calpurna sighed. "Very well, very well. But it still *rankles*. And that pompous old fool has put me all at sixes and sevens by delaying our breakfast . . . Koru, help your father to prepare the table, and I'll see what I can salvage for our meal." She turned toward the inner door and Indigo, seeing an opportunity for a private word, said, "I'll help you, Calpurna."

The household's cooking was done in a small room at the back of the building. Calpurna refused to call it a kitchen, although to Indigo's eyes it seemed adequate enough. The Agantian woman muttered darkly to herself as she set about stirring and seasoning what looked and smelled like a kind of lentil porridge over the wood fire while Indigo cut bread and Ellani fetched plates and bowls from an incongruously elegant cupboard that stood against one wall. As the child went out with her load precariously balanced, Calpurna suddenly stopped her grumbles in midsentence, turned, and smiled a rueful apology.

"What am I thinking of? Here I am allowing you to be hurled into the midst of this chaos, and I haven't even asked you if you slept well! Please forgive me, Indigo. I'm not usually so graceless, but that *dreadful* old man always brings out the worst in me!" She gave her spoon another ferocious twist as though imagining that it were Choai and not porridge boiling in the pot. "*Did* you sleep well?"

"I did, thank you." Indigo glanced quickly over her shoulder to ensure that Ellani wasn't returning, then added, "But there was one thing . . ."

"Oh?" Calpurna looked concerned. "Not the children, I hope. Did they disturb you? They always rise so early; I *told* them to be quiet this morning, but—"

"No, no; it wasn't the children." Indigo told her of the strange whispering she'd heard in the night, the small, far-away voices that seemed to be speaking in the local tongue. When she finished, Calpurna frowned.

"There was no sign of anyone outside, you say? Well, no, that would make sense of course . . . the local people don't set foot in the Foreigners' Enclave without a very good reason. And these were *children*'s voices?"

"I can't be sure, but I think so."

Calpurna's frown deepened and the porridge was momentarily forgotten. "How strange," she said.

Indigo was alerted. "In what way?"

"Oh, it's just that when Ellani and Koru were little they both used to say that they heard voices in the night on occasion. It didn't happen very often, but they were both quite terrified by them."

That, Indigo thought, could explain Ellani's strange reaction earlier in the day. "Did you ever discover what lay behind it?" she asked.

"No, we didn't. We simply assumed that it was nothing more than a fancy." She smiled. "Young children have such very vivid imaginations—and anyway, they soon grew out of it." She hesitated, and an odd expression crept across her face. "Or Ellani did, anyway."

"Koru still hears them?"

There was another pause. "Well, he *says* he does; but then he's only eight years old yet, and at that age it's often very hard to separate invention from truth." Abruptly then—

just a little *too* abruptly, Indigo thought—Calpurna's face cleared and she smiled. "I don't think we need worry about what Koru says. I'll ask Hollend to investigate the matter for you. Doubtless there's something about the house, some loose tile or strut, that's causing these sounds. Hollend will soon find it and put it right."

Indigo looked back at her, nonplussed by her attitude. She seemed unwilling or unable to do anything other than dismiss the story, and moreover to dismiss it with an explanation so bland that it was almost absurd. Was she hiding something? Indigo wondered. It seemed unlikely; Calpurna's expression was too open, too ingenuous, and she didn't seem to be the stuff of which good liars were made.

Cautiously probing, testing, she said in as casual a tone as she could contrive, "Are you sure that's what it is, Calpurna?"

Calpurna was attending to the breakfast again, but she paused to turn and give her guest another bright if slightly baffled smile.

"But of course I'm sure, my dear," she said. "After all, what other explanation could there possibly be?"

# ·CHAPTER·III·

The "juvenile" who came to escort Indigo to her new workplace was a thin, underdeveloped girl, probably thirteen or fourteen years old, though she looked younger. She seemed very reluctant to utter a single unnecessary word; Indigo learned that her name was Thia, but other than that she could discover nothing about her.

Before she left the house, Calpurna had taken her aside. Her hostess's manner was apologetic as she said, "Indigo, forgive my presumption, but may I give you a little advice?"

"Certainly." Indigo was thankful for any counsel that might help her through the maze of protocol and custom that so rigidly defined life in Joyful Travail.

Calpurna smiled. "It isn't so difficult if you just remember to follow a few simple rules," she said. "Bow to everyone you meet—a deeper bow to those who wear colored sashes, for they are the Uncles and Aunts, like Choai, and they consider themselves important. Always wait for them to address you first, but speak as freely as you please to others." The smile became a shade conspiratorial. "As a physician you'll be entitled to respect, despite the fact that you're also a foreigner, so take no nonsense from the lower ranks. And don't *suggest* remedies to your patients—*instruct* them, firmly and sternly. They expect that. Politeness may well be a fixation in this country, but it goes only one layer deep. Beneath the surface, most people here are quite remarkably rude."

Indigo laughed, then quelled the laughter lest the waiting Thia should overhear. "I'll remember. Thank you!"

"Oh, and you'd best wear this." Reaching into a deep pocket of her overskirt, Calpurna brought out a narrow white sash, which she handed to Indigo with a moue of distaste. "I'm sorry; it smacks somewhat of branding an animal, but it's the protocol here. We all have to display the foreigners' rank color whenever we venture outside the Enclave. White, I'm afraid, denotes the lowest of the low." She helped Indigo to slip the sash over her shoulder and tie it, then added, "You'd best go."

On impulse, Indigo kissed her cheek. "Thank you again, Calpurna. I couldn't have coped without your help!"

"Oh, nonsense. You've twice the intelligence of these wretched little people and it won't take you long to unravel their wiles. Don't let Choai work you to a shadow on your first day; if he tries to persuade you to stay beyond sunset, refuse. We'll see you this evening."

Walking out through the Enclave gates in the wake of the taciturn Thia, Indigo felt as if she were entering an entirely new and alien world. Having spent the hours since her arrival under the roof of Hollend and Calpurna, she had seen little of Joyful Travail, except as a vague sprawl of buildings beyond the Enclave fence. Now though, in the chilly but bright light of day, a jumble of impressions crowded into her mind.

Joyful Travail's main thoroughfare—less a street and

more a broad lane, Indigo thought—ran in a precisely straight line toward the square at the center of the town. A narrow strip to one side was paved with slabs of roughly cut stone, but the rest of the roadway consisted of nothing more than hard-packed, reddish-brown earth. It was impossible to judge whether the single-story buildings lining the street were dwellings or workplaces, for they were all identical: unadorned, unpainted, fronted by plain doors and uncurtained windows that gave no clue to what lay behind the facades.

Mutely, Thia led Indigo toward the square. She took a path that kept them as far as possible from the paved strip and, as two women wearing green sashes went by in the opposite direction along the paving, Indigo realized why. The pavement, it seemed, was reserved for those of higher status; lowly individuals—and foreigners—were expected to keep a respectful distance. The women's glances slid sidelong as they passed; the white sash was noted and the two faces looked aloofly away. Indigo began to wish that she hadn't persuaded Grimya to stay with Calpurna. Without the wolf to keep her company it seemed she'd be lacking for a single friendly word or face until she returned to the Enclave. But Hollend had advised against allowing the wolf to accompany her. Pet animals, he said, were frowned upon unless they were clearly useful, and even a creature of Grimya's intelligence could find little to occupy her in a physician's consulting room.

Thia hurried on. The thoroughfare was growing busier: women with baskets on their backs were converging on the market square; two men pushing a laden barrow followed a boy driving a flock of poultry; and a smaller flock of children laden with agricultural tools hastened behind him. Two carts, one drawn by oxen and the other by an underfed pony, rattled by. This, it seemed, was the heart of Joyful Travail, and as she emerged in Thia's wake into the square itself, Indigo slowed her steps to take in the scene that confronted her.

The square was a hard-trodden earth arena, featureless but for a large and cumbersome water pump at its center. It was flanked on all sides by more of the dreary, characterless houses, their uniformity broken only by one building, larger than the rest but equally drab, with double doors that stood resolutely shut.

The daily market appeared to be in full swing. Trestle tables set in serried ranks displayed foodstuffs, household implements, clothing, crude wooden furniture; beside their tables the stall holders watched potential customers alertly and with an air of suspicion that bordered on hostility. Coming onto the scene as a stranger, an outsider, Indigo felt an alarming sense of alienness, as though she had entered not merely into another country but into another dimension, and as her mind began to absorb the images before her she suddenly realized what lay at the root of it. Busy though it was, bustling and alive with activity, the square was almost totally silent. Goods were pointed at in silence, wooden tokens changed hands in silence, purchases were stowed into baskets or hefted on backs and carried away with no more than a nod of acknowledgment between vendor and client. No one sang, no one whistled; there were no stall holders declaring loudly that their wares were better than their neighbors', no groups of chattering men, gossiping women, or boisterous children. It was a stark and shocking contrast to the markets of so many other lands Indigo had visited— the chaotic and noisy bazaars of Huon Parita, the grand trading fairs of Khimiz, even the modest farmers' gatherings held at harvest time in western towns like Bruhome—and as she stood staring, a peculiar sense of unreality assailed her, bringing with it a formless and illogical dread.

Thia turned her masklike little face in Indigo's direction. "Please not to delay," she said with frosty politeness. "To waste time would be most unproductive."

With an effort Indigo shook herself free from the inertia that had taken hold of her and, as the child set off across the square, hastened after her. There was something unnerving about plunging into the midst of that quiet, unsmiling crowd, but the psychic wave of hostility that Indigo had expected didn't materialize. One or two gazes lit briefly on her white shoulder sash, but even these looks weren't overtly antagonistic. The townsfolk were simply as uninterested in the foreigner as they seemed to be in everything but their own immediate concerns.

Thia led her to the far side of the square, and a house with an unpainted door to which a wooden triangle had been nailed. The juvenile rapped on the door with a confidence that surprised Indigo, and moments later it was opened by a small, wizened woman. She wore no sash, and when she saw Indigo she made an obsequious bow.

"This is the widow of Physician Huni," Thia said without any greeting or other preamble. "She has no useful place now and so is shortly to leave this house. You will practice your healing skills in the room that was Physician Huni's." She turned to the old woman. "Please to show the way."

Still unspeaking, the woman turned back into the house, and they followed. She led them up a flight of dark, narrow stairs, at the top of which a door opened onto a large room. Two wooden stools, a table, and a rickety cupboard with double doors were the only furnishings; the walls and floor were bare, and the single lamp burning on the tabletop gave off an unwholesome smell along with its weak, parchment-yellow light. There was one window, but it looked straight out onto the featureless wall of another house. The room's whole atmosphere was drearily depressing.

The old woman bowed again and now spoke for the first time, though she addressed Thia and not Indigo. "The first patients are waiting below."

Thia started to say, "Send the first—" but Indigo interrupted her. She felt suddenly angry—angry at Thia's arro-

gant manner toward Huni's widow, and angry, too, at the
child's presumption that she herself had no mind or will of
her own.

"Thank you, Thia," she said acerbically. "I am quite able
to answer for myself." She smiled at the widow, and made
a bow of such courtesy that the old woman was visibly startled.

"I shall need five minutes to settle myself, madam," she
said. "Then, if you will be so kind, I shall see my first patient."

Huni's widow blinked in puzzlement. Perhaps, Indigo
thought, she hadn't expected a foreigner to speak her language so well. Then she gave a small shrug, said, "It will
be as you wish," and withdrew.

Indigo put her bag of herbs down on the table. The brief
flare of anger had settled below simmering point now, but
Thia's attitude still rankled, and she said, "Thia, you will
please me if you are less discourteous to Physician Huni's
widow in the future."

The child looked as surprised as the old woman had. "In
what way was I discourteous, please, Physician?"

"In what *way*?" Indigo echoed incredulously. "To speak
to her as though she were some menial, to speak to me
about her as though she were not there, and not to even
trouble to introduce us—*that* is the way, Thia!"

Thia's expression didn't change one whit, and suddenly
Indigo realized that her confusion was genuine. "But," Thia
said, "what function can the widow of Physician Huni perform? She is too old now to do useful work."

Sweet Earth Mother, Indigo thought, so *that* was at the
nub of it. Function. Use. Practical value. She remembered
some of the words Uncle Choai had used, first when they
met on the road and later at Hollend's house; speaking of "a
useful and worthy profession" and promising "an estimation
of your usefulness." Hardheaded practicality was virtually a
religion among these people—indeed, she thought, that

might be literally true, as they seemed to worship no gods or spiritual powers whatsoever. Thus Physician Huni's unfortunate widow, too old, as Thia said, to have any capacity for work, had been demoted on her husband's death to the status of a superfluous and potentially burdensome nuisance. What was worse, she seemed to accept it without question or demur. That was why she had been so taken aback by Indigo's courteous address.

"I think," Indigo said aloud, and with a wintry smile, "that I have a great deal to learn about Joyful Travail."

Thia inclined her head. "That is true of all foreigners, Physician. But Uncle Choai has wisely said that proper ways are learned with time."

Indigo raised an eyebrow at the clear implication that Choai had discussed her with Thia. Juvenile she might be, but the girl clearly had enough "useful" attributes to give her far more status than a mere foreigner. However she made no comment and turned instead to the cupboard. It wasn't locked, but its contents were a disappointment: only two rolled bandages, unwashed since their last use, and a collection of small earthenware pots and bottles containing the dregs of the Earth Mother alone knew what herbal nostrums. Hastily Indigo shut the cupboard again. She'd just have to manage as best she could with her own supplies; at least, she thought wryly, it seemed that she had little cause to worry about living up to Physician Huni's standards.

Well, there was no point in deferring the inevitable for longer than she must. Time to pay Uncle Choai for his token and prove her worth.

She opened her bag and sat down on the nearer of the two stools. "Very well, Thia," she said. "I'm ready. Fetch my first patient, please."

By sunset that evening, Indigo was in a daze of exhaustion. Thirty patients, Choai had said, but the true number had been more like fifty. Most had had only minor ailments or injuries: mild fevers, persistent coughs, or small wounds sustained in the fields that needed attention if they weren't to fester and rob the sufferer of valuable working time. Even so, Indigo felt drained to the marrow, not by the work itself, not even by the numbers of patients filing through her door, but by the sheer strain of having to deal with the people of Joyful Travail.

To begin with, they were clearly suspicious of her. She could see it in their eyes, in the sudden closing of their expressions when they realized that they must explain their maladies to a foreigner and not to one of their own. Yet this entrenched and instinctive attitude clearly clashed head-on with the deference—almost reverence—which protocol demanded must be shown to a physician as a matter of principle. So one after another they had sat stiff and silent, or squirming and evasive, on the opposite side of the table, while Indigo called on all the forbearance she could muster to persuade them to reveal what was wrong. As things turned out, and against her expectations, she had cause to be very thankful for Thia's presence; for those patients—and there were a few—who flatly refused to speak directly to the foreign healer were willing to describe their symptoms to the girl, and a procedure was established by which Thia solemnly conveyed what she had been told to Indigo, and Indigo instructed Thia which herbs to prescribe as a draught or mix as a poultice. The whole thing was farcical and made Indigo want to laugh aloud, but she pushed the impulse firmly down. Thia, for her part, seemed to find no humor whatever in the pantomime.

Midway through the afternoon, Indigo had insisted on a short respite from work. This, again, was something that Thia appeared to find incomprehensible, but she obeyed dutifully enough. Hungry and thirsty by now, Indigo offered the girl a wooden token that Calpurna had given her and asked her to go out into the market and buy them both something to eat and drink. She received a blank look and was informed that no such things were available in the market. Each citizen of Joyful Travail saw for his or her own sustenance as required. Prepared food and drink were not items to be *sold*.

"I have, however, a pasty that is to be my day's ration," Thia added. "I will share it with you, if you wish."

She brought something wrapped in a clean cloth from a satchel over her shoulder, and displayed it. A flat slab of grayish dough enclosing lumps of meat and vegetables—by the look and smell of it, unspiced and half raw into the bargain. Indigo forced a smile, trying not to make comparisons with Calpurna's fine cooking.

"Thank you, Thia, but I won't deprive you of your proper ration," she said. "I'll do well enough without. Though perhaps you might ask Physician Huni's wife if she will spare me a drink of water."

Thia bowed. "As you wish, Physician Indigo."

So while Thia munched her unappetizing pasty, Indigo tried between sips of brackish water to draw the girl out a little and find out more of her home and family. She soon realized that this, too, was a new concept to Thia's mind. The art of conversation for its own sake was alien to the girl, and she was convinced that there must be something more to Indigo's curiosity than a simple effort to be friendly. However, a few snippets of information were proffered, though reluctantly. Thia, it seemed, was the eldest of four daughters, a fact that seemed to please her, for it meant that with no brother to take precedence over her she was the kingpin of her parents' pride and ambition.

"I had learned to read and write and count by the time I was ten years old, and so no time was wasted before I was able to begin useful work," she told Indigo. "I am more intelligent and more diligent than others of my age, and so I shall do very well in life."

Indigo hid a smile at this complete disregard for anything

resembling modesty. "What do you do when you're not helping me?" she asked.

"Whatever the Uncles require of me," Thia said. "There are many useful tasks for someone of my talents, although I am still a juvenile. I copy documents for the Uncles and for the Foreigners' Duty House, I am assigned to many newcomers—like you—to help them carry out their duties. I convey letters and messages to people of high rank. And of course I assist my mother in her household." She smiled suddenly. "Although next year I shall marry and then I will have a household of my own to order."

"Marry?" Indigo was taken aback.

"Yes," Thia said blithely. "I have been chosen for the eldest son of Uncle Choai's nephew. He is younger than me, but when he reaches eighteen years and is an adult, he will have a place in the Trading Office and six bounds of land for his own use. His rank-color will be orange, and that is very worthy."

How old was Thia? Indigo wondered anew. Fourteen? Younger? She sounded more like a cynical middle-aged woman than the child she truly was, and Indigo said gently, hoping that her tone wasn't too ironic, "I hope you'll be very happy."

"Of course I shall." That smile again; it had no warmth in it. "Uncle Choai says that his great-nephew is both pleasant and industrious. We will suit each other very well."

*Uncle Choai says* . . . "Do you mean you haven't yet *met* your future husband?"

"There has been no need for us to meet." Thia looked faintly puzzled by the notion. Then, before Indigo could say any more, she swallowed the last mouthful of her pasty, folded the cloth neatly, and put it away, at the same moment standing up. "I have finished my meal. Thank you for permitting me to eat. Shall I call in your next patient?"

Indigo sighed. Thia, and Thia's attitudes, were beyond

her. "Yes," she said. "Yes, you may as well. I don't doubt that time spent in idleness is time immorally wasted."

Sarcasm was lost on Thia, and for the first time her smile looked utterly genuine. "That is just what Uncle Choai would say!" she declared firmly. "For a foreigner, Physician Indigo, you are very well versed in our ways. This will be of great pleasure to all!"

So now Indigo sat at the table, desultorily gathering her belongings back into her bag while Thia fussily helped her. The girl was clearly restless, and at last Indigo said,

"If you wish to go, Thia, I can manage well enough on my own."

The girl's face brightened. "Thank you, Physician Indigo. With your permission, I will leave."

Indigo suppressed a yawn. "I should be the one thanking you. You've been of great help to me." She paused. "Do I owe you any tokens?"

Thia bowed. "No, thank you. Juveniles are not permitted to accept payment for their services. If, however, you wish to give me a gift on any occasion, that will be quite acceptable."

"Then I'll do so." Indigo smiled at her. "What would you like? Some small jewels, to wear in your hair or around your neck?"

The girl looked blank. "Jewels are useful to those who wish to trade at the Foreigners' Enclave, but there is no purpose to be served by displaying them on one's person," she said; then, after a few moments' earnest consideration: "Two fowls in their first year of egg-laying would be suitable, or one sapling fruit tree, or one handspan of winter vegetable seed that can be sown this season before it loses vitality. I thank you for your generosity, Physician Indigo, and I will gratefully receive whichever of those choices you please to offer me." She bowed again and took a step toward the door. "I will attend on you tomorrow. I wish you a nourishing meal and a healthy night's sleep."

Indigo stared at the door as it closed behind Thia, and listened to the sound of her feet pattering down the stairs. She didn't know whether she wanted to laugh at the way in which Thia had neatly turned the possibility of a gift into the firm promise of a gift, or to lament at the depth of the girl's cold and unwavering pragmatism, which seemed to have not the least spark of humor or imagination to leaven it. In the end she did neither, but pushed Thia to the back of her mind and continued to gather up her effects, thinking instead of Grimya's eager welcome when she returned to the Foreigners' Enclave, and of the hot meal that Calpurna had promised would be waiting for her. She must find a way to repay Hollend and Calpurna for their hospitality, though she didn't know how best to do it. Certainly they didn't need money, and they'd probably be offended if she offered it, though she had more than enough to pay her way. Perhaps if—

Her speculations paused midstream as someone tapped on the door.

"Please?" It was a child's voice. "Please, is the physician at home?"

Indigo struggled not to let her spirits sink. Fifty patients in the space of an afternoon, and now, just when she'd thought she could rest at last, a newcomer . . . but if she had the temerity to call herself a healer, then she also had a healer's obligations. Besides, at this late hour it might well be an emergency.

She began to unlace the straps of her bag again, and tried not to sound resigned or irritable as she called out, "I am at home. Come in."

There was a pause, during which she heard what sounded like several more young voices whispering outside the door. Then the latch clicked and, diffidently, the door was pushed open.

There were three of them, none over seven or eight years old—or at least that was what Indigo thought at first glance. Their faces were thin and pinched, their eyes disproportionately huge as they stared at her in wonderment. Ragged hair, extraordinarily soft and fine, small, almost stunted bodies that made it impossible to tell whether they were boys or girls. They were all holding hands, as though to boost their flagging confidence, and suddenly they went into a huddle, whispering together again. There was a high-pitched giggle, and Indigo overheard the words *"white sash," "foreigner,"* and *"too soon."*

Beginning to lose patience at what appeared to be some kind of children's prank, she said a little sharply, remembering Calpurna's advice about being firm, "Come now! I haven't time to waste with games. What do you want?"

All three of her visitors stopped their muttering and looked at her. Then the middle one, who appeared to be their leader, said in a husky little voice,

"Do you *know* any games?"

It was such an extraordinary question that it threw Indigo completely and, as she floundered, another child piped, "We have seen you. We know you are the foreign healer. Will you heal us?"

Indigo had no warning but, as the child spoke, intuition suddenly and shockingly displaced logic, and the shock was redoubled as, at the same moment, she realized that she could see the contours of the drab hall not only behind the children, but *through* them. Their bodies were translucent.

She only had time to say, "Sweet Mother, I—"

The three children vanished.

# ·CHAPTER·IV·

"A most unfortunate occurrence." Uncle Choai bowed to Hollend in the peculiar, sidelong manner that conveyed apology. "I blame myself entirely. It is clear to me now that Physician Indigo was not sufficiently restored after the rigors of her journeying to be properly prepared for her work, and the fault for failure to recognize this is mine alone."

"No, no, Uncle," Hollend protested. "Indigo is my guest, and I take full responsibility for her well-being. *I* am to blame."

Choai bowed again. "You are most gracious. However, my conscience cannot be entirely assuaged by your kind words and will continue to trouble me. I have been hasty, and I trust"—here he gave Indigo an ingratiating smile—"that my folly may be overlooked."

Indigo tried to smile back at him, but it was a pallid effort, for she was still feeling the sting of acute embarrassment. She had come face to face with Choai on the stairs of the physician's house and there had been a confused exchange between them, she shocked and incoherent, he at first puzzled and then, when he finally comprehended what she was saying, solicitous and placatory together. He had firmly insisted on escorting her back to the Foreigners' Enclave, where he sorrowfully informed Hollend that Indigo appeared to have suffered some form of hallucinatory lapse, doubtless brought on by overtiredness. Indigo hadn't contradicted him; she was too dispirited by the results of her earlier efforts to convince him of the truth to try a second time, and now she sat silent while further compliments and thanks were exchanged. Elaborate farewells were made and Uncle Choai finally departed after expressing his hope that Physician Indigo would be fit to resume her work after a day or two of rest and recuperation.

Hollend and Calpurna both saw the official to the door. As soon as they left the room Indigo turned to Grimya, who sat on the floor at her feet.

"Grimya, before they come back—"

*Be careful!* the wolf warned silently. *The children aren't far away. Say nothing aloud.*

Indigo had forgotten about Ellani and Koru, and hastily she, too, switched to telepathic speech. *Grimya, I haven't been able to tell you before, but it happened again! The voices, the strange voices—only this time—*

Grimya's second warning interrupted her suddenly, and she drew back from the wolf in the instant before Hollend's voice hailed her as he walked back into the room, Calpurna close behind him.

"Well, Indigo, you've certainly made an impression on Uncle Choai!" Hollend was grinning. "I never thought I'd live to hear him apologize for anything! He must consider you a very valuable asset to Joyful Travail—what did you do, raise one of your patients from the dead?"

"Never mind what Indigo has or hasn't done to impress Choai." Calpurna's sharp tone showed that she considered her husband's remark to be in poor taste. "Indigo, I had no *idea* that you were so exhausted! I thought that a good night's sleep would be enough to restore you; I didn't *realize*—"

"Calpurna—Calpurna, please, listen to me." Indigo reached out to lay a hand on the Agantian woman's arm. "What Choai told you wasn't the whole story, not by any manner of means."

Calpurna hesitated. "What do you mean?"

Indigo told them what had happened: the knocking at her door when Thia had left, the three children who had put the bizarre question *"Do you know any games?"* before asking if she could heal them and then vanishing at the very moment when she realized that their bodies were as transparent as those of ghosts. For several seconds Indigo had been unable to do anything but stare witlessly at the empty doorway, then, violently, she had leapt to her feet and run from the room and down the steep stairs. Though what she had seen gave the lie to it, she had an irrational conviction that the children were still there, that she could pursue and catch them. Instead, at the open street door, she collided head-on with Uncle Choai. Why he had come to the house Indigo neither knew nor cared; disregarding all propriety she had caught hold of his sleeve.

"Uncle! The children—did you see them? Which direction did they take?"

Choai blinked very rapidly as curiosity supplanted his initial indignation. "Children, Physician Indigo? There are no children here."

She'd tried to explain what she had seen, but as soon as Choai began to grasp her meaning she knew that she'd made a great mistake. Quite simply he either wouldn't or couldn't believe her. People, whether children or otherwise, did not vanish before the eyes of their observers, he said. Such things were not possible. Indigo attempted to argue, but the old man was adamant. She must, he told her with an air of benign concern, have suffered a temporary unbalance of mind and senses due to overtiredness. It was quite clear that he was in error for assuming that she was fully fit to begin her work, and he would now make amends for his misunderstanding by personally escorting her back to the care and comfort of her hosts.

"He led me back here as though I were a half-witted invalid," Indigo finished, aware that Grimya was listening to her as intently as Hollend and Calpurna. "The rest you know, but for one thing. I'm not overtired and I did *not* hallucinate, whatever Uncle Choai might like to believe. I saw those children. They were there, they spoke to me, and then they vanished, exactly as I've described."

There was a long silence, broken only by a faint, worried whine from Grimya. Hollend and Calpurna exchanged looks that Indigo couldn't interpret, and it was Hollend who spoke at last.

"Indigo . . . I don't want to cast doubt on what you think you saw. But you have to admit, don't you, that old Choai was right?"

"Right?"

Calpurna took hold of her hand, squeezing it in a motherly way. "My dear, of course he was. As he said, such a thing simply isn't possible!" She smiled kindly, continuing in a tone she might have used to soothe a troubled child. "We all know that, don't we? Of course we do! You must have drifted off to sleep for a few moments, and dreamed it. Dreams can be like that." She glanced at her husband. "Falling asleep at your work's nothing to be ashamed of, as Hollend will testify!"

Appalled by her bland dismissal, Indigo started to say, "But Calpurna, you don't seem to—"

*No, Indigo. Don't argue with her.* Grimya's silent message came swiftly and urgently before she could get any further. *I have seen something in her mind, and in Hollend's, too. It's better that you say nothing. I will explain later, when we're on our own.*

"Now." Calpurna clapped her hands together, as if to signal that the subject of Indigo's lapse was comfortably resolved and thus closed. "We must see to it that the same mistake isn't allowed to occur again. You will rest, Indigo, and I mean *rest*, until your strength and vitality are completely restored. And your recuperation will begin with an excellent meal!"

She didn't give Indigo time to reply, but moved gracefully toward the kitchen. Hollend's expression flowered briefly into a look of relief and Indigo realized that her hosts were both discomfited by what she'd told them. Or perhaps *embarrassed* was closer to the mark; as though she'd committed some fundamental error of decorum by telling them about her uncanny experience or by even admitting that it had happened. She recalled her exchange with Calpurna in the kitchen that morning, following the disturbances of the night, and the revelation that Ellani and Koru had suffered from similar "delusions" in the past. Then, as now, Calpurna had seemed very eager to draw a curtain over the subject and dismiss any but the most rational of explanations, and Indigo couldn't understand why that should be.

From the kitchen now came cheerful noises as Calpurna prepared to serve the evening meal. The two children had prudently disappeared when they saw Uncle Choai approaching the house, but now Ellani emerged from the upper floor and, with a nod and a shy smile in Indigo's direction, hurried to join her mother. Indigo followed her as Hollend began to prepare the table, but Calpurna waved away her offer of help.

"No, no; Ellani is all the help I need." She smiled brightly; a little *too* brightly, Indigo thought. "Why not go up to your room and rest for a while? I'll send one of the children to fetch you when the meal's ready."

"If you're sure . . ."

"Of course I am. Go on now."

Grimya followed Indigo up the steep stairs, and as soon as the guest-room door had closed behind them, the wolf said in an urgent, guttural whisper,

"Good! Now we can talk—and I can tell you why I thought it would not be wise to argue with Calpurna."

Indigo glanced over her shoulder. "We'd best not discuss it aloud," she said, pitching her own voice softly. "The house's inner walls are flimsy, and sound might carry."

*Very well.* Grimya changed her mode of speech. *Listen, Indigo. You were very surprised when Calpurna and Hollend agreed with what the old man, Choai, said had happened to you. But I wasn't surprised, for I could sense something of what they were thinking.*

Though the wolf couldn't precisely read minds, her acute mental senses were often attuned to people's prevailing moods and stray unguarded thoughts. Indigo waited to hear more, and Grimya continued. *They did not believe you because they could not believe you. Something has happened to them both, I think, in the years they have lived here. They have become like the people of this country. They have lost the ability to believe in anything that is not very logical.*

Indigo began to comprehend. *Like voices in the night?*

*Like that, yes. And like children who appear from nowhere and then disappear back into nowhere again,* Grimya paused. *You must have seen it for yourself. All the people here are the same. It is as if they have forgotten how to dream.*

As if they have forgotten how to dream . . . With her uncanny talent for reaching straight to the heart, Grimya had exactly encapsulated Indigo's own disquieting impression of Joyful Travail—indeed, of this entire country—and its inhabitants. Did the sly Uncle Choai, or the primly calculating Thia, or any of their fellow countrymen and women know what a dream was? Were they capable of perceiving anything beyond the strict limits of their physical senses, or of imagining anything beyond the narrow confines of a future planned and mapped to the last icily pragmatic detail? Everything she had seen so far suggested that Grimya was right. So, faced with a sudden anomaly in the form of a foreigner who claimed to have come face to face with three ghosts, their reaction was one of blind and resolute rejection. They did not believe in such things, therefore such things could not exist. There was no room for error; no *possibility* of error. The foreigner was wrong and that was the end of the matter. But surely Hollend and Calpurna didn't share that senseless prejudice? They were outsiders, they hadn't been immersed from childhood in the dogmas of this alien culture, and so they must surely have more open minds. Yet, in this at least, they seemed to be as blind as Choai.

Grimya, who had listened to Indigo's confused thoughts, said: *Perhaps the years in this country have changed them. Perhaps they have caught this thing, this unbelief, like a disease.*

Was it possible? For a weak or foolish mind, or to the vulnerable consciousness of a young child, perhaps. But Hollend and Calpurna were both too intelligent and strong-willed to fall prey so easily to outside influences. They looked down on the people of Joyful Travail, almost despised them, albeit with an element of affection in their disparagement. It didn't make *sense*.

She turned to the wolf again. *I don't know what lies behind this, Grimya. But whatever Hollend and Calpurna and Choai say—whatever anyone says—I know what I saw! And I wasn't dreaming!*

Before Grimya could answer her there was a light rap at the door, and a small, hesitant voice called her name. Indigo started violently as her mind flashed back to the physician's room—but the voice was familiar.

"Koru?"

He came in, bobbing his head at her in a way that blended, oddly, the greeting courtesies of both Agantia and

Joyful Travail. "Mother says the meal will be ready in a few minutes."

"Oh . . . oh, yes. Thank you, Koru. I'll come down in just a moment."

She expected him to bob his head again and leave, but instead he lingered, and it was obvious that he was striving to overcome his innate shyness to say something more. Puzzled, Indigo queried gently, "Koru? What is it? Is something wrong?"

Koru fidgeted guiltily, pressing one foot down on top of the other and clasping his hands behind his back. Then, in a rush, he blurted,

"I didn't mean to listen! But I couldn't help it!"

Grimya's ears pricked suddenly. *He means the old man Choai. He must have heard what was said—and what you told his parents.*

Koru's face was painfully red with shame and he might have lost courage and bolted before Indigo could speak again, but Grimya suddenly moved toward him, tail wagging, and reached up to lick his chin. It was a wise and perfectly timed gesture, for Koru was already utterly fascinated and disarmed by the she-wolf and entertained secret fancies that, one day, he too might have such a "dog" of his own. Gratefully he buried his hands in the dense fur of her ruff, hiding his face, and with it his embarrassment.

Indigo flashed Grimya a warmly grateful glance and addressed the boy kindly.

"There's no need to worry, Koru," she said. "I don't mind that you listened—and I won't tell anyone if you don't want me to."

Slowly Koru looked up, his expression hopeful. "I didn't *mean* to," he said again. "It was just that I've . . ." Then he faltered as his nerve failed him once more.

Indigo's mind made a sudden intuitive leap and she decided to gamble that she was right. She leaned toward him, her voice soft. "You've seen them, too? Is that it?"

Koru stood very still. Then, emphatically, he nodded.

She let out a breath that she hadn't even realized she'd been holding. "Three children, like the ones who came to me?"

"No. There were only two. But I could see *through* them, just the way you said!"

Indigo's heart was quickening by the moment. "Did they talk to you?"

Another nod. "They wanted me to go out and play with them. I . . ." He glanced uneasily toward the window. "I said no. It was night, and I was scared. So they went away again, just like the ones you saw. But . . . sometimes I still hear them outside. They call me. They call my name, and they say, 'Come and play. Come and play.' "

Again the question *"Do you know any games?"* echoed in Indigo's memory, and a strange, chilly shiver ran the length of her spine. Koru looked up at her. Suddenly his eyes were fearful.

"You won't tell, will you, Indigo?" he pleaded helplessly. "Not *anyone!*"

"Of course not. I promise."

"You see . . . I told Ellani, but she hit me and said I must never say anything about it ever again."

"She *hit* you?" Indigo was shocked; it was impossible to imagine the sweet-faced Ellani being moved to such extremes, especially against her brother whom she seemed to love dearly. But somehow she didn't think Koru was lying.

*It begins to make a pattern,* Grimya's voice said somberly in her mind. *Ellani first, this morning, and then Calpurna, and now the story Koru tells us. These are the same voices and the same creatures that followed us on the road, but no one here believes in them, except for us and Koru.*

*And Ellani,* Indigo nodded.

*Yes, and Ellani. But she is too frightened to admit what she knows. That is why she was so angry with her brother.*

The soft but clear sound of a copper gong shimmered suddenly from below, and Koru's eyes widened with alarm.

"That's Mother! The meal's ready—I said that I'd only be a moment—"

Indigo hastily gathered her wits. "Don't worry," she reassured the boy. "I'll tell her that I invited you to stay and play with Grimya. No one will know what you've told me, Koru. I promise you that."

Relief suffused his face. "Thank you!" He turned to go, then: "Indigo . . . do *you* believe those other children were real?"

She hesitated, wondering if it was wise to be completely honest. Koru was so young, so impressionable; she knew how his mother would have wanted her to answer such a question and felt that she had no right to go against Calpurna's wishes. She wrestled with her conscience—then abruptly found herself stung by a keen spark of anger. Whatever her reasons, Calpurna was trying to deny the truth. And the truth, Indigo decided, was something that not even a child's own mother had the right to withhold from him.

"Yes, Koru," she said. "I believe they were. I believe they *are*."

The boy stood motionless for a few seconds while his expression went through an extraordinary ferment of different emotions. Then one emotion triumphed—sheer, exuberant, and open wonderment.

"Oh, yes," he said. "Oh, *yes*! They must be real, mustn't they? After all, we've both seen them now!" He opened the door and took a step onto the landing, then his voice dropped to a conspiratorial whisper. "This will be our secret, won't it? Ours and no one else's. And now that you're here, now that they've found someone older than me who believes in them, they'll come back, I *know* they will. And this time, I won't be afraid to play with them!"

# ·CHAPTER·V·

That night Indigo had a strange and vivid dream. She seemed to wake from a deep sleep to find herself climbing down the ladder-stairs that led to the house's lower floor. There was light below, and a murmuring of voices, and as the main room came into view below her Indigo saw that it was filled with people. Or, rather, the *shadows* of people. She blinked, rubbed at her eyes, looked again, and it was the same: shadows, moving purposefully this way and that, yet with no physical forms to cast them.

"Hollend?" Her own voice echoed strangely against the murmuring background. "Calpurna?" She looked for some familiar figure among the shifting, two-dimensional shapes, but the shadows were constantly changing as they passed over walls, across furniture, and it was impossible to make out any distinguishing feature.

Without quite knowing how, she had reached the foot of the stairs, and suddenly one voice spoke out above the rest, from behind her. It said crisply:

"And what was *your* name?"

Indigo whirled. The light in the room was misty, like the sun filtering through deep water, but she could see well enough to make out a large lectern standing, incongruously, where the kitchen doorway should have been. There was someone behind the lectern. His head was bent over a large, open book and he was writing busily, with an absurdly large quill pen. On his head, something dully metallic glinted.

Indigo stared at him, and he repeated with a tinge of impatience, "Come, come. The question is perfectly clear. Your name, please."

He was speaking her own language, the tongue of the Southern Isles ... Involuntarily Indigo took a step toward the lectern, and abruptly the man's head came up. She realized then that what he wore on his head was a crown, old and tarnished and decorated with sharp spikes, some of which had broken or crumbled away. It might have been made of bronze or of some other metal discolored by the patina of age; it was impossible to tell. But there was, she thought, something unclean about it.

The face below the crown was staring at her. Brown eyes, large and soft and almost bovine. Hair the salt-and-pepper of black turning to gray, neatly cut in a sharp fringe above brows of the same color. A long, narrow nose, peculiarly twisted as though at some time it had been broken and badly reset. Heavy jowls, and between them a mouth so small and plump and vividly red that it looked as if it didn't truly belong to him but had been stolen from another individual entirely.

He smiled, not altogether pleasantly. "I assure you, this is as tedious for me as it is for you, but the proper procedures must be observed. For the third time, what was your *name*?"

Awake, Indigo would have been alerted by the question's strangeness. Not *is*, he had said, but *was*. In her dream, though, she simply opened her mouth and said, "Anghara Kaligsdaughter, of Carn Caille on the Southern Isles."

Shock went through her like a painful physical jolt. What had she said? She'd given him her true name—the name she'd been forced to relinquish half a century ago!

"No!" Her voice cracked. "No, not that! I was wrong, that isn't—"

She stopped. The brown eyes were regarding her, and the smile vanished as the red mouth pursed tightly.

"The entry has been made and second thoughts cannot be allowed for. Name: Anghara Kaligsdaughter. Function: physician. Status: foreigner. Purpose . . . ah, yes—now we come to the most important question. What is your purpose?"

She didn't understand and he clearly knew it, for impatience flickered once again in his face.

"*Purpose,*" he repeated with the resigned air of a sage faced with willful idiocy. "You must have a purpose, or you would not be here. What is it?"

"I have no *purpose,*" Indigo said, still unsure of herself. "I intend only—"

"Wrong." He interrupted her with indifferent but absolute certainty. "That is the wrong answer, and cannot be recorded. Tell the truth."

And behind her, the shadow-voices began to whisper, *"Tell the truth, tell the truth, the truth, the truth . . ."*

This was insane . . . "I *am* telling the truth!" Indigo protested vehemently, as anger at last began to break through the hold the dream had over her. "Who are you to question me, and to doubt my word?"

The man's strange, rosebud mouth widened suddenly in a peaceable and utterly confident smile. "I am the Benefactor. All know the Benefactor. All must answer to me in one way or in another. There are no exceptions."

"*I* do not know you," Indigo retorted sharply.

The smile remained. "Then you would be wise to learn of me, or you will find little to content you here." With a decisive flourish the quill pen made a mark in the ledger, and the man nodded at her. "Go back to the quarters assigned to you, and consider your purpose. Two paths are open to you: decide which you will follow, and when you have decided, I will grant you a second interview."

Close behind Indigo, something giggled. Involuntarily she looked over her shoulder, but saw only the misty light and the anomalous shadow-shapes drifting, apparently aimless, about the room. She turned back again—but the lectern and its occupant had vanished, and instead Calpurna was emerging from the kitchen, a welcoming smile on her face and a steaming china dish in her hands.

"Welcome, Indigo!" Her lips didn't move, but her voice floated clearly. "Stay with us, Indigo! We will teach you! We will be friends!"

And from the room at her back, other voices, children's voices. *"No, no. No, no. There is another choice. There are other people."*

"Where's Grimya?" In the illogical way of dreams, Indigo asked the question for no reason. Again Calpurna's lips didn't move; again her voice came clearly.

"Grimya is with the children. Grimya is at work, with the children."

*"No, no. No, no. Grimya has come to play with us instead. Grimya plays with us. Play with us, too, Indigo. Play with us; play your harp and sing. Do you know any songs? Do you know any games?"*

As Indigo stood confused and suddenly frightened in the middle of the floor, Calpurna reached her and, insubstantial as smoke, walked through her and on across the room.

Indigo yelped with shock, and woke in an icy sweat amid a tangle of disordered blankets.

"We'll send word to Uncle Choai that you must have at least three days' rest, and if he doesn't like the idea then he may do as he pleases!" Calpurna's tone was firm, and she set Indigo's breakfast down on the table with a decisive thump before looking long and hard into her guest's face.

"My dear, you're positively gray. Are you *quite* sure you shouldn't be taking a sleeping draught at nights?"

"If she needs one, my love, she's well able to prescribe it for herself," Hollend said.

Calpurna shot him a scathing look, but Indigo insisted that she had no such need. "Truly, Calpurna, I *did* sleep well." She smiled. "My only problem was with dreams, and I don't think there's a physician in the world who knows a remedy for those."

"Dreams?" Calpurna's pleasant face became sympathetic. "Ah, well, that's something that never troubles us; isn't that so, Hollend?"

Hollend grunted assent. "I can't remember when I last had a dream. Must have been years ago." He raised an expressive glance heavenward. "And thankful I am to be rid of them, too."

"Koru still has the occasional nightmare, but then of course he's so young," Calpurna went on, adding comfortably, "he'll grow out of it soon, I'm sure. Now, Indigo, let me help you to some of this new seed-bread. It's Ellani's own baking and she's very anxious that you should try it."

Ellani, sitting at the far side of the table, blushed, and Indigo realized that once again Calpurna had deftly steered away from what seemed to be an undesirable subject and onto safer ground. Remembering what Koru had said she thought perhaps it would be better to let the matter drop— but for one odd factor, one memory from the dream that wouldn't let her alone but kept echoing in her mind.

She took a bite from the bread Calpurna had set in front of her. It was very good—Ellani had a burgeoning talent for cookery—and she praised it lavishly, at the same time not failing to notice the look of profound relief on Calpurna's face. Then, quite casually, she said, "Oh, Calpurna, I've been meaning to ask you. Have you ever heard of someone called the Benefactor?"

She'd anticipated either blank incomprehension or another of those sudden, nervous silences. But to her surprise Calpurna smiled broadly, and Hollend laughed.

"Well, well. I see they haven't wasted any time. Who's been extolling the virtues of the Benefactor to you—Choai, was it? Or is that juvenile they assigned to you, Thua or whatever her name is, earning herself a few extra tokens by drumming up more trade for the House?"

"The House?" Indigo was nonplussed. "What's that?"

"Good grief, three days in Joyful Travail and she hasn't yet heard of the House? The Committees are growing lax!" Hollend grinned as he helped himself to more of Ellani's bread. "This is good, daughter, very good. You're improving rapidly." He took a bite, then waved his knife at Indigo and continued speaking with his mouth full. "But seriously, Indigo, it might be worth your while paying a visit there. Everyone does sooner or later, and they have some interesting old artifacts on display."

Curiosity—and something else, something indefinable—had begun to nag at Indigo like a sore tooth. "But what *is* the House?" she asked. "And what does it have to do with this Benefactor?"

"Well, you see, it all happened many hundreds of years ago, or so the locals say—" Hollend began, but Calpurna interrupted him.

"Hollend, don't talk through your food—you're becoming as mannerless as the natives. What will Indigo think of you?" And to Indigo: "If he starts trying to explain it you'll be sitting here until past noon, so I'll tell you myself. The House—and actually, for once, it's not so grand a term even by the standards of these parts—stands a mile outside town, on a hill overlooking the southernmost fields. It's what you might call a museum—"

"More of a mausoleum," Hollend interjected, still eating.

"Museum or mausoleum, as you please. The locals are very proud of it, for they say it was the home of some great leader, a king or a Takhan, I don't know what title they used in this country. No one seems to know his name, for he lived centuries ago, but they refer to him as the Benefactor."

*All know the Benefactor. All must answer to me* . . . The words of the man in her dream echoed in Indigo's mind, and she suppressed a small shiver. "He was their ruler?" she asked.

"So it would seem. I know what you're thinking: it's hard to imagine a country so riddled with Committees having one individual to reign over them, but it seems things were different then. Anyway, they hold this Benefactor in great regard—"

"Almost reverence, you might say," Hollend put in.

"Well, yes, I suppose you might . . ." Calpurna looked a little puzzled by the term but then returned to her topic. "And when he died they preserved his house as a memorial to him. There's yet another Committee, formed for the sole purpose of keeping the House in good order. They're very proud of it, and very keen to show visitors around, especially foreigners, of course. They claim that to this day it looks exactly as it did on the day the Benefactor died."

Hollend, still eating, made a dissenting noise and hastily swallowed his mouthful of bread. "No, my dear, you're wrong there. The Benefactor didn't die, he *disappeared*. That's part of the story, don't you remember from our own visit to the House?"

"Oh . . . yes, now that you mention it I believe I do recall . . . Well, anyway, whatever he did, whether he died or disappeared or went to live somewhere else, the locals have kept his home as a showpiece. You really should go and see it, Indigo. It's quite educational."

The were interrupted at that moment by the arrival of Koru, with Grimya padding at his heels. The wolf tended to wake and become restless at dawn, and Koru, with a small boy's boundless energy, was only too ready to accompany her around the Enclave for early-morning exercise. Now he politely said his good mornings to Indigo and his family and scrambled onto his chair to devour ravenously the breakfast his mother set before him. Hollend, smiling fondly, leaned over to pinch his son's cheek.

"You've got a healthy color this morning, Koru. Grimya's company is clearly doing you good!"

Koru smiled back. "She's fun, Papa. I wish *I* could have a dog."

"Well, we'll have to see. All depends on whether we can find a good use for one, doesn't it?"

"I can think of lots. For instance—"

"Yes, dear, I'm sure you can," Calpurna intervened soothingly, "but not now. Eat your breakfast, or you'll be late for your lessons. I expect Grimya's hungry, too, Indigo. If you'd like to bring her to the kitchen when you've finished, there's plenty of yesterday's meat left over."

Grimya's ears pricked eagerly and she wagged her tail, making Hollend and Koru laugh.

"I do believe she understood you, my love." Hollend shook out his fine linen napkin—another import from Agantia—and folded it neatly. "Now, Koru, we were just telling Indigo about the Benefactor's House, and that she should see it."

Koru stopped chewing and his eyes lit. "Oh, yes! Oh, Indigo, you must!" He squirmed round in his chair, breakfast momentarily forgotten. "Papa, couldn't I take her? You know how much I like the House! Let me, please!"

Hollend beamed. "That's a sensible idea. Indigo, will you allow Koru to be your escort? I'll tell you this much—he'll be a more interesting guide than the walking corpses of the House Committee!"

"Now, Hollend," Calpurna said disapprovingly, "Koru has his schooling and his work."

Like all children in Joyful Travail, Koru and his sister spent half of each day at lessons and the other half at work. Ellani's afternoons were taken up with what Joyful Travail considered "proper" duties for a girl, while Koru, too young yet to be of much practical help to Hollend in his business, worked with other boys from the Enclave in the fields outside the town, receiving a share of produce as payment for his efforts.

"Oh, a day's leave will do him no harm. He's but eight years old, my dear; he needs a little respite now and then."

"*I'll* be working today," Ellani said a little resentfully. "I don't see why Koru should be excused."

"Well, then, my chick, you may go, too." Hollend ignored his wife's frowns. But Ellani shook her head.

"No, thank you. I don't like that place."

Aware of tension among the family and embarrassed to feel that she was the cause of it, Indigo hastily tried to soothe Calpurna's and Ellani's ruffled feelings. "I don't want to be a nuisance—" she began.

Hollend waved her protest aside. "No, no, you're no such thing! A day's leisure won't ruin Koru, and the Uncles can mutter to their hearts' content. If he wants to go with you to the House, he may do so. And if he escorts you politely and properly, and can answer all your questions, then we'll call it work and I'll pay him the proper token. All right?" He looked up at Calpurna.

Calpurna tried to resist the amused chuckle that came to her but failed. "Oh, very well. It'll probably benefit Indigo to be seen visiting the House, anyway. The townsfolk will take it as an indication that she wishes to learn their ways." She smiled at Indigo. "I'll pack you some meat rolls and a flask of fruit juice. It's an arduous walk up that hill, and the guided tour is long and tedious. Koru can take enough tokens to pay your entrance fee."

Her last words, though carelessly and naturally uttered, brought a sudden pang of guilt to Indigo's mind. For three days now she had enjoyed the family's free and generous hospitality, with never a mention of how, or even if, she might repay their kindness. And however Uncle Choai and his ilk might view the matter, Indigo felt that it was time to make recompense.

She said so, and was immediately shouted down. Hollend and Calpurna would hear of no such thing. Her society alone, they insisted, was payment enough; and besides—without wishing to give offense—what could she offer them that they didn't already have? By the standards of Joyful Travail they were wealthy; they needed no money, for they already had more than enough to buy anything that this country could offer, and what Joyful Travail couldn't provide was amply supplied by the regular shipments from Agantia. They had made a new friend whose company they enjoyed; that was repayment, they said, in abundant measure.

Indigo was touched by their words and by the sincerity that she knew had prompted them, but all the same she couldn't in all conscience let the subject go at that. That was how she came to say the thing that, later, turned her stomach to ice when she thought back on it.

"Well," she told them, half laughing, self-conscious at their fulsome arguments, "if that's true, then I thank you. But perhaps there's still one thing I can do, though the Mother knows it isn't much." She gestured diffidently in the direction of the stairs. "In my room, I have a harp. I'm no bard, but I play well enough, and I sing, too. If I can do nothing else, maybe I might at least sing for my supper?"

There was a small silence. Not an unpleasant or tense silence, simply one of bafflement. Then Calpurna said, "Sing . . .?"

"Yes." Indigo's puzzlement matched theirs. "I make no claims to any real talent, but . . ." Her voice trailed off. Hollend and Calpurna were both smiling at her, but it was the smile of indulgent parents faced by the unfathomable reasoning of a very small child for whom allowances must naturally be made.

"Well," Hollend said at last. "That is very thoughtful of you, Indigo."

"Yes." Calpurna chimed in quickly, as though grateful for her husband's lead. "*Most* thoughtful. And of course, if you would like to play and sing, we will be pleased to hear you. But . . ." She and Hollend exchanged a glance over the bowed head of Koru. "There really is no need, Indigo. I mean . . . Well, there's no *purpose* in music and singing, is there?" She gave Indigo a strange, pallid little smile. "And what is the value of something without purpose?"

# ·CHAPTER·VI·

Though they would probably have objected strongly to the term, the people solemnly making their way up the hill toward the Benefactor's House had the look of pilgrims approaching a shrine. Indigo, Grimya, and Koru overtook three individuals and one small group toiling along in the dry, dusty heat, and each face bore the same look of rapt eagerness fortified by a distinct aura of self-righteous piety. None wore foreigners' white sashes, but all except one middle-aged woman condescended to return Indigo's polite bow as she passed them. Judging from what Koru had told her, it seemed that regular visits to the House were very much the done thing for any man or woman who had a position to maintain, and foreigners who made the arduous trek up the hill were held in greater esteem—or at least in less disdain—as a result. Why this should be, and what unspoken tradition drew the folk of Joyful Travail back to the House time and again throughout their lives, was still a mystery to Indigo. Certainly the place had no religious significance, for, as she was rapidly learning, spiritual concepts had no place whatever here. Hollend and Calpurna could offer no explanation other than to say that it simply *was* a tradition, and Koru was too young to be interested in whys and wherefores. But, still haunted by her dream, Indigo couldn't shake off the feeling that something strange, untoward, and as yet unexplained lay behind the blank wall that had shut the House away from any casual gaze for so long.

They walked on, drawing away from the other walkers on the track. The palisades of Joyful Travail had fallen behind them now, and the House's oddly symmetrical hill dominated the view, rising above the wide, green-and-brown sweep of cultivated fields. Of the building itself little was visible, for the hilltop was surrounded by a high stone wall crowned with savage iron spikes; only the pointed and moss-encrusted apex of a tiled roof showed above these defenses. With a child's boundless energy Koru was setting a fierce pace along the track, and though Grimya had no difficulty in keeping up with him, Indigo was beginning to flag. Autumn in these latitudes was often heralded by a heat wave, and by the time she trudged up the last few yards of stony road in Koru's wake she could feel sweat prickling on her skin under her light clothing. Where the road ended, a wooden postern gate had been set into the wall, and a number of early arrivals were already waiting for the appointed time when the gate would open to admit them. According to the hard-faced and superior young man whom Indigo had encountered earlier behind the desk at the Foreigners' Duty House, tours of the House were conducted by authorized Committee Guides twice each day, the first tour commencing one hour before noon, the second three hours before sunset. A young couple wearing white sashes smiled self-consciously at Indigo and Koru; the others ignored them save for baffled and faintly disapproving glances in

Grimya's direction, clearly wondering what possible function her presence here could be serving.

As the last stragglers came up to the wall, a bolt clanked on the far side of the postern and the gate swung open to reveal a diminutive woman wearing a severe black tabard and trousers, with a red sash at her shoulder. She uttered no greeting but simply said in clipped, well-rehearsed tones,

"I am a representative of the Benefactor's House Committee, and your authorized guide. My name is Aunt Nikku. Please to pay your fees and then to follow me." Unsmiling, she moved to each visitor in turn, one hand palm upward, checking the value of each token as it was passed to her before secreting her tally in a leather pouch with a strong clasp. Indigo and her companions were among the last in line, and as she reached them Aunt Nikku pointed at Grimya.

"You have brought an animal. What is the purpose of this?"

Indigo bowed courteously but her eyes gleamed. "Is there a rule forbidding animals to enter the House?"

"There is no rule. But I see no necessity for the animal to come in."

Koru, anticipating trouble, spoke up quickly. "The dog is well trained, please, Aunt Nikku." He, too, bowed to the small woman. "This new foreigner is Physician Indigo; she is lodging with my father, Hollend the Agantian. We will of course insist upon paying the proper fee for the animal, too." And with great aplomb he produced a high-value token and held it out.

Despite his tender years Koru had the measure of these people, Indigo thought as after only a moment's hesitation Aunt Nikku took the token and slipped it into one of her own pockets instead of adding it to her bulging pouch. "This is a legitimate request," she agreed with a gracious nod. "Provided that the animal is clean and makes no noise, its presence will be acceptable."

Suppressing a smile, Indigo watched her march self-importantly to the head of the line. "We will begin," she announced. "Please to follow. Questions of relevance may be asked when the tour is completed." Without another glance in the direction of Indigo and her friends, she led them through the postern and into the walled grounds beyond.

Indigo's immediate reaction when she had her first clear sight of the Benefactor's House was one of surprise quickly followed by disappointment. From Koru's eager descriptions she had anticipated some magnificent and ornate mansion set amid sumptuous gardens and with myriad windows glittering in the morning sun. Certainly the House was unusual, for instead of following the customary foursquare style of local architecture it was built in the shape of a hexagon with four floors, each floor slightly smaller than the one below, and the whole crowned with an overhanging roof that rose to a central point, like a bizarre hat. But despite its uncommon shape the building was unadorned and functional, and the gardens that surrounded it were not gardens of shrubs and lawns and trees but simply an acreage of tilled land on which vegetable crops grew in regimented rows. Certainly the House was large by the standards of Joyful Travail, but beyond its size and its unusual configuration there was nothing to mark it as the dwelling place of a great and noble ruler. Indeed, Indigo thought, in many of the countries she had visited—in Khimiz, say, or even the modestly prosperous farmlands of the Western Continent—the home of anyone above the status of small vintner or minor merchant would have been built on a more exalted scale than this.

Grimya, who had gleaned her thoughts and shared them, gazed around her with a baffled air. *This is very strange,* she said silently. *There is nothing grand about this house. Why do people feel such reverence for it?*

Why indeed? But there *was* an air of reverence, almost

of rapture, in the expressions and demeanors of their fellow sightseers that didn't match Indigo's impressions of Joyful Travail's natives. Even the two young foreigners seemed to have caught the prevailing mood, surreptitiously holding hands and staring at the house with wide, respectful eyes.

Aunt Nikku, however, was not inclined to tolerate loitering. Clapping her hands imperiously to call her charges to order, she set off at a brisk pace along a path of wooden slats, one of several laid in a crisscross pattern over the vegetable beds to keep visitors' shoes clean. Three or four laborers were tending the crops but none looked up as the party went by, and Aunt Nikku ignored them. She had begun a monologue that Indigo, near the end of the line, couldn't fully make out but that seemed to be about the productivity of the soil and the diligence of the House Committee in maintaining the highest standards. Abandoning her efforts to hear better, Indigo concentrated her scrutiny on the House now looming ahead. As they approached the open front door she decided that the Committee's standards, however lavishly Aunt Nikku might praise them, left something to be desired; for although the House was in good repair, little if anything had been done to show it to its best advantage. The stone walls were unpainted, the door likewise, and the windows were so grimy that it was obvious no one ever took the trouble to wash them. Another paradox— that Joyful Travail's greatest pride and joy should be marred and diminished by such simple yet fundamental neglect . . . and yet, she thought, perhaps that in itself was yet further confirmation of local attitudes. After all, if the House was no longer occupied, what would be the value of cleaning its windows? Simply an unnecessary expenditure of time and effort, like so much else that might have made life in this peculiar land more pleasant.

*There is a word for what you're thinking,* Grimya said,

and her mental tone was faintly disapproving. *But I can't remember it.*

Indigo's lip twitched with amusement. She knew what the wolf meant, what the word was, and that she couldn't hide anything from her friend for long. *Cynical? Yes, perhaps I am, Grimya. But the more I see of the people hereabouts, the harder it is not to think in such a way.*

An odd sound that was Grimya's equivalent of a human sigh echoed in her mind. *I know. Yet I don't believe they think and behave as they do on purpose. They simply don't know any better.*

*They don't* want *to know,* Indigo said firmly. *That's the worst of it. Even the foreigners who have lived here for any length of time seem to catch the same disease, the—*

Grimya interrupted her. *Indigo . . .*

The vanguard of their party had reached the House's front door, and suddenly the wolf halted, her ears pricked forward and her nose twitching.

*What is it?* Indigo asked. *What's wrong?*

*I saw something. By the door. It moved too fast to be clear, and now it's gone. But it looked like a little child.*

An elderly man behind them cleared his throat pointedly, and Indigo realized that she, too, had stopped and was holding up the people behind her. Bowing an apology she stepped aside to let the others pass, then looked at Grimya.

*Are you sure you didn't imagine it?*

*Quite sure. And I smell something, too. Not a proper smell, but a . . . a . . .* She groped for the word but couldn't find it. *You know what I mean.*

Indigo did. Something psychic—now she could feel it, too, as she stared at the entrance only a few yards ahead. The House's atmosphere was spilling out, reaching toward them . . . and it reeked of power.

She turned to the wolf, her face shocked. *Grimya what—*

"Not to dawdle, please!" Aunt Nikku's sharply reproachful voice cut into the half-formed question, and Indigo looked up to see the little woman glaring at her from the House's threshold. "All visitors must keep together and not delay the tour!"

Again Indigo made the sidelong bow. "My apologies." And silently to the wolf she added, *Say nothing more for now, Grimya. But stay alert. I suspect we might find more here than either of us had bargained for.*

"And before you now you will see the couch upon which the Benefactor rested each night. Please to note that this couch takes up no more space than is strictly necessary, and also that it is placed in such a position as to permit its occupant to rise and reach the stairs to the lower floors with the minimum of effort wasted."

Aunt Nikku paused briefly for her listeners to absorb this piece of information, then continued, word-perfect and monotonous. "It is a documented fact that the Benefactor needed no more than two hours' sleep each night, thus saving much time to be put to valuable use. This example is one that we will all do very well to follow, for it is well known that sleeping hours are wasted hours, and wasted hours afford no profit to the idle. The Benefactor made it clear that not all may have the strength to emulate him in this, but to strive is to earn, and credit comes to all who do their best."

She moved on and the party dutifully followed her, filing past the couch on its roped-off dais. Their faces, even those of the foreigners, all wore properly respectful expressions; one or two nodded their heads sagely as though savoring the indisputable truth of Aunt Nikku's homily. Indigo, though, stared thoughtfully at the blanketless and obviously very uncomfortable bed on its six squat legs, and felt again the nagging sense of unease that had been growing in her since they had set foot inside the building.

She'd paid no attention to Aunt Nikku's droning lecture and very little to Koru's eagerly whispered and frequent asides. Instead she had tried to bring her more subtle senses to bear on what her eyes and ears were telling her. And she was beginning to reach an unnerving, if not entirely unexpected, conclusion.

To all appearances the Benefactor's House was indeed nothing more than a museum, a memorial to one man whose life had epitomized all that was held most dear by the people of Joyful Travail. Calpurna's assertion that the place had been preserved exactly as it was when the Benefactor died wasn't quite accurate, for the House Committee or their predecessors had ensured that the relics in their care were carefully shielded from curious or acquisitive fingers by rope barriers that obliged visitors to follow a narrow and strictly defined route through the House's many rooms. For nearly two hours Indigo and Grimya had followed silently in Aunt Nikku's wake as she led her party first through the kitchen, laundry, and ablutions rooms on the ground floor, then up an open and alarmingly creaky staircase to the workrooms above, then to the third story, which housed sleeping accommodations for the Benefactor, servants, and guests. All the levels were dully alike, the furniture and objects on display no more interesting than those to be found in any local dwelling, and the little sunlight that was able to penetrate through the high, grimy windows cast a depressing patina over everything. But despite the dullness, despite the monotony, Indigo knew with an instinct as sure as any of her physical senses that what they were seeing was only a small part of the true picture. Grimya knew it, too, and so, she suspected, did Koru, though he wasn't consciously aware of it. As the tour progressed she'd watched the little boy, and believed now that she had an inkling of why he had been so eager to return to this place. It wasn't the exhibits that fascinated him, and it most certainly wasn't Aunt Nikku's lectures. It was the House's atmosphere. Koru hadn't yet fallen prey to the creeping malaise of materialism that pervaded Joyful Travail; unlike his parents, and even his sister, he was still young enough to be immune to that joyless, spiritless infection. He had seen the ghost-children. Did he see them now? Or did he at least feel their presence? For they were here. Hiding in shadows, invisible and noiseless and unwilling to reveal themselves, but *here*. And this House, Indigo believed, was inextricably linked with them and with whatever strange, unearthly realm they inhabited.

A sharp sound startled her, snapping her back to earth, and she realized that Aunt Nikku was clapping her hands once more to call everyone to attention. "With this we conclude our inspection of the third story," the small woman announced. "We shall move now to the final stage of our tour as we climb the stairs to the top floor. These stairs are steep, and the infirm may elect to remain behind if they so wish. However, for those who have the strength and the will, a great privilege awaits."

No one wished or would admit to wishing to stay behind, so the small crocodile filed after Aunt Nikku toward the last flight stretching away into the musty gloom above. Suddenly Koru reached out and grasped Indigo's hand.

*"Just wait, Indigo!"* he stage-whispered ardently. *"This part is the best of all!"*

Indigo bit back a reflexive warning to be careful as he bounded ahead of her and started to climb, ignoring the disapproving frowns of his elders. She followed at a pace more sedately suited to the rest of the party . . . and then, as she neared the top of the flight, she felt the same tingling surge of power that had assailed her when she first approached the House. Her hand gripped the stair rail more tightly and she peered upward, trying to see past the slowly moving file of people ahead of her. Whatever lay up there held the key to this mystery, and her heart quickened with an almost oppressive sense of excitement as at last she and Grimya emerged onto the top floor.

It seemed for the first few moments that there was noth-

ing here to see that was worth the trouble of climbing up
from the floor below. The single large chamber was surrounded on all six sides by high windows, as grimy as the
rest and letting in only a dismal trickle of daylight, and even
in the heavy shadows Indigo could see that it was almost
completely unfurnished. In the angle between two of the
windows stood something tall and oval, covered with a dust
sheet. What it was Indigo didn't know and had no chance to
ask, for Aunt Nikku was fussily shepherding her charges toward the only other object in the chamber, which stood at
the exact center of the room.

"Now at last," she said, her voice echoing under the cav-
ernous ceiling that sloped up to the roof's apex, "we have
arrived before the final artifact, and one that causes the
hearts of the House Committee to swell with the pride of
achievement. By our skills we have maintained this relic in
the exact condition in which the Benefactor bequeathed it to
us upon his departure. And it is the only—I repeat, the
*only*—item of his personal belongings that has survived the
decay of centuries to be displayed here for the benefit of
all." With a practiced, almost melodramatic movement,
Aunt Nikku stepped aside to reveal the Committee's pride
and joy—and a psychic jolt shot through Indigo like a knife
blade.

There was a plinth at the center of the room. Like everything else in the mausoleum it was cordoned off, but this
time with double ropes as though to emphasize that this was
no ordinary exhibit but something of especial value. On the
plinth was a cushion—in itself a rarity in Joyful Travail.
And on the cushion lay a crown. It was made of a metal that
looked like bronze, and many of the sharp, regular spikes
that crenellated it were broken or crumbled with age. It
must have been many, many centuries old.

Indigo sucked an involuntary, harsh breath between her
teeth as her dream came back to her with jolting clarity. She
saw again the man's face under its fringe of gray hair, the

dark eyes with their deceptive softness, the crooked nose, the rosebud mouth. She could almost hear his voice as it had been in the dream, crisp and businesslike, demanding to know her name and her purpose in coming to Joyful Travail.

And in her mind, like ghostly echoes, rang the sound of children's laughter . . .

# ·CHAPTER·VII·

Aunt Nikku was only too pleased to answer Indigo's questions when the tour was over. She clearly liked nothing better than to show off her knowledge, and seemed to consider that the foreigner's interest in the Benefactor reflected great credit on herself. But Indigo's efforts to discover what she really wanted to learn were stymied by the little woman's implacable judgment of what was relevant and what was not.

The idea that some portrait or sculpture of the Benefactor might exist seemed utterly to confound Aunt Nikku. Just as Thia had been nonplussed by the notion of using jewels as adornment, the Aunt could see no purpose in making a picture of anyone, living or dead, for such a thing could have no possible use. No, she said; details of the Benefactor's physical appearance were not known, and such details weren't important. All that mattered was that in stature, strength, and stamina he had set an example to be followed by all right-thinking persons. Had he been a what? A king?

Aunt Nikku was not familiar with the word. Ah, a ruler. Yes, this was the case, for in those days it had been the practice in the Nation of Prosperity for rulership to be inherited, passing from father to son. However, the Benefactor had known that this was not the proper way of things. And when he rose to leadership in his turn, he revealed and embraced the great verity that only through the auspices of many wise minds in Committee could true progress be made. From this time on, the Benefactor decreed, the people should have not one ruler but many leaders, and those leaders should be chosen not by privilege of birth but by privilege of merit. So from his shining example had come correction and improvement, and the sweeping away of all that did not directly contribute to betterment through diligent work.

At this point Koru began to grow restive, so when Aunt Nikku finished her sermon and inclined her head to invite the next question Indigo politely demurred, thanked her, and took her leave. When they were back on the dusty road, with others of the party filtering more slowly out of the postern gate behind them, Koru said,

"You asked a lot of questions, Indigo. Are you *really* that interested in the Benefactor?"

Indigo smiled. "Not really, Koru, no. I just like to learn. I'm sorry if you were bored."

He blinked, surprised. "I wasn't. It's just that *I* could have told you all the things that Aunt Nikku said. I asked before, when Mother and Papa brought me here. We had a different guide but he told just the same stories."

"Oh," said Indigo. "I see." She glanced sidelong at the little boy striding beside her. "Did you mind hearing them all again?"

Koru grinned. "Not a bit. I like them." Suddenly he looked up, and his eyes, which were very bright and as blue as Calpurna's, met hers with sheer innocent delight. "I think the Benefactor must have been a sort of magic person, don't you?"

Grimya made an odd sound, quickly truncated, and Indigo stopped. "Magic?" she echoed. "Why do you say that, Koru?"

A faint cloud came over the small boy's face, as though belatedly he feared that he might have made a dreadful mistake. "Well, of course," he said hastily, "everyone knows there's no such *thing* as magic . . ."

Grimya, knowing Indigo's thoughts, communicated silently, *Yes. Be truthful*, and Indigo dropped to a crouch, reaching out to take Koru's hands.

"I don't, Koru. I believe in magic."

"Do you?" He still looked dubious, unsure of himself.

"Yes."

He thought hard, still wary but wanting to trust her; wanting, she realized, to trust *someone* who shared his own belief. At last desire overcame caution. "Well . . ." One foot scuffed in the dust. "Well . . . it's that crown, you see. The Benefactor's crown. It *is* magic; I can feel it. And I always think that . . . that if they'd let me touch it, or hold it, I'd . . ." His voice trailed off and his cheeks reddened. "It's silly. But if only I could *touch* it, I really truly believe that I could see into another world, where things are different and people are more happy."

Unknowing wisdom from the lips of a child . . . With a stab of pain and pity Indigo thought, *Is this what life in this land brings to all who fall under its influence?* Joylessness, spiritlessness—the inability to know or experience any pleasure beyond the grim satisfaction of material gain. She thought of Thia and her cold, narrow contentment at the prospect of marriage to a husband she'd never met but who had much merit in the community and was likely to be rich. She thought of Uncle Choai, sly and greedy and ever ready to use others for his own advancement. She thought of Calpurna and Hollend, ensnared by the same seductive web and now no longer able to enjoy pleasure for pleasure's own sake. No art, no music, no playing of games. Nothing that made life palatable. Even Ellani had succumbed to the infection, though she was but ten or eleven years old. Of all the souls she'd met in Joyful Travail only Koru still had a bright spark burning within him—and how long would it be, Indigo asked herself, before the pressure became too great and he, too, was lost?

In her heart Indigo believed she knew what lay at the core of this terrible malaise, and the thought of it invoked a cold, ugly sense of despair. If she was right, then fate had played a terrible joke, for it seemed that the very thing from which she was fleeing and which had driven her to take refuge in this land had been here all along, waiting for her, waiting to challenge her to take up again the quest she had tried so hard to abandon.

Indigo had found her sixth demon.

At first she refused to think about it, trying not even to acknowledge what she knew to be the truth. Grimya was aware of her thoughts but said nothing, for this was a dilemma that Indigo had to resolve without reference to anyone else. Besides, the wolf was far from sure about her own feelings on the matter. Until a year ago it had been different, but that was before their stay on the Dark Isle. In her nightmares Grimya still relived the time they had spent in that humid, sweltering land; Dark Isle had been, for her, a living hell, and she had wanted to howl with the sheer joy of relief on the day when they at last set foot on the ship that was to carry them away from its fetid and disease-ridden shores. But before they left, Indigo had made a decision and taken a step that had broken the pattern that their lives had followed for more than half a century.

Long ago, Indigo had received a gift, a pebble at whose heart a tiny, shifting golden spark lived and moved. For fifty years she and Grimya had followed where that lodestone led, seeking the demons that Indigo's own impulsive hands had released from the Tower of Regrets, finding those demons, and destroying them. Before Dark Isle Indigo had never questioned what she must do, but that ordeal and its aftermath had changed everything. On the night they left the cliff-citadel for the last time she had thrown the lodestone from the towering stairway, down, down into the great, glittering lake that lay far below. It was an ironic offering to the lake's dark deity, thanks for a lesson learned, and as the water glinted briefly in acceptance of the tribute, Indigo had made a resolution. She would no longer be led, no longer be commanded, for she was beginning to understand both the nature and the extent of her own powers, and she meant to use them for a cause far dearer to her than the hunting down of demons. When the Tower of Regrets fell, her lover, Fenran, had been trapped in a tormented limbo beyond the world's physical dimensions; alive but beyond her reach. For fifty years, as she struggled to fulfil her quest, Indigo had believed that only when the seven demons were destroyed could she and Fenran hope to be reunited. But on Dark Isle she had learned that that wasn't necessarily so—and the choice between continuing her quest and turning to a new goal was hers and hers alone.

For Indigo the choice had been clear. So she had turned her back on the lodestone and what she saw as its tyranny, put aside all thought of demons, and sworn that she would dedicate herself to the one thing that mattered to her above all else in the world: to find Fenran, and to set him free. In the Nation of Prosperity she had sought a respite, time to rest and recoup and to make her plans. But it seemed now that, however strong her will, those old obligations were unwilling to relinquish their hold on her, and a new demon had followed in her footsteps and risen to haunt her.

In the first throes of the anger that she felt—anger which, she knew, was a close companion to fear—Indigo determined that she would not be goaded. She had made a vow to herself and to Fenran; she would keep that vow, and no demons or spectral children or long-dead Benefactors would sway her from the path she'd chosen. So on the day after her ill-fated visit to the House she threw herself into a turmoil of work. It was an act of defiance, and also the surest means she had of shutting out the thoughts and the fears and the speculations that crowded in on her mind.

Uncle Choai was both surprised and gratified to learn, via the Foreigners' Duty House, that Physician Indigo would be ready to receive patients at the house in the market square as of the following morning. Thia, who called for her punctually at the end of the breakfast hour, relayed the message that Uncle Choai proffered his felicitations at Indigo's most expeditious recovery, and trusted—a small sting this, but unmistakable—that there would be no recurrence of her unfortunate lapse from full health. As they walked to the square among the early crowds Indigo was aware of an occasional covert but curious glance from the juvenile, and suspected that Thia knew all about her "lapse," though the girl was too politely reticent to make reference to it or to ask any questions.

At the physician's house Huni's widow again bowed them up to the bare room at the top of the stairs. The old woman had a set, introverted look on her face this morning and there was a good deal of activity on the lower floor, furniture and other artifacts being moved, men arguing in low but emphatic voices. When Indigo asked what was afoot, Thia shrugged her shoulders indifferently and said that Huni's widow was to find new lodging today and was doubtlessly engaged in selling those household effects that were left now that her sons and daughters had taken their share.

"Where will she go?" Indigo paused at the door of the physician's room, looking back at the bustle below.

Another shrug. "That will depend on how many tokens

she receives. She will probably have enough to pay lodging to her youngest daughter."

"You mean—she must *pay* her own children to house her?"

Thia gave her a blank look. "Of course. She is too old to work, so how else is she to be of value?" She surveyed the shabby dispensary with a critical eye. "There will be many patients waiting. Shall I summon the first?"

All that day Indigo was kept busy. On her first foray into this new role she had met with a great deal of suspicion, but now it seemed that attitudes had shifted somewhat. In fact she had a strong impression that many of her patients were motivated more by curiosity about the foreign physician than by any real need for her skills, although no power on Earth would have dragged such an admission out of any one of them, and she wondered what tales Uncle Choai might have been spreading about her prowess. Thia took everything in her stride, as might have been expected, and with a smug air reminiscent of Aunt Nikku's seemed to assume that Indigo's popularity reflected great credit upon herself.

At noon Indigo again stipulated a pause for rest and refreshment—this, as she told Thia, was a habit to which anyone who worked for her must become accustomed—and while they were eating (Calpurna had provided Indigo with bread and meat) Thia surprised her by suddenly speaking up without prompting.

"Physician Indigo, is it permissible for me to ask you a question?"

Indigo looked up, startled, then hastily swallowed her mouthful of food. "Of course, Thia. What do you wish to know?"

Thia inclined her head with careful gratitude. "I am told," she said after a moment's pause, "that you have an animal of your own. A dog."

"That's right. Her name is Grimya."

"The animal has a name? Ah. That is . . . most interesting. I would like to ask you, what purpose does this animal
serve for you?"

Indigo hid the ghost of a smile behind her hand, disguis-
ing the gesture by appearing to clear her throat. "Grimya
has many uses and many talents, Thia. She's a skilled
hunter, so she can provide meat. She's also my guardian,
which allows me to venture into places that might otherwise
be unsafe for a lone woman."

Thia smiled. "That need, of course, does not arise in Joyful Travail, although I understand that in other areas codes
of conduct are different." Another pause, then: "Would such
an animal as she— this Gri . . ."—she struggled with the unfamiliar word—"this Grimya, also be skilled at guarding
livestock, or perhaps even herding them?"

Indigo began to see the direction in which Thia was leading, and tried to imagine Grimya in the role of sheep- or
cattle-dog. Reserving judgment, she said, "Grimya is highly
intelligent. Yes, I think she'd have such skills. Why do you
ask?"

"As I think I have mentioned before, my husband-to-be
will have six bounds of land as his own. That is sufficient
to support a profitable sheep flock, and a reliable dog to
herd them would be a most useful asset." Suddenly Thia's
eyes took on an odd gleam that Indigo had never seen in
them before. "A gift has been mentioned, Physician Indigo,
for which I am greatly obliged to you. Perhaps it might be
considered fitting for me to have a dog like yours?"

As the girl finished speaking, Indigo had a startling and
quite unexpected flash of insight. For the first time since she
had encountered Thia she had detected something more than
cold and pragmatic logic in her tone. Hard though it was to
credit, Thia had, just for a moment, sounded *wistful*.

"Well," she said, nonplussed and not quite sure how best
to answer, "I don't know, Thia. If it's possible to find a dog,
then of course I'd be happy to buy one for you. But I must

say that ... a dog is more than simply a useful thing to own. A dog needs ... well, it needs care, attention ..." She couldn't add "love," for that would have baffled Thia utterly, but she had to try to make the girl comprehend. "A dog will look upon you as a companion and a friend, and you must treat it accordingly."

To her surprise, Thia nodded eagerly. "Oh, yes, Physician, I entirely understand!" she declared. "That is what I want, most certainly. A friend." Again the wistful note crept into her voice, and with it a little frown, faintly puzzled and faintly sad, as if for a moment she had glimpsed some far happier and more pleasant prospect beyond the room's dreary confines. "A real *friend* ..."

Then, as the juvenile's words trailed off in a small sigh, Indigo saw something that made her skin crawl with shock.

The image of a girl-child was materializing in the room. She stood directly behind the chair where the real Thia sat and she was dim and insubstantial, a specter, a phantom, the door clearly visible through her slight frame. The vision smiled, and its ghost's hands, like the hands of the children who had visited her here two days ago, reached out in a gesture of helpless appeal, its dark eyes filled with mute longing. And though the hair was different, longer and softer and not clipped into severe shape, the spectral child had Thia's face.

Indigo made a sound; a choked, inarticulate noise that she couldn't stem and couldn't control. Instantly, Thia—the real Thia—was on her feet.

"Physician, is something wrong?"

The phantom had vanished, gone as though it had never existed. But it *had* existed. She'd *seen* it.

"I think some food has caught in your throat." With brisk efficiency Thia crossed to the table and picked up a flask that stood there. "I would recommend water, to clear the blockage."

Indigo didn't argue but took the flask and drank from it, fighting to get her mind and body under control.

"Th . . ." She swallowed, coughed, swallowed again. "Thank you, Thia. Yes, yes; that's quite enough, I'm recovered now." She watched as the girl replaced the flask on the table, trying and failing to make the sudden return to normality tally with what she had just seen. In her mind, silently, savagely, an inner voice said, *No! I will not be led! I will not be commanded! Leave me—leave me alone!*

"We were speaking of dogs." Thia sat down again.

Indigo blinked. "Of . . . dogs?"

"Yes." Thia smiled, and all traces of that momentary, wistful other-Thia had vanished, as though a child's writing slate had abruptly been wiped clean. Thia had no thoughts now of companionship or friendship or love. She was herself again, and for her, as for any good citizen of Joyful Travail, a dog was nothing more than a potentially valuable asset.

"I would be most pleased to accept a dog as a gift, Physician Indigo," she said with smug detachment. "Such a creature would be a most *useful* possession, I think."

The afternoon was warm and humid, the room in Huni's house stifling, and by the time her last patient bowed his way out Indigo felt fit for little more than a long night's sleep. Thia had departed after dropping another oblique reminder about the promised gift, and the activity below had ceased. Indigo wasted no time in leaving the house herself. With both today's unnerving experience and the previous eerie visitation sharp in her mind she wasn't anxious to stay in the dispensary a moment longer than necessary; the bleak room made her uneasy, and she was thankful to get out into the fresher air of the square.

The market had finished its business for the day, which, Indigo thought as she glanced upward, was probably just as well, for the sun had vanished and the sky had taken on the ominous, brassy tint that heralded a thunderstorm. The air was still and clammy and the empty market stalls had a look of hunched and skeletal abandonment. No lights showed yet in the windows of any of the houses, despite the false gloom, and but for the distant clucking of chickens and a glimpse of a solitary woman bustling down a side lane the entire town might have been deserted.

Indigo started across the square. A slight, short-lived breeze whisked from the southwest, and far away she thought she heard a faint rumble. Reaching the main thoroughfare she encountered several other people also hastening homeward to beat the coming rain; a lanky boy strode past her without so much as a glance, a middle-aged couple passed by on the pavement reserved for higher ranks, and ahead of her a young girl, her foreigner's white sash almost luminescent in the stormlight, was hurrying toward the Enclave. Indigo quickened her pace to a brisk jog, hoping to catch up with her. The Enclave gates were guarded during the busier hours of the day, and although in theory its residents could come and go as freely as they pleased, some of the guards took a perverse delight in being awkward, and two would stand a better chance than one of averting tiresome delays.

The girl was walking quickly, and the Enclave gates were in sight by the time Indigo drew close enough for hailing. She cupped a hand to her mouth, ready to call out, then suddenly jolted to a halt as her heart almost stopped beating under her ribs.

Where a moment before there had been one hurrying figure ahead of her, suddenly there were two. And the second—which looked exactly like a younger, more childlike version of the girl, save for the fact that Indigo could see the gates clearly through its insubstantial body—turned its head and looked back at her.

A sharp, pretty little face smiled coquettishly, and the phantom raised one hand and waved. Indigo's heart lurched and restarted; she shut her eyes tightly, an oath on her lips—

When she looked again, the doppelgänger was gone.


"You're very quiet." Calpurna closed the door of the brick oven beside the kitchen fire and smiled over her shoulder at Indigo, who was preparing vegetables for the family's evening meal. "Tiring day?"

Indigo returned the smile, forcing herself out of her preoccupation. "It could have been a lot worse," she said. "I suspect half my patients only came for curiosity's sake, to look at the outlandish new healer."

Calpurna laughed. "Don't worry, your novelty value will soon wear off and they'll go back to their normal sullen selves. Are those ready? Good; put them in the pan, and you'll find salt in the jar on the top shelf of the cupboard. Thank you." She glanced out of the window at the lowering sky. The storm hadn't yet broken, but the thunder's grumbling was closer and more frequent, and occasional flickers of lightning made shadows dance in the kitchen. "I hope Hollend has the sense to bring Koru home before the rain starts. We'll have both of them down with the lung-chill if they get caught in it."

"I expected to be caught myself," Indigo told her, and again the image flashed before her inner eye, of the fairhaired girl in the foreigner's sash hurrying ahead of her along the road. Time and again she'd tried to push that image away, and time and again it came back . . .

She nibbled at her lower lip. "Calpurna, how many families live in the Foreigner's Enclave?"

Calpurna was a little surprised by the change of subject, but didn't query it. "Oh . . . about a dozen, I think."

"Do you know them all?"

"Well, we're all on speaking terms, of course, because we are rather thrown together; after all, if we had to rely on the locals for our society . . ." A raised eyebrow completed

Calpurna's point eloquently. "But I wouldn't say that many of them are great *friends*. Why do you ask?"

"It was just that someone else went into the Enclave ahead of me." Indigo hoped that her voice sounded casual enough not to arouse Calpurna's suspicions. "A girl, a few years older than Ellani, with fair hair. I simply wondered who she was."

"Fair hair . . . about shoulder length? Ah, then it was probably Sessa Kishikul, the ore-trader's daughter." A pause. "You didn't speak to her?"

"No."

Calpurna shook her head sagely. "She's an odd one. Rather sad, in fact. The family are Scorvans; decent people, though they tend to be a little reserved. There's something wrong with Sessa, I think." She tapped the side of her head. "In her brain. I don't know the proper term for it, but the poor girl must be all of seventeen now, yet she still has the mind of a child."

The door latch clacked at that moment and Ellani came in. Two small metal churns swung from a yoke over her shoulders, and as she set them down thankfully on the tiled floor she said, "Father and Koru are on their way. I saw them coming through the gates."

"That's a small mercy, anyway. Here now, give me the water." Calpurna took the churns, adding a few acid comments about the Foreigners' Committee and their imposition of such primitive and inconvenient facilities. "Go and wash your hands, then you may prepare the table. Oh, and Ellani—you know Sessa Kishikul, don't you?"

Ellani looked wary. "Ye-es."

"Of course you do; you have lessons with her. How old is she?"

Ellani shrugged. "I don't know. Rosiris Pia says she's eighteen, but that can't be true. She doesn't *behave* like an adult. Anyway, I never have anything to do with her."

With that sweeping aspersion Ellani left the kitchen. As

she went out, lightning flashed silently outside once more. It might have been an illusion created by the momentary flicker in the room—and Indigo tried to convince herself that that was all it could have been—but it seemed to her that, just for one instant, another Ellani looked back over her shoulder and gave her a secretive, conspiratorial smile.

# ·CHAPTER·VIII·

The events of that day were, as Indigo soon discovered, only the beginning and only a mild taste of what was to come. For from the next morning onward her waking hours were relentlessly and alarmingly haunted by more and more of the doppelgänger visions.

At first she could see no pattern to the illusions. They seemed to manifest at any time and under any circumstance, and there seemed to be no common factor to link any one with any other. A boy driving sheep through the market square, hitting stragglers with a heavy stick and constantly shouting at his charges in a raucous voice, suddenly had a twin dancing and skipping by his side. An ancient man in a high-rank blue sash, being helped and guided along the reserved pavement by a sour-faced servant, was briefly followed by a juvenile and translucent little caricature of himself. A mother, deeply suspicious of the foreign physician but propelled by necessity, brought a child with an ulcerated leg for treatment, and for a moment it seemed to

Indigo that two children stood before her instead of only one. All through the first day the manifestations grew more and more frequent, and by evening Indigo's nerves felt strained almost to breaking point. Even in Hollend's house she couldn't find sanctuary, for twice more she saw Ellani shadowed by a smiling twin.

Then at last she realized that there *was* a common factor after all—and that factor was childhood.

"Or rather, not childhood itself," she said to Grimya as they sat together on the bed in her room late on the second night, "but a childish *mind*. Do you remember my telling you about the old man and his servant? He could obviously do very little for himself; I think his mind must have regressed to infancy as the minds of very old people sometimes do. Then there's the ore-merchant's daughter, Sessa Kishikul. Calpurna says she's afflicted, that she still has the mind of a little girl. And all the others . . ." She paused, thinking back. Ellani, Thia, the shepherd boy, the patient with the ulcerated leg . . . yes, she was right. "All the others were children. All of them."

"Then you th-ink," the she-wolf said in her husky voice, "that *only* the children have these strrrange double-creatures?"

"Yes. Or perhaps . . ." Another possibility was lurking at the back of Indigo's mind but she couldn't quite formulate it. "I don't know, Grimya. Perhaps those are the only ones that we can see."

Grimya was silent for some time. She, too, had witnessed the manifestations, not only in Indigo's company but also in Koru's, for with nothing to interest her at the physician's house she'd taken to accompanying the little boy to the fields, where she found ample opportunity to make herself useful. Whether Koru himself had been aware of the phantoms she didn't know. And there was something else, something that was beginning to puzzle her.

At last Indigo said, "What are you thinking?"

The wolf blinked, staring at the square of the window through which only faint starlight was visible. "I am th . . . *inking* two things," she said slowly. "First, I am wondering why it is that we see these shadow-creatures while others do not. And then I am wondering why it is that Koru does not seem to have one."

Indigo stared at her in surprise as she realized that that was true. Of all the children in Joyful Travail Koru was surely among the most likely of all to attract a spectral twin, yet thus far no such twin had manifested.

"I hh-ave spent many hours with Koru in the fields," Grimya added, looking round at Indigo. "But I've never once seen anything."

"No. No, neither have I. Yet he's so much more of a child than Ellani is; you'd think, wouldn't you, that he would be far more likely than her to have a shadow-double?"

"Unless," Grimya said thoughtfully, "he does not *need* one?"

Indigo stared at her. "What do you mean by that, Grimya?"

The wolf shook her head. "I don't know. It is just a thought, and I don't know why I think it. But it seems to me that per-haps Koru has not yet grown *enough* for this to happen to him." She licked her own muzzle, as she often did when perplexed. "When I was a very small cub, I found no need to look for wonder in the world. It was there for me in everything. Only when I grew a ll-ittle older did the wonder start to fade as I learned that life could be very hh . . . *ard*. Now I ask myself if these people who have the minds of children have also learned that life is hh-ard."

"And Koru has not?" Indigo began to understand her meaning.

"*Yess*. At least, that is the only answer I can th . . . ink of."

Despite the warmth of the autumn night Indigo suddenly felt a deep chill in her marrow. It wasn't what Grimya had said; it wasn't anything logical or explicable. But she felt, without knowing how or why, that some intelligence whose nature she didn't yet comprehend was gently but heartily laughing at her.

"Then what are they?" she whispered, and the chill was in her voice, giving it a peculiar, shivering quality that she couldn't overcome. "What *are* those shadow-creatures?"

Grimya whined softly. "We cannot be sure," she said. "But if what I have said is true . . . then I th-ink they are the ghosts of what these people might have been."

As though the same intelligence that had laughed in Indigo's mind that night had chosen now to mock and tease her, the phantoms began to appear more often and more clearly. Almost every child or juvenile that Indigo encountered, whether in the street or the square or her own dispensary, was tracked by its own smiling twin, each one beckoning to her, appealing to her, sending out a silent call from which she would turn sharply away with her heart pounding anew. And at night the ghost-children returned. Grimya heard them first, waking sharply from sleep and running to the window. Front paws on the sill, she gazed defensively, uneasily out into the empty darkness where nothing moved, then turned back into the quiet bedroom to find Indigo also awake and listening to the small chorus of voices that murmured to her to *come to us, come and play, play with us.* On the following day there were glimpses of small, sad yet eager faces, peeping from behind a market stall, or gazing from the heart of a corn sheaf in the fields, or smiling in the shadowed corners of the stairway as Indigo climbed to her work in the physician's house. As three more days and nights went by, and the faces and the callings grew ever stronger, Indigo knew that that intelligence, that *something*, was slowly but surely gaining a hold on her.

She fought it, fought it with all her strength. Whatever it was and whatever it wanted, she was determined that she wouldn't listen to its importunings. Demons might haunt her dreams but they no longer had the power to manipulate her. She would not be tempted, she would not be challenged. She was done with demons—she'd made that pledge on Dark Isle—and would have no more of them. All she wanted, all she craved, was *peace*; peace to recover her inner resolve, and to give her the strength and the guidance to embark on her new quest to find Fenran.

To add to her tribulations, but on a more prosaic level, there had been some trouble with Physician Huni's widow. According to Thia, and as she had predicted, the old woman was now living with her youngest daughter, but it seemed that the arrangement wasn't a happy one, for the widow—whose name, Indigo learned, was Mimino—had taken to returning to her old home. She made no attempt to enter the house but simply stood in the market square at a circumspect distance from the door, staring at the upper floor where Indigo worked. Twice, seeing her there, Indigo went down the stairs and out into the square, wanting to talk to her and ready to invite her back into the house that had been her home for so many years. But the moment she appeared in the doorway Mimino shook her head in a chiding way, made the odd, lopsided bow of apology, and scurried away before Indigo could come close enough to speak. Thia only shrugged at Indigo's concern and said that the old woman was senile and thus worthless; the physician should not waste her time on one who no longer had value and was she ready for her next patient? But the small, sad figure of Mimino continued to haunt Indigo even as the ghost-children haunted her, and she couldn't forget the wistful look in the widow's eyes as she stood sentinel outside the house that had once been her home and her comfort.

Two nights later, Hollend and Calpurna were summoned—there was, Calpurna sourly said, no other word for it—to a reception organized by Joyful Travail's Foreigners' Committee. These events took place three or four times each year and were, as Calpurna added with further rancor, an excuse for the high-ranking Uncles and Aunts to oil the wheels of the outland trade that kept their miserable little community on its feet, and to call in payment for favors done and concessions granted. Hollend, more sanguine than his wife, said that the event was simply a rare opportunity to eat passable food at the Committee's expense and to pave the way for some new and profitable transactions. But it was no place for children, so would Indigo oblige them by looking after Koru and Ellani for the evening, seeing to their meal and ensuring that they went to bed at the proper time?

Indigo was pleased to agree, for she felt it would be some small recompense for the Agantians' hospitality, which to date they had refused to let her repay. She had amassed tokens in plenty now, for Uncle Choai had been back to the house and had made a great show of handing over payment for her physician's services—everything in Joyful Travail had its price and the healer's arts were no exception, though Indigo suspected that a generous percentage of her patients' fees found their way into Uncle Choai's ample sleeve-pockets. But still Hollend and Calpurna wouldn't accept one single token in recompense. She was their guest, Calpurna said, and also their friend. Even in this uncivilized land they maintained the standards of Agantia, and a guest and friend did *not* pay money for her lodging.

Indigo's hosts left the house under a sky turning black not only with dusk but also with the approach of another storm. Calpurna muttered that they'd look like two drowned dogs by the time they returned, but Hollend said philosophically that at this time of year they could expect little else and it would do no harm to the growing crops. Indigo watched them walk arguing cheerfully toward the Enclave gates, then closed the door. Back inside the house she found Koru going from window to window, carefully closing and latching the inner shutters.

"Is that a good idea, Koru?" she asked, smiling at him. "It's very warm tonight. We don't want to be stifled."

The small boy looked round at her with a mixture of concern and embarrassment, and Ellani, who was sewing at the table, said disparagingly, "He's frightened of storms. You'd think he'd have grown out of that at his age, but he hasn't."

Koru's cheeks reddened and Indigo gave Ellani a sharp glance. "Well, I hardly think that's anything to be ashamed of, Ellani." She gestured toward the wolf, who had padded in behind her. "Storms make Grimya nervous, too." And silently she added, *Please forgive the lie, love, but it's for Koru's sake.*

*I don't mind,* Grimya communicated. *Though I don't understand why Ellani is being so unkind. It isn't like her.*

Relief spread across Koru's face like the coming of dawn, and he said stoutly, "I'll be all right, Indigo. Grimya and I can comfort each other."

"That's right." Indigo smiled at him. "Now we'd best see about our meal. Ellani, perhaps you'd like to put your sewing away and prepare the table?"

"Yes, Indigo." Ellani was still watching Koru, and her face wore an extraordinary look—part angry and part resentful, Indigo thought, and with an inexplicable hint of fear. Baffled but not wanting to stir up trouble by questioning the girl, she headed toward the kitchen.

The storm broke while they were eating. Even through the shutters the first flash of lightning made shadows in the room jump vividly, and Koru jumped, too, knocking over his cup of diluted fruit juice. As thunder rolled over the roof Ellani raised her eyes heavenward in an exasperated gesture and got up.

"I'll fetch a cloth," she said in a world-weary tone, and to her brother, "You are so *clumsy.*"

As she flounced out Grimya glanced meaningfully at Indigo, then made a whimpering sound and moved under the table, pressing against Koru's legs. Koru bent to stroke her, then looked up. "I *am* all right," he said in a small voice. "Really I am. It just made me jump."

"I understand. Listen now, eat your meal quickly and we'll find something to do that stops you from thinking about the storm."

Ellani came back and would have made a great show of mopping the spilled drink, but Koru grabbed the cloth from her and stubbornly did it himself. He flinched again when a second lightning flash flickered through the room but bit his lip, carried the cloth back to the kitchen, and then sat down again to finish his food. The meal was completed in an atmosphere of tacit hostility between the two children, and Indigo was thankful when at last the table could be cleared and some other distraction sought. Ellani fetched her sewing again and sat down near the largest of the lamps, where the light was best, and Indigo said, "Well, now, what would you like to do?"

"Koru should be in bed soon," Ellani told her.

Koru looked at her anxiously. "I don't want to go to bed. I couldn't sleep, Elli, I *couldn't*, not until the storm's gone!"

"Don't be so silly! It's only thunder, it can't hurt you. Think of Mother and Father—they've got to walk all the way back from the Committee House in the storm, but *they're* not afraid!"

Indigo decided it was time she put a stop to the bickering. "Now, Ellani," she said, though not unkindly, "I think we can make an exception just for once, especially as your mother isn't here. It probably won't be long before the storm passes"—another crash of thunder put the lie to that, but she continued nevertheless—"and until it does we'll all find a way to keep ourselves occupied together."

Ellani shrugged. "All right, if you say. What should we do?"

"Well . . . I have my harp upstairs. I could play it for you, and maybe we could sing some songs."

"I don't know any songs," Ellani said.

"I do!" Koru's face lit. "I know one—"

His sister turned on him. "No, you don't!"

"Yes, I do, and so do you! It's that one Sessa sang that time—"

"You don't know it and neither do I, and anyway, Sessa doesn't sing it anymore."

Koru subsided into unhappy silence, and Indigo, nonplussed, said, "Well then, *I'll* sing for you. Would you like that?"

Koru nodded and, after a few moments' pause, Ellani said, "If that's what you wish, Indigo."

As she fetched the harp from her room, Indigo puzzled over Ellani's strange behavior. She'd never known her to be so snappish with her brother, and the reason behind the extraordinary look that she'd given him earlier, before the meal began, was a complete conundrum. Perhaps Ellani felt uneasy with a stranger in the house and her parents not present, but Indigo didn't think that was it. This was something more fundamental.

When she rejoined the children, Ellani had returned her attention to her sewing and Koru was curled up in the corner farthest from any window, with Grimya beside him. Indigo sat down and, a little diffidently, tuned the harp before playing a few bars of melody. Grimya made a happy sound—she loved music—and Koru's eyes widened appreciatively. Ellani looked up, too, but her smile was uncertain and a little artificial. Feeling suddenly like a performer stepping on stage before a reluctant audience, Indigo said, "I'll play you a song I learned when I was about your age, Ellani. There's a very easy chorus, so you can both join in if you like."

She thought after a couple of verses that she heard Koru humming along, but Ellani only sat with the artificial smile fixed on her face, politely listening but clearly unmoved. When the song finished Koru clapped his hands and asked for another, and, hoping to entice Ellani out of her mood,

Indigo played a comic song she'd learned from the Brabazon Fairplayers in Bruhome years before. Ellani didn't laugh, and when she finished Indigo stroked a soft arpeggio from the harp and said gently, "Did you like that song, Ellani?"

The girl's smile became a shade more forced. "Yes, thank you," she said. "It was . . . very nice." A pause, then: "Do you play and sing often?"

"Yes, quite often."

"Why? What does it achieve?"

Indigo was quite taken aback by the question. "Well, I . . . simply enjoy playing and singing. But as to what it *achieves* . . . I don't really understand what you mean, Ellani."

Ellani was staring at the harp as though it were some alien thing whose mysteries she was trying to fathom. "Father says that in other countries some people earn tokens by playing and singing. Is that true?"

"Yes, it is. I earned my own living with my music for some years, in the Western Continent."

"Oh." Again that blank look. "That seems very strange. I mean, what *benefit* is there from paying to hear music?"

"Perhaps," Indigo said gently, "the benefit depends on whether or not the music gives pleasure to those who hear it."

Ellani frowned, but before she could continue the debate Koru intervened. "*I* like the songs. Another, Indigo! Sing another!" he begged. His sister's gaze slid sideways to him, then, very decorously, she set her sewing aside.

"I think, if you don't mind, I shall go to bed," she said. "I'm very tired."

"No—no, I don't mind at all." Indigo started to put the harp aside. "Would you like me to come up with you?"

"Thank you, but I can see for myself. May I take one of the lamps?"

"Of course . . . well, good night, Ellani."

"Good night, Indigo." The little smile flicked again, still as puzzled as ever, and she added as though belatedly remembering her manners, "Thank you for your interesting music."

There was a long silence after Ellani had gone. Koru was staring at the floor, and Indigo felt too deflated by the girl's attitude simply to pick up her harp again and carry on playing. At last Koru looked up.

"Please, Indigo, don't take any notice of my sister. She doesn't understand."

Indigo sighed. "I didn't mean to bore her. I thought she might be entertained by the music."

The little boy shook his head emphatically. "No. She doesn't like music because she can't see why anyone should want to listen to it. It doesn't *do* anything, you see." Suddenly, alarmingly, his face took on an expression of understanding far beyond his years. "Everyone thinks that. Even Papa and Mother do. But I know it isn't really true—and you know, too, don't you?"

"Oh, Koru . . ." Indigo didn't know what to say. She could feel Koru's confusion and distress and she pitied him deeply. But had she any right to go against his parents' influence? Koru wasn't her child; was it fair, then, to help him fight the creeping influence of this land's cold, joyless philosophy, when she would soon be gone while he must stay and live his life here?

Then, to her chagrin, Koru said: "I saw what happened to Ellani. I saw the ghost that was following her."

Indigo froze. There was an odd look, almost a sly look, in Koru's eyes as he watched her reaction, and with a small shock she realized that he had read her better than any child of his age should have been capable of doing.

"I know you've seen it too, Indigo. You tried to pretend it wasn't there, but I know." Abruptly he cast his own gaze down. "It's happened to me lots of times, but I've stopped telling anyone about it because they only get angry and say

I'm wrong. I'm *not* wrong." He looked up again, challengingly. "Am I?"

Indigo couldn't deny it. "No," she said very quietly. "You're right."

"And it isn't just Ellani. There are others, lots of others. I keep seeing and hearing them, like the children I told you about." He paused again. "And now I know who they are."

Indigo stared at him. Lightning flickered through the room again, but Koru didn't so much as twitch. He had other matters on his mind now, matters more important than his fear of the storm.

Slowly, cautiously, Indigo said, "You *know* who they are?"

"Yes. I used to think they were ghosts; that's why I was scared of them, because ghosts are dead people. But now I don't believe that. I think they're every bit as real as we are, but they live in a different world from ours." Another hesitation, while Koru stared at his own small hands clasped in his lap. Then: "Indigo, do you believe there are other worlds?"

Indigo couldn't bring herself to lie to him, not even for his parents' sake. "Yes," she said. "I believe there are other worlds than the one we see around us. Many others."

Koru nodded. "Everyone else says there *are* no other worlds. We're the only ones who believe in them. So that's why we're the only ones who can see the children, isn't it?"

His gaze met hers, and there was a look of such solemn certainty in his eyes that Indigo was momentarily confounded. Before she could speak, though, Koru continued, leaning forward now, conspiratorial.

"Ellani *has* seen them, though she pretends she hasn't. But because she wants to believe what everyone tells her, she's frightened, and so she gets angry if I try to talk to her about it. I think . . ." His expression suddenly furtive, he shuffled closer to Indigo. "I think she knows that she's got something following her, and she's been trying to make it go away."

"Has she said so?"

"No. But I've seen her look over her shoulder sometimes as if she can feel something behind her, and then she goes upstairs and she won't talk to anyone for hours, and sometimes I've heard her crying. *I* think—"

A peculiar sound from Grimya, half growl and half strangled yelp, stopped him in midsentence. Alerted at the same instant by a quick but despairing surge of warning from the wolf's mind, Indigo looked up.

Ellani was standing in the doorway, by the foot of the stairs, where the lamplight couldn't reach. Her face bore a look of fury, outrage, and betrayal, and as Koru saw Indigo react and swung round, Ellani strode across the room and grabbed him by the hair.

"You horrible, dirty, sneaking little *liar*!" she screeched. "Telling tales behind my back—I'll *hurt* you, I'll *kill* you—"

*"Ellani!"* Indigo was on her feet, the harp toppling as she sprang to separate the two children. Grimya, knowing better than to intervene, scrambled hastily aside as Indigo pulled Ellani away from her brother. Koru cowered as Ellani stumbled back; then suddenly the girl turned on Indigo.

"Leave me alone!" she shouted, her face distorted with furious tears and her hands flailing against Indigo's restraining grip. "You're as bad as *he* is! I heard everything you said, and it's all *lies*!"

"No, it isn't!" Koru, his confidence restored now that he was no longer under direct attack, fired back at her. "It's true and you *know* it is, only you pretend it isn't!"

"I don't! *You're* the one who—"

"Stop it!" Indigo's voice was sharp; she shook Ellani, then pointed her free hand sternly at Koru. "You, too, Koru, be quiet!" A resentful silence fell, the children glaring first at her and then at each other, and then with stiff dignity Ellani disengaged her arm.

"I apologize for losing my temper," she said in a tight, remote little voice. Her eyes, meeting Indigo's, reflected pure hatred. "I shall go back to my room until Mother and Father return." Then a small, triumphant, and unpleasant smile pulled at the edges of her mouth. "But when they do, I intend to tell them *exactly* what has happened. Koru hasn't heard the last of this, Indigo—and neither have you!"

Without waiting for a reply she turned on her heel and, head high, walked out of the room.

"So I'm sure, Indigo, that you understand our feelings." Hollend wouldn't meet Indigo's eyes directly for more than a few moments at a time. "We simply can't have this sort of thing happening again, and Koru is a very impressionable boy. I don't believe in being too strict with children, but I think it's time to draw the line."

"I understand, of course. I'm only sorry that I caused this trouble."

"You're not to blame, Indigo," Calpurna said firmly. "Koru was entirely responsible, and he must learn that these silly notions are simply not to be tolerated any longer. Now," she stood up, "let's say no more of it. The children must be asleep by this time, so I think we should all go to bed and consider the matter closed."

Indigo acquiesced, but despite Calpurna's mollifying words she knew that she wasn't in the best of standings with her hosts. They might not blame her as such for what had happened, but they were clearly at a loss to understand why she had, as they saw it, encouraged Koru in his foolish and reprehensible fancies. With discomfiting accuracy Ellani had told them all she had overheard, and Koru had received a stern and shaming lecture from both his parents before being sent tearfully to bed. To add to his chagrin, Calpurna had made him promise that never again would he embarrass and compromise Indigo by asking her to play her harp and sing for him, and, most of all, never *ever* again would he try to lead their guest into talking of such foolish and nonexistent things as ghosts from other worlds.

Ellani, as she followed her brother soberly up the stairs, had worn a self-righteous expression that made it clear she was pleased with her night's work. She hadn't addressed a word directly to Indigo since her parents' return, but she obviously felt that she had done nothing less than her duty.

"I don't understand her," Indigo said to Grimya when all were in bed at last and the household quiet. "She seemed . . . I don't know, almost *vindictive*. I didn't believe Ellani had such a streak in her."

*Fear is a very powerful thing,* Grimya observed silently. *It can make anger out of nothing, and turn the kindest of us to cruelty.* She looked round at her friend. *We both know that for ourselves.*

"I suppose that's true. But she's so young . . ." She sighed. "I must try to make amends, Grimya. I must try to smooth things over between the children, and between Koru and his parents."

*He was crying when he went to bed,* Grimya said. *It seems unfair that he must be the one to suffer when he has done nothing wrong.*

"I agree. I'll try to make it up to him in some way, though the Mother alone knows how." For though they'd not expressed their feelings to her directly, Hollend and Calpurna had been quite unequivocal: there could be no more music for Koru, no songs, no stories, no harmless games or pastimes. That, Indigo thought as she lay sadly down to try to sleep, left little else to gladden the heart of a young boy.

She thought she wouldn't sleep that night, but sleep came at last and when she woke it was to find watery daylight filtering into her room from a colorless, overcast sky. Grimya was gone; there were sounds of movement below and, not knowing the hour, Indigo dressed quickly and started downstairs.

She was almost at the bottom of the flight when she realized that there were many voices in the main room. She heard Calpurna, sounding shrill and agitated, then unfamiliar tones speaking the local tongue. A second later the outer door banged, then the inner door opened and two people appeared. One, a stranger, hurried through to the kitchen. The other was Ellani.

Ellani saw Indigo, and stopped. Indigo was nonplussed by the expression on her face, and she said hesitantly, "Ellani—what's going on? Is something amiss?"

"Oh, yes, something's amiss." Ellani looked back at her with undisguised disgust. "Koru's gone. His bed hasn't been slept in. He's disappeared—and it's all your fault!"

# ·CHAPTER·IX·

**I**t was Grimya who had alerted the household. She'd woken at dawn, as always, and had padded quietly to Koru's tiny bedchamber, thinking that she might find him awake and hoping to cheer him a little. Koru wasn't there, and one look at the neat, untouched bed told the wolf immediately that he hadn't risen even earlier than herself and gone out.

Grimya had wasted no time. She hadn't wanted to wake Indigo, she told her later, because Indigo was tired and needed sleep; so instead she had run straight to the room where Hollend and Calpurna slept, whined and scratched at the door until she roused them, then led them back to Koru's room to see the truth for themselves.

Indigo wished that Grimya had woken her, but it was too late for regrets now. Only an hour had passed since the she-wolf had made her discovery, but already the house was in turmoil. Hollend's first action had been to rouse his neighbors, and quickly they had scoured the Enclave. It took only a short time to establish that Koru wasn't there, and as soon

as this became clear one neighbor's eldest son was sent flying on long legs to the Duty House with the news that Koru
was missing. Two Uncles and an Aunt from the Foreigners'
Committee quickly arrived, and Hollend, grim-faced and interrupted frequently by the distraught Calpurna, told them of
the previous night's upset and said he had come to the reluctant but inescapable conclusion that Koru had run away.

For all their pomposity and formality, when it came to an
emergency the officials of the Foreigners' Committee were
well organized and impressively swift to react. By the time
Indigo came on the scene a small army of juveniles, field laborers, and even some younger Uncles and Aunts who
didn't consider the task beneath their dignity had gathered,
and instructions for a search of Joyful Travail were being issued by Uncle Choai, who appeared to have taken charge.
The family's Enclave neighbors, so Indigo learned from
Hollend, had already mustered a search party of their own
and had set off a few minutes earlier. Every extra hand
would be welcomed, Hollend said, and after one look at his
drawn face, and at Calpurna, disheveled and distracted and
close to hysteria, Indigo made no attempt to commiserate
but simply said, "Tell me where I'll be of most use."

She was assigned to one of the parties setting out to
search the fields surrounding Joyful Travail, a party picked
for its youth and stamina. Thia was among them, she was
surprised to see; glimpsing Indigo, the juvenile made a
grave bow and shook her head in a way that managed to express both polite sympathy for Hollend and Calpurna and
tacit disapproval of Koru's precipitate flight.

They had left the house and were nearing the Enclave
gates when a small, solitary figure appeared, hobbling determinedly toward them. Indigo was surprised to recognize
Mimino, Physician Huni's widow, and more startled still
when as the party hurried by the old woman called out
shrilly: "Physician!"

Heads turned, eyebrows were raised. Indigo left the press of people and went to meet Mimino.

"Madam." She bowed courteously. "Can I be of service to you?"

Mimino's gaze darted from side to side, then fixed on a spot slightly to Indigo's right. "It has been heard at my daughter's house about the little foreigner," she said furtively. "Therefore it occurs to me that the physician will not be at her post today. If it is wished, I shall wait at the square to tell the physician's patients of the reason for her absence."

Indigo was touched by the concern that Mimino was trying with little success to hide. "That is very kind of you, madam. But I wouldn't want to put you to any trouble."

"It is not a trouble." Briefly, and with strange candor, Mimino looked directly at her. "I have nothing else to do. And I would be pleased, for the little one's sake, to be of use."

Indigo hesitated a bare moment, then impulsively reached out and clasped the old woman's wrinkled hands.

"I am grateful, Mimino," she said. "Thank you. You are very kind."

Mimino pulled her hands free and made a self-deprecating gesture. "No, no. It is less than nothing." But she looked pleased. "That the little one is found, that is what matters. I wish you good fortune, Physician Indigo." Then, to Indigo's utter astonishment, she smiled a smile that lit her face like a star. "Yes. I wish you good fortune."

And without waiting for any answer Indigo might have made, she turned and hobbled away back toward the Enclave gates.

The search parties returned to the Foreigners' Duty House soon after sunset, and somberly reported failure. Not one sign of Koru had been found, not one soul in the town or in the fields for miles around had seen him or could give any clue to where he might be. Even Grimya's sensitive nose had proved useless, for the rain hadn't abated until near morning and any trail Koru might have left was obliterated.

Indigo, however, had expected little else, for as the day wore on she had become more and more convinced that she knew where the little boy had gone—or at least, where he had intended to go. Combing the fields with her companions, Grimya padding beside her, her gaze had frequently been drawn southward to the distant, solitary hill where the Benefactor's House stood behind its high wall. She didn't speak of her suspicions even to Grimya, and at first she had tried to dismiss them, telling herself that it was an impossibility, that even had Koru tried to reach the House the wall's barrier was enough to defeat a grown man, let alone an eight-year-old child. Besides, another group of searchers was covering the area around the hill, so if Koru was there they would surely find him.

But now darkness had fallen, the search had been called off for the day, and no clue had been found to Koru's whereabouts. Calpurna was worryingly quiet now after her earlier frenetic state, and sat mutely at Hollend's side in the Duty House while Uncle Choai—who seemed to have assumed overall control of the search operation—reported the parties' findings, or lack of them, with a relentlessly detailed formality that made Indigo wince. Tomorrow, he said, the hunt would continue, and those who through their industry owned horses would be required to loan their animals so that the searchers could travel farther afield. Until then, with great regret, he must state that there was nothing more to be done.

Hollend pallidly thanked Uncle Choai and the teams of helpers, then took Calpurna home, Ellani walking beside them and Indigo and Grimya following a short way behind. At the house there were neighbors waiting to meet them and offer both sympathy and company; a Scorvan woman who

Indigo guessed was the mother of the afflicted girl, Sessa, had cooked a meal, and as the main room filled with people Indigo retreated to her room. She needed to think, for with the searchers' failure her hope—almost, she admitted, her expectation—that Koru would be found in the vicinity of the Benefactor's House had been dashed.

She sat on her unmade bed for several minutes, not speaking, gazing at the window but blind to the night outside. Then, very gently, Grimya broke the silence.

"He is there, Indigo. I know he is there. And I th-*ink* you know it, too."

Indigo's shoulders relaxed as her refusal to accept the obvious gave way at last to resignation. "Yes, Grimya. It's the only possibility that makes any sense, isn't it? After what he said last night, and after the lecture that Hollend and Calpurna gave him, the House is the one place where he'd think to go to salve his hurts."

"When we were there," Grimya said, "he ss-eemed to look on it as another home."

"I know." Indigo made a helpless gesture. "But surely, if he'd managed somehow to get in, one of the Committee guides would have found him."

"They might not. There are many places to hh . . . *ide* in that house, or in the gardens around it. Besides," the wolf added darkly, "we do not know where he might have gone *afterward*."

It took Indigo a few moments to realize what Grimya meant by that, but when she did she felt a sudden, stark chill take hold of her. "He told us that he believes in other worlds . . ."

"Yess. And we know that he is right." Grimya blinked her amber eyes. "Indigo, if he went into that house, and if he—"

"Don't say it." She reached out to lay a hand on the wolf's muzzle as in her mind she heard Koru's voice and remembered what he had said to her about the Benefactor's crown. *"If only I could touch it, I really truly believe that I could see into another world, where things are different and people are more happy."*

They were both silent for a few moments; then quietly Indigo spoke again.

"We must go after him, Grimya. If he's broken through into whatever other dimensions that house contains, we *have* to try to follow and bring him back!"

Grimya gave a soft sigh, and Indigo knew that she had been hoping for this though she hadn't liked to say so. Grimya was very fond of Koru . . . and suddenly that knowledge crystallized Indigo's own uncertainties into clear, cold resolution.

"We'll go tonight." Her voice was crisp. "When the household is asleep." Her eyes narrowed as she stared at the window again. "If I'm right about that place, then midnight would be the most appropriate hour."

"Will we tell anyone?"

"No. I don't want to raise Hollend and Calpurna's hopes . . . and anyway, how could I possibly explain our reasoning to them? They'd think I was mad." *And maybe,* said a small, bitter inner voice, *they'd be right. Because this is exactly what I've been trying to avoid since we first came to Joyful Travail.*

It was ironic—so ironic that perhaps, in another mood, Indigo might have laughed. For despite her lofty determination to ignore the lures and challenges laid in her path, this new demon had finally used her own conscience as a weapon against her, and that had succeeded where all else had failed.

Very well then, she thought. Very well: she would pick up the gauntlet after all. Not for her own sake, not for the sake of the quest that she had determined to abandon, but for Koru. Like it or not, she felt she had no choice. And she couldn't entirely deny that, if nothing else, she was curious to learn what the demon had in store for her.

\* \* \*

Good luck was on Indigo's side that night. The kindly
neighbors departed with promises to return at dawn ready
for a new day of searching, and when the last visitor had
left Hollend persuaded his wife to go to bed. Indigo had returned to help with the host's duties, and when Calpurna,
heavy-eyed and despondent, had climbed the ladder-stairs to
the upper floor Hollend came into the kitchen where she
was clearing away cups and banking down the range fire for
the night.

"There's no need to do that, Indigo."

She smiled sympathetically. "I'm glad to. It's little
enough."

Hollend scrubbed at his face with one hand. He looked
weary, drawn; old, she thought. "Calpurna says she won't
sleep. I suppose . . ." He hesitated. "I suppose there isn't
anything you could give her, is there? If she lies awake worrying all night she won't be fit to face the morning."

Indigo had hardly dared to hope that this might happen,
but she took care to hide her relief and eagerness. "Of
course, Hollend. I'll mix an herbal draught. It will ensure
her a night's rest and there won't be any aftereffects tomorrow." She put the last of the washed cups away and gave
him an assessing look. "Maybe you'd like another draught
for yourself, as well?"

His frame relaxed visibly. "I won't say that I wouldn't be
grateful. Thank you, Indigo. You're very kind."

So within the hour Hollend and Calpurna were both
sleeping. Indigo had closed the lower floor's shutters and
extinguished all the lights, then waited in the darkness with
Grimya until she judged that it was safe to risk the small
noise of the front door opening. They slipped out into a
night cleared of clouds and with a sharp, autumnal chill in
the air, and headed toward the Enclave gates. The gate
guard was relaxed three hours after sunset, by which time
all right-thinking folk were expected to be abed, and the two

of them walked quietly through a town utterly silent and deserted and without one single light showing at a window. Indigo was nervous, and Grimya knew she was thinking of the ghost-children, fearing and half expecting that at any moment a small, phantasmic face might appear smiling in the dark ahead. But nothing save for their own gliding shadows disturbed the stillness and before long they were at the town palisade. Through another unwatched gateway, then before them the rough southward road stretched away like a faint, pale ribbon into the hills.

If the town's silence had been discomfiting, the soft night sounds that pervaded the terraces of fields were eerier still. Small, erratic breezes rustled the foliage of tall beans on their serried ranks of poles; insects whispered and clicked in the grass verges; once, some lithe, fast-moving animal streaked across their path to vanish among the lower-growing crops, and moments later came a small shriek, quickly silenced, as it sprang on the prey it had been stalking. Shapes were stranger and more deceptive out here away from the familiarity of streets and buildings, silhouettes took on semblances of life to which the wind added an illusion of movement, and Indigo found herself lured into thoughts of things uncanny and nightmarish; old legends from her homeland, tales of horrors half seen in darkness, memories of other lands and other encounters. She said nothing and tried to keep her thoughts from Grimya, but she was thankful when the road began to wind more steeply upward and against the stars' glitter she saw the outline of the high wall surrounding the Benefactor's House on the crest of its hill. Perverse though it might be, she would be thankful to reach their destination.

They arrived at the postern-gate at last, and Grimya gazed up at the wall towering before them.

"The gate will be locked." Her voice registered sudden dismay. "How shh-all we get in?"

Indigo smiled. She'd considered that problem before leaving and had decided that this was no time for subtlety, so from a small bag at her belt she pulled her knife, together with a heavy meat skewer that she had "borrowed" from Calpurna's kitchen.

"I'll break the lock." She moved toward the door. "It's half rusted anyway; I noticed that when we came here the first time. It'll be easy enough to pry it off, and as there's no one here at night the bolt can't be drawn on the far side."

"It will be known in the morning that ss . . . *omeone* has been here," Grimya said dubiously.

"I don't care." Deftly, Indigo started to insert the skewer into the door's locking device. "They can think what they will; it doesn't—" She stopped.

From the lock had come a faint but distinct *click*, and the door seemed to tremble momentarily. Indigo's hand fell away from the skewer, which dropped to the ground with a soft thud. She and Grimya stared at each other. Then Grimya said: "Try the door . . ."

It opened even as she touched it, swinging back with a creak of neglected hinges. Grimya uttered an instinctive growl that she swiftly quelled, and together they peered through the open postern into the deep shadow of the garden beyond.

"Well," Indigo said at last, very quietly. "It would seem that someone is expecting us."

The wolf showed her teeth. "Or sss-ome*thing*."

"No." Indigo bent to pick up the skewer, slipped it back into the bag, then touched the hilt of the sheathed knife that hung beside it; just a small gesture, to reassure herself. "No, I don't think so, Grimya. I think that what we shall meet here is human." She smiled to herself in the darkness, then stepped over the threshold. "Or was, once."

Still the children didn't appear. Indigo was disconcerted by that, for she had expected that here in the House's garden, even if nowhere else, they would make at least some sign of their presence known. But as she and Grimya walked along the slat paths toward the strangely shaped bulk of the House itself, nothing disturbed the quiet. Even the breezes were still, shut out by the high surrounding wall, and the only light they had to guide them was the faint shimmer of stars, augmented by a slowly strengthening glow from the moon as it began to rise. When Indigo looked up at the tiered building, whose silhouette seemed to lean drunkenly toward them, she saw moonlight reflecting in two of the topmost windows, creating the bizarre illusion of eyes gazing down at them from a huge, blank face. Quickly looking away again she followed Grimya to the House's front door.

"It's open." Grimya spoke in a tone that suggested she had expected nothing else. She glanced up at her friend. "I w-will go first, Indigo. I am not afraid of this place."

"No, Grimya, wait—" But before Indigo could voice her own half-realized fears, the wolf had disappeared through the open door into darkness. There was a brief pause, then came the sound of Grimya's claws clicking on an uncarpeted floor and her voice drifted back, hollow in the enclosed space.

"It is *hh*-ard to see very well. But I can make out the shape of the stairs. If we climb up, there may be more light."

Cautiously, resisting an urge to look back over her shoulder, Indigo entered the House. Her own eyes were nowhere near as acute as the wolf's, but after a minute or so she began to discern faint differences in the shades of darkness, allowing her to make her careful way across the room to where Grimya waited at the foot of the stairs.

*There is nothing to interest us down here.* Grimya switched to telepathic speech as Indigo joined her. *I sense that clearly. I think that we must go to the topmost floor of all.*

Indigo agreed. She too felt intuitively that whatever awaited them lay above, and together they began to climb.

The second floor, like the first, was still and deserted; their soft footfalls created empty echoes as they moved toward the next flight of stairs. On to the third story, and again the pattern was the same: stillness, quiet, no sign of any other presence. As they approached the third and final staircase Indigo felt her heartbeat quicken and become irregular, and with it a sense of queasiness in the pit of her stomach. She forced the sensation down, reminding herself that she had faced infinitely worse terrors than the mere darkness of an old, empty house, but nonetheless as she started up the flight her palms were clammy on the stair rail.

There was light on the topmost floor. Moonlight, thin and new and weakened by the grimy windows through which it shone, but it was enough to show the plinth with its double surrounding ropes in the center of the hexagonal room. One shaft of the moonlight, penetrating a pane that was either broken or cleaner than its neighbors, slanted across the Benefactor's ancient crown and illuminated the tarnished bronze in an eerie, phosphorescent halo.

Grimya's voice in her mind said, *Yes . . . yes. There is something here. I feel it.*

Indigo felt it, too, but she didn't reply, only stood staring at the plinth and at the crown on its cushion. Still nothing moved, still the presence, whatever it was, showed no sign that it wished to make itself known. Yet it was here. An awareness, a consciousness, watching them and waiting to see what they would do. It was almost as though the room itself was alive . . .

Very slowly Indigo moved forward until her thighs touched the rope barrier that kept the crown safe from the taint of curious hands. She began to reach out, then stopped as she realized that she didn't want to touch the thing. And for no apparent reason something else had suddenly come to mind—a brief and seemingly insignificant memory from her first visit here.

She stepped back from the barrier and turned round. Yes,

it was still there: the shrouded object between two of the windows. Aunt Nikku had made no mention of it and so it had no obvious importance. But . . .

*Indigo?* Grimya queried, curious. Indigo made a gesture warning the wolf to silence, then moved toward the object. She had an irrational impulse to adopt a hunter's tactic as she approached, almost as though whatever lay under the dust-sheet wasn't some inanimate object but a living animal. Her hand stretched out, caught hold of the rough fabric, twitched it—

The sheet slid to the floor with a soft noise, dust rising from it in a billowing cloud, and Indigo and Grimya found themselves confronted by a rectangular mirror, tall as a man's height. Their own images gazed solemnly back at them, strangely lit by the moon; in the glass's depths the crown on its plinth glowed dully amid shadow.

"A mm-*irror.*" Grimya moved hesitantly forward, her voice filled with wonder. Since her first encounter with a looking glass in Khimiz many years ago she had been fascinated by mirrors, though never quite able to banish an innate suspicion of them. She padded closer, stopping only when her breath began to mist the glass, then looked up at her friend. "This is very strrrange."

"Very." What, Indigo asked herself, could the Benefactor possibly have wanted with such a thing as this? Joyful Travail had no use for mirrors; they were an alien idea. And the House Committee had taken care to hide the glass under a sheet, instead of displaying it with the other relics of a lost age. Obviously they were anxious that no one should see it. That fitted well enough with their philosophy, but if they considered it worthless, why hadn't they simply destroyed it?

Grimya was stretching toward the mirror, sniffing with great interest. As her nose touched the surface, she started to say, "It smells of—" and instantly the words turned to a yelp of shock as bright light suddenly flared out of the glass and into the room. The wolf sprang back; Indigo, too, re-coiled violently—and when they recovered their wits enough to look again, they saw that their own reflections had vanished and the glass now showed the image of an-other and utterly different world.

"Sweet Mother!" Indigo struggled to quell the painful, shocked thumping of her heart. Grimya whined fearfully, crouching behind Indigo with her ears laid flat to her head as she stared at the scene in disbelief.

The mirror showed a landscape of gently rolling hills, clothed here and there with small tracts of woodland. No sun was visible, but the scene shone with the clear, bright light of a summer noon. Far off in the distance was the glimmer of what might have been tall towers, pastel-colored and vivid in the brightness and, appearing from the foot of the mirror, a stony path led away into the distance. To the right of the path were meadows filled with flowers and be-yond them the glimmer of water. To the left was a glimpse of more woodland, crowding up to the mirror's frame so that, tantalizingly, only the edge of the tree canopy was vis-ible.

And as Indigo looked closer, the leaves agitated with a brief disturbance.

"Grimya!" She reached out to the wolf, urging her for-ward. "There, look—something is moving!"

Grimya was recovering her wits and composure, and she, too, stared at the glass. "Yes!" she said after a moment. "I see it—there, at the edge of the wood."

"Can you tell what it is?"

"Nnn . . . no. It has stopped now." She glanced up at In-digo and bared her fangs uncertainly. "Per-haps an animal? If so, it is a big one."

Together they peered at the mirror again. Then, so ab-ruptly and unexpectedly that for a moment Indigo's mind couldn't register the significance of what her eyes saw, a shape stepped out of the trees and onto the path. Fair hair, a small, sturdy figure—recognition hit Indigo like a physical blow, and she cried out, *"Koru!"*

The little boy took not the slightest notice. His back was to the mirror and he had already set off along the path. Behind him, from the wood, other small figures were emerging. Children—there must have been a dozen or more of them, scrambling from the undergrowth, clasping hands, running and skipping in Koru's wake. They were laughing, Indigo could see, but the sound of their laughter couldn't penetrate the mirror's barrier.

"Koru!" Indigo cried. "No, Koru, come back!" Desperate to make herself heard she sprang forward, beating her open palms on the glass. There was a high-pitched ringing noise that filled her head—then the glass seemed to splinter into a thousand glittering shards. Indigo fell forward; losing her balance, she pitched into a brilliant kaleidoscope of light and sprawled painfully on all fours. She felt the hard boards of the House's floor beneath her knees, while her hands—

Her hands scrabbled among the dust and stones of the path in the otherworld.

Dizzily Indigo raised her head. Light and darkness spun around her in mad, dancing patterns. Behind her in the moonlit room Grimya was barking her name, but before her the small figures of the children, with Koru now in their midst, ran and skipped away along the path. Confusion and disorientation were suddenly eclipsed by the frantic need to reach him, and Indigo yelled out, *"Koru! Koru, wait!"*

The little boy slewed to a halt and spun round. His face registered shock, and hard on shock's heels came horror.

"No!" His voice carried back to her like a clear but distant birdcall. "No! Go away, leave me alone! You can't come in here! Leave me *alone!*" And with a speed that stunned Indigo he raced from the path and back toward the woods. The other children streamed after him like the tail of a comet, and within moments the entire group had vanished among the trees.

*"Koru!"* Indigo cried despairingly. *"Koru!"* She started to scramble to her feet, thinking to run after them, but a conflicting force pulled her back. The scene before her lurched violently; she felt something dragging at her—then the world within the mirror shattered into fragments as Grimya gave a final, desperate tug, and Indigo tumbled back into the dark room.

"Indigo, Indigo!" The wolf bounded around her, licking her face in a mixture of agitation and relief. "You were disappearing into the m . . . *irror!* I couldn't ss-ee you!"

Sprawling, breathless, Indigo stared at the glass again. Her own face stared back, Grimya's shadowy form beside it. The wood, the meadows, the path, the entire brightly lit scene, were gone.

From behind them came a soft, rich chuckle.

Indigo whirled so fast that she lost her balance again, and her right knee thumped painfully against the floor. The roped-off plinth was no longer there. In its place was a lectern; and behind the lectern, quill pen poised over a large, open book and the ancient bronze crown glowing dully on his head, stood an all-too-familiar figure.

Indigo stared at the neatly cut graying hair, the dark eyes, the crooked nose above a small, rosy mouth. *"Oh, Goddess . . .,"* she said softly.

The Benefactor gazed back at her, and humor with a small suggestion of malevolence glinted momentarily in his eyes. Then the plump red mouth smiled.

"I had expected you a little sooner than this, Physician Indigo," he said. "Still, a tardy visit is better than none at all. Sit down, please. I believe we have some business to discuss."

# ·CHAPTER·X·

"I have been aware of your progress since you came to Joyful Travail," the Benefactor said. "And I find it most interesting, even if at times a little hard to comprehend."

Indigo stared at him. Already crouched on one knee, she'd fallen ungracefully back at the shock of his first words and now sat, as he had requested, on the dusty floor, bereft of speech. He looked so *substantial*. Flesh and blood, not a shadowy phantom. Yet he'd been dead for centuries . . .

The red mouth made a small moue. "Have you recovered sufficiently to speak? If you have, it might save time and inconvenience for us both if you would do so."

Indigo found her voice at last. "You are—" She coughed as dust tickled her throat. "You *are* the Benefactor?"

"Yes. Or so I understand." The moue became a dry smile. "The epithet was not applied until some while after my . . . disappearance is perhaps the proper word, and so its aptness might be a matter for debate."

Indigo's mind whirled. What manner of being was she confronting? Ghost? Illusion? He looked too substantial.

He spoke again before she could gather her wits. "However, the question of my proper title is not especially relevant at present. The important question concerns you, and your intentions."

"My intentions?" Involuntarily, Indigo flung a glance over her shoulder to the mirror.

"You have already plumbed the secret—or I should say, one of the secrets—of this doorway. Indeed, I was greatly impressed to see that you almost broke through at your first attempt. Normally, only children can do that. It was most encouraging."

Children . . . Of course, Indigo thought. The mystery was starting to make sense at last.

"So they *are* under your control," she said harshly. "I begin to understand."

The Benefactor shook his head regretfully. "I rather think you don't, Physician Indigo. But I hope that I will be able to explain everything to you, and that when I have done so you and I shall be allies with a common cause."

The sheer audacity of that statement made Indigo choke back a snort of incredulous laughter. *"Allies?"* she repeated. "When you've lured Koru away and trapped him in your ghost-world to become like those other poor creatures? You presume a very great deal!"

The Benefactor seemed unmoved by her outrage. Very deliberately he leaned forward and made a small notation in the book before him. Then he said,

"Mm, yes. I see we are at cross purposes."

"I see very well we are *not*!" Indigo retorted indignantly. "You have stolen a child, led him to this mausoleum, and tricked him into—"

He interrupted her, as mildly as though she hadn't been speaking. "Do you think I am another of your demons, Physician Indigo?"

Indigo's jaw froze rigid and she was utterly silent. The Benefactor made another note in his ledger, then looked up. "Well?" he repeated pleasantly. "Do you?"

A muscle twitched violently in her throat. "You can't know about—"

"About the quest that has kept you roaming the world for half a century and that you have now arbitrarily decided to abandon? Yes, I know a very great deal about it."

Grimya snarled softly, and Indigo said in an unnaturally high-pitched voice: *"How?"*

"Because I know you. Or at least, I know what I might best term an aspect of you; considerably better than you know it yourself, I think. Now, to return to my question—and Grimya, little wolf, don't snarl at me again. Contrary to appearances I am not flesh and blood, so your teeth would have little effect upon me." He bestowed a smile on Grimya. "Speak, if you have anything to say. I know your secret and I assure you I'm not about to broadcast it to this world."

Grimya looked at Indigo, appalled. *He knows I can speak!* she communicated. *How does he know? How?*

Indigo only shook her head, and the wolf turned a furious frightened face to the Benefactor.

"I hh-ave nothing to say to you!" she growled.

The Benefactor regarded her for a moment, then raised his gaze to Indigo once more. "I asked if you believe I am a demon. Grimya appears to have made up her mind that I am. But what do *you* think?"

Indigo turned her head away. She felt sick. "I see no reason," she said, her voice hard-edged now with bitterness, "not to agree with Grimya. And I want nothing to do with you. I came here to escape from demons, not to confront yet another one." She swung back to face him again. "Whatever challenge it is you want to throw in my face, I have no intention of accepting it!"

The Benefactor steepled his fingers and stared at them.

"Sadly," he said, "you may find you have little choice in the matter. For it seems to me that you haven't sufficiently considered the true nature of demons in general, and yours in particular."

"You're talking in riddles!" Indigo said disgustedly.

"No, no. Not at all. I am, perhaps, viewing the matter from a philosopher's standpoint, which to the untrained mind may seem unwieldy at times. But ask yourself this: you have faced, and conquered, five powers, which for the purposes of our debate we shall call demons. But what *were* they? Were they men of flesh and blood? No, they were not, although some might have imitated or even taken possession of the bodies of men when it suited their purpose. Were they, then, the ghosts of men? No. Or deities? Again no, though one seemed to have that semblance for a while. So, we come to—"

"Wait." Indigo cut across the flow of words. The Benefactor stopped in midsentence and smiled solicitously. "Yes? You are beginning to understand?"

"No! This is *insane!*" She flung an arm out, encompassing the moonlit chamber and all it contained. "I came here to find a lost child, not to sit arguing with a—a—a *shade!*" With a violent movement she scrambled to her feet. "Only one question matters to me. Will you or will you not release Koru from your ghost-world?"

For several seconds there was silence. Then the Benefactor sighed. There was such melancholy in the sound that it took Indigo completely by surprise.

"Ah, Physician Indigo, perhaps I was foolish to invest my hope and my trust in you. Perhaps I should have acknowledged that you, like me, are no more than human and thus prey to all the many human flaws. But then, optimism was *my* greatest flaw for many years."

"Don't dissemble with me, Benefactor." Indigo forced herself to turn away from the ambivalent tributary down which her thoughts were trying to flow. "I want only an answer to my question."

The soft brown eyes focused on her once more. "Very well, then I shall answer it. I cannot release this child from the place that it pleases you to call my ghost-world. It is not in my power to release him, for I do not hold him prisoner. Koru entered that world—which, incidentally, is not mine in the sense that you imagine—of his own free will, and he may return from it at any time he chooses. However"—a small, poignant smile pursed the rosebud mouth—"it would appear that he does not wish to return. And that, I think, brings us back to considering the nature of demons."

Unbidden, the image of Koru's face when, halfway through the mirror-gateway, she had cried out to him, rose in Indigo's mind. The little boy's face had registered horror at the sight of her, and with a sudden sharp flash of insight Indigo realized why. Koru had run away from home. He hadn't been abducted by ghost-children or by any other force; he had gone, as the Benefactor said, of his own free will. Koru was searching for a sanctuary where his childish delights wouldn't be crushed out of existence, and where he might find friends who wouldn't punish him for daring to believe in something beyond the harsh tenets of Joyful Travail. To his mind, Indigo now represented the unkind world from which he had fled. He'd seen her as an enemy come to drag him back to the bleak hearthside of reality, and he had run from her in fear. Koru had demons of his own, and he counted Indigo among their number.

The Benefactor was watching the changing expressions on Indigo's face. She couldn't look at him; the confusion within her was too great. But at last, quietly, he spoke.

"What *is* the nature of demons, Physician Indigo? We both know that they have no true form but are abstract things. We may give them names from time to time, yet a name is not a reality but only a convenient label. The reality of demons comes from within, I think. So might it not be said that they find their only true form in the fears and burdens that beset us all?"

Beside her Grimya whined, but Indigo's fingers clenched in the fur of the she-wolf's ruff, exhorting her to silence.

"You have given names to many of your demons," the Benefactor continued. "Tyranny, Entropy, Vengeance, Hatred ... Yet were not all those forces, all those demons, a part of you? Did you not carry the shadow of each one within you, and wasn't each triumph in fact a victory over your own dark self ... over the being that you have learned to call Nemesis?"

An ugly emotion lurched through Indigo as the softly spoken words went home. Her mouth opened, words of denial crowding to her tongue—but she didn't give them voice. An image was in her mind of a smiling, silver-haired child, the evil creature that followed in her footsteps and mockingly called her *sister*. Nemesis, created from the malignant depths of her own psyche, her corrupt and murderous sibling who had sought to thwart her at every turn. Nemesis had led her many times into a demon's snares. Yet each time she had prevailed, and with the death of every demon the influence of that evil child had weakened, until it no longer had the power to torment her. It had been a long, long time, Indigo reminded herself, since she had been plagued by that cruel, ever-smiling face ...

If the Benefactor was privy to her thoughts he showed no sign of it. "We all seek scapegoats to embody those things within ourselves that we hate or fear," he said reflectively. "Even Koru has made that mistake, as you saw but a few minutes ago. And you, Indigo—you may have resolved to leave your demons behind, but how can you do so while the being that, in your eyes, is the embodiment of them all still lives a life of its own?"

"That isn't true!" Anger made Indigo's voice shrill. "Nemesis no longer has a life of its own! I have overcome it. It is *gone*."

"I think not. I think it still lives, and that you must meet it again." He paused. "Look into your heart. Wherever you go, do you not carry Nemesis with you? You have found another demon here in Joyful Travail. The form it takes within you is reflected in this land, but if you turn your face away and leave, it will follow you." Suddenly the dark eyes grew intense. "You came here as a healer. But can you heal yourself, Physician Indigo? Can you purge this demon from your soul, and so purge my people of its taint?"

Indigo's pulse felt thick and heavy in her veins. "*Your* people?" she echoed.

"Yes. Even after all this time they are still mine, for my words and my deeds are the law of Joyful Travail. That is my burden, you see. That is the curse I brought upon them, and upon myself." The rosebud mouth smiled, and the smile was bittersweet. "We share a mutual sorrow, you and I."

In Indigo's mind, a voice spoke. *Indigo, there is something strange here. I cannot be sure, and I know we have made such errors in the past. But I do not believe that this Benefactor is a demon, or even a demon's servant. I sense no evil in his mind. Only sadness . . .*

Indigo looked down at Grimya, and the wolf whined softly as she returned the gaze. Her eyes were troubled, and she licked her own muzzle with a tremulous movement, a sure sign of her confusion.

The Benefactor was watching them. "She speaks to you?" There was an oddly wistful note in the question.

Indigo nodded. "Yes. She . . . says it's possible that she has misjudged you."

"And do you agree with her?" Now, it seemed, hope was added to wistfulness.

Indigo and Grimya exchanged another look, and Indigo felt Grimya's eager urging. The wolf's instinct was almost always reliable, but Grimya's change of heart had taken her by surprise. She couldn't quite bring herself to trust it.

"I don't know." She turned her head aside, not wanting to look at his face.

In her mind Grimya said, *Indigo—*

*No, love,* she told the wolf firmly. *Don't try to persuade me. Whatever you might have sensed or seen, I can't bring myself to trust him. Not yet, not like this. I must have proof.*

The Benefactor sighed. For a moment he stood motionless, lost in thought; then, quite gently, he reached to the ledger on its lectern before him and closed it. The air shimmered; slowly the lectern and its burden faded from sight and the plinth with its surrounding ropes reappeared. His expression still pensive, the Benefactor lifted the ancient bronze crown from his head and regarded it for a few moments with a mingling of regret and distaste before setting it carefully back in its ordained place. The crown glowed momentarily then reverted to dullness. Then the Benefactor stepped through the ropes, his outline melding briefly and disturbingly with them, and walked to where the tall mirror still reflected the dim image of the room.

"Very well," he said. "I am aware that no reasonable man could expect you to change your view so swiftly. We are both, after all, only human."

*"Human?"* Indigo had been badly startled when he had walked through the ropes; she had thought him corporeal and now she was floundering.

"Indeed, yes. I am as human as you, Physician Indigo. Not a ghost and not a shade, though perhaps not quite a living man in the ordinary sense. And most certainly not a demon." A faintly self-mocking smile shadowed his mouth as he turned his head to regard her. "I can prove that to you, if you will allow it."

Indigo swallowed, collecting herself. She wanted proof, yes—but what proof could he hope to give her? Words weren't enough. There had to be more. And, she reminded herself, even if the Benefactor himself was not a demon, a demonic presence was awake and working here.

The Benefactor was waiting for her to reply. At last, frowning, she looked at him again.

"You say you can prove your claim. How?"

He indicated the mirror again. "You came here to find the little boy Koru. Your intention is to rescue him from the world beyond the mirror and restore him to his family. As I have already said, the child is not my prisoner and I cannot directly influence him. But I can help you. Indeed, without my help you may well find that the task you have set yourself is impossible."

"Is that a threat?" Indigo glanced at the mirror, her eyes speculative.

"No, it is not. You have already shown that you have the ability to pass through the glass, and I have no power nor any wish to prevent you from going where you please. But your eyes are not yet fully opened to the truth of what lies beyond that mirror. I can help you to open them. And when that is achieved, you might find and bring back something of far greater significance than simply one little lost boy. Something of inestimable value to you, and also to Joyful Travail."

Her eyes narrowed as she returned his gaze. It was an old, all-too-familiar pattern, and she could feel the lure of the trap. Quietly but with underlying venom she said, "You want me to rid you of a demon."

The Benefactor's shoulders lifted fractionally. "You might say that is true. But then, as we have already agreed, the demons without are also the demons within. To free Joyful Travail from its bondage would also be to free yourself." His dark gaze shifted and he stared down at the floor. "Unless that can be done, Physician Indigo, you will learn that it might be a greater kindness to leave Koru where he is."

For a moment, thinking of Koru's plight, she was almost convinced. But on the heels of her uncertainty came a sudden flash of skepticism. It didn't fit; there was one great anomaly.

She said: "No. Your argument isn't convincing, Benefactor. If the people of Joyful Travail are *your* people, as you claim, why don't *you* help them? Why should you have need of me?"

"Because," the Benefactor said simply, "I do not have the power to do what must be done."

"And you think that I have?" She felt the sharp thrust of anger within her.

"I know that you have. And I can show you how to use it; not only for Koru's sake but for your own."

Ah, that cryptic hint again. *Not only for Koru's sake but for your own.* Implying that without his help she could achieve nothing, and at the same time trying to embroil her in some bizarre scheme of his own ... No, Indigo thought, it wouldn't do. Despite Grimya's changing feelings she couldn't shake off her own suspicions and bring herself to trust the Benefactor, be he ghost or living man or anything else. Her purpose was to find Koru, and she wasn't prepared to take risks with his life.

"No," she said. "I came here with one intention, and I don't intend to be distracted. If this other world of yours has secrets, they're no concern of mine—and neither are your tribulations or those of Joyful Travail. I'm sorry, Benefactor. But I won't be your champion."

The Benefactor smiled an odd, embittered little smile. "Very well," he said. "I see now that I cannot sway you. I had hoped, but ..." He made a small, almost dismissive gesture. "So be it, then. Follow the child and persuade him to return. If you can."

Indigo didn't unbend. "I shall."

"That's as you please. I believe, however, that you will fail in your endeavor. When you do, I hope that you will reconsider my words and accept the help that I alone can give you."

Deep in Indigo's psyche a worm of uncertainty stirred, but she pushed it down. Beside her, Grimya was silent, and she glanced at the she-wolf, silently communicating. *Grimya? Am I doing the right thing?*

Grimya's reply was emphatic. *I cannot say. But you have made a decision. And where you go, I go, too.*

The Benefactor had moved toward the mirror. As he stood before it Indigo saw that the glass showed no reflection of his face and form but only the empty room behind him. Then he uttered another heartfelt sigh and turned away.

"It is only polite to wish you good fortune," he said a little stiffly. "And I do so. However, I also venture to hope that your good fortune will not take the form that you presently anticipate. If that is so, we shall meet again."

He faced her and made a deep, courteous bow. For a moment, as he straightened up, their eyes met, and Indigo was shocked by the sad intensity of his gaze. Then there was a small shimmer in the air, a tiny shifting as of dust-motes dancing on a breeze, and the Benefactor vanished.

For some seconds Grimya stared at the spot where he had been standing. The air in the dark room was utterly still. On its plinth behind the protective ropes, the ancient bronze crown gleamed sullenly. The wolf looked round at Indigo.

"I w ... *onder*," she said hesitantly, "where he h-has gone?"

"Who knows? Perhaps he's still here but invisible, watching us." But she didn't think so. There was a sense of emptiness in the House now, as of a presence and a life—of sorts—withdrawn.

Unwilling to speculate further about the nature of the Benefactor's existence, Indigo reached down and touched the she-wolf's head reassuringly. "Are you ready, love?"

Grimya's tail wagged, though a little uncertainly. "Yess." She looked up once more. "But if we don't find Koru ..."

"We will. We must."

Indigo reached out and laid the palm of her hand against the mirror. This time she was prepared for the shock of the change, but still her heart skipped a beat as light flooded from the mirror's core and into the room. And there in the glass the green, rolling landscape of the ghost-world appeared once more.

The doorway was open. Indigo could feel the tingling touch of warmer air on her outspread fingers, as though something breathed gently on them. She extended her arm an inch farther, saw her hand begin to vanish into the glass . . . She drew a deep breath; then, with Grimya following close on her heels, she stepped through the glass as easily as she might have stepped across the threshold of a welcoming house, and entered the world of ghosts.

# ·CHAPTER·XI·

The first thing that struck them both was the silence. Not an ominous silence or in any way threatening, but an extraordinarily still and peaceful quiet. There was a soft, almost translucent quality to the air, and though as before no sun shone in the sky, the entire scene was bathed in mellow light. They stood on the same path along which Koru and the other children had fled; to their left was the dappled shade of the woods, while to the right the gleam of water that Indigo had glimpsed in the mirror had resolved into a slow, broad river meandering through lush meadows where summer grass grew waist high. Ahead, the view hazed into a distant prospect of green hills; between two of those hills a tint of brighter color might mark the location of the towers Indigo thought she had glimpsed earlier, though the soft light made it impossible to be certain. It was an idyllic scene, and yet something wasn't quite right. Indigo couldn't pinpoint it, but she felt certain that some element, some basic and obvious ingredient, was missing. Was it that this dimension was less substantial than the world on the far side of the mirror? No, Indigo thought; that wasn't what was wrong. In fact, in many ways this world seemed *more* real than the land they had left behind, its air sweeter, its colors more intense. But something was missing.

Grimya, who had followed her thoughts, suddenly pricked her ears. "I kn-know," she said. "There is no bird song. Listen, Indigo."

She was right, Indigo realized. Even in Joyful Travail birds were abundant, fluttering among the rooftops, squabbling for food in the fields and the market square, their chattering and chirruping a constant and delightful background to leaven the town's dourness. But here, where they might have expected to find them in their hundreds, not one solitary whistle impinged on the silence.

Grimya raised her head and stared at the wood a short way to their left. "No rr . . . rustling in the trees," she added, bemused. "It isn't simply that the birds do not sing. They are not even here."

No song, no birds . . . What else was missing from this place? Indigo wondered. She remembered the children; the small sprites laughing behind the closed infirmary door, the doppelgängers skipping beside their oblivious twins. Phantoms not fully able to manifest in a physical dimension . . . Was this their world, and could only ghosts exist within it? Yet Koru had entered without hindrance, and she and Grimya, who were also flesh and blood, had been able to follow . . .

Her heart lurched nervously at that thought, and quickly she looked down at her own body as though expecting to see herself transformed into an insubstantial wraith. The fear was unfounded; she felt and looked as solid as ever. But it focused her mind with abrupt clarity.

"Grimya, we must waste no time." She kept her voice low, unable to dismiss entirely the suspicion that someone or something might be eavesdropping. "We must search for Koru."

Grimya's tongue lolled. "I agree. But where should we start?" She dropped her muzzle to the ground. "I have tried to find a track, but there is nn-othing. No scent at all."

"Well, we're standing on the path that he and the children took when they ran from me." Indigo tried shielding her eyes with a cupped hand, but with no sun glare to overcome it made no difference to her vision. "Your eyesight's far better than mine. Can you see where the path leads?"

The wolf stared hard into the distance. "I th-*ink* so. I th-ink it goes between those two tall hills."

"Where the towers are—if they are towers?"

"Yess. And they are towers. I can ss . . . see them quite well."

"Then we'll follow the path." There was a fair chance that Koru and his strange companions would have made for the towers; logically, the little boy was likely to reason that they offered a more secure hiding place than the patches of woodland.

They set off, and as Grimya fell naturally into her steady, ground-eating lope, Indigo discovered to her surprise that she had no difficulty in keeping up with her. Grimya often forgot that her friend had only two legs, but for the first time Indigo seemed able to match the wolf's speed. It was a disorienting but delightful experience. Indigo felt almost as if she were swimming, but without the drag of water to hamper her. Her body seemed to have no weight and the soles of her shoes barely skimmed the ground as she ran, although there was enough contact to reassure her of the path's rough solidity beneath her flying feet. And they were moving so *fast*. Trees skimmed by in a blur and the slow river was already curving away and falling behind them.

"Grimya!" Her voice came in a breathless gasp, snatched away by the warm wind in her face. "What's happening to me?"

"I d-do not know!" came the wolf's eager reply. "But I feel it too, Indigo! I hh-ave never run so fast as this! It is—it is strrange, and wonderful!"

Strange and wonderful and invigorating—suddenly Indigo started to laugh with sheer exhilaration. Such speed, such freedom, such a *race*—yes, they were racing, racing each other, running just for the delight of it!

"Indigo!" Grimya cried out. "Catch me! Catch me, if you can!" And before Indigo could respond, the wolf swerved from the path and away into the woods. The leaf-canopy danced and sprang back behind her, and with a flick of her plumed tail she was gone.

"Grimya?" Indigo slithered to a halt. "Grimya! Where are you?"

From the woods came a distant call. "*Yess*! Where am I? Find me!"

Laughter and breathlessness together made Indigo's lungs hurt, but she revelled in the feeling. "I'll find you!" she shouted back. "You can't hide from me!"

She plunged in among the trees, into cool, moist gloom dancing with patterns of light and shadow. There were briars and bushes all about her and deep leaf mold underfoot, but nothing hampered her as she pushed through seeking for Grimya.

There—a clearing ahead, and in the clearing a gray shape. Grimya was crouched, muzzle low, haunches high, like an excited cub; as Indigo emerged from the trees the wolf made an extraordinarily agile leap sideways and raced away again, cutting straight across her friend's path even as Indigo reached out to grab at her and streaking away back to the track. Indigo turned after her and broke from the wood again to see Grimya waiting on the path, tail wagging furiously, tongue lolling and all four legs braced for flight.

"Rrr ... *un*!" Grimya cried. "Rrrun! Catch me! Catch me!" And she was away.

The chase was wild, mad, and wonderful. How long it

lasted neither of them could later have guessed, but at the time it seemed endless: an anarchic, childish, and joyous game of catch-as-you-can across lush meadows and the short, springy turf of greenswards, through copses and over tiny streams, zigzagging this way and that. Now Grimya led the chase, now Indigo; shouting exuberantly to each other, running, diving, jumping, oblivious to everything but their own unconfined frolic. At last there came a moment when Indigo caught up with Grimya—or Grimya with her—at the top of a shallow, grassy knoll. The she-wolf leapt up; Indigo, crying with laughter, grabbed at her ruff, and they lost their balance and rolled together down the smooth green slope to land in a tangle of fur and hair and limbs at the bottom. Scrabbling upright, Indigo struck her elbow against a stone half-hidden in the grass—and the momentary jarring pain in her arm had a sudden and shocking effect.

*What are we doing?* Realization hit her as powerfully as though cold water had been thrown in her face, and she shook her head as though waking from a violent dream. Playing games—playing games like children, when they should have been searching for Koru—

"Indigo!" Five feet away Grimya spun in a triple circle, tail wagging crazily. "I will rrr-ace you back to the top!"

"No!" As the wolf bunched her muscles to begin the chase anew Indigo's arm shot out in a frantic gesture, forestalling her. "No, Grimya, don't!"

Grimya's ears flicked backward then forward, and the eager light in her eyes took on a tinge of confusion. "Indigo? What do you mean? What is wrrrong?"

"Grimya . . ." Very slowly she started to get to her feet. The pain in her arm was gone, but what it had triggered still held fast, and she felt her heart begin to thump as though there were hammers beneath her ribs. "Grimya, what are we *doing*? We came here to seek Koru. Yet we've . . ." She couldn't express it, couldn't find the words she wanted to say. Suddenly she put both hands to her face, pressing fingertips hard against her temples. "What's *possessed* us?"

Abruptly, the spell that had already been broken for Indigo broke for Grimya, too. The she-wolf's tail and ears drooped and understanding crept into her amber eyes, quickly followed by dismay.

"How did it hh—*appen*? I don't understand! One moment we were just running, and then—and then—"

Indigo was upright, now, and walked a little unsteadily to the wolf's side. She still felt dazed, and shook her head in an effort to clear it of the confusion and banish a residual urge to start laughing helplessly again.

"I don't understand it either." She sat down again on the grass and hugged Grimya close to her. "I can't imagine what manner of crazed notion took hold of me. Perhaps it was—I don't know; perhaps the speed we were going, the excitement of it ..." They'd been like children, racing and shouting and laughing ... She paused and drew a deep breath. "But it's passed now, it's lost its hold. Are you all right?"

"Yess." Grimya dipped her head. "All rr-right now." She flicked her ears then looked up again—and abruptly her body tautened. "Indigo! Look there, over your sh ... *oulder*! Look where we have come!"

Surprised, Indigo looked back. No more than a quarter of a mile from where they sat, smooth stone walls shimmered in the hazy light.

"The towers!" Indigo's voice rose sharply in astonishment. Only minutes ago, or so it seemed, that strange, shining structure had been a vast way off, barely visible between the folds of two distant hills, yet somehow the hectic, zigzagging game had brought Indigo and Grimya to that hill and almost to the towers' feet. They couldn't have covered such a distance, Indigo thought; it wasn't *possible*; and she rubbed at her eyes, convinced that her vision would suddenly clear and the towers dissolve and vanish.

But they didn't vanish. They stood tall and slender and solid, rising in a graceful cluster from behind their high curtain wall that spanned the space between the two sheltering hills. There were five, all apparently built of marble, but each one shining a different subtle pastel shade, green and blue and gray mingling with pink and gold. Numerous windows reflected the daylight like diamonds set into the walls, and crowning each tower was a bright, fluttering pennant.

Indigo scrambled to her feet again. She said nothing but started up the gentle slope of the hill, her gaze fixed on the smooth curtain wall ahead. Grimya bounded after her, catching up within a few strides, and together they climbed toward the towers, which seemed to reflect the light like mirages.

The high wall was no more than fifty yards ahead when the wolf abruptly halted.

"Indigo!" she called out, stopping Indigo in her tracks. "I can hear singing!"

Suddenly alert, Indigo listened. Faint but clear—she, too, heard it: the distant sound of children's voices in bright if faintly uncertain harmony, coming from behind the wall.

Indigo glanced speculatively up to the wall's top. It must have been a good twelve feet high, and sheer, without a single handhold anywhere in its smooth surface. Impossible to climb; yet there was no sign of a gate or any other means of entry. How had the children got in?

The song ended abruptly and there came sounds of giggling followed by muffled whispers, as though the children were debating something among themselves. Quickly taking advantage of the respite, Indigo cupped her hands to her mouth and made to call out. But before she could make a sound Grimya said silently, *Wait! Listen!*

The children were beginning to sing again, the sound ragged at first but growing stronger and surer as more and more voices joined in. For a few moments, perhaps because it *was* so familiar, what they were singing didn't consciously register in Indigo's mind, but Grimya recognized it instantly. The wolf's amber eyes widened and she looked up at Indigo's face, her tongue lolling.

*That song! It is the one you sang to Koru the night before he ran away!*

And as the children sang, Indigo remembered.

> *Canna mho ree, mho ree, mho ree,*
> *Canna mho ree na tye;*
> *Si inna mho hee etha narrina chee*
> *Im alea corro in fhye.*

The words, in the lilting language of the Southern Isles, were corrupted, as though the children had simply heard and repeated them like babies' doggerel. But Indigo had known that song since she could barely toddle—and on that calamitous night she had sung it for Koru, while Ellani stared sullenly from her corner . . .

"Koru must have taught it to them!" Her voice was a whisper. "He remembered it, and he taught it to them. He must be with them, Grimya, behind the wall . . ."

The first verse ended, but it seemed that the children were less sure of the second verse, for their singing petered out and they began to whisper and murmur once more. Indigo drew breath, and before they could begin again her voice rose strong and clear.

> *Canna mi har, mi har, mi har,*
> *Canna mi har enla sho;*
> *Si anna lo mhor essa kerria vhor*
> *Por incharo serra im lho.*

The hills echoed her singing back in a strange, sweet carillon, and as she finished and the last notes died away there was absolute silence from the far side of the wall. Then:

"*Pretty.*"

*"Yes. Pretty."*

*"I like the song. And she sings it so nicely."*

*"Better than us. Better than us. She knows it better than us."*

*"Does she know other songs? Does she know games?"*

*"Oh, yes. Yes, she must. She must, mustn't she?"*

*"Shall we ask her to sing them and play them?"*

*"Yes! Yes, ask her. Ask."*

There was a long pause. Indigo waited, not daring to speak lest she provoke the children into fleeing again. Then, cautiously and a little diffidently, one individual spoke up.

"Singing lady?"

It wasn't Koru's voice, but still Indigo let her breath out in relief. "Yes, I'm here."

"Will you sing us another song?"

"I'll be glad to," Indigo called back. "And I can show you a dance. It's very easy to learn."

A chorus of eager voices broke out. "Oh, yes, yes!"

"But," Indigo added, "I can't show you the dance unless we can see each other. The wall is between us." She hesitated, exchanging a quick glance with Grimya. "Will you come out, or may I come in?"

There was a great agitation of whispering at that, but try as they might neither Indigo nor Grimya could hear what the children were saying. Indigo was just beginning to fear that they were having second thoughts when Grimya projected a telepathic alert.

*Look! Over there, by the hill!*

Indigo turned quickly. Where the curtain wall met the gentler slope of the hillside a light was glowing. It formed an arch at the base of the wall, like a tiny earthbound rainbow, shimmering with a spectrum of color. Then within the arch the outlines of a door appeared, ghostly at first but gaining solidity to become a little wooden gate, white-painted, with a gold latch.

The latch lifted, and the door swung back a little way.

There was more muttering, a stifled giggle, then a small, solemn face in a frame of unruly black hair looked out. Large eyes regarded Indigo and Grimya carefully for a few moments, then the child said,

"Are you the singing lady?"

Indigo smiled. "Yes."

A pause. Then: "Koru said you have an instrument that makes music. Where is it?"

"My harp? I didn't bring it with me." The child looked crestfallen and Indigo added, "I'm sorry."

The small features knitted together in a thoughtful frown. "You know some more songs, though? And games?"

"Yes. Songs and games and dances."

The child continued to consider for a few moments, then abruptly and emphatically nodded.

"Yes! It's all right. You can come in and play with us." And she stood back, pulling the door open wide.

Hesitantly at first, then more swiftly for fear that the children might change their minds, Indigo went toward the door with Grimya at her heels. She ducked under the arch, and immediately small hands were reaching out toward her, clasping, clutching at her clothes and her arms and her hair, pulling her into the security of the enclosing wall.

Indigo entered a garden. She found herself standing on a smooth greensward starred with white daisies, while all around the wall other flowers blossomed in profusion: briar roses and honeysuckle, bright, upturned faces of yellow sunflowers, tall, elegant spires of foxglove and valerian. Amid the riot of color the five towers, pale and shining, rose gracefully skyward with their pennants fluttering high above her head. But she had time for no more than this one brief impression of the sanctuary before a babble of voices rose up around her like the chatter of happy birds.

"The singing lady, the singing lady!"

"Sing us another pretty song!"

"Dance with us!"

"Play with us! We know lots of games!"

A little giddy with the multitude of impressions crowding in on her, Indigo turned her attention to the children. There must have been twenty or more of them, boys and girls alike, skipping and jumping excitedly as they closed in around her. They were dressed in an extraordinary motley of colors, far removed from the dull styles of Joyful Travail—and they were, she realized, as solid and as real as she herself. No ghosts, these. Or at least, not in this dimension.

Some of the children were now hugging and petting Grimya, exclaiming over her soft fur, and Indigo couldn't suppress a smile at the wolf's obvious delight in their adulation. But as she scanned the small sea of eager faces she couldn't find Koru among them. She tried to ask where he was, but her anxious questions were swept aside.

"Sing a song! Sing a song, and we shall dance. We know a dance, we'll show you! Sing a song for us!"

They were rushing to form a circle around her, linking hands, beaming with anticipation, and Indigo knew that she couldn't hope for any help in finding Koru until she had satisfied their ardent demands. She thought of projecting a message to Grimya, asking her to look for Koru while she entertained the children; but Grimya was already happily preoccupied, lost to the lure of the attention she was receiving. She would simply have to bide her time.

She recalled the comic Fairplayers song she'd sung for Koru on the ill-starred night before his disappearance. It might be taking a risk to repeat it now, but at the time Koru had enjoyed it and it had a splendid dancing lilt. There was just a chance that it might lure him from his hiding place.

Indigo clapped her hands to announce the song and began. For a few bars the children stood motionless, heads tilted alertly, listening. Then one small boy began to move his feet in a simple skipping step, and almost immediately others joined in until the entire group was circling round her, their feet twinkling over the grass. There was no pattern and no real rhythm to their dance, but youth and sheer exuberance gave them a grace of their own and their delight and energy were infectious. When the song ended they hugged each other, hugged Indigo, jumped up and down on the spot, and clamored for more.

"Pretty, pretty!"

"It was fun!"

"More songs, more dances!"

"Teach us a new dance!"

Suddenly their pleas gave Indigo an idea. There was another Fairplayers dance, a favorite with the youngest members of the Brabazon family, which involved calling partners by name into the center of a ring. It was simple, the children would revel in it—and it might succeed in enticing Koru where the first song had failed.

She held up her hands for quiet and said, "Very well. I'll teach you a dance. A lovely dance. But before we begin, I must know some of your names."

They looked at her blankly. Then one said: "Why?"

"Because I will call you, one at a time, into the circle to dance with me. Now," she smiled encouragement at a girl with an impish expression, "what's your name?"

The child giggled. "Wind. Grass. Flower. Singing Lady."

Nonplussed, Indigo turned her attention to the boy next to her. "What's *your* name?"

All the children were beginning to laugh now, as though this were some new and intriguing game. "River!" the boy declared. "Tree! Pretty!"

Didn't they understand? Or was this some peculiar joke at her expense? Or—and the thought shook Indigo as it occurred to her—did they *have* no names of their own? Whatever the truth of it, it would clearly achieve nothing to persist with her questions so, thinking swiftly, she changed tack.

"Well, then, it doesn't matter. The song has a chorus; each time I sing the chorus I will point—like this, you see?—and the one I point to must come into the circle to dance the next verse with me."

She didn't know if they comprehended but it hardly mattered; if they picked up no more than the rudiments it would be enough to please them and would serve her own purpose. She sang the chorus through once for them, letting them jump and prance and spin as she did so, then she launched into the first verse. As she sang, she communicated to the she-wolf:

*Grimya, I will call you first, to show them how it's done. Then I'll let one or two of them have a turn. And then I'll call Koru.*

The words of the verse were simple, almost nonsensical. Indigo reached the end, then, pointing at the wolf, called out: "Grimya, Grimya, play and sing! Dance with me in the merry ring!"

Grimya had few inhibitions, and in the old days with the Brabazons she had enjoyed nothing better than to take part in their shows. She loved an audience, and now she bounded into the ring where Indigo waited and began a dance of her own devising, turning round and round with her tail wagging joyously. The children were enraptured, and when the next verse and the wolf's display ended they all shouted to be next. Indigo pointed to the solemn little girl who had opened the gate to her—she made up a doggerel name on the spot; it seemed to make no difference— and the child joined them as the third verse began, doing her best, it seemed, to copy Grimya's capering. Next came a tousle-headed boy, then another, then a taller girl; by this time the dance was fast and furious and the children utterly captivated and determined that the fun shouldn't end until each and every one of them had been summoned into the center of the circle.

Then, after the seventh verse, Indigo didn't point but instead held up both arms. "Koru, Koru, play and sing, dance with us in the merry ring!"

No one came forward. Confused, the children shambled to an untidy halt and stood looking at one another. So far, so good, Indigo thought. She called again. "Koru, Koru, play and sing, dance with us in the merry ring!"

Still there was no sign of a tow-haired boy among the children's number. Indigo made a show of looking carefully around, then shook her head sadly.

"He won't come. He's spoiled our dance!"

Understanding dawned on the circle of small faces, and with it indignation.

"Koru! She called Koru!"

"He isn't here. Where is he?"

"He must come. Koru!"

"Find him, find him, or the fun will all be spoiled!"

"Where's Koru? Find Koru!"

And in eager chorus, "Koru! Koru! You mustn't stay away! Come out, Koru, come out and dance with us!"

Grimya communicated suddenly: *There he is—by the green tower.*

The green tower was the nearest of the five, and in a low doorway at its foot stood a small, solitary figure. He was trying to hide in the shadows, but the other children had seen him now and they rushed toward him in a happily shouting horde.

"Koru! Why did you hide?"

"Come and see the singing lady and her lovely dog!"

"Come and play!"

They pounced on Koru, kissing him and patting him like a long-lost brother, and hurried him back to where Indigo and Grimya waited. As they approached Indigo saw Koru's face clearly. His expression was stark with fear and misery, and there was terror in his blue eyes.

Indigo dropped to a crouch as the children brought him to her, putting her face on a level with his so as not to intimidate him. "Hello, Koru," she said gently.

He jerked his head aside. "I won't come back!"

His companions were apparently oblivious to his distress; they chirped and chirruped, urging Indigo to begin the calling dance again. Grimya whined softly, and Indigo said,

"Koru, there's no need to be afraid of me. I only want to talk to you."

"No, you don't!" He looked at her again, and suddenly his voice was filled with desperate venom. "You don't! I know! You've come to take me back, you've come to make me go with you! Well, I won't, I *won't*, and you can't make me! You're not my friend anymore. Go away! You're no different from any of the others, from Papa and Mother and Elli and all the Aunts and Uncles! You do whatever they tell you, because you're just like them! I thought you weren't, once, but you are! They've made you *dead*!"

There was a long and dreadful silence. Even the children now realized that something was badly amiss, and they drew back from Koru, staring at him with wide eyes. Several put their thumbs into their mouths in worried chagrin and one very small girl started to cry.

Koru stood alone and defiant, glaring at Indigo like a small but ferocious animal. Indigo was searching desperately for something to say, but could find nothing that didn't threaten to make the situation even worse. And Koru's last words still rang in her mind. *You're just like the others. They've made you dead.*

Then, unexpectedly, Grimya stepped forward. She moved with great care and very slowly, her amber gaze fixed on Koru's face. The boy saw her, glanced at her, and frowned as though for a moment his resolve had wavered. Then to Indigo's astonishment Grimya spoke.

"K-Koru . . . ," she said in her rough, halting voice. "Am *I* dead, like all the others? Do you hh-hate me, too?"

Koru's eyes widened in shock. "Grimya . . . you—you can *talk*!"

"Yess. I can talk." The she-wolf sent a silent message to Indigo: *Say nothing; do nothing.* She dipped her head in the diffident way she had. "W-we did not tell you before. We did not d ... *are* tell even you, Koru. Not because the others said so, but because we feared what they would do."

Koru dragged his lower lip down with an uncertain finger. "*You* were afraid of them, too ...?"

"Yess. They would not have under ... stood, and they would have driven us out. That is why ..." She hesitated, and Indigo heard her silent apology for the white lie that was to follow: "... that is why we came to this place. Not to take you back. To be with you."

Indigo stared at the wolf in astonishment. She'd never dreamed that Grimya could be so devious—but no, devious was an unjust term. Grimya understood Koru on a deep and fundamental level that she herself could never achieve; for Koru was a child, and Grimya, too, was childlike. She knew and shared a child's simple yet vital hopes and dreams and fears; clear and untrammelled emotions that for Indigo, as for most humans, were lost beyond recall when childhood was left behind. Suddenly the memory of Grimya running and leaping and barking in their wild chase across the meadows and through the woods came to her mind, and with it another image that Indigo had never witnessed but often imagined: the small, eager cub exploring the strange new world of the Horselands forest where she had been so recently born, before her own kind had learned of her mutation and driven her out as a pariah. Distressed, she put a hand to her face—

"Indigo." It was Koru's voice, quite changed. "You're crying!"

"No ..." The denial was unthinking, a reflex; Indigo sniffed and wiped her eyes with the back of one hand. "No, I'm not. Not now."

"Mother says it's wrong to cry, but I don't believe her. It isn't wrong, not here. I . . ." Koru struggled with himself for a moment; youth and innocence held him back from more than a glimmer of understanding. "I . . . didn't mean what I said. About you being dead. I'm sorry, Indigo."

She couldn't answer, but only made a cancelling gesture.

"If only you'd *told* me about Grimya." Koru gazed at the wolf, wonder in his look. "If I'd known, it might all have been different. But I thought you'd come to take me away. And I won't go back." He shook his head. "I *won't*."

"Koru—" But Grimya's mental voice cut across what Indigo had been about to say. *No, Indigo. I think it would not be wise to argue with him yet.*

Indigo bit her words back and sighed. Then, suddenly, she felt a tug at her sleeve.

"Singing lady." It was the solemn-faced girl. Bolder than her companions, she had come forward and now gazed at Indigo with greatly serious intent. "It's Koru's turn to dance."

The sheer incongruity of her preoccupation, stated so firmly, brought a bubble of unexpected laughter to Indigo's throat. Koru grinned.

"Yes, Indigo! Let us dance!" He paused. "I was in the tower. I heard you and I wanted to join in, but I didn't dare. I know better now." Suddenly he reached out to her, offering to pull her to her feet. "I wish you'd brought your harp; I like that. But it doesn't really matter, because I expect the Benefactor can make you another one if you ask him."

She had allowed him to help her up before she realized what he'd said.

"The Benefactor? Koru, tell me about the Benefactor. What is he? *Who* is he?"

Koru's face screwed up thoughtfully. "Well, I don't exactly *know*," he said. "You see, I've only seen him once, and then not to talk to. But all my friends know him. Sometimes we all pretend he's a king. That's fun—I had a book once with kings in it, so I know all about them and I can tell the others."

Indigo was aware of Grimya watching Koru intently. She hesitated, then ventured, trying to keep her voice casual, "So he doesn't . . . keep you prisoners here?"

"Prisoners?" Koru's eyes opened very wide and then he laughed gustily. "Indigo, you have such silly ideas! All my friends like the Benefactor. They say he isn't what they think he is in Joyful Travail, and that everyone there has got the story all wrong. I think that's very funny, don't you?"

Grimya intervened before Indigo could reply.

*Indigo, don't ask him any more questions. Not now. We hold his trust by a thin thread, I think, and it would be better to make sure of it before we try to persuade him home. Besides,* she wagged her tail tentatively, *I would not wish to disappoint all the children.*

There was a faintly wistful note to her mental voice, as though she wasn't convinced that Koru should be persuaded to return home at all. Indigo was about to protest when she realized to her consternation that she couldn't entirely disagree. The contrast between Koru's happiness here and the life that awaited him back in Joyful Travail was a stark one. Wasn't it possible, just possible, that the little boy would be better off in this world . . . ?

The insidious thought appalled her. She couldn't allow herself to consider such a thing. It was unconscionable and a terrible betrayal of Hollend and Calpurna, who had been so good to her. She shook her head, banishing the doubts, and realized that the children were crowding round her again.

"Singing lady, singing lady!"

"Let's finish our dance!"

"No, no—let's begin it all over again. It will be even more fun!"

Koru tugged at her hand. "Come on, Indigo! Begin again, sing the song!"

Grimya barked, her tail swirling eagerly now, and Indigo gave in. The children formed a new circle and began to skip around her, the wolf and Koru among them. Indigo looked up at the five shining pastel towers, so gracious and peaceful as they soared into the sky. Then she drew breath, and began to sing.

# ·CHAPTER·XII·

The revelry went on and on until Indigo's sense of time was quite lost. The children seemed tireless, and the ending of each dance or game brought loud and impassioned pleas for another until at last Indigo felt she could sing no more.

She held up both hands, protesting as yet another cry for further play went up. "Please, please!" *Sweet Mother,* the thought flicked desperately through her mind, *how many hours have passed? What's happening in Joyful Travail— what must Hollend and Calpurna be thinking?*

"My throat is too tired!" She clutched at it and poked her tongue out, making an outrageous face. The children giggled and Indigo played up to them. "I'm much too old to keep up with you for very long!" She put her other hand to her back and performed an ungainly hop like a crone in a comic play. Peals of laughter greeted this, and Indigo was a little shocked to find how easy and appealing it had become to slip into the role of playmate and entertainer. She was enjoying this hugely, she realized, just as she had enjoyed her earlier game with Grimya, forgetting all else in sheer, self-indulgent delight.

But was there any harm in such simple pleasure? The children's rapturous faces would have been reward enough under any circumstances; in these beautiful, peaceful, yet somehow exhilarating surroundings the enchantment was multiplied tenfold.

They'd fallen silent now, or as silent as their ebullience would allow. Indigo dropped her comic pretense and said, "I must rest for a while. My voice is weary, and you've almost danced me off my feet." Somehow she had to find a way to get Koru away from the others without arousing his suspicions or theirs. She *had* to talk to him.

One of the children spoke up. "I know! *We'll* sing a song for *you*." She turned to her immediate companions. "We know songs, don't we? Lots of songs!"

A babble broke out. "Oh, yes, yes, lots! Let's sing one now!"

"Which one?"

"I like the skipping song best."

"No, no, we've done that one. Let's sing the other one. *You* know, the one about the boat."

"What's a boat?"

"I know what a boat is! It goes on water, and it floats. Yes, let's sing that one!"

There was a chorus of general approval, and two small girls ran forward to pat the grass in a brisk, almost motherly manner and persuade Indigo to sit down.

"There, singing lady, sit here and we will sing for you." They saw her comfortably settled, then sprang up again. "Come on, Koru! You can lead us."

Koru, his cheeks flushed with pleasure, grinned at Indigo. "They taught me this song," he said a little bashfully. "I don't know it *very* well yet, but I'll try."

The others were growing impatient. "Come on, Koru, come on!"

Koru drew himself up and, in a piping but surprisingly true treble voice, began to sing.

And Indigo felt as though her heart had stopped beating.

It was impossible—or so she told herself—to be sure, because the tune wasn't quite as she recalled it and Koru didn't know all the words. And there was always the chance that the song, old as it was, had somehow found its way to Joyful Travail and into the minds of these ghost-children. But the song that Koru sang was as familiar to her as that first chorus had been. A Southern Isles song—a sailors' shanty from her homeland, which she'd not heard for more than half a century.

As Koru continued to sing she sat staring at him, bewildered, uncertain, and when the other children's voices joined in, swelling to a blithe chorus, she barely noticed. The song ended at last and still Indigo stayed motionless, still staring.

For several seconds there was a silence that grew more and more uncomfortable. Koru glanced surreptitiously at his friends but found them as nonplussed as he was. He moved toward Indigo, peering at her face.

"Indigo, have we done something wrong? Don't you like the song? What's the matter?"

The other children closed in, too, twittering and whispering worriedly.

"What's wrong?"

"Is the singing lady not well?"

"How can we make her better?"

Suddenly Indigo seemed to snap out of her trance. She blinked, and her eyes focused on the huddle of troubled faces before her.

"Koru . . . where did you learn that song?"

One of the children glanced sidelong at Koru. "Don't you like it?" she asked.

"Yes—oh, yes, I like it very much. But—" She turned her

head slowly, looking at them all in turn, "Where did you learn it?"

The children frowned and muttered. One or two scratched their heads in puzzlement. Then a boy spoke.

"We learned it from Koru."

"No, we didn't," objected another. "We *taught* it to Koru. We just said so!"

A third piped up. "That's right." He smirked. "*I* know where we learned it."

"Where?"

"At the tower in the wood. Remember? When we went to see the tower. The tower sang it to us."

"Don't be silly! Towers don't sing!"

"This one does. You know it does. We've heard it."

"That wasn't the *tower*, silly. That was the sleeping man."

"Koru wasn't here then."

"No, that's why we had to teach him the song later. But it was the sleeping man." The boy looked triumphantly at Grimya and Indigo in turn. "The sleeping man. He sang it."

A peculiar sense of excitement moved in Indigo, and she asked, "Who is the sleeping man?"

The boy shrugged. "We don't know, really. He lives in the tower. Sometimes he does, anyway, though he isn't always there."

"Where is this tower?"

"In the woods." A hand pointed vaguely beyond the curtain wall. "It's quite a long way, so we don't go there very often."

"We thought it was the tower singing to us," a girl volunteered. "But that's silly, because towers can't sing."

"Yes they *can*! It *does*!"

"No, no, no. The *man* sings. Sometimes, when he's there, he sings in his sleep, and we remembered some of his songs. That was clever, wasn't it? Remembering them. It was clever!"

Indigo's mind raced as she tried to comprehend the children's quicksilver prattle. A "sleeping man," sometimes there and sometimes not, who knew Southern Isles shanties and sang them in his sleep? It didn't make any sense. What did the children mean? The workings of their minds were impossible to follow logically, for they flitted like birds from one topic to another, putting their own indecipherable interpretation on everything. Ghost-minds . . . She suppressed a shiver that crept up and tried to take her by surprise. She had to find out what lay behind this. Perhaps it would lead nowhere, come to nothing. But—and at that moment she couldn't have explained why—she had to *know*.

"Children." She started to get to her feet. "Children, I would very much like to see the sleeping man. Will you take me to him?"

Faces fell. "Oh, but we want to sing more songs!"

"It's a long way. *Such* a long, long way."

"Better to stay here. Better to play more games!"

Frustration welled in Indigo but she quelled it. "Please," she said, and then, with a flash of inspiration. "I've run out of songs to sing. If the sleeping man's in his tower today, maybe we can learn some new ones from him!"

This clearly hadn't occurred to them and they greeted the idea with cautious interest. As they whispered and debated, Indigo turned to Koru.

"Please, Koru, can you persuade them to take me?"

He looked back at her, his blue eyes solemn and filled with a sudden peculiarly adult perception. "Is this something important, Indigo?"

She nodded. "I think it might be."

He didn't say any more but reached out and touched her arm lightly in a reassuring gesture. Then he turned to the other children.

"Come on, let's go and see the sleeping man! It isn't *that* far. Indigo wants to see him, and she's our friend!"

The simple logic worked. First a few, then more, then all of the children took up Koru's words.

"Yes, let's go!"

"Koru's right; it isn't *that* far!"

"And the wood is nice. I like the wood!"

"Come with us, singing lady. Come and see the sleeping man and see if he'll sing us a new song!"

Like a small flock of starlings wheeling with a single mind toward their roost, the children swirled as one toward the curtain wall where the door by which Indigo and Grimya had entered the garden still stood ajar. Koru hung back briefly, gazing curiously at Indigo.

"Are you sure?" he said.

Grimya, in her mind, added, *Indigo, we don't know what we might find. There could be danger here.*

Indigo didn't look at either of them. She was staring at the wall, her eyes focused far beyond it, not, it seemed, into another place but into another time. She nodded.

"I'm sure."

"It wasn't that I *wanted* to run away." Koru looked up at Indigo with an expression of helpless sorrow. "But I had to. After what happened and what Mother and Papa said. I didn't want to make them unhappy. But I *had* to go. You understand, Indigo, don't you?"

They were following the children over the springy turf of another gently rolling hill, the third or fourth they had crossed since leaving the towers and the garden. Indigo knew that Koru would rather have gone ahead to join his friends, whose voices rang cheerfully as they ran and jumped and indulged in mock battles, chasing each other across the grass. But the ties of friendship, coupled perhaps with a residual sense of duty or guilt, had prompted him to stay at her side and try to explain what he had done.

Indigo said, "Yes, Koru, I do understand." It would have been easy to add that though she sympathized with him she also sympathized with his grieving family, and to ask him to think of the unhappiness he had caused them. But she shared Grimya's view that the time for persuasion wasn't yet right, and that, anyway, to try to manipulate Koru's conscience would be unfair. The little boy was clearly well aware of the consequences of what he'd done, and to play on that would only add more confusion to his already troubled mind. But there were areas where it was safe to tread, and now she said:

"How did you find your way here, Koru? How did you know that this world even existed?"

He thought long and hard about that before answering. "I think . . . I've always known it was here. Whenever I went to the Benefactor's House I used to sort of *feel* it. And then, when . . . well, when I—that night—I just knew I had to go back to the House. I thought I'd be scared of it in the dark, but I wasn't. The gate was open when I got there, so I went in." Suddenly a vivid smile lit his face. "They were waiting for me, all my friends were waiting. They said they knew I'd come, and they showed me how to get through the mirror."

Indigo smiled. "You talk of your friends as though you've known them all your life."

Koru looked faintly perplexed. "Well . . . I haven't really, of course. But I'd *seen* them, when they used to come and call to me and want me to play, and now I feel as if I've known them for ages, so it doesn't really matter." Again he gave her that quick, brilliant smile. "It's like that with real friends, isn't it?"

Indigo chose her next words with great care. She needed to ask the question, but she was also aware of how precarious her hold on Koru's trust still was, and how easy it would be to alienate him.

"Koru . . ." She glanced ahead to where the children shrieked and laughed and chased each other. "Do you think that your friends are . . . ghosts?"

"Ghosts?" She'd anticipated indignation, possibly anger, even fear. What she hadn't expected was the laughter that bubbled from Koru's throat, as though she'd told him some great joke.

"Oh no, they're not *ghosts*!" He veered a little closer to her and added in a confiding tone, "I used to think they might be, and that's why I was afraid of them. But they're not ghosts, Indigo. They're people, just like us."

"But they aren't *quite* like us, are they?" Indigo persisted cautiously. "How do they live? What do they eat?"

Koru shrugged. "They don't have to eat anything. No one does, here. That's what's so wonderful—we don't have to do anything we don't want to! We don't have to have lessons, or work in the fields, or go to bed when we're told. We can just play games and sing and dance and have fun all the time, and there's *no* one to tell us it's wrong, or that we can't believe in things, or . . ." Abruptly his voice trailed off as he realized, a little belatedly, where Indigo's gentle probing had been leading. His face clouded and he looked at her with something approaching suspicion.

"I'm not going to go back." Defiance colored his voice. "I meant what I said before, Indigo. I didn't mean to say it so horribly, but it was true all the same. All the people in Joyful Travail, even Mother and Papa—they don't *feel* anything; they never laugh, they never play or sing. That's just like being dead, isn't it? When all the happiness and fun inside you shrivels up and isn't there anymore, and they say it wasn't real anyway and you mustn't ever talk about it again." His mouth twitched unhappily. "*They're* the ones who are like ghosts, not my friends."

Grimya spoke silently in Indigo's mind. *I understand him, Indigo, and I think he is right. That is a kind of death. And all Koru wants is to stay alive.*

Indigo bit her lower lip. She'd been greatly moved by Koru's words and pitied his plight. But she also pitied Hollend and Calpurna. Whatever he thought of them, however bitter and betrayed he might feel, Koru hadn't witnessed their grief. She couldn't abandon her duty to them.

"Koru." Heedless of the fact that the children were shouting to them to hurry, she stopped walking and turned to face the little boy. "Koru, your mother and father—they *do* love you very dearly. And they're desperately worried about you. I know you weren't happy in Joyful Travail, but maybe if I helped you to talk to them, helped to explain—"

"Explain what?" Koru said miserably.

"About this world. About your friends, and the things you want to do—"

"No." He shook his head so emphatically that she realized even before he said another word that her cause was lost. "They wouldn't believe you. They'd say it was all lies and we were making it up. They've already done that to Ellani; she used to believe but she doesn't anymore."

Indigo made one last effort. "But if they *saw* your friends—"

Koru's vivid blue eyes met hers with frighteningly adult understanding. "But they won't see them, will they?" he said. "Even if they look they won't see anything, because they don't want to." Abruptly, then, he turned away. "Please, Indigo, don't let's talk about it anymore. I know you're my friend and I know you're only trying to help and do what you think is best. But I'm not going to change my mind. I *will* miss Mother and Papa, and Ellani, too. But I'm *happy* here. And I'm going to stay, forever and ever."

*Forever and ever* . . . The words had a chilling ring in Indigo's psyche as she realized that they might well be literally true. *No one has to eat here,* Koru had said. And: *We can do anything we want to.* She recalled the pastel towers, and the gateway in the wall that had appeared only when the children wanted to enter or leave. She remembered racing with Grimya, flying over the ground faster than any living creature could run. A world not of ghosts, she thought, but of dreams . . . and in dreams, a child had only to wish and the wish would come true.

Renewed cries from the other children impinged suddenly, and she looked up to see that the whole group had stopped and some half-dozen were running back toward them.

"Singing lady, singing lady!"

"Why aren't you running with us? It isn't very far now!"

"Come and see the sleeping man! Come and see the tower!"

"The wood's nice, you'll like the wood!"

"Let's run and play!"

"Koru, come *on*!"

Small, determined hands grasped at Indigo's arms and tried to pull her along. She looked from one to another of the eager faces bobbing around her. They were so happy, so simple, so shallow . . . Could Koru live like they did, become as they were? Surely not, she thought. Surely, like Joyful Travail, this world could offer him only half a life.

But it was too late to explain, to try to make Koru understand. Already he was skipping off hand in hand with two of the children while the other four bounced impatiently on the spot and urged Indigo to follow. She darted a quick, helpless glance at Grimya, which the wolf returned intently.

Grimya projected: *I know what you are thinking. But I still must ask myself which would be worse, Indigo? To be half alive here, or half alive in Joyful Travail? I have asked that question before and I still do not know the answer.*

The wood where the sleeping man had made his home lay in the fold of a small valley. From a distance the trees seemed to form a solid, impenetrable mass like a dark lake, but as the party drew closer Indigo realized that there were clear spaces beneath the leaf-canopy. Tall conifers dominated the wood, though there were patches of broadleaf trees among their crowding numbers, and as they started down the slope toward the wood's edge the children ceased their games and marched ahead hand in hand.

Since their small confrontation it seemed that Koru was

determined not to give Indigo another opportunity to speak. He wasn't precisely avoiding her, but whenever she came within speaking distance he took great care to ensure that at least one and preferably several of his friends were at his side. However, as they neared the trees' edge he came toward her, one of the girls dancing alongside him.

"This is the place," he said eagerly. "We have to go into the wood, but we all know the way, so you needn't fear getting lost."

"We *never* get lost," the girl informed Indigo proudly. "We're clever, aren't we?"

From up ahead the other children called out, "Come on, come on!" and a boy added, "You'll like the wood. *We* do." Without waiting for a response he started forward again, and the others fell into single file behind him as he led them all into the shadowy quiet.

Indigo, following with Koru and the girl, asked, "Where does the sleeping man live?"

"In a tower," Koru told her. "You can't see it until you get very close, though, because it isn't anything like as big as our towers. It isn't as nice as our towers, either, but I suppose he must like it or he wouldn't live there."

"What does he look like?"

"I don't exactly *know*," Koru said. "You see, I've only been here once before, and when I came, he wasn't there, so I haven't seen him yet."

"Where had he gone?" she asked.

A shrug. "Somewhere. He only comes to the tower sometimes, you see, and we never know when he'll be there and when he won't."

"And have you—or rather your friends—ever talked to him?"

Koru shook his head. "No. When he's here, he's always asleep."

"We try to wake him up," the girl volunteered brightly, "but he won't. He must be *very* tired. Still, he sings us some nice songs," she added, as though singing in one's sleep were the most natural thing in the world.

From the dim shade ahead of them a voice called back. "Koru! Singing lady! Where are you?"

Koru grabbed Indigo's hand and tugged. "Come on, or the others will leave us behind."

They hurried after the children and Koru said no more. But as they penetrated deeper into the wood Indigo pondered the few tantalizing facts she had gleaned from him about the sleeping man. What, exactly, was he? she wondered. An inhabitant of this world, like the children themselves?—though that in itself posed yet more unanswerable questions. Or someone who, like Koru and herself and Grimya, had found a doorway between this dimension and the physical world, and who had learned to move at will between the two? That could explain his frequent absences. But why did he sleep, and why could the children never wake him? Was he under some spell? Or was there a stranger answer that as yet she'd not even guessed at?

Ahead of her, the children had begun to sing a song with a walking rhythm in the tongue of Joyful Travail. Koru and the girl joined in and after a minute or so Indigo did, too, caught up in the song's infectious cheerfulness. Then she realized that the trees were beginning to thin out, and moments later a clearing came into view ahead, with a solitary tower standing in its center.

It wasn't in the least like the five pastel towers of the children's garden. In many ways it resembled a strange, squat tree rather than a building fashioned by human hands, for its shape was gently undulating and its walls, only two stories high, were thickly clad with moss and ivy and luxuriantly ramping honeysuckle, through which small, round windows peeped. There was something reassuring about the tower's sturdiness, a sense of permanence and, Indigo thought to her own surprise, of welcome. Approaching through the undergrowth and listening to the children's voices still piping their song, she had a sudden fleeting understanding of how a wandering troubadour might feel on unexpectedly finding a friendly house in the midst of wilderness. The thought brought a faintly wistful smile to her face; then the song ended and the little party reached the tower.

The last bright chorus echoed away through the wood and, as though by unspoken agreement or established custom, the children spread out into a half-circle before the tower.

"Sleeping man!" A girl's lone voice rose out of the quiet. "Sleeping man, are you there? We've come to hear you sing, and we've brought a new friend to see you."

Koru whispered to Indigo: "Perhaps he hasn't come back yet. But if he is there, he might sing a song."

Other voices joined in with the girl's.

"Sleeping man, sleeping man!"

"Are you there, sleeping man? Sing for us! Sing a song!"

"We've learned new songs and new games. The singing lady taught them to us."

"Wake up, wake up, please wake up. If you wake up, the singing lady will sing a song for *you*!"

They waited, but no answer came. Among the tangle of scrambling greenery at the tower's foot Indigo could now make out a low, arched wooden door. But the door was closed and stayed closed, and there was no creak of a casement opening in any of the upper windows.

The girl who had been the first to call out sighed. "He isn't going to come out. He won't wake up."

Indigo was still gazing at the door. "Perhaps he isn't there," she said.

The children all gave this earnest consideration. "Perhaps he isn't. But if he is, why doesn't he wake up?"

"He never wakes up."

"Yes he does, he does!"

"No he doesn't!"

"But he sings to us—"

"In his *sleep*. He sings in his *sleep*."

"Oh. Oh, yes. In his sleep. No, he doesn't wake up, does he?"

"And sometimes when we go into the tower he isn't even there. Perhaps he isn't there now. Perhaps that's why he won't sing to us."

From among the tangles of their obscure and illogical argument a phrase caught Indigo's attention. *When we go into the tower* . . . She sent a quick mental message to Grimya.

*Grimya, I think we should go and see for ourselves.* Her gaze took in the children, still chattering together. They seemed to have forgotten her.

Grimya agreed. *If we wait for the children, we will wait a long time.* Something like a silent sigh echoed in Indigo's mind. *They are very hard to understand sometimes. So much of what they say makes little sense.*

Smiling wryly, Indigo moved toward the tower door. The old wood felt warm to the touch; the latch lifted and the door moved easily. That surprised her, for she'd expected—though logically she didn't quite know why—that it would be locked.

Abruptly then there came a shout from behind her.

"Singing lady, singing lady!"

"Singing lady, where are you going?"

"She's going into the tower. She's going to see if the sleeping man's there."

"That's very clever! The singing lady's clever!"

"We'll go, too, shall we?"

"Yes, we'll go, and see if the sleeping man's at home."

"Wait for us, singing lady, wait for us! We'll come, too!"

The children crowded after Indigo and Grimya, eager and clamoring. Indigo fought down a flash of irritation at their irrepressible cheerfulness, which suddenly clashed with her own mood. Unconsciously her left fist was clenched at her side as her right hand pushed the door open. She hesitated a bare moment, then ducked her head and entered the tower.

The single, circular room was surprisingly light. The leaves of the encroaching creepers filmed the windows and gave the light a greenish tinge, but it was a pleasant shade, not in the least oppressive. What surprised Indigo above all, though, was the fact that the tower was empty but for a solitary chair, broad-armed and high-backed, set at the far side of the room and facing away from her toward the wall.

The other children had followed her in and now jostled together, muttering and giggling.

"Is he there?"

"I can't see! Is he there, singing lady? Is he?"

"In his chair! That's where he'll be."

"*Shh!* She's clever, she knows that! Don't push!"

Indigo stared at the chair. She'd thought it empty, but now, as the last of the children found room in the tower and their bodies no longer blocked the light from the doorway, she realized that someone was indeed sitting—or rather, slumping—in its depths. She moved forward . . . Then her steps slowed, faltered. She was suddenly afraid to go on; afraid of what she might find.

Then, as she moved a little to one side and her angle of vision changed, she saw. Hands limp on the chair's armrests, head propped by the high back, dark, unmoving, a recumbent figure. Her heart seemed to contract as though a hand had grasped and squeezed it, driving the breath from her and tightening her ribs with pain. *She knew*—

She stepped up to the chair, and her eyes saw what the shock of intuition had already revealed. He looked as still and as peaceful as though he'd simply fallen asleep on a quiet afternoon before a comfortable fireside. Black hair, a little wild; the so-familiar bones of his face, the curve of his lips, the dark lashes casting shadows on his cheeks. Fifty years hadn't changed him one iota. And every muscle and every nerve within Indigo seemed to shut down as she gazed at the sleeping man.

In a voice so chokingly soft that only Grimya could hear, she whispered:

"*Fenran . . .*"

# ·CHAPTER·XIII·

This time, she wasn't deluded. This time there was no blizzard, no deceptive lantern-light, no daze of exhaustion to lead her mind astray as had happened once before in the Redoubt. This time there could be no mistake. Since her exile began she had seen him only in her dreams, or in agonizingly brief instants when her own half-realized powers had momentarily breached the barriers that held them apart. But now, for the first time in half a century, Indigo looked upon the living face and form of her lost love.

She couldn't speak. She had whispered his name but could say or do no more. On an unreal level, as though from another world, she sensed Grimya's anxious thoughts in her mind, heard Koru's worried voice from behind her as he, too, realized that something was very wrong. But she couldn't respond to them, couldn't even think. She only stood unmoving, unbreathing, staring down at Fenran's sleeping figure.

The other children, blithely oblivious to her plight, began to clamor again.

"Sleeping man, sleeping man!"

"Is he there? Will he wake up?"

"Wake up, sleeping man; wake up and see the singing lady!"

"We can all sing some more songs!"

They were pressing closer, elbowing one another in their efforts to peer at the chair and see what Indigo had found. Suddenly something within Indigo snapped. She whirled, and to Grimya it seemed that in a space of a few seconds she had aged twenty years.

"Koru, make them go! Take them out of here, take them *away*!"

Koru's eyes widened with chagrin. "Indigo, what's wrong? What have we done?"

They hadn't done anything; it wasn't their fault, for they hadn't known what was afoot. But if they didn't go, and quickly, Indigo knew that she would lash out blindly without thought for the consequences.

Grimya saw the roiling emotions in her mind and turned, blocking Koru's path as he started to move toward Indigo. Her stance was protective, but as Koru shrank back nervously he saw that there was no aggression in her amber eyes, only sadness.

"Koru," Grimya said gently. "P . . . lease. Do as Indigo asks, and lead the children outside."

Koru was bewildered. "Why?" he asked helplessly. "What's wrong with her, Grimya?"

Grimya made a sound very like a human sigh. "I c-annot explain it all to you, for I thhhink you would not understand."

"Is it the sleeping man? Is it something about him?" Koru flung a glance toward Indigo's motionless figure by the chair, then looked at the wolf again as intuition sparked. "Does Indigo *know* him?"

Grimya dipped her head. "Yess. She knows him."

Koru's face became woeful. "Oh, Grimya, I didn't mean

to upset her!" Hope lit his face abruptly. "Perhaps we can wake him after all! Perhaps—"

"Not now, Koru. Pl . . . *lease*. Make them go."

The depth of feeling and urgency underlying the wolf's appeal must have reached through to Koru, for he nodded soberly and turned to his friends. What he said to them Indigo didn't know; her mind was frozen, locked within the small tableau of herself and Fenran, and she wasn't even aware of the exchange between Grimya and the little boy. But at last, slowly, as though stirring from a terrible dream, she realized that the children had wandered outside and only the wolf remained, watching her in a silent agony of concern.

"*Sweet Mother . . .*" But then Indigo's teeth clamped down hard on her tongue, biting the words away before she lost control and began to repeat them, uselessly, crazily, over and over again. At last, when she made no further sound, Grimya ventured gently:

"Perhaps he *can* be woken. Perhaps it is possible."

"The children said . . ."

"They may be wrrr-ong."

Indigo looked at her, and wild hope flickered to life like a furnace fire in her eyes. She couldn't pretend to herself that she even began to comprehend what was happening to her; it was too incredible, almost too grotesque to believe. *Fenran, here . . .* But—

"Yes," she whispered. "Oh, yes, yes. They may be wrong!" In her heart she prayed silently, desperately, *Please, Great Goddess, let them be wrong!*

Indigo dropped to her knees beside the chair. Slowly her hands reached out, and her fingers touched Fenran's still form.

He was real. Flesh and blood, not a phantom but alive and *real*. His skin was warm, browned by sun and wind, just as she remembered it. And beneath her shaking fingers she felt the final proof that this was no illusion: the steady pulse of his heart.

"Fenran." She whispered his name like a litany. "Fenran. Oh, my love. My love . . . Wake. Please, my dearest one. Wake. *Wake.*"

But she knew even as the words poured from her that her pleas and prayers would be in vain. She held his hands, she kissed his lips, her tears fell on his face as she begged and entreated. Yet Fenran slept on, peaceful as a child, unmoving and unaware.

Grimya had slipped quietly out of the tower. She couldn't bear to witness Indigo's grief; she felt like an intruder and there was nothing she could do to help. Indigo didn't see her go. Every part of her being was focused on Fenran.

So when the new voice spoke to her out of the shadows, the shock of recognition was all the greater.

The voice said: "You cannot wake him, Indigo. Not yet— and not alone. But I can help you."

Indigo's head came up as swiftly and violently as if someone had struck her on the jaw. She turned, saw, and her right hand flew to her belt, looking to snatch her knife from its sheath. But the knife wasn't there. She'd left it behind, dropped it at the Benefactor's House when she had tried to force the lock of the gate. All she could do was stare, raging, disbelieving, at the figure confronting her.

Nemesis, child-demon of her own dark self, didn't flinch. Its eyes glinted like silver coins in the gloom; its small, feline face was like the face of a ghost. Then it said: "Sister—"

"Don't *dare* to call me that!" Indigo's fists clenched furiously as on the heels of the first shock came a surge of loathing: memories of Nemesis's evil deeds and trickeries, memories of bitterness and hatred, and the scars of an undying, implacable enmity. She wanted to scream in the being's face but could find no words foul enough. She wanted to tear out its silver hair, gouge out its silver eyes, smash her fist again and again into that hateful, eternally smiling countenance—

But Nemesis was not smiling. Slowly and almost subliminally Indigo began to realize that, for once, there was no mocking leer on its lips, no malice in its eyes. The look of cruel triumph that had haunted her dreams for half a century had gone, replaced by an expression of wistful yearning. The realization shook Indigo's resolve. She was suddenly unsure of her ground, and though she could barely speak, she forced the words out.

"What do you *want*?"

"Sister," Nemesis said again. "We can wake him. Together, you and I. We have the power."

Something caught in Indigo's throat as an intuition that she didn't want to acknowledge clawed at her. *Together?*

"No!" Intuition collapsed as the ugly memories came boiling to the surface again, and with a violent movement Indigo sprang to her feet, barring Fenran's slumped body from Nemesis's view. "Damn you! You won't touch him. You *won't*! Try, and I'll *annihilate* you!"

Nemesis hesitated. Then, from the chair, came the sound of a soft sigh.

*"Fenran!"* Indigo spun round, almost losing her balance as hope and terror surged like a tide.

The chair was empty. Fenran had vanished.

*"NO!"* Indigo screamed like a banshee, provoking an echoing howl from Grimya and cries from the children beyond the door. There was a scrabbling of paws outside, a voice—Koru's—shouting her name in alarm. Nemesis turned its head, and as Grimya's shadow fell across the doorway, the figure of the demon-child winked out.

"Indigo!" The she-wolf rushed to her side, eyes feral and teeth bared to attack whoever or whatever menaced her friend. "Indigo, what is it? What's wrr-ong?"

At first Indigo couldn't speak. Her body shaking, her

hands barely under control, she pointed wordlessly at the chair. Grimya looked.

"He is gone! But—"

"N-Nemesis." Indigo's voice came at last, quavering and shot through with an undercurrent of terrible violence. "It was here, Grimya. It w-was *here*. It said—it said—And then Fenran, he—he *vanished* . . ." She covered her face with her hands.

Grimya stared from Indigo to the chair and back to Indigo again. She didn't understand, but before she could try to calm her friend enough to ask any questions, Koru came running in.

"Indigo, Indigo, what's amiss?" He was breathless. "You screamed!"

Indigo had got a grip on herself, and she waved a hand in a quick, negating gesture. "I'm all right, Koru. There's nothing to worry about."

Far from reassured, Koru glanced at the chair. "Oh," he said then, believing that he understood. "The sleeping man's gone." Furtively he glanced at Grimya and added in a whisper, "Was that it, Grimya? Was that what upset Indigo?"

Grimya didn't even attempt to answer his question. Indigo was moving toward the door, slowly, stiffly. She was clearly dazed still and the wolf hurried to her side, gazing up anxiously. Koru moved aside as she crossed the floor, but she ignored him. Then she stopped.

"I'm going back to Joyful Travail, Grimya. I—I can't stay here. I *can't*."

Outside, the children's voices rose with sudden renewed eagerness. Grimya paid them no heed; she had no interest in whatever game they were playing now. "Indigo, w . . . wait," she entreated. "I don't under-stand."

Indigo shook her head. She didn't have the words to explain. Later, maybe, it would be possible, but not now. She started forward again—and then they both heard what the children outside were shouting.

"He's here, he's here!"

"He's come to play with us!"

"Come and play with us! Come and see the singing lady and her gray dog!"

And one lone, piping voice: "Oh, we *so* hoped you'd come and play!"

Indigo and Grimya both froze, and the wild possibility tumbled through Indigo's mind. *Fenran! He'd come back—*

She ducked under the low lintel, ran outside into the dappled sunlight—and stopped.

The children had already surrounded him, eager and excited as a litter of puppies greeting a much-loved master. They clutched at his sleeves, tugged at his robe, reached up toward his face. In their midst, chuckling and teasing and clearly revelling in their adulation, the Benefactor spread his arms in an all-embracing gesture of welcome.

Indigo's shoulders slumped and she turned her head away, biting back tears. For a moment, just for a moment, she'd believed that . . . But she should have known better, of course. The hope had been false. Nemesis's presence had proved that.

"Indigo?" The Benefactor had seen her.

She refused to look at him. "I'm returning to Joyful Travail. Don't try to dissuade me; don't even try to *talk* to me, or I'll . . ." The words trailed off as she realized that she wouldn't *do* anything. Even if it were possible, there would be no point. Under her breath, she said again the words she had said to Nemesis. "*Damn* you . . ."

"Ah." Grimya had also emerged from the tower, and she saw the look in the Benefactor's eyes even if Indigo didn't. "I think I understand." He glanced at the children clamoring around him and raised both hands, signaling them to silence. "Little ones, little ones! Of course I shall play with you, but in a while."

"*Ohhh!*" Wails of disappointment went up.

"Hush, hush! There is something I must do first. As soon as I have finished, we shall play a new game."

They blinked at one another, only partially mollified. "Well ..." one said uncertainly.

"Look!" The Benefactor clapped his hands together. "I have a present for you." His hands parted, and a ball, shimmering with jewel colors, materialized between his fingers.

"Catch the ball, little ones! Catch the ball, if you can!" The Benefactor hurled the glittering toy into the air. It hovered like a bird, then with a volition of its own darted away into the trees. With shrill cries of delight the children raced after it; Indigo saw Koru's hand snatched by the little girl who had accompanied them into the wood, and he, too, was borne off on the rushing, shouting tide.

The Benefactor gazed after them until they were lost from view, their voices now distant and barely audible in the wood's depths. Then he turned to face Indigo.

"So," he said, "you have found what you were seeking."

At last Indigo did meet his steady brown eyes, but her face was haggard. "What sort of a creature are you?" she said softly, venomously. "If you wanted to torment me, or play another mindless children's game with me, couldn't you have found another way?"

"Ah, yes. I see. So you don't yet understand."

"I understand very well!"

"No, I don't believe that you do. I did not conjure an image of Fenran to torment you, Indigo. The man you saw sleeping in the tower is no less real than you are; no less real than Grimya, or Koru, or even the children whom you still persist in thinking of as ghosts."

Emotion surged. *"But I couldn't wake him!"*

"That is true. Nor will you wake him, until and unless you learn the real nature of this world and find again the lost part of yourself that dwells here."

He had taken several steps toward her as he spoke; her head came up sharply and he paused. "Part of myself?"

The Benefactor nodded gravely. "Yes. The part that you call Nemesis."

Her face froze. "I won't accept that! You can't tell me—"

The Benefactor interrupted her. "Indigo, look into your heart. You have known for many years that Nemesis is a part of you, and you have sought to destroy it. But if you should succeed, what then? You would lose your one chance to become what you once were, before your trials began. You would lose, forever, the chance to be *complete*. For you and Nemesis are both a part of one and the same entity; an entity who, long ago, was called Anghara."

Indigo didn't want to listen to him. The memory of Nemesis was still too clear, the hatred too strong. But somewhere in her a tiny flame of uncertainty was alight. Uncertainty, and something else. *Longing . . . ?*

"Do you know the true nature of this world, Indigo?" the Benefactor asked gently. "Do you know why the children live here in their helpless, pitiable simplicity? Why your own lover, Fenran, rests in this tower, in the sleep from which no one can wake him? And why Nemesis has sought, and found, a kind of solace here? I will tell you. It is because this world is a sanctuary of spirits. Not spirits of the dead, for the body of each one still lives and breathes in the world of physical flesh. But those whose spirits have found refuge here are incomplete. They have lost—or forfeited—their wholeness, lost that precious essence of themselves that makes them more than mere flesh and bone. And so, cast out and unnourished, those essences have taken another form and have fled to a place where they may live in safety. The friends Koru has made here, those happy, eager children, are the spirits of the people of Joyful Travail; the spirits who, unlike their physical selves, have not destroyed their own ability to dream."

Indigo was staring at the Benefactor; a strange, almost blind stare. *The body of each one still lives and breathes in the world of physical flesh,* he had said . . . "You are telling me that Fenran . . . that Fenran's soul is here?"

"His soul. His spirit. His essence." The Benefactor made a helpless gesture. "So many different names for something that words cannot encompass. But, like the children, his mind has sought a refuge."

"And . . ." She hardly dared articulate the question. "And his body . . . ?"

"That I cannot say, for I do not know. All I can tell you is that when his body sleeps, his spirit finds a hiatus here, for the unconscious mind can traverse the gateways between dimensions."

"Then he is truly alive . . ."

"Yes, he is truly alive. But you knew that, Indigo. What else could have given you the strength and the will to search for him these fifty years past?"

Indigo drew a deep, racking breath. This was monstrous—he was trying to twist her mind, trying to turn her toward some crazed ambition of his own . . . And then she remembered their previous encounter. This was the bait, the trap set to lure her. Fenran—or Fenran's image, for although she'd touched him and felt him she still couldn't trust anything in this world—set before her like a glittering prize to be won. And the price? Help my people, he'd asked her. Purge them of a demon's taint . . .

"What do you want?" She hissed the words through clenched teeth. "What do you *really* want of me?"

The Benefactor sighed. "Nothing more and nothing less than I have already told you. Your help in making the people of Joyful Travail whole again."

"And for that—for that, you are offering me Fenran?"

"No." He shook his head. "I cannot give your love back to you; I am not a worker of miracles. But if you will do as I ask, *you* will gain the power to awaken him."

A muscle was trembling violently in Indigo's cheek and she couldn't stop it. "How?"

"By reuniting all these lost spirits with their own selves, so that they no longer need to seek sanctuary in this world. But if you are to heal them, you yourself must also be healed." The mild brown eyes grew suddenly intense. "That is the only way to help them Indigo—and it is the only way in which you can hope to awaken your Fenran to full life. You have found him, but there is still a barrier between you. If you would break it down, and help my people along the way, you and Nemesis must be reconciled." He paused. "It comes hard to one such as me to beg, but I beg you now. Help us, Indigo. Accept Nemesis, be complete again, and lead these lost souls home."

He fell silent then, his shoulders lifting in a small shrug as though expressing that he had striven his best and there was nothing more he could do or say. For a long time Indigo stood looking at him as the knowledge of what he was asking sank deeper into her mind. To trust Nemesis ... it was mad; it was an obscenity. Nemesis was her deadliest enemy, its very existence dedicated to her downfall.

The silver-eyed child's words echoed in her mind. *Sister, we can wake him. Together, you and I. We have the power.*

"No!" The word snapped out at last. The Benefactor was tempting her with her heart's deepest desire, promising her the happiness that for fifty years had been her one and only dream. But it was just that. A dream. She couldn't trust him.

"No," Indigo said again, and this time the timbre of her voice carried absolute finality. Suddenly, she was utterly calm. "You tell me that if I would awaken Fenran, I must first help the people of Joyful Travail, and you say I have the power to do it. Very well. If that's so, then I shall move the stars themselves to achieve what must be done! But I'll do it alone. Nemesis is no longer a part of me. I have overcome it, and now I reject it. I have no need of that demon-child, for I *am* complete!"

The Benefactor gazed steadily back at her. "You are wrong, Indigo," he said with heavy sorrow.

Her lip twitched in a cold smile. "I beg to differ, Benefactor—and I think I know myself better than you will ever do. I'm going to return to Joyful Travail. I'm going to carry the good news that Koru is found, and I'm going to show your people the truth about this world and what it contains!"

She swung round, turning her back on the Benefactor. Behind her, she heard a sigh.

"Be it as you wish, then. Go back to my people. Tell them the truth, and show them the folly of their disbelief."

The air shimmered, and suddenly Indigo found herself looking at a dimly glowing rectangle hanging unsupported before her. In its depths the topmost room of the House in Joyful Travail was just visible, spectral and gloomy.

"I have no need of the mirror to move between worlds," the Benefactor said. "It is merely a device; one of many. If and when you wish to return here, you may use whatever means your will dictates. You carry my good wishes with you, but I think you will find that hope and goodwill are not remedy enough to grant sight to the blind."

His words were calmly resigned; his face when Indigo looked back at him was impassive. He seemed to have accepted defeat, and she was taken unawares by a fleeting feeling of intense sadness. She *couldn't* trust him; she still didn't even know what manner of being he was. Ghost or revenant, friend or enemy. But whatever he might be, or once have been, he was no demon. Indigo pitied him—and, strange though the knowledge was, she knew that under other circumstances she could have felt great affection for him.

She looked down at Grimya, and her voice was oddly gruff. "Are you coming, love?"

Grimya didn't reply immediately. She hadn't uttered a word or projected a single thought to Indigo since the Benefactor's arrival, and now she was gazing back at him and at the tower, her eyes remote and unhappy. Then she licked her muzzle.

"Yess. I am coming."

Indigo stepped up to the softly shining rectangle, then, as Grimya had done, looked back to where the Benefactor stood.

"I'll prove you wrong. I can—and I will."

Her hand passed through the light, arm and shoulder following. She took another step; there was a shimmer, like dark water briefly disturbed, and she was gone.

As Grimya made to follow, the Benefactor spoke.

"Little wolf. If you should have need of me, you will always find me at the House."

Grimya hesitated. She felt she wanted to say something but the right words weren't in her mind and wouldn't come to her. Her ears and tail drooped and, uttering a small, sad whine, she followed Indigo through the gateway.

As the wolf vanished there was a scuffle in the trees on the clearing's edge, and the sound of young voices. The Benefactor looked up. His hands moved and the rectangle of light vanished as the children, with Koru at their head, came running and scrambling into view.

"We caught it, we caught it!"

"We caught the ball!"

"Aren't we clever? Aren't we?"

They danced round him, shouting and laughing. Then abruptly Koru floundered to a halt and looked around. His blue eyes widened. "Where's Indigo?"

The Benefactor smiled gently down at him. "She has gone back to Joyful Travail, Koru."

"Oh! But I thought she was going to stay with us . . ."

He shook his head. "She could not stay. She has . . . some work to do."

Koru was crestfallen. "Will she come back? I thought she might stay. I hoped she would—forever and ever." The corners of his mouth turned down sorrowfully. "I'll miss her."

"Will you?" The Benefactor's gaze grew more thoughtful. "Surely you're happy enough here with all your friends around you?"

"*Ye-es*. But . . ." Koru gave an odd little shrug. "They only want to play games. I love games, too, but sometimes I . . . I'd like to do other things as well." He paused, then sighed. "I *will* miss Indigo and Grimya."

"You could have gone with them, back to Joyful Travail."

An emphatic shake of the small blond head. "No, I couldn't. I *couldn't*."

The Benefactor said no more. The other children were clamoring loudly for the shining ball to be thrown again, and two of them ran to Koru and caught hold of his hands, wanting him to join in their frivolous dance. Koru allowed himself to be pulled away; but as the little boy turned, the Benefactor saw the faintest glimmer of an uncertain tear at the corner of one blue eye.

Again there was the gentle and subtle shift between worlds, the sense of simply stepping over a threshold. Even as she felt herself merging with the supernatural doorway Indigo smelled the dry, musty air of the House in Joyful Travail and felt the tickle of dust in her nostrils. Gloom folded around her and she found herself back in the top room, the Benefactor's sanctum.

There was a second disturbance in the mirror, a rippling of the glass, and Grimya appeared, writhing and wriggling as she crossed the barrier. The wolf sprang onto the floor and shook herself, blinking.

"We are back!" She sounded relieved, then she twisted round to look over her shoulder. "The other-world has gone."

The glass of the mirror showed only their own reflections now, and the watery light of early morning streamed in through the easternmost of the six grimy windows above their heads, illuminating the bare room, the tarnished crown on its roped-off plinth, the mirror with its dust-sheet discarded on the floor. Indigo rubbed at her eyes like someone coming slowly out of a dream, and for some seconds stood motionless. Then:

"I'm going back to the town, Grimya. I'm going to see Hollend and Calpurna."

She didn't want to talk about what had happened and the wolf said nothing, only dipping her head in acquiescence. They started across the floor toward the stairs—then Grimya stopped and her ears pricked alertly. "Indigo! I hh-*ear* something!"

She was staring at the dark maw of the stairwell, and a moment later Indigo also heard the sound. Someone was moving on the floor below. For an irrational instant Indigo was half convinced that the Benefactor had returned to the physical world and reached it before them. Then, shattering the suspicion, a shrill female voice called out.

"Who is there? What are you doing?"

Indigo ran to the banister and looked over at the outraged face of Aunt Nikku, the House guide.

"What is this?" Aunt Nikku started up toward them, her wooden-soled shoes rapping out a sharp staccato on the stairs. Her eyes narrowed to furious slits as she gained the top of the flight and confronted Indigo, bristling with indignation. "What is this?" she demanded again. "The House is forbidden at this hour! Explain at once, please!"

Indigo opened her mouth to speak, then realized that she couldn't give any explanation that this officious little woman would comprehend, let alone accept. Aunt Nikku's sharp gaze scanned the room and lit on the uncovered mirror.

"What?" she cried, pointing. "What? What have you done here?" Pushing past Indigo she rushed to stand before the mirror and stared at it in horror as if expecting it to disintegrate before her gaze. Then she whirled round.

"No object in the House is to be touched! This is a great

disobedience!" She bent to gather up the dust-sheet, shaking it out vigorously before trying to put it back in place over the mirror. She was too short to reach the top of the frame and with some thought of placating her Indigo went to help, but Aunt Nikku uttered a shriek and batted at her hands.

"Ah! Ah! Now you attack me! You are a criminal! You are a thief!"

Indigo's temper flared. "Don't be ridiculous! I'm only trying—"

"Thief!" Aunt Nikku cried. "I know! *I* know! You have come here to steal the House's treasures and carry them away!" She started to bat wildly at Indigo again; Indigo made a grab for her arms, trying to restrain her; Grimya rushed in to Indigo's defense, and in the confusion matters were suddenly out of hand. The commotion lasted only a few seconds, but at the end of it Indigo's arm had been scratched by Aunt Nikku's nails while Aunt Nikku herself sat on the floor in the tangles of the dust-sheet, nursing a bleeding hand that Grimya had bitten. For a moment there was silence. Then:

"Ahh!" There was far more fury than pain in Aunt Nikku's cry as she tried to scramble upright, tripped over the sheet again, and finally stood, swaying on her feet. "The animal has savaged me! It has savaged me!"

Indigo rubbed her arm, glowering at the little woman. "She was defending me from you. And it's only a shallow wound; the bleeding's stopping already. I'll clean it for you and—"

"This is not the point of the matter!" Aunt Nikku shrilled. "I have been attacked! Such a thing is not to be tolerated!"

"Aunt Nikku, please calm down!" Indigo cast a quick glance back at the mirror. "There is a great deal to explain—"

"Indeed so! And it shall be explained at once, before the Committee!"

"Please, will you *listen* to me! I came here—"

"I am well aware of why you came here! To steal! To rob! You will answer for this misdeed, and the proper punishment will be exacted!"

There was no reasoning with her, Indigo realized. The little woman stood, tiny but fearsome, like an outraged shrew, her eyes ablaze with righteous fervor. Suddenly and dramatically Aunt Nikku pointed at the mirror.

"You will replace the sheet upon that artifact, and then you will come with me before the proper Committee! At once!"

Indigo sighed. It would have been a simple matter to push Aunt Nikku out of the way and leave her fuming but impotent as she and Grimya made their escape from the House. But that would only complicate the situation. Better to let the little woman have her way, at least until Indigo could reach the Committees with the news she had brought back to Joyful Travail. That and nothing else was of paramount importance. She *had* to show the people of Joyful Travail the truth about the ghost-world and the children who inhabited it. Not with the help of the Benefactor, not with the help of Nemesis, but by her own will.

She didn't speak to Aunt Nikku, but gathered up the fallen dust-sheet and settled it over the mirror once more. For a moment she stared into the glass, but only her own image looked back. The ghost-world was invisible . . . and waiting. Indigo draped the last fold of cloth over the mirror, hiding it entirely from view, then, still without a word, turned and followed Aunt Nikku toward the stairs.

# ·CHAPTER·XIV·

Uncle Choai didn't often raise his voice, and so the shock of his sudden bellow for silence had the desired effect and succeeded where all else had failed. Even Aunt Nikku's shrill accusations halted in midstream and she stood staring at him, mouth open in astonishment.

Uncle Choai drew himself upright with an air of injured dignity and scanned the agitated, interested, or simply baffled faces around him.

"This is not the estimable behavior expected from diligent citizens of Joyful Travail," he announced sternly. "Such uproar is not seemly and will not be allowed to continue! There are proper procedures, and they shall be followed, please."

Gazes slid away as people seemed suddenly reluctant to look anyone else in the face. Someone made a show of clearing his throat. Only Indigo continued to watch Uncle Choai, but—at least for the moment—said nothing. It was sheer chance that Choai had happened to be paying a rou-

tine visit to the Foreigners' Duty House at the moment
when Aunt Nikku marched in ablaze with virtue and loudly
declaring her grievance against Indigo and Grimya. As a
member of the Foreigners' Committee, and the only elder
immediately available, Choai had at once appointed himself
arbiter of the quarrel and demanded to know what was
amiss. Aunt Nikku launched into a voluble tirade; others,
curious, came to see what was to do, and within minutes the
area in front of the Duty House's reception desk was
crowded with onlookers, many of whom were joining in the
argument with questions and opinions of their own. Thia
was there, Indigo saw, and at the back of the crowd she
even glimpsed the timid face of old Mimino, Physician
Huni's widow; but to her frustration there was no sign of
Hollend or Calpurna or anyone else from the Enclave.

She didn't think she could keep her temper in check for
much longer. At first, with Aunt Nikku refusing to listen to
a word she said, to go to the Committee had seemed the
only sensible course of action; now, though, she was fast
coming to regret that decision. Uncle Choai was clearly bent
on seeing that formality was rigidly observed, and that
didn't bode well.

"Respected Aunt Nikku." Choai spoke into the restored
quiet, bowing stiffly to the little woman and giving her a
look that made his dislike of her quite clear. "I understand
that you wish to make a complaint against the foreigner
Physician Indigo, and that you claim an ignoble assault
upon your person. Please to explain further."

Aunt Nikku needed no second invitation. She began immediately to recount her own dramatic and highly colored
version of events: her discovery of Indigo and Grimya in
the Benefactor's House, her unmasking of the foreigner as
a base criminal intent on pillage and robbery, and the sav-
aging of her own person, most certainly at its mistress's
command, by the foreigner's dog. She thrust her bitten hand
toward Uncle Choai, displaying Grimya's teeth marks, and

demanded that justice should be done, preferably in the form of a stiff penalty imposed on the culprit and paid to herself. Her audience were agog and began to make comments of their own, and suddenly Indigo could stand it no longer.

"Uncle Choai!" Her voice cut across Aunt Nikku's piercing tones, surprising the small woman into silence. Heads turned, eyes widened with shocked disapproval at such a breach of protocol. Ignoring them all, Indigo made the customary bow to the elder, but the movement, and her voice, were sharp with impatience. "Your pardon, respected Uncle, but there is no time to go about matters this way! I have news, very urgent news—"

"Physician Indigo!" Choai was outraged. "This is not proper! You will have your turn to speak in good time; until then, please to be silent."

"You don't understand—this is *important*! It concerns—"

"What it does or does not concern is not relevant until the proper time!" Uncle Choai interrupted admonishingly. "I say to you again, please to control these outbursts and remain silent!"

His tone was so peremptory, his manner so patronizing and haughty, that it snapped the threads of what little forbearance Indigo had left. Abandoning caution and with it any hope of redeeming herself in Choai's eyes, she yelled, "Damn you, you old fool, will you *listen! I've found Koru!*"

For perhaps three seconds the room was utterly still—then uproar broke out. Uncle Choai, his wrath eclipsed by Indigo's revelation, was thumping the desk and shouting for order, but no one heeded him. People crowded round Indigo, prodding her, shaking her, hurling questions; Aunt Nikku shrilled that the foreigner must be lying, others agreed and began arguments with neighbors who took Indigo's side. Only two people didn't join in the fray. Old Mimino had already withdrawn from the Duty House, aware of her lowly status and anxious not to be noticed. And Thia, pushing her way through the crowd, reached the door, slipped through, and began to run in the direction of the Enclave.

Hollend and Calpurna entered the Duty House a few minutes later. The gathering was in complete disarray, with everyone talking at once and Uncle Choai still striving to assert his authority, but the arrival of the lost boy's parents, with Thia smiling self-effacingly behind them, brought a sudden sober hush.

Calpurna pushed through the crowd. Her face was tear-stained and drawn, making her look far older than her years.

"Is it true?" she cried. "My little one—have you found him? Where is he, *tell me!*"

Immediately the babble broke out afresh, and chaos would have reigned again but for Hollend. Uncle Choai was clearly not pleased when, by sheer force of personality, the Agantian took charge and managed to restore some semblance of quiet and order and at last Indigo was able to speak.

"Yes," she said in answer to Calpurna's frantic questions, "I've found Koru—or at least, I know where he is. He's alive and well, but—"

Calpurna interrupted. "Where, Indigo, *where?*"

"At the Benefactor's House."

Aunt Nikku, who had been listening as intently as anyone, visibly bridled. "What?" she cried. "This is not so! If true, I would have known of it!"

"Please, listen!" Indigo held up both hands, and at a glare from Hollend Aunt Nikku's protests subsided to a sullen mutter.

"Koru *is* at the Benefactor's House, but there is a reason why Aunt Nikku—with respect"—Indigo bowed with a measure of sarcasm to the angry little guide—"didn't find him."

"I'm sorry," Hollend said. "I don't understand."

"It's very hard to explain ... I went to the House to

search last night—what prompted me to do that isn't important at the moment—and I found a—a way through to another place . . ."

"Some sort of secret hideaway, you mean?"

It was as close an analogy as they would believe at this stage, Indigo thought. She nodded. "Yes. Aunt Nikku doesn't know of it; in fact I doubt if any living person does. But I found it, and that's where Koru is."

"Why didn't you bring him back?" Calpurna cried. "Why not? Is he hurt, is he *trapped* somewhere?"

"No, no, he's quite unharmed. But . . ." Indigo hesitated, then decided she had to be honest. "He wouldn't come with me, Calpurna. I tried to persuade him, but he wouldn't listen. He . . . doesn't want to be brought home."

Calpurna made a choked noise and clutched her husband's arm. For another second or two Hollend continued to stare at Indigo as though trying to read in her eyes all that he suspected she hadn't said. Then he turned to face the company at large.

"Then why are we standing here wasting time? For pity's sake, let's go to the House at once!"

Everyone present in the Duty House wanted to join the party that set off soon afterward, but Hollend, firmly backed by Uncle Choai, who was anxious to salvage as much of his lost ascendancy as he could, argued against it. Too many people would frighten Koru, he said, and if the boy was indeed afraid or unwilling to come home of his own volition, a large crowd to confront him would only make matters worse. This common sense prevailed at last, and five people—Hollend and Calpurna, Indigo, Uncle Choai, and Aunt Nikku—eventually left for the House. Grimya was about to join them when Uncle Choai held up a hand.

"Not the animal," he said firmly. "The animal will stay here. The matter of the creature's disgraceful assault upon the respected Aunt Nikku has still to be considered and the proper steps decided upon. Until then, the animal will remain at the Duty House in custody of the Foreigners' Committee."

Indigo objected vociferously but Uncle Choai was adamant and at last, rather than hold the party up any longer, she gave in.

*I'm sorry, love,* she said silently to the wolf. *But he gives us no choice. Don't worry; as soon as we return I'll ensure that this nonsense is resolved.*

Grimya licked her own muzzle. *I will come to no harm. But I shall worry for you.* She paused. *Are you sure that you are doing the right thing? If the Benefactor was right in his warning, this may make yet more trouble.*

*I know. But I don't believe he was right. I can do this, Grimya.* She remembered Nemesis's face. *And I don't need the kind of help the Benefactor offers!*

The obsequious, ever-present Thia had not been able to inveigle herself into the search party but, as a token of his approval for her quick-wittedness in fetching Hollend and Calpurna, Choai charged her personally with taking care of Grimya until their return. Thia was most satisfied with the commission, and as soon as the door of the Duty House had closed she caught the wolf by the scruff of her neck and marched her toward a back room, imperiously ordering that a dish of water be brought to quench the animal's thirst. Not wanting to compound her present troubles any further, Grimya made no protest, but when the water was brought and Thia carefully set it on a shelf above her reach before turning to face her, the wolf began to feel distinctly uneasy. Her telepathic mind could sense the gist of Thia's thoughts; they were covetous, and underlying that greed was a glimmer of something even less pleasant.

In fact Thia had her own private plans for Grimya. She had already suggested to Physician Indigo that the animal, or one similar, would make a suitable and acceptable gift in

payment for the services she had rendered, and was offended that the hint had not been taken. Now that she herself was in good standing with Uncle Choai and Indigo less
so, Thia considered it likely that she would soon be able to
resolve the matter in her own favor. Possession of this dog
would make her the envy of her peers, and the animal
would prove most useful to her if properly trained. Training,
Thia firmly believed, was, as with all beasts, simply a matter of discipline.

She stared down at the wolf. "You shall have water if you
obey me, but not unless." Obviously the creature couldn't
understand human speech, but she had been told that dogs
were capable of learning to recognize certain word-sounds if
they were repeated often and emphatically enough. She
pointed to the bowl and then to the floor to illustrate her
point, then clapped her hands. "Sit down, please!"

Grimya had taken a dislike to Thia from their first encounter. She stared back, affecting bafflement, and Thia
frowned.

"Sit *down*, please!" There was an angry edge in her
voice, but again Grimya didn't respond. The girl sighed impatiently. This would not do; it was not good enough. Indigo clearly had control over the animal, and there was no
logical reason why she herself should not exert the same
dominance. The dog must learn—*would* learn—who was
mistress here.

Her jerkin was fastened by a plain leather thong at the
waist. Thia untied the belt and brandished it.

"You will learn," she said imperiously. "Do you understand me? You will learn!" She stropped the belt through
her fingers, then raised it and brought it down like a whip-
lash, aiming for Grimya's muzzle.

Grimya moved fast. She twisted about, snapped as the
makeshift lash came at her, and her teeth clamped on the
thong, jerking Thia's arm almost out of its socket. The girl
gave a shriek of surprise and outrage, stumbled forward two

paces, and found herself staring into the wolf's enraged amber eyes. Grimya hauled on the thong, worrying it as though it were prey; then with a contemptuous movement she dropped it and her lips drew back from her fangs in a snarl as her hackles rose aggressively.

"Touch me again," she said in her grating, guttural voice, "and I will tear your thhhroat out!"

Thia's eyes bulged. *It spoke! The animal spoke to her!* Then in a giddy rush of sick fear, denial came on realization's heels: *No, not so, such things are impossible!*

She took three cautious paces backward, then bolted for the door, scrabbling, fumbling at the latch. She flung one last wild look in Grimya's direction, not knowing whether she was more frightened of physical attack or of the mad, unthinkable, *untenable* fact—no, not fact, not fact, it had been a delusion, a momentary lapse of mind—that the wolf had spoken to her in her own language. Then Thia fled and, ruefully, but with a certain satisfaction, Grimya heard a bolt being drawn on the far side of the door. She was a prisoner now. But at least she had had the pleasure of ensuring that Thia would not return.

Aunt Nikku made much ceremony of unlocking and opening the postern-gate in the surrounding wall of the Benefactor's House, at the same time loudly lamenting the disruption that would surely be caused by this unheard-of departure from her proper routines and procedures. All the way to the House she and Uncle Choai had conducted a savagely polite argument on the question of precedence, and only the intervention of Hollend, angered by the effect of their quarrel on the already distraught Calpurna, had finally silenced the debate. To the relief of everyone—excepting possibly Aunt Nikku—it was still too early for the arrival of any visitors for the first tour of the day, and so at last the gate was opened and the small party entered the House's precincts. Several laborers were at work in the regimented garden, but at Uncle Choai's order they all set down their tools and, curious but silent, filed through the postern to wait outside until the elders and their party were done.

The familiar musty smell tickled Indigo's nostrils as they entered the House. Aunt Nikku led them into the claustro-phobic gloom, then turned and faced her challengingly.

"What now, please?"

Indigo nodded toward the stairs. "The top floor," she said.

They clattered up the three staircases without a further word. At the last flight Calpurna's nerve almost failed her, but Hollend put a comforting arm around her shoulders and she continued on.

The topmost room was as Indigo and Aunt Nikku had left it, only some scuffed marks in the dust showing where the small fracas had taken place. Calpurna seemed unwillingly fascinated by the crown on its plinth; as her husband led her round the room she couldn't tear her gaze from the ancient artifact, and twice she shivered as though touched by a cold, invisible breath. At last they grouped together before the shrouded mirror, and four expectant pairs of eyes focused on Indigo's face.

Indigo had had time to consider what she would say at this moment, and was as ready as she could ever hope to be.

"Hollend—Calpurna." She looked from one to the other. "What I have to show you now won't be easy for you to ac-cept. But I think—I *hope*—that I can prove the truth of all that I've said to you."

Uncle Choai was frowning, Aunt Nikku sullen; Hollend and Calpurna only stared at Indigo in tense silence. Indigo turned and pulled the dust-sheet from the mirror.

"A glass?" There was an edge to Hollend's voice. "What has this to do with the passageway you told us of?"

"Please, Hollend, listen to me. I told you that Koru has found a—a secret hideaway was your phrase for it, I think. It isn't quite as simple as that. Where Koru has gone is not a hideaway in the sense that you understand it, but . . . another world."

*"What?"* Hollend was incredulous, and Calpurna's lower lip began to tremble. "What in the name of all that's rational are you *talking* about?"

Indigo had counted on her suspicion that Hollend at least hadn't entirely fallen prey to the ethos of Joyful Travail and so would be willing, if reluctant, to acknowledge the possibility of the ghost-world's existence. But as she saw the hard, furious glitter in his eyes she felt suddenly and horribly apprehensive. The Benefactor had tried to warn her; Grimya, too, had tried in her own way. At the time, incensed and defiant, she'd dismissed their arguments, but now she started to realize that she might have made a terrible mistake.

Desperate not to acknowledge her doubts and aware that she'd gone too far now to withdraw, she plowed on desperately. "Hollend, please, bear with me—let me show you. I *have* found Koru, and I can take you to him." She turned again to face the mirror. "Look—look what happens when I touch the glass!"

She reached out to the mirror. Her hand met an unyielding surface, and when she pressed against it the mirror only rocked gently in its frame.

"No!" Indigo whirled, staring past her four companions' hostile faces, staring at the crown on its plinth. "Don't play this joke on me, you can't, you *can't! Open the gateway!*"

Calpurna burst into tears. Uncle Choai looked at Aunt Nikku, and Aunt Nikku made an expressive moue.

"It is as I have already tried to tell you. The foreigner is attempting to deceive us and disguise her real intentions. Either that or she is quite mad."

Indigo heard, and turned on her. "I am not mad! I'm telling you the *truth*! The mirror is a gateway to another world, another dimension! Koru found it, and he fled there because he was punished for believing that such things were possible! Oh, sweet Mother, you are all so *blind*!" She rocked the mirror again, violently, almost tipping it over, and strode to the roped-off plinth. "Your precious Benefactor, whom you all revere so greatly—*he* knew! I've *seen* him, I've *talked* to him—he may have been dead for centuries but his spirit, his ghost—something, I don't know—still lives; and it's *here*, it controls the gateway! I know! I've seen the ghost-world— I've *been* there, and Koru is there, too, and . . ."

Her voice trailed off then as a spark of reason somewhere deep inside her mind brought her suddenly back to Earth. Frantically she looked from one face to another, but there was no help and no understanding to be had. Calpurna had hidden her face against her husband's shoulder and was sobbing bitterly, while Hollend fixed Indigo with a look of sheer, disgusted contempt. Aunt Nikku's expression was one of sorrowful vindication, while Uncle Choai only gazed emotionlessly, his face a chilly mask.

It was Choai who broke the awful silence at last. "Hollend, my respected friend." It was all but unheard-of for an elder of Joyful Travail to address a foreigner in such terms, and a sign of the greatest esteem. "It will be well, I think, if you take your brave and noble wife away from this place and offer her what comfort you may find under these unhappy circumstances."

Hollend's gaze slid briefly to the elder, then he nodded. He didn't look at Indigo again as he led Calpurna away and down the stairs. When he judged them out of earshot, Choai turned to Indigo.

"Physician Indigo." His voice was icily remote. "I am not in possession of all the facts and so am not yet able to pronounce final judgment upon your behavior. It may be that you are ill, as has been believed to be the case once before. Or it may be that you are of a cruel and most undesirable disposition that finds satisfaction in pretending to a display of insanity. If this is so, the penalty will be most severe." He nodded graciously to Aunt Nikku. "We will return now to the Committee House, where the truth will be ascertained." And, as Indigo opened her mouth to protest, "Not to speak, please. Outside the House are strong and loyal citizens, and force will be used if your behavior makes it necessary." He indicated the staircase. "Kindly proceed."

There was nothing Indigo could do or say. In the space of less than a minute her sense of triumph had collapsed into the depths of desolate failure, and she silently and furiously railed against herself. She was as blind as the people of Joyful Travail! Blind and vain and stupid; she had let her own arrogance overrule reason and wisdom and, like a spoiled and self-centered child, had expected the closed minds of these people to open at her command. The mirror's failure to reveal its secret had no relevance now; even had the ghost-world opened before them, Hollend and Calpurna would have been oblivious to its presence. She should have known, should have *understood*. Now all she had achieved was to bring further misery on them and condemn herself utterly in their eyes.

This time she didn't even look at the mirror, knowing that it would show nothing but her own defeated image. She nodded once, curtly, to show that she acquiesced, and for the second time that morning turned her back on the House and all it contained.

Hollend and Calpurna had gone ahead; neither wanted to be in Indigo's presence now. The laborers bowed respectfully as Uncle Choai and Aunt Nikku left in their turn with the tall foreigner walking silent and somber before them, then returned to their work. As dust settled in the topmost room of the House there was no one to see the peculiar play of light, seemingly without a source, that glimmered suddenly about the ancient crown on its plinth, and no one to hear the faint, spectral echo of a sound that might, with a little imagination, have been taken for a gentle and sorrowful sigh.

# ·CHAPTER·XV·

This time there was nothing impromptu or informal about the delegation that gathered that evening in an upper room of the Committee House overlooking the market square. Indigo had been kept an effective prisoner in the Duty House throughout the afternoon, unable to see Grimya and unable to speak with anyone she knew. She'd been given food and water, but her questions and protests and entreaties met only with stony silence until, shortly before sunset, she was escorted to the Committee House to face the tribunal.

They were ready for her when she entered. Six elders, of whom Uncle Choai was the lowest-ranking, had taken their places behind a long table, while a gaggle of secretaries, notaries, and other minor officials sat cross-legged in a row to one side of the room. On the other side were ranged Hollend, Calpurna, and Ellani, who had now joined her parents, together with Aunt Nikku and, somewhat to Indigo's surprise, Thia. A solitary three-legged stool had been set alone in the middle of the room, and here Indigo was told to sit.

She had not been permitted to bring Grimya to the inquiry. Later she realized that she should have foreseen the implications of the ban, but with more urgent preoccupations to concern her she gave it no immediate thought beyond irritation at the elders' entrenched attitude. That, as she soon discovered, was a mistake.

The senior elder, an aged, hatchet-faced woman by the name of Aunt Osiku, who wore a blue sash and an expression of permanent distaste, wasted no time with preliminaries. The matter laid before this temporary Committee, she said, was a simple one. The foreigner Indigo, but a short time ago welcomed with open arms into the happy and peaceable community of Joyful Travail, had abused both her privilege and her duty by attempting to make a mockery of those who had been kind enough to befriend her. It was now known to the Committee that she had attempted to subvert the impressionable mind of an eight-year-old child entrusted to her care; the child had then run away from his home and was yet to be found. It was quite clear to any right-thinking person, Aunt Osiku declared, that the seditious actions of the foreigner Indigo were solely and entirely responsible for the boy Koru's disappearance. Now, as if such a betrayal were not sufficient, she had brazenly attempted to lure not only the child's own parents—who, most certainly, had already suffered enough—but also two respected Committee elders into the same tangled web of nonsensical fabrication with which she had already seduced the hapless child. Furthermore, thanks to the evidence of Aunt Nikku, whose honorability was of course of the highest caliber, an underlying motive had been revealed, for Aunt Nikku had personally apprehended the foreigner Indigo in the very act of attempting to plunder the treasures of the Benefactor's House.

Indigo listened to this damning homily with growing incredulity and outrage. Several times she opened her mouth to make a furious protest, but the words simply wouldn't come; the attack on her was such a monstrous distortion of all that had happened that it defied reason and robbed her of speech. She looked once toward Koru's family, but Calpurna immediately turned her head aside and only Ellani met her gaze. The girl's eyes were bright with a vindictiveness bordering on hatred, and Indigo looked away.

"So, then," the sour-faced elder said, "it is now for this Committee to rule on the appropriate action to be taken in this matter."

"Respected Aunt." Suddenly Thia rose smartly to her feet, bowing toward the table. "If a lowly juvenile might be permitted to speak, it would be a great boon."

The elder looked at her in surprise. "Juvenile ..." She consulted her notes. "Juvenile Thia. Do you have information of useful value to the Committee?"

Thia bowed again. "Yes, respected Aunt. It concerns a further complaint against the animal that belongs to the foreigner Indigo."

Indigo's pulse quickened, and the Aunt's expression grew keener. "You may inform the Committee of what you know. Speak, please."

Thia's mouth curled in a smug little smile. "Respected Aunt, I was entrusted with the responsibility of guarding this animal, which is a large and strong dog, while the foreigner Indigo sought so disgracefully to deceive the esteemed elders and the child Koru's unhappy family. The Committee is aware that this animal had already made a savage and quite unjustified assault upon the person of respected Aunt Nikku. It is now my correct duty to inform the Committee that, whilst in my care and without provocation, the creature also attacked me."

Indigo cried, *"What?"* and Aunt Osiku turned a searing gaze on her.

"The foreigner Indigo will please be silent." As Indigo reluctantly subsided, the elder looked at Thia again. "This is most serious, juvenile Thia. Was a wound inflicted?"

"No, respected Aunt. By swift thought and prudent action I was able to evade the animal's teeth."

"I am happy to hear that. What has become of the animal now?"

"It is securely locked in a room at the Foreigners' Duty House, respected Aunt. I deemed it unwise to remain in the creature's presence, and I have duly given warning that for an unprepared person to enter the room would be dangerous."

Aunt Osiku nodded sagaciously. "Most judicious, most judicious. You have acted properly and assiduously." She signaled to one of the secretaries at the side of the room. "Let it be a matter of record that this Committee recognizes and commends the responsible conduct of juvenile Thia." The secretary bowed and scribbled while Thia and her mentor, Uncle Choai, made little effort to conceal their delight. Aunt Osiku waited until the secretary had finished writing, then nodded her satisfaction.

"Very well. Now, this Committee notes that Hollend and Calpurna, parents of the missing child, claim redress and distraint upon the foreigner Indigo in proper payment for her offense against them. Aunt Nikku also petitions for distraint, and in addition requests the destruction of the foreigner Indigo's dog as a menace to public safety—"

Aware that her earlier interruption had done nothing to help her, Indigo had been struggling to control herself and stay silent. This, though, was too much, and she sprang to her feet, sending the stool toppling. "*Destroy* Grimya?" she yelled. "That is *monstrous*! By the Mother, I'll not tolerate any more of this—"

The elder made a gesture, and before she could say another word Indigo found her arms pinned to her sides by two men. She hadn't even known they were in the room; they must have come from behind her, and she had no doubt that they had been set to guard against any such outburst on her part.

Aunt Osiku glared at her and snapped out, "The foreigner Indigo will *sit*!" One of Indigo's captors righted the fallen stool while the other jerked Indigo's arm viciously. She threw him off with a furious movement and, white-faced with anger, subsided back onto her seat. Her heart was pounding but she forced herself to hold her tongue.

Aunt Osiku returned her attention to Thia, who had watched the fracas with an expression of pitying disdain. "Juvenile Thia, do you wish to add your name to those of Hollend and Calpurna and Aunt Nikku in this petition for distraint against the foreigner Indigo?"

Thia bowed very low. "If that is permitted, respected Aunt, that is my wish."

"Very well." Another nod to the secretaries, another scribbled note. "Return to your place please, juvenile Thia."

As Thia sat down, the six elders gathered close together and began to confer in whispers. There was much nodding, many obsequious gestures from Uncle Choai, but though she strained to hear what they said, Indigo couldn't pick up a single word. At last, Aunt Osiku straightened and clapped her hands.

"Very well. This Committee has consulted, and is now ready to give judgment."

For a moment Indigo didn't believe what she was hearing. Her jaw dropped. *"Judgment—?"*

Silence fell. The elders all stared at her. Then Aunt Osiku said coldly, "Quite so."

"But—but this is *ludicrous*! You've heard only one side of the story!"

The Aunt seemed to look straight through her. "All evidence necessary to this Committee's deliberations has been given and duly considered. No more is to be said. The foreigner Indigo will be silent, please, or it will be found necessary to remove her and pronounce judgment in her absence."

"Damn you, I will *not* be silent!" Indigo shouted, jumping up again. The two men hastened forward but this time she was ready for them; with her right hand she pushed one forcibly away while a well-timed blow from her left elbow sent the other stumbling backward, winded.

Aunt Osiku rose to her feet, red-faced with indignation. "This is not to be tolerated!"

"You're quite right, respected Aunt—it is most certainly not to be tolerated!" Indigo fired back. "How can you possibly pronounce judgment without hearing what I have to say? If I'm on trial here—as I obviously am—then I have a right to speak!"

"It is well known that a culprit may speak only at the discretion of the Committee before which he or she is brought," the Aunt said with asperity. "If this is desired, proper representation must be made and permission sought."

"Then I make that representation now!" Indigo said through clenched teeth.

The Aunt nodded yet again to her secretary. "Let it be a matter of record that the foreigner Indigo pleads permission to state her case before this Committee. Let it also be a matter of record that such permission is not granted." Her cold stare slid to Indigo again. "The culprit will sit down."

Not even *foreigner* now, but *culprit* . . . "This is a travesty!" Indigo protested. "A travesty, a mockery—Goddess help me, what manner of blind, bigoted fools *are* you?"

Aunt Osiku was quite unmoved by her tirade, and abruptly Indigo realized that nothing she might say and nothing she might do would make one whit of difference. The Committee had judged her and found her guilty. However violently she protested, their decision was made, and neither reason nor any other form of appeal would alter it. Stunned by that knowledge Indigo felt all strength drain suddenly out of her, and involuntarily she sat down hard on the stool, her face bleached.

There was an expectant hush. Aunt Osiku cleared her throat.

"This Committee finds merit in the complaints laid against the foreigner Indigo, and the foreigner Indigo is deemed entirely culpable in all aspects. Let it now be a matter of record that penalty shall be applied thus: the culprit's person is no longer desirable in the vicinity of Joyful Travail, and so she shall be conveyed to a place five miles eastward from the town and there sent upon her way; this action to be taken one hour after sunrise tomorrow. Permission to return to Joyful Travail at any time in the future is not granted, and the punishment for disobedience shall be swift and severe."

Indigo stared at her, nonplussed. Mere exile? She'd expected far worse . . .

The Aunt continued. "Upon the petitions of distraint received from Hollend and Calpurna, from Aunt Nikku, and from juvenile Thia, the Committee rules thus: that the goods and possessions of the culprit Indigo are forfeited to the petitioners in turn, in a ratio of three, two, and one, the total value of this distraint to be set at one hundred and fifty tokens."

Ah, so *that* was the nub of it. Bitterness filled Indigo as she realized the extent of these people's cynicism. What purpose could be served by imprisonment, or even execution, when instead there was profit to be had? A prisoner took up productive space and ate costly food, and a corpse was of no possible use to anyone. A heavy financial penalty was a far more pragmatic option.

She looked across the room at Hollend and Calpurna. Calpurna was composed, sorrowful still but nodding sober agreement at the elders' judgment. Hollend looked weary but relieved. And Ellani . . . Ellani was smiling. Was that all Koru meant to them? Indigo asked herself with an inward shiver. Had they been so tainted by the ethos of this monstrous country that they valued their own son's and brother's life only in terms of money? She couldn't believe that of them. Surely, *surely* it wasn't possible.

Her unhappy speculations were interrupted as Aunt Osiku spoke again.

"Lastly, we arrive at the question of the culprit's dog. It is clear from the evidence laid before this Committee that the animal in question is also not desirable within the bounds of Joyful Travail. Already it has launched two assaults, both without provocation, upon upright and innocent citizens. Blame for these assaults is assigned to the culprit Indigo, for it is well known that a mere animal does not possess the power of reason and therefore cannot be deemed responsible for its actions. However, it is the obligation of this Committee to consider not only the continuing safety of Joyful Travail's own good citizens but also the welfare of the inhabitants of other districts into which the culprit might stray in future. The animal has proved itself a menace to the maintenance of peace and order, and to allow it freedom to roam abroad would be a dereliction of our proper duty to our neighbors. Thus, this Committee rules that the animal shall be confiscated and destroyed."

Indigo froze rigid. She couldn't move a muscle, couldn't even breathe—

The Aunt smiled with benign satisfaction at the room in general. "The business of this Committee is concluded, I think. All may be dismissed."

The other elders were rising, nodding and talking to one another. The secretaries and notaries were gathering up their papers. Hollend began to usher his wife and daughter away; behind Indigo someone opened the double doors, letting in a wave of cool air . . .

And, shattering the quiet bustle, Indigo screamed, *"NO!!"*

She resisted them. She fought with all her strength when three more men came running at Aunt Osiku's cry to assist the two already struggling to hold Indigo down, but though the first pair hadn't been a match for her she had no chance against five. They bound her hands behind her, then when

she still tried to kick them they bound her feet, and finally
she was carried unceremoniously from the room in full view
of the assembled company.

Aunt Osiku watched the removal with an air of disapproving sorrow, and only when Indigo and her guards had
disappeared down the stairs did she sigh ruefully, shake her
head, and gather up her papers in readiness to leave. Catching Hollend's eye, she signaled to him.

"Foreigner Hollend." Her bow was courteous. "The Committee regrets this unfortunate outburst. Most distasteful,
and an affront to your good wife, who has already suffered
so much at the culprit's hands."

Such a clear apology from the lips of an elder of blue rank
was a rarity, and Hollend returned her bow with emphasis.
"Your kindness is deeply felt and appreciated, respected
Aunt."

A gracious nod. "The distraining of the culprit's possessions will take place one hour after sunset this evening, I
think. That will be a convenient time for all concerned. I
shall assign two monitors to return with you to your house
and collect all relevant goods for inventory and evaluation,
and interested parties may gather at the Duty House at the
appropriate time."

"Thank you." Hollend hesitated, then: "In truth, respected
Aunt, my wife and I want nothing from Indigo."

"Nothing?" The elder looked surprised.

"We both feel that to—to have anything that—reminds us
of this unhappy episode would be . . . unpleasant." He met
her curious gaze. "And no wealth in the world could compensate us for the loss of our son."

It was obvious that Aunt Osiku found such a thing impossible to understand, but, allowing for the peculiar ways of
foreigners, she made the best she could of it. "Well, that
choice is yours to make, of course. However, I would advise
you to remember that the law of distraint is intended not

only to compensate the wronged victim but also to properly punish the wrongdoer."

"Of course, yes, I understand that." Hollend paused again. "There is just one artifact that my daughter would greatly like, and which I ask might be assigned to us."

"Which is?"

"A musical instrument. I don't know what it's called, but it is made of wood, of a triangular shape, with a number of strings stretched on the frame. I understand that Indigo . . . played it for Koru, on the night before . . ." His voice trailed off.

"A wooden frame for making musical sounds? I see no virtue in such a thing."

"Quite so. But my daughter asks that she be granted custody of it."

Completely baffled now, the elder shrugged her shoulders. "Very well. I shall order that it be set aside." She nodded graciously to indicate that she had no more to say, and made to move on. Then she stopped and looked back.

"*Why* does your daughter want this instrument? Do you know?"

Hollend smiled thinly. "Yes, respected Aunt. She wishes to burn it to ashes."

"I don't care," Indigo pleaded desperately. "I don't care what you take, what you have—you can have it *all*; my ponies, my money, my belongings, everything I possess—but *don't harm Grimya!*"

Yet she knew even as she beseeched them yet again that it was useless. The Committee had ruled, and nothing, not pity, not mercy, not even bribery, would persuade them to change their minds. Grimya was condemned to die and there was nothing she could do.

They had brought her from her makeshift cell in the Duty House to witness the distraining of her goods, and under other circumstances the scrupulous way in which the pro-

ceedings were conducted would have been hollowly laugh-
able. Whilst fully intending to rob her of almost everything
she owned—a hundred and fifty tokens bought a very great
deal in Joyful Travail—the Committee made a great show
of demonstrating to her that not one iota more than the imposed fine would be taken. And for that they expected her
to be grateful.

Indigo barely listened as the squabbling and bartering
went on. Most of it—no, in fairness, *all* of it—was between
Aunt Nikku and Thia, both of whom wanted one of Indigo's
two ponies. That dispute was settled when a notary announced that the value of each pony had been set at thirty
tokens and thus juvenile Thia, with only twenty-five tokens
accruing, could not claim it. Aunt Nikku made no effort to
hide her delight, and for her remaining twenty tokens demanded the pony's harness, the best of Indigo's clothes
including her heavy wool coat, her knife and its sheath—
which she herself had found where Indigo dropped it at the
House, thus, Aunt Nikku said, confirming her claim—and
her cooking utensils, which were made of higher-quality
iron than anything available in the district. Thia, seething,
began to argue over the clothes and the knife, and another
wizened little elder, whom Indigo had never seen before,
was forced to intervene and arbitrate until finally both parties were satisfied.

Throughout the wrangling and squabbling, Hollend and
Calpurna had stood together at one side of the room, watching silently but playing no part. Now and again some assid-
uous functionary would make an attempt to draw them in,
urging them to take what was rightly theirs, but each time
they only shook their heads and refused whatever was offered. There was an air of sad and stoical dignity about
them both that, despite her earlier feelings of contempt, Indigo found painfully moving, but they never once looked at
her.

Ellani, however, was another matter. From the moment

the proceedings began she had been staring at Indigo, and
the expression in her eyes bore the same hatred Indigo had
seen earlier, though magnified now by gleeful triumph. And
when at last Thia's and Aunt Nikku's portions had been settled and everyone else in the room looked expectantly at
Hollend and Calpurna, it was Ellani who stepped forward.
She bowed respectfully to the elders present, then pointed at
an angular leather bag that lay on the floor among the rum-
mage of Indigo's possessions.

"If you please, respected Uncles and Aunts, I would like
to have that," she said.

Indigo stared in astonishment. Her harp? She didn't understand. Then, unexpectedly, Calpurna spoke. She was
looking directly at Indigo for the first time, and her face
bore a look of bitter misery.

"We claim this instrument and nothing more," she said
coldly. "We will not soil our hands with any other goods of
the creature who betrayed our trust so cruelly. But this . . ."
She gestured toward the harp and shuddered. "This, at least,
we will take and burn, so that it may never be used again
to taint the mind of an innocent child!" Then, as Indigo
stared at her in bewilderment, her voice dropped to a husky,
hollow pitch. "How could you have done such a thing to
us? How *could* you?"

"My dear . . ." Hollend drew her back and she turned
sharply away, biting her lip as her eyes filled with tears. "I
want to go home. Take me away, Hollend, take me out of
her sight. I want to go home!"

"Calpurna—" Indigo tried to start up from the stool on
which she'd been placed, but the restraining hands of three
of Joyful Travail's most heavily built men pushed her down
again. "Calpurna, wait, please! If you'd only—"

"You will be silent!" one of the men barked. And already
Hollend was leading Calpurna away. She wouldn't listen,
wouldn't hear. Suddenly Indigo covered her face with one
hand and began, softly and despairingly, to cry.

Aunt Osiku, who had presided over these proceedings as over the mockery of a trial, clapped her hands. "All is completed now, I think. This meeting for the purpose of distraint against the culprit is at an end. The confiscated goods may be claimed one hour before noon tomorrow, when all inventories and proper procedures have been completed. That is all now. Go, please." As everyone began to shuffle toward the door in Hollend and Calpurna's wake, she turned to Indigo's guards and made an imperious gesture. "The culprit will be locked in a secure room until the hour when she is to be escorted from Joyful Travail. If she wishes a meal before her departure, she may purchase one at a fee of three tokens."

She turned to go, but Indigo cried out. "Wait! Please—"

The elder stopped. She turned again, but her eyes focused on the wall and not on Indigo's face. "There are no questions to be answered and no further requests to be considered," she said in a clipped voice.

"Respected Aunt, I *must* ask one question of you. *Please.*" It was a last, desperate effort, and if she had to grovel, Indigo thought, then grovel she would. "Grimya— my dog—where is she? Is she still . . . alive?"

The Aunt's gaze didn't waver. "As the reply will not benefit or abet the culprit, this question may be answered. The animal is secured elsewhere. It is still alive."

*Sweet Mother, at least that was something.* "What will happen to her?" Indigo asked.

For a moment she thought the Aunt wouldn't reply, but then came the careless little shrug of the shoulders. "The creature will be killed in the proper way of dispatching animals, by the cutting of its throat. This task will be performed by the slaughterman, tomorrow or the next day, as is convenient."

Tomorrow or the next day . . . So, Indigo thought, there was still a thread of hope. Somehow, *somehow*, she must find a way to escape from this place before they came for her in the morning. Or if that should fail, a means of returning to Joyful Travail unseen. For of one thing she was certain. If she should fail to rescue Grimya, then nothing else—not Koru, not the secrets of the ghost-world, not even her quest to awaken Fenran—would matter to her anymore.

Thia was not in the best of moods as she left the Foreigners' Duty House. The disputes over her rightful portion still rankled, and she was particularly enraged by the fact that the foreigner's ponies had been assigned a value beyond her reach. Aunt Nikku would be insufferable now, and Thia was resolved to even the slate between them at the first possible opportunity.

Dusk had fallen and the others who had been at the Duty House were already dispersing, so Thia was surprised to see a human-shaped shadow lurking near the wall. She stopped, peered into the gloom, and her sharp eyes made out a familiar figure.

"You!" Her voice cut imperiously in the quiet. "What are you doing there?"

The figure shambled forward with a nervous, sidling motion and Thia stared contemptuously at the bowed head of old Mimino, Physician Huni's widow.

"What do you want, worthless heap of bones?" she demanded viciously. "There is nothing here for the likes of you, old carrion! Go away—crawl back to your midden and huddle among the animals, and do not dare to show your face here again, for you are of no use to anyone!"

Mimino didn't protest at the girl's cruel and calculated insults, didn't so much as utter a word. Her head dipped several times, like a bird making a strange obeisance, then she backed away into the shadows as swiftly as her enfeebled limbs would allow. Thia's lip curled in a sneer and she strode off along the road toward the center of the town. Confident that she had put the old woman in her place she didn't look back, and so didn't see Mimino watching her departure with eyes that were strangely bright and alert. The old woman gazed at Thia's receding back for a few moments longer. Then she smiled, an odd, very private smile. Oh, yes, she knew what was what; for hadn't she found a place at the back of the crowd inside the Duty House tonight, and heard all that had happened? Mimino knew. Mimino knew *much* more than anyone could guess. The foreigner, the new physician, had been kind to her. And Mimino meant to help her if she could. Mimino meant to be *useful*.

She waited a few moments more, until she was certain that Thia was out of sight and no one else was approaching. Then she turned, and moved with a facility that belied her usual crabbed and crooked stance toward the Duty House.

# ·CHAPTER·XVI·

Grimya was frantic. No one had come near her since the time—hours ago now, it must be, though she had no way of being sure—when she had been bundled unceremoniously into a wooden crate and carried from the Duty House to an unknown destination. When her captors had gone she had bitten her way out of the box, which was flimsy and half rotten, to find herself in a featureless, windowless, and empty room with a bare-earth floor. The room stank of unclean things: old blood, and meat so rancid that not even the lowest of scavengers would touch it. There was a human smell, too, of men who did not cleanse themselves, unpleasant and sickly and thick on the air. Beyond this, though, there was nothing whatever to give her a clue to her whereabouts.

Her first thought had been to find Indigo, but when she mustered her telepathic senses she found to her dismay that she couldn't make contact. That, the wolf realized, must mean that Indigo was too far away for a link between them to be established. Where, though? Still at the Benefactor's House? Had she found the way through the mirror again and returned to the ghost-world, or had she and her companions come back to Joyful Travail and was something terribly wrong? Grimya had learned nothing from the men who had come to carry her away, for they hadn't spoken a single word to each other, let alone to her. But the fact that she had been removed from the Duty House to a more secure prison made her fear the worst. Why had her captors taken such pains to separate her from Indigo? Why didn't Indigo come back? What was to become of them both?

For a long time, then, Grimya had tried to get someone's—anyone's—attention. She had barked and yelped and whined at the door of her prison, scratching the grimy, unpainted wood with her claws and pausing every so often to listen intently for any answering sound from outside. But there was nothing, and at last she came to the conclusion there was no one else in the building to hear her. Miserably, head and tail drooping, she lay down on the floor, staring at the door and wishing with all her heart that will power alone could make it swing open. Where was Indigo? And why, *why* were they being kept apart?

How long she lay there, helpless and frustrated to the point of despair by her enforced inactivity, Grimya didn't know. She sensed that dark had fallen but, with no window to look out of, had no means of judging the hour with any accuracy. Over and over in her mind she tried to picture what might have happened to Indigo, but the possibilities defeated her imagination.

Then, unexpectedly, her sensitive ears picked up a small sound beyond the door.

Instantly Grimya was on her feet, hope and dread rising in equal measure. Indigo? No, for the quick telepathic call she sent out met with no answering welcome. Yet someone was out there. She could feel their presence ... And there was that sound again, cautious, almost furtive, as though whoever it was was anxious not to be seen or heard.

The sounds approached the door; stopped. Then came a harsh, groaning squeak, as of unoiled and rusty pieces of metal grating together, and the bolt on the far side was drawn back. Grimya backed quickly away, hackles up and ready either to spring if an enemy appeared or to run if the opportunity came, and waited. The door shook a little, as though sticking, then opened. And the wolf's eyes widened in surprise as she saw an old woman framed in the doorway.

Mimino smiled and put a finger to her lips. *"Shh!"* she said in a penetrating whisper. "Not to make a sound, please." She slipped into the room, nodding and smiling, her small eyes almost vanishing among sheaves of wrinkles as she closed the door behind her.

"You must not be afraid," she said. "I am friend to Physician Indigo, for she has been most kind to me, and now I shall be friend to you, too." A shade of collusion crept into her smile. "I know your secret, gray dog. I know that you can talk, for I have watched you and I have seen. Many times I have seen you, though you did not see me. I watch and I listen, and I have come to understand much that others do not."

Grimya remembered now that she'd encountered Mimino once before. The old woman had approached Indigo at the Enclave gates when their search party had been setting out to hunt for Koru, and had offered to wait at the physician's house to explain her absence to patients who came calling. Later Indigo had told Grimya that she was Physician Huni's widow, now considered worthless as she was too old for useful work. Indigo had felt sorry for her and had taken an instinctive liking to her. Now Mimino was apparently anxious to repay the compliment—and, moreover, she had witnessed Grimya's uncanny ability and accepted it as though it were the most natural thing in the world. Mimino, it seemed, of all the citizens of Joyful Travail, had no need of a shadow-double. But could she be trusted? That was the question the wolf couldn't answer.

As though aware of Grimya's dilemma, Mimino bent down until their faces were almost on a level.

"I will not give away your secret," she said. "Even if so, I could do you no harm, for who would believe this worthless heap of bones"—she chuckled at herself for repeating Thia's vicious words—"if she should tell them that the gray dog can speak?"

That was true . . . Grimya hesitated, then suddenly decided that she must take the opportunity. A second chance might not come.

She drew breath, and said softly, huskily, "Whh . . . ere is Indigo?"

"Ah!" Mimino clasped her hands together. "You speak, you speak! This is good. You will trust me now, I think, and I will tell you what you must know. There is much trouble for Physician Indigo, and much trouble for you, too."

Grimya's ears pricked sharply. "Indigo has returned?"

"Yes, yes. They did not find the little one, I think, and now Physician Indigo is to leave Joyful Travail in great disgrace. But for you there is worse still, for the elders have said that you are to die."

As Grimya stared in amazement, Mimino told her all she knew. Her account was fragmented, for she had witnessed only a part of the Committee hearing and the later distraint proceedings, but by watching and listening where she could she had pieced together enough to make a coherent picture.

When the old woman finished her story, Grimya growled softly. "I mm-ust go to Indigo! I must go to her at once!"

"No!" Mimino held up a warning hand. "That would not be an enlightened thing to do, for if you are seen before the time of Physician Indigo's departure you will be captured again. You must hide, I think, until Physician Indigo has left Joyful Travail, and only then to be reunited with her."

Grimya saw the sense in that. A hiding place . . . Where

could she find a safe hiding place? And then she remembered what the Benefactor had said to her. *You will always find me at the House* ...

Since leaving the ghost-world Grimya had said nothing about her own feelings on the matter of the Benefactor, but her instinct had led her to a very different conclusion from Indigo's. From what Mimino had said, she surmised that something had happened at the House to prove the Benefactor's claim that Indigo could not succeed in her endeavor. If that was so, then the Benefactor had proved his integrity. He had done his best to warn Indigo, and the wolf's telepathic mind had sensed the depth of sorrow in him when he had failed. Very well then, Grimya thought. She would return to the House, and she would ask the Benefactor for help.

She looked at Mimino again. The old woman had returned to the door and was holding it open, smiling, nodding and gesturing for the wolf to precede her. Grimya hesitated.

"I sh-all do as you say and hide until morning. When Indigo is driven out of the town, which way will she go?"

"I have heard the Aunt say that they will send her eastward," Mimino told her. "Seven miles along the Splendid Progress Road there is a well-house, to serve the crops with water, but the fields there are fallow now so the well-house is not used. Physician Indigo will pass that way, I think, and it would be prudent to meet her there."

Grimya's ears pricked forward and her next words came in a grateful rush.

"I d ... do not know what I can do to repay you for your kindness. But I shall find something. I prrromise it!"

Mimino beamed. "You are a good friend, gray dog. The physician is a good friend, too. No more can be asked."

She was still smiling as Grimya slipped through the door and away into the night.

* * *

The moon was up, though a veil of thin cloud diffused its light enough to give Grimya good cover as she made her escape from Joyful Travail and sped away toward the Benefactor's House. Though she hated to be fleeing the town without Indigo, she had accepted Mimino's assurance that Indigo was in no danger. Her own life was the only one at risk, and to seek out Indigo now would be foolhardy. Mimino had also promised that she would try to get word to Indigo that Grimya was safe and unharmed. It would be well if she did, the old woman had added sagely, for otherwise there would be great adversity when the time came for the physician to leave the town in the morning.

The high surrounding wall of the Benefactor's House loomed black and forbidding against the skyline as Grimya loped up the hill. Approaching the postern-gate, dismay filled her suddenly as she realized that at this hour of the night—and especially in the wake of recent events—the gate would be locked. In her eagerness to find the Benefactor she had overlooked the question of how she was to get in.

Reaching the postern, Grimya stopped and stared at it. She could reach the latch easily enough, but an experimental push with one paw told her that the door was firmly secured on the far side.

Then, behind the door, a voice giggled.

Grimya's ears shot forward. *Someone was there.* Softly, urged by a precarious but clear instinct, she whined. And immediately an answer came back.

"Gray dog? Is that you, gray dog?"

The ghost-children were there . . . Hope leapt, and Grimya called back, "Yess, I am here! But I c-annot get in!"

There was a pause, during which she thought she heard faint, conspiratorial whispering. Then:

"The door is barred and bolted. But we can undo the bolts; we can let you in." Another pause. "The Benefactor is waiting here to see you. *He* says it's all right. He says we should let you in." Another ripple of youthful laughter was followed by a scraping sound, more whispers, a querulous but muffled question. Then the gate creaked, shuddered, and opened. Three small faces peered out at Grimya, and she recognized three of the same children whom she and Indigo had encountered in the strange otherworld. Now, though, their forms were no longer solid. Moonlight cast a strange, faint aura about them and the wolf could see the contours of the House and its garden through their wraithlike bodies.

She wriggled through the gate, wagging her tail in thanks. "Whh-ere is Koru?" she asked.

They shook their heads solemnly. "Koru isn't here. He didn't want to come. But the Benefactor is waiting for you. Come on, gray dog, come on!" As one they turned and ran toward the old building looming in the darkness, and Grimya raced after them.

The Benefactor was standing by the House's main door. As the wolf approached he bowed to her with great courtesy, and the rosebud mouth beneath the sad, dark eyes smiled kindly. "I am glad to meet you again, Grimya—but I am also sorry that the circumstance could not have been happier."

The three children had melted away into the darkness of the garden, and Grimya and the Benefactor were alone. She lowered her head, her muzzle almost touching the ground.

"Indigo has f-failed." Her voice was mournful. "I do not know what happened, but the people would not believe her. Even Koru's own mother and f . . . father." She looked up again. "You were rrright."

The Benefactor nodded. He was vindicated but he clearly took no pleasure from the knowledge. He turned and pushed the door open. "There is much to be done now. Come inside, Grimya. Come into the House, and let us talk."

He walked away into the gloom of the interior, and a little uncertainly the wolf followed. Among the artifacts displayed on the ground floor was a high-backed and uncomfortable-looking chair. The Benefactor seated himself on it, and Grimya sat down on the floor.

"I am very sorry," the Benefactor began, "that it has come to this. So much time and effort could have been saved if only Indigo had trusted me."

Grimya growled faintly. "I do not blame her for that!"

"No, I see you don't, and doubtless you are right. But the time has come now to put mistrust behind us." He looked hard at Grimya. "Can you do that, little wolf?"

She hesitated. "I c . . . annot speak for Indigo . . ."

"I do not ask you to. I ask you only to speak for yourself. Will you trust me, Grimya?"

She held his gaze. Logic said no; Indigo had said no. But logic and Indigo weren't enough to gainsay her own animal instinct. Besides, she reflected, what was the alternative?

"Yess," she said. "I will. I think that I must."

The Benefactor bowed acknowledgment. "Thank you, little wolf. I hope you will not think it presumptuous of me to say that you are wiser than you know."

"I w-would not agree with that. But I have said that I will trust you, and I do not break my prr-omises." Grimya paused. "What do you want of me?"

"I have seen the nature of the bond that exists between you and Indigo," the Benefactor said. "And I believe that you have the power to persuade her to help me. That is what I want of you."

The wolf considered this for a few moments. "You mean, to help you in the way you asked her to do before? To . . . make your people whole again?"

"Yes."

Grimya recalled the laughter and the joyful faces of the otherworld children. And she remembered what Koru had said; that to return to Joyful Travail would be akin to dying. Would it be wise, would it be *right*, to do what the Benefactor desired?

"I do not know," she said at last, uncertainly. "The children are hh-appy in that world, and I was happy there, too. It is a *glad* place."

"Is it? Oh, I know that it appears delightful and carefree, but ask yourself this, Grimya: how long would your happiness in that world have lasted before you began to yearn for something more than endless games? You were a cub once. But would you have wanted to remain a cub forever? That is the children's fate."

The wolf dipped her head. "No, I w ... ould not have wanted that. It would not be a *life*." She whined softly. "But then, to remain in Joyful Travail is not a life, either. That is why Koru ran away, because in Joyful Travail they would not ll-et him be himself."

"That is true. But neither can he be himself in the other-world, as I think he is beginning to understand." The Bene-factor remembered the tear in Koru's eye when he learned that Indigo and Grimya had gone away and were unlikely to return. "Poor Koru. Whichever world he chooses, the prob-lem for him is the same. It is not, as you say, a *life*." His expression softened. "And that is why the healing I desire must take place. I don't want to bring sorrow to the children of the otherworld, Grimya. I love them too dearly for that. But in their hearts they know that they are not complete, and they yearn to be whole again. Oh, they sing their songs and play their games and dance their dances—but theirs is a very shallow happiness. And when there are no more games left to play and no more songs left to sing, they pine for what they have lost, and then they venture back to their old world, seeking their other selves and trying to reach out to them. But those other selves—the people of Joyful Travail—are unaware of them. They are like blind creatures, and they will not see.

"I love my people, Grimya, just as I love the children. I want them to be cured of their blindness; to believe again, as they once did, that their spirit selves exist and that there is more to life than material greed. I want to reunite them with the souls they have abandoned, so that both they and those souls may find genuine happiness in completion." He paused. "Without that there can be no glad future for Koru, or for any of them."

Grimya blinked slowly. She remembered the games she had played with the children, recalled the sound of their laughing voices. It *had* been a joyous time, but . . .

*Would you have wanted to remain a cub forever?*

She looked up at last. "Yess," she said. "I th-*ink* that I understand." A soft whine grew and then died at the back of her throat. "If this thing could be done, I . . . I thhink that it would be a good thing, the right thing. But . . ." She hesitated, her gaze scanning the Benefactor's face earnestly. "But how can Indigo hope to ach . . . ach-*ieve* it? And"— this was the most important thing, she knew, and the hardest question of all to ask—"how will it help her to awaken Fenran?"

For almost a minute the Benefactor didn't answer. He seemed to be contemplating, debating inwardly with himself, and Grimya's telepathic abilities could sense nothing of his thoughts. At length, though, his eyes refocused and he looked down at her.

"Little wolf, it will not be easy. I know this, and I will not pretend otherwise to you. There is one way, just one, in which Indigo can heal my people and gain her own heart's desire. But she has shown herself deeply unwilling to do it, and I do not know if even you can move her."

Grimya uttered a soft exhalation, almost a growl. "You mean . . . Nemesis." She didn't have Indigo's instinctive revulsion for the name, but speaking it aloud gave her a chill frisson nonetheless.

The Benefactor nodded. "I do." His look grew suddenly keen. "She cannot escape the truth forever, Grimya. Inasmuch as the bodies and spirits of my people must be reconciled if there is to be any hope for them, so Indigo must one day be reconciled with Nemesis. Nemesis is a part of her being. Until she accepts it and becomes one with it, the wheel that she set in motion all those years ago can never come full circle and lead her back to Fenran."

The Benefactor had tried to say this to Indigo by the tower in the otherworld, Grimya remembered; but Indigo, still suffering from the shock of Nemesis's appearance, had furiously and bitterly repudiated his words. At the time Grimya had been confused and unable to coordinate let alone interpret her own feelings, but since then—and particularly during her imprisonment—she had thought long and hard about what the Benefactor had said. Indigo, she knew, still wouldn't accept it. But Grimya had made up her own mind, and she believed that Indigo was wrong. The thought of going against her was disconcerting to the wolf, for her instinct had always been to defer to her friend in all things. Now though, for once, she was prepared to dissent.

She whined softly again. "You are rr-right," she said. "I will help you in any way that I can. Indigo must be persuaded. She *must*."

Abruptly, the Benefactor leaned forward from his chair and, to the wolf's surprise, his hands cupped round her muzzle in a gesture not only of gratitude but also, backed by a sudden warm surge from his mind, of genuine affection.

"Little wolf." His voice caught with an emotion that made Grimya feel suddenly and strangely sad. "You are the truest friend that any soul could wish for ... Thank you, dear Grimya. Thank you."

Grimya wriggled, pleased and disconcerted together. She *liked* the Benefactor, she realized. Whatever he was—or whatever he had been, which was a conundrum she felt beyond her simple comprehension—he was a good man.

"In the morning," she said, "they will drive Indigo from Joyful Travail. I know this; the old woman told me. I m-must meet her. I must bring her here. What should I say to her?"

"Say nothing of our talk, little one." The Benefactor's hands still stroked her face. They felt as solid and as real, she realized, as Indigo's own hands ... She uttered a soft sound, almost a croon, in the back of her throat, and the Benefactor, her friend, crouched forward, his dark eyes suddenly intent. "Listen now. Listen, and I will tell you what I wish you to do."

The elders of the Committee that had pronounced judgment upon Indigo were surprised and not a little relieved to discover that she allowed herself to be escorted out of Joyful Travail without the anticipated fuss. As Aunt Osiku remarked later to Uncle Choai, it was clear that after a night's sober reflection the culprit now recognized and repented of her folly; even her protests over the unfortunate matter of the dog had ceased. An excellent consequence, the Aunt declared, though not, of course, enough to redeem her crime. All would now proceed as arranged, and the unhappy episode could be forgotten.

The only incident that marred Indigo's departure was the discovery that, at some time during the night, the harp that had been promised to Ellani had disappeared. A thorough search was made of the Duty House; Indigo's depleted belongings, now strapped to the back of her one remaining pony, were unpacked and reexamined, but no trace of the instrument could be found. The elders were baffled, but Indigo showed no interest in the turmoil. She believed she knew where the harp had gone, and thought it unlikely that she would ever be able to retrieve it, but that was no longer important, for she had far more vital matters to preoccupy her.

Late last night, while she lay sleepless and tormented by her fears for Grimya, a footstep had shuffled in the street outside her cell in the Duty House and a small, self-effacing voice had whispered her name. Startled, Indigo scrambled upright and ran to the high, barred window. She could see only the shadow of a human figure, but she recognized both the silhouette and the gentle tones of Mimino. The old woman spoke softly and rapidly; Indigo listened, and then, clinging to hope, yet hardly daring to trust what she'd heard, hissed, "Mimino, where will I find Grimya? Where should I meet her?"

The shadow-figure tapped her own nose with a conspiratorial finger. "She has left Joyful Travail now. She has gone to a place where she may hide from those who wish to harm her. Make no complaint when they drive you from the town, and the gray dog will meet you. I have told her of a safe place, and she will await you there." She described the location of the unused well-house, then hesitated. "There is one more thing to tell, Physician. It concerns your instrument, the one that makes music. There is great commotion because the instrument is nowhere to be found. I am able to assure you that however diligently the elders may search, they will not find the instrument—and it will not be burned."

She made a small, bobbing bow in the direction of the window, and then, just one small patch of darkness among many, she melted away before Indigo could even find the words to thank her.

Now, with the early sun hidden behind a layer of cloud and the threat of rain in the air, Indigo looked back for the last time at the palisades of Joyful Travail. Her remaining pony stood patiently beside her, flicking one ear back and forth, as her gaze roamed over the drab vista of square, unadorned houses, the higher roofs of the Foreigners' Enclave and, in the far distance, the green hummock of the hill where the Benefactor's House gazed down over the town. No one had come out to see her away; the only witnesses to her departure were the two men whom the elders had deputized to carry out their orders, and who now stood, arms folded, waiting for her to move on. They were armed with heavy staves and neither looked overly intelligent; Indigo knew they were under instructions to exchange no words with her, and so after one indifferent glance at them she turned without speaking, clicked her tongue to the pony, and walked away.

Her guards followed her for the better part of two hours, passing field after regimented field, never looking to one side or the other and always keeping a meticulous distance between themselves and her. At last though, she looked over her shoulder and saw that they had turned, unnoticed and without a word or signal, and were marching back toward Joyful Travail. Glancing to the roadside verge Indigo saw a stone slab with a figure '5' cut crudely into its surface in the plain script of the region, and smiled cynically. The men had discharged their duty precisely as instructed and had no intention of taking a single step more than was expected of them.

Well, she was free of them and free of Joyful Travail, though at a heavy price. The distraint had left her with little more than the clothes she walked in, her bags of herbs, one cooking pot and a few utensils, and of course the pony. Even her crossbow and quiver of bolts had been taken, claimed gleefully by Thia despite the fact that such weapons were unknown in Joyful Travail and the juvenile would never develop the skill to use them. That level of pettiness made Indigo feel bitter, but a far greater source of bitterness was the awareness of her own stupidity. She had come to Joyful Travail seeking to forget anything and everything to do with her quest, and had allowed herself to be lured into yet another evil tangle, which had ended in disaster. Koru was lost, Hollend and Calpurna's friendship had turned to hatred—with good reason, she acknowledged—and she herself was now a pariah in the eyes of the people she'd wanted only to help.

And she had come so close to finding Fenran, only to lose him again . . .

Indigo's vision blurred, and angrily she rubbed the tears

away. She mustn't think about Fenran, not now, not yet, and she mustn't dwell on her hideous experience at the tower in the wood. She didn't believe what the Benefactor had told her, she *wouldn't* believe it, and she wouldn't be snared by his scheming. The sleeping man had been a trick, an illusion. She would find the *real* Fenran, and Nemesis would have no part to play in the search. *Look to the future,* she told herself. *Look ahead. Grimya will be at the rendezvous now. She will be waiting.*

That thought lifted a little of the gloom and Indigo increased her pace to a long-legged stride, the pony breaking into a trot beside her. The Splendid Progress Road, though hardly the great highway that its name implied, was easy going in good weather; before long she had passed another milepost, and soon after that she saw the thatched roof of a well-house a short way ahead. The fields hereabouts were indeed lying fallow as Mimino had said, and the well-house stood unguarded and apparently deserted.

Eagerly, Indigo sent out a mental message, seeking for the she-wolf. But no answer came, and she frowned. Perhaps Grimya hadn't yet arrived . . . She tugged on the pony's reins and jogged toward the well. Still there was no response to her telepathic call, and as she reached the thatched turret she slowed and halted.

*Grimya! Grimya, are you there?*

Nothing. The well-house door stood ajar and, leaving the pony to graze at the roadside, Indigo approached cautiously. The door gave at a touch and she ducked under the low lintel. The space inside the well-house was cramped, but though her own body blocked the doorway, small gaps in the thatch overhead let in enough light to cast a reflection of the well's surface on the wall. And there, sitting on the floor and silhouetted against the reflection's bright undulations, was Grimya.

"Grimya!" Relief and delight flooded through Indigo in

equal measure, and she ran forward to hug the she-wolf, dropping to her knees. "Oh love, you're safe, you're safe!"

Grimya wriggled involuntarily with the pleasure of the embrace but she said nothing. Indigo, however, was too absorbed to notice.

"*Bless* old Mimino! She came to me last night, she told me what she'd done—I'll never forget her kindness!" She rose to her feet again, gazing round at the well-house's cramped confines. "There must be a way to repay her, even if we shan't be able to see her again ourselves. Once we're safely away from the district I'll think of something. But now we should go, and quickly. I want to put as much distance between us and Joyful Travail as I can before nightfall." She started toward the door.

Grimya didn't move. She had been dreading this moment but she was determined to go through with it, for she believed that what she was about to do was right. Besides, she had given the Benefactor her promise, and to break a promise was unthinkable.

She said, firmly and distinctly, "No."

Indigo stopped, turned, and stared. "What?"

"I said, n-no. I w-ill not go with you." The wolf's eyes were unhappy but she forced herself to hold Indigo's astonished gaze. She had rehearsed what she wanted to say and she knew it must be said now, before her resolve wavered and failed her.

"I am not going to leave Joyful Travail," she said, the words coming in a husky rush. "I am sorry, Indigo, but my mind is made up and you c-*annot* change it. We tried to help Koru and we failed. I am going to try again. I am going back to the ghost-world."

Stunned, Indigo started to cry out, "Grimya, you can't—" but her protest was truncated as suddenly the shimmering oval reflection on the well-house wall seemed to erupt. Light streamed from it, illuminating the turret as though the roof had been violently stripped away, and clear and steady in the brilliance the familiar vista of broad, sweeping grasslands and green hills sprang to life.

Grimya took a step toward the shimmering scene. "The B . . . *Benefactor* showed me this doorway," she said. "It is only one of many, he says."

"Grimya, don't! Come away—"

"No. I am going, and I want you to come with me."

Indigo shook her head wildly. "I can't go back there, I *can't*!"

"Then I must go alone." The wolf's voice was filled with sadness. "I am sorry, Indigo. I don't w . . . want to leave you, but if there is no other way to do this, I will do it without you." She whined softly. "I am sorry . . ."

Before Indigo could react, she sprang toward the shining oval. The reflection and the scene beyond rippled briefly, then Grimya reappeared on the far side. She looked back briefly and seemed to be speaking, but her voice was inaudible. Then she turned and ran away from the gateway, away from Indigo, across the sward of the ghost-world.

# ·CHAPTER·XVII·

"She may not come." Grimya looked up at the tall, calm figure who stood beside her at the edge of the wood. "That is what I am so afraid of. She may not come."

The Benefactor reached down to touch the top of her head lightly but reassuringly. "I think she will, little wolf. Be patient."

Among the trees crowding behind them, voices whispered and murmured together and there was a sudden giggle, quickly shushed. Grimya looked over her shoulder, but the children were invisible in the light-and-shadow patterns of the leaves. Her heart was beating painfully and she didn't know how much longer she could endure the strain of waiting. If Indigo didn't come, didn't follow her through the gateway, what would she do? The thought of losing her was unbearable. And if Indigo believed she had been betrayed, abandoned, that Grimya no longer cared for her—

Resolutely she pushed the thought away, telling herself

that she could achieve nothing by fretting. If another minute passed and still Indigo didn't come, she would—

"There." The Benefactor's voice broke into her musings suddenly, and he pointed. "Look, Grimya. Look."

Grimya's ears shot forward and she stared down the long slope of the hill that fell away from the wood's edge. Below, and far off still, a figure on horseback was moving toward them.

Grimya began to tremble with relief and excitement. "It is Indigo! It *is*!"

"Hush!" The Benefactor laid a warning finger on her muzzle. "She must not hear you, not yet." He was smiling, Grimya saw, and then he turned toward the trees and beckoned. "Koru, little son, come out! It is time for our new game to begin."

There was more muted whispering and giggling, then Koru emerged from the shadows. "Is Indigo coming?" His voice was eager.

"Yes, she is coming. Look there, near the foot of the hill. And she has brought her pony with her." The Benefactor glanced at Grimya and his smile widened. "You see, little wolf? Indigo will not abandon you. It must have given her great trouble to persuade her pony to step through the gateway, but she would not leave it behind for she does not know when she might return. Clearly she means to search until she finds you, no matter how long it may take." The wolf's tail began to wag eagerly and he added warningly, "Careful now, be careful. Do not let Indigo hear your thoughts and discover where you are. Koru"—drawing the little boy toward him—"are you sure of what you must do?"

Koru nodded. "I know what to *do* . . . but I'm still not sure *why*." His blue eyes looked searchingly at the Benefactor's face. "It seems a very strange game."

The Benefactor turned to fully face him and dropped to a crouch, taking hold of both of his hands. "It is a strange game, yes, Koru . . . but I promise you that if we can play it well, it will bring much happiness to all of us." His fist closed gently, fondly, on the small fingers. "*All* of us, Koru. Not just you and your friends, but Indigo and Grimya, too . ·. and your mother and father, and all the people you left behind in Joyful Travail."

Koru bit his lower lip at this mention of his family. "You said before . . . you said that there was a way to make them believe in magic things. Is that what you mean?"

"That is what I mean. To make them believe, and make them alive again."

"Then I . . ." The words broke off; Koru sniffed, wiped his eyes on his sleeve. "I *do* miss them," he said in a small voice, then blinked rapidly. "Yes. Yes, let's play the game. I want to try. I *do*."

"Good. That is good." The Benefactor released his hands and stood up. Then, his smile returning and becoming faintly conspiratorial, he reached into one of the voluminous sleeves of his robe and brought out a small sphere that at first sight seemed to be made of clear glass. Rainbow reflections swirled and winked across its surface and it looked no more substantial than a bubble.

"Here, Koru." He offered the sphere to the little boy. "Here is the ball I promised to bring you for the game."

Koru's eyes widened with delight. "It's beautiful!" He reached out, then hesitated. "Won't it break?"

"No, it won't break."

"And you—you've put the magic in it, as you said you would?"

"Yes, little son, I have. Take it, now. You know what to do with it. Grimya will give you the signal."

The figure on the pony was by now no more than fifty yards away. Koru took the glass ball, holding it with great care. The Benefactor turned to Grimya.

"All is ready, little wolf." He bowed. "I wish you good luck, and I hope fervently to see you when the game is complete."

Grimya dipped her head. When she raised it again, the Benefactor was gone.

The pony wasn't inclined to hurry. After the fright of being forced through the gateway it was delighted by the new world in which it found itself, and wanted to make the most of the lush grass. Indigo kept it on a tight rein, spurring it regularly with her heels, but she intended to halt at the top of the hill and let the pony graze while she scanned the surrounding landscape for any trace of Grimya.

She was still angry with the wolf, but her anger was rapidly commuting into a cold, hard knot of worry at the pit of her stomach, a feeling that grew by the minute as her eyes found nothing and her telepathic calls produced no response. She didn't understand why Grimya had behaved as she had; such a rebellion was utterly unlike her, and Indigo was convinced that an outside influence must have been at work on the wolf. Which could only mean, she thought bitterly, the Benefactor. But why had Grimya been so foolish, so gullible, as to succumb to his persuasions? Unless—and this was a chilling possibility—Grimya had had no choice in the matter . . .

Then, abruptly, a voice spoke in her mind.

*Indigo.*

"Grimya?" Indigo pulled so hard on the pony's reins that it reared and whinnied an indignant protest. Rapidly she switched to silent speech. *Grimya! Where are you?*

*In the wood ahead of you, at the top of the hill.*

Indigo stood up in the stirrups, peering at the trees above her. *I can't see you!*

For a few seconds there was no reply. Then, from the leafy confusion of the low-hanging branches, Grimya appeared and padded slowly toward her. A mixed wave of fury, relief, and bafflement swept over Indigo; swinging out of the saddle she left the pony to its own devices and ran to meet the wolf.

"Grimya, where have you *been*? I called and called but you didn't answer!" She dropped to her knees, reaching out. "Why didn't you answer? What's *wrong* with you, Grimya, why have you done this?"

Grimya writhed free from her embrace and backed off a pace. In Indigo's head her voice spoke clearly.

*I want you to see the Benefactor.*

"The Benefactor?" Indigo stood up as a mental alarm sounded, and looked quickly toward the wood as though expecting to see the Benefactor lurking malevolently in the trees' shadows. "Did he do this to you, Grimya? Has he got some hold over you?"

*No. He has done nothing to me, except to open my eyes. Now he can open yours, too. I want you to see him.* She paused. *It is as I said to you before. I want to help Koru— and I want to help you. This is the only way, Indigo. I know you don't want to leave Joyful Travail, but at the same time you are too afraid to face what you found here. The Bene- factor can help you; he can show you. He is not a demon. But he knows how demons can be conquered.*

It was a long and impassioned speech for Grimya, but even as she made the plea she saw that it wouldn't succeed. Indigo's mind was closing against her words, rejecting them. Mere persuasion, as the Benefactor had predicted, wasn't enough to overcome her innate prejudice and the dread it engendered. She must resort to the more drastic plan.

Indigo was moving toward her again, trying to catch hold of her ruff. Grimya danced back, then twisted her head round and uttered a sharp, high-pitched bark.

"Grimya, what—" Indigo began.

From the trees above her a familiar voice called out:

"Catch the ball, Indigo! Catch the ball!"

"Koru?" Nonplussed, Indigo looked up. High overhead, capturing the vivid light of the otherworld, a glittering sphere spun and twinkled and fell toward her. Instantly she realized that something was afoot and, alarmed, she tried to tear her gaze away. But she couldn't. The sphere was so beautiful; it captivated her, and suddenly she wanted it, oh, she *wanted* it, to hold and to have and to play with!

"No! No, I won't be trapped—" But already her hands were reaching up toward the shimmering ball and she couldn't control them; the desire to touch it and hold it was too great. With a part of her mind that still struggled to maintain reason she saw Koru emerge from the wood and stand watching, his face apprehensive and eager together, and then she forgot him and forgot everything else as the wonderful ball came spiraling down toward her.

It landed in her upraised hands and it was lighter than feathers, frail as a bubble, strong as steel. For one horrifying moment Indigo knew what it was and sensed the power it could wield—then the sphere seemed to explode with brilliant light and a huge shock wave coursed through her. She cried out and stumbled backward, losing her hold on the sphere—

*"Catch the ball, Indigo! Catch the ball!"* It was Grimya's voice, barking a joyful challenge, and suddenly other voices joined in.

"Singing lady, singing lady!"

"Catch the ball! We'll all catch the ball!"

"Run, singing lady, run!"

"Run and play, Indigo! Play with us!"

"Play with us, princess! Play, Anghara! Catch the ball!"

Her mind whirled. *Indigo, singing lady, Anghara*—she didn't know who or what she was; time and place were both spinning out of control and she was a child, a woman, a wife, a daughter, a lost soul—

Suddenly she was running. The shimmering ball, her treasure, her toy, had sprung from her grasping fingers and danced out of reach on the breeze. She *must* retrieve it, *must* catch it!

*"Catch the ball, catch the ball!"* Others were joining in

the race, emerging from the wood and running to meet her.
Children—the children, so many children, her friends, all
crying the litany over and over again, *"Catch the ball, catch
the ball!"* as they swept her up and carried her along on
their tide while the beautiful toy spun away above them.

She would be first, Indigo thought wildly; she *would*. No
matter that she was little, that her legs were too short to
keep up with the others; she was a princess and she would
*win*! Hair flying, silk skirt whirling (silk skirt? No, surely
not; she hadn't worn such clothes since—since—) she raced
over the turf, feeling as though her feet skimmed across its
surface and barely touched ground. The glittering sphere
was falling, lower and lower, faster and faster, and she ran
faster, too, chubby arms reaching out and hands reaching
upward to claim her prize. A squeal of delight escaped her
as the beautiful, shining thing seemed to glide directly to
her clutching fingers, and she held it triumphantly above her
head.

"Throw the ball! Throw the ball!" Her friends—she
couldn't remember who they were, but she knew they were
her friends—set up an eager clamor. "Throw the ball, and
see where it lands!"

Indigo, child-Anghara, laughed and nodded and drew
breath, crouching, ready to hurl the ball upward again with
all her strength. But instantly the ball became so heavy that
her small hands could barely hold it. She gasped, swayed—

"I will help you!" One child ran to her side from the
throng. She had an impression of silver eyes, silver hair;
then the newcomer's hands closed on the ball with her own
and suddenly the weight was gone and it was light as feathers again.

"Together!" the silver-haired one cried. "Together! Throw
the ball!"

They leapt as one, hurling the sparkling toy skyward. It
speared up and up, growing smaller; then just as child-
Indigo began to fear that it would vanish and be lost to

them, and was ready to cry for disappointment, it curved over and began to fall.

"Over the hills!" There was a great brindle-gray wolf among them, and it was *her* voice, shouting, barking. A wolf that could talk! *Grimya? Who was Grimya? She knew, she knew, but*—The wolf bounded to her and though Indigo knew she should have feared it, she felt only delight as the creature cried again, "Over the hills!"

Indigo jumped and clapped her hands. "A race, a race! Run after the ball!"

And they were away. As she ran with the wind in her face and her feet seeming to fly over the grass, Indigo was filled with a bizarre conviction that this had happened before—or would happen again, far, far in the future—and she almost cried out fearfully for the others to stop. But the race was on and couldn't be halted; something had hold of her, had power over her and over them all, and she could no more have broken the spell than stopped the sun and moon in their tracks. On they went, jumping over tussocks, splashing through streams. In an instant of astonishing clarity Indigo realized suddenly that they would never find the glittering ball again, but it no longer mattered. All that *did* matter was running the race, playing the game. The game was everything: it was life, it was joy, it had stripped away the years and the burdens and made a carefree child of her again. The game must never end; it must never, *ever* end, for she was a princess, and all her dear friends were with her, and they were calling her name, *Indigo, Indigo, Anghara, Anghara* . . .

Oh yes, Oh *yes*, there were games for them all to play. They didn't find the glittering ball, as she had known they wouldn't, and at last they tired of the chase and the search and sat down on the crown of a gentle green knoll to catch their breath. Indigo tried to count the children's numbers, but she hadn't enough fingers. What did it matter? They were all her friends. And her *best* friends, her *dearest* friends, were close by. The talking wolf lay at her feet, the boy with the golden hair (Koru? Was that his name? She'd never heard such a name before . . .) held her right hand, while the other one, the *special* one, the one with the silver eyes and hair, held her left. They sang some songs, but soon, bored with inactivity, they were up and away again. Now there were dancing-games and skipping-games, and Indigo sang in her childish voice: *"Canna mho rhee, mho rhee, mho rhee; Canna mho rhee na tye. . . ."* They found a streamlet small enough to jump across, so on its banks they played Sea Dragon, where only those who wore the Dragon's chosen color could cross the water in safety, and the silver-eyed child was Dragon and Indigo-Anghara won because her fine clothes had many colors in them, and because she was a princess. Then when that was done and they were all breathless again and splashed with water, a game of Follow the Hunter began, and away they went in single file, dancing and twisting and leaping as they strove to mimic whatever the Hunter did.

No one knew or cared how long that game went on, but at last, with the day still warm and the light unchanging, they came to the edge of another wood. With the strange clarity of vision that this world seemed to bestow, Indigo had seen the dark mass of trees from a great distance, and as they drew closer she became more firmly convinced that she had visited this place before, though she couldn't recall when or how. The wood lay within a shallow valley, and from a higher vantage point the treetops seemed almost like a still, dark lake. A part of her mind protested that it didn't want her to go closer, still less enter the wood, but her friends were moving toward it, and the silver-eyed child held her hand and said that it would be all right, and she trusted and believed.

On the edge of the woodland they halted. It was very quiet; no birds sang, and the breeze now was too slight to ruffle the leaf canopy. Indigo frowned and stared down at

the grass beneath her feet. She didn't want to venture in,
and yet she did want to. What awaited her? Something was
there. Happy or sad? Good or evil? Right or—

The speculations broke off as she thought determinedly,
*Whatever it is, I shall meet it! I am a princess, and prin-
cesses are not afraid of anything!*

Her small fists clenched with resolve, and she cried out:
"Birds in the Bushes! Let's play Birds in the Bushes!"

Somehow, though she sensed that none of them had ever
played the hiding game before, they all seemed to know it
just as well as she did.

"Hide, hide!" she shouted to them. "I'll find you all!"

They scattered as she covered her eyes and began to
count. She could count to a hundred now, and she was
proud of that; it was a fine achievement, for she was only
. . . how many years old was she? Six? Seven? She wasn't
sure, but she knew she was older now than she'd been when
they sat and rested on the knoll. She'd had to count on her
fingers then, but now—

*Now she was—*

But the brief, uneasy frisson fled and she finished her
counting aloud.

"Forty-eight, forty-nine—*fifty*! I'm coming to find you,
I'm coming to catch you!"

There was no sign of anyone when she looked up, but a
telltale trail of newly trodden grass zigzagged away into the
trees. Indigo-Anghara smiled and, pleased with her own
hunter's sharp eye, set off in pursuit. But wherever she
looked, however stealthily she crept round the trunk of a
tree or peered behind a thicket of brambles, she couldn't
find any of her friends. Soon she began to feel piqued. Surely no one could hide themselves *that* well? She was *good* at
this game; she should have discovered *someone's* hiding
place by now, and they couldn't have moved after she'd finished counting, for that was against the rules.

At last she gave up. Hands on hips she stared at the trees

crowding and towering around her, and called, "Oh, all *right*! I can't find you. Come out!"

Nothing stirred. She frowned, tapping her foot. This wasn't the way the game should be played. She'd admitted defeat; her friends should now emerge from wherever they'd concealed themselves.

"Where *are* you?" she shouted again, and a petulant note began to creep into her voice. "Come *out. Now!*"

Still no answer came, only a slight shifting of the breeze among the branches above her head. Indigo-Anghara uttered a wearily adult-sounding sigh, and set off on her search once more, taking what she judged to be the easiest path through the trees and keeping a sharp eye open for any sign of movement. She was angry with the others. A joke was well enough, but they had gone too far now. When she found them, she would tell them exactly what she thought, warn them that they couldn't treat a princess in such a way, even if she had allowed them to be her friends. She would tell them—

The combative train of thought fell away as she walked round the bole of a vast oak and came upon the clearing.

Briefly, memory stirred, trying to snatch her out of her childish consciousness to another and far less pleasant level of awareness. *She had been here before . . .* But the recollection was past and gone in an instant, and only interest remained as Indigo-Anghara stared at the squat tower standing alone in the small glade. Covered and all but obscured by ramping greenery, the tower seemed to gaze mildly back, its round windows like benevolent owl's eyes. She'd never seen anything quite like it before—*oh, but she had, she had*—and she put one forefinger in her mouth, staring with rapidly burgeoning curiosity as she wondered who might live here or whether, if no one did, she might claim it for her own.

Then as she continued to stare at the tower the click of a

latch sounded sharp against the wood's deep silence, and at the tower's foot a door opened.

Curiosity flared into sheer fascination as Indigo-Anghara looked at the figure emerging from the tower. A child, like herself—but the face had an adult cast and the eyes, silver eyes, were filled with old experience. Silver eyes and silver hair; a catlike little countenance that she found beautiful in a peculiar way. There was something familiar about it, and her mind sought for the connection. *Catch the ball* . . . Hadn't they played together? Hadn't they been companions? And there had been others, among them a golden-haired boy and a wolf that talked—

Immediately the idea of a talking wolf struck her as so nonsensical that Indigo-Anghara uttered an involuntary giggle of laughter. The silver-eyed creature put its head to one side and gave her a quizzical smile.

"Why do you laugh, Sister? Is this meeting so humorous?"

*Sister?* But this wasn't her brother Kirra, and she had no other siblings. Indigo-Anghara was baffled but, remembering her rank and the manners it demanded, she bowed with great dignity and said, "Good day to you. I believe we have not been introduced. I am . . ." But then the words trailed off as a small serpent of disquiet began to uncoil within her. *I am . . . who am I? Who?*

The silver-eyed creature stepped gracefully toward her. "Don't you know me, Anghara? Don't you remember?"

A huge confusion of emotions welled in the child that Indigo had become. She *did* know this being, she *did*. But the name wouldn't come to her, and when she struggled for the memory of the games they had played together she couldn't recall a single detail.

"Remember me, Sister." The being extended a small hand toward her, but though she longed to reach out and touch it she couldn't bring herself to do so, and she didn't know why. Conflicting emotions of love and hatred were seething through her mind, and with them a sense of such miserable yearning that she felt it would break her heart.

Indigo-Anghara made a small, frightened sound, like a whimper. She didn't understand this and she wanted to turn and run from it, run to somewhere safe, but her feet refused to obey her. Why couldn't she remember? *What was happening to her?*

"Who am I?" Her voice rose in a childish wail. *But I'm not a child! I'm—* "I can't remember, I can't!" She backed away a pace. "I don't know! I can't remember! *I don't know who I am!*"

Nemesis stepped forward, its hand still extended. "You can remember, if you will. Remember the child you once were. Remember the woman you have become. Remember me, Sister, for I am a part of you." The fingers were an inch from her own now. "Touch me, Anghara. You, I, us— there's no difference; it is all one. Let it *be* one again."

Very slowly, feeling as though she were on the edge of a precipice, Indigo-Anghara reached out. Lightly the tips of their fingers touched and something like a violent stabbing sensation shot through her. She felt a prickling sensation at the back of her eyes, and her throat was suddenly dry and hot—then the memories came crashing back into her mind, clear and savage and terrible. In a single instant she was a little girl running and playing under the slanting sun of the Southern Isles; and she was a nervous but excited adolescent riding out on her first hunt; and she was a young woman, in love and longing for her marriage-day; and she was on the tundra, the forbidden tundra, and the Tower of Regrets was falling and Carn Caille was burning, and she was screaming Fenran's name to the sky as she cradled his bloodstained corpse in her arms, and—and—

With a last violent shock her vision cleared. The past had fled, the child-princess was gone. She was herself again.

And before her, holding her hand, stood Nemesis. Not a demon, not her enemy in the way she had always believed, but *herself.* Child and adolescent and woman, Nemesis had always been within her; she knew it now as she never had before. And without Nemesis, without that dark companion whom she had striven for so long to deny and destroy, Indigo knew that a part of her would die.

She stared into Nemesis's silver eyes, and for a moment, recalling other days and other meetings, she awaited the surge of savage emotions that she'd come to know so well over the years: loathing, contempt, cold fear, and blind hatred. But they didn't come. There was only a sensation of faint bewilderment, and of sadness.

Nemesis did not smile. Softly, so softly that Indigo could barely hear, it said:

"Haven't we striven against each other for too long, to no purpose?" The being paused, and the silver eyes were filled with longing and sadness. "Sister, I do not want to die; but that choice is yours and yours alone to make. I can only ask you, beg you—can we not be reconciled at last, and be one again?"

Indigo held Nemesis's gaze and knew that it was too late for equivocation. The decision must be made, the enduring conflict resolved once and for all. *You, I, us—there's no difference.* It was true; she could no longer deny it. She could no longer deny *herself.*

Her fingers tightened their hold on Nemesis's hand, and in a small, unsteady voice Indigo said: "Help me . . ."

The being moved toward her. She felt its arms go round her and suddenly they were clinging together in a fierce embrace. Waves of heat and cold flooded through Indigo and tears streamed down her face. She heard Nemesis whisper, *"Anghara, Anghara,"* and her own lips formed and echoed the name, her old name, her true name. *"Anghara . . ."*

The scene around her began to spin. Though her feet were not moving, it seemed to her febrile mind that she and Nemesis were turning, faster, faster, beginning to whirl as though in a wild dance over which there could be no con-

trol. The tower, the trees, the sward, all blurred into a giddying kaleidoscope of green and brown, light and shadow,
and at the heart of it all Nemesis was a flicker of silver,
merging, melding, heat and cold, fire and water. She felt a
charge of tremendous energy building up within her. Then
darkness swelled, light flared; she felt as though her head
and feet were being pulled apart by a terrific force, and she
knew she was going to black out and that there was nothing
she could do—

She was unconscious before she hit the ground.

# ·CHAPTER·XVIII·

**F**ar away, like something half heard in a dream, someone was calling her name.

"Indigo. Anghara. Wake, my sister. Wake."

She stirred, and the sigh she uttered seemed to take on a life of its own and drift away. At last, languidly, she allowed her eyes to open.

She was lying on the soft grass of the woodland clearing, the creeper-hung tower a looming dark mass at her back. Nothing stirred in the clearing or among the surrounding trees, yet Indigo felt an overwhelming conviction that she wasn't alone. Another presence was here . . . or had been here . . .

Then in her mind the voice she had heard calling to her spoke again.

*"Not another presence, my sister. No longer that."*

She had been making a move to rise to her feet, but at this she checked, motionless, and suddenly her uncertain senses coalesced as memory returned. *Nemesis . . .*

*"Yes, Sister. We are one again—and I am so very glad."*

Slowly, very slowly, Indigo's muscles unlocked and she stood upright. She remembered it all now: the chases, the games, the melding of past and present into a new understanding and a new perception. She remembered Nemesis's hands holding her own, she remembered the being's appeal—*Haven't we striven against each other for too long, to no purpose?*—and her own answering plea: *Help me!* And in the wild, uncontrollable moments that had followed, in the embrace and the dance and the spinning out of consciousness, Indigo and her oldest enemy, who was no enemy at all, had been reconciled.

She began to realize how she had changed. She felt strong in ways that she had never been before. She felt aware. She felt alive. She was . . . *complete.*

*"Sister, we are whole again!"* The words seemed to sing within her skull as the part of herself that had been Nemesis spoke again. *"We have the power now; the power we have sought for so long. Anghara, Anghara—let us turn to the tower. Let us put the last sorrow to rights, and set Fenran free!"*

Indigo felt a surge of excitement, heady as the bright air of the ghost-world. It was true—the power was in her, she felt it, *knew* it. The long years of heartbreak were about to end, the final and most wonderful reconciliation was within her grasp. Now, at her touch, at the sound of her voice, the sleeping man would wake.

She spun, eager as the child whose echoes still lived within her, turning toward the tower that dreamed behind her in the gentle, never-changing light—

And stopped.

Grimya and the Benefactor had emerged from the cover of the trees at the clearing's edge and stood beside the tower. Indigo couldn't tell how long they had been hidden there and how much they had seen, but she had a sharply uneasy conviction that they were aware of all that had taken place.

Grimya's amber gaze was fixed on her, unblinking, unswerving, but the she-wolf made no movement and no sound. The Benefactor, too, looked steadily at Indigo, his expression quiet but strangely wistful.

*"Sister,"* the inner voice urged, *"why do we wait? Fenran is here."*

He was; she knew it. Even now he slept in the chair in the tower. One touch, one word . . . Heart pounding against her ribs Indigo took three steps toward the tower door, then paused again. Still neither Grimya nor the Benefactor moved and she realized that, contrary to her first suspicion, the Benefactor wouldn't attempt to intervene, to persuade her or cajole her or compel her to aid his own cause. She could enter the tower unhindered. She could be reunited with Fenran, and together they and Grimya could leave the ghost-world, leave this land, and never once look back on Joyful Travail and its troubles.

And at the same moment she knew that, for her, that simple resolution was impossible.

A rush of misery overtook her and she looked at Grimya as her mind reached out to touch the wolf's thoughts. *Grimya—Grimya, I love him so much and I've waited so long for this! I can't be turned aside now; and yet* . . . She couldn't explain the confusion within her, the words simply wouldn't come.

Grimya's answering mental voice was sad. *I cannot tell you what to do, Indigo. I cannot say, it is not my place to say. You alone must decide.*

It would be such an easy decision to make. Turn her back, harden her heart. Fifty years of striving—hadn't she done enough, suffered enough, to have earned the right to be selfish now? Yet without the Benefactor this chance, this moment, would never have come. He had opened the door, shown her the way and offered her the prize from the very beginning even in the face of her own unwillingness to help him in return. And Grimya . . . but for Grimya she would by now have been miles from Joyful Travail, walking the Splendid Progress Road with her hopes in ruins, and she knew that it must have cost the wolf dearly to stand against her and force her to open her eyes. She owed Grimya a debt—she owed them both a great debt. And though the wolf was too diffident and too loyal to voice her own thoughts, Indigo knew what her friend wanted her to do.

She looked longingly at the tower door and her resolve quavered. But she had made her decision. She wouldn't change it.

"Just for a while, my love," she whispered, though she knew that the sleeping man in his tower would not and could not hear her. "I'll be back." She paused, feeling again the presence of that part of her that had been Nemesis, and smiled piquantly. "*We'll* be back. We promise." Then she turned and walked toward the two silent, waiting figures at the clearing's edge.

Grimya came forward to meet her, pushing her muzzle into Indigo's outstretched hand.

"Oh, Grimya . . ." Indigo's voice caught a little. "I'm sorry, love. I'm sorry for doubting you."

There was a strange radiance in the depths of the Benefactor's dark eyes as he looked at her. "I think," he said gently, "that all is well now. Is that not right, Indigo?"

She raised her head, meeting his gaze. "Yes. All *is* well. And I also apologize to you, Benefactor. I was wrong; I made a great mistake. I discovered it when I tried to convince the elders of the truth, but I was too proud—or too stubborn—to admit it then." She blinked. "I admit it now, and I ask your pardon."

The Benefactor made a self-effacing movement with one hand. "For all its small value, it is yours."

"I want to help you, if I can." Strange, she thought, how the words came easily now. "If what I've learned here—

what I've found here—can also be given to the people of
Joyful Travail, then I'll do it, if I have the power." She
looked back at the tower, and suppressed an involuntary
shiver as she recalled something the Benefactor had once
said to her. "This world shouldn't exist," she said. "It
shouldn't *need* to exist; that's the greatest tragedy. But will
the children leave it willingly? It is their haven and they
seem so happy here. Mightn't it be too late for them to return?"

Grimya made a soft sound at the back of her throat.
"They s-seem happy, yes," she said. "But even they understand, somewhere within them, that for all its beauty this
world cannot give them a ll ... *life*."

Indigo looked at the wolf in surprise but the Benefactor
smiled. "Your friend repeats only what she has already said
to me, Indigo. She is more of a philosopher than she cares
to admit, I think."

"Grimya is wiser than I am." Indigo's mouth quirked.
"She always has been."

Grimya swung her head from side to side. "No. I brought
you here, that is all. The rrrest ... that was your doing. That
was your choice." She blinked. "But I am g-glad that you
chose as you did. Not just for Koru's sake, but for yours."

Indigo didn't reply to that, but knelt down in the grass
and hugged the wolf close to her. There was no need for
words; Grimya understood. After perhaps a minute she
looked up at the Benefactor.

"*Is* it too late for the children?"

"With your help, no, it is not." He seemed sad, she
thought, and wondered why. Then he smiled and the cloud
lifted from his face. "It will be the happiest and greatest
game of all for them. And if you are successful, it will be
the last they shall ever play here." A pause. "Even though
I cannot play the game with them and with you, and thus
will not see its outcome, I shall treasure that moment."

She hesitated, suddenly confounded. "You will not see its outcome?"

"No. My visits to the physical world cannot be prolonged. Too many years—too many centuries—have passed since I sought refuge here, and to return to the world I left behind for more than a few minutes at a time would mean my death. But I will wait and I will watch, and I will give you what little help I can."

Indigo stared at him. "But if the children leave—" Then she stopped as the Benefactor raised a finger to his lips. He was smiling again, the smile conspiratorial, and she realized that he didn't want her to ask the question that had sprung to her mind. Did he know the answer? Did he know what would become of him if the children he loved should depart from the ghost-world forever? Or was his future simply an unknown quantity that he preferred not to consider?

She dropped her gaze, aware that she had no right to ask for an answer and—perhaps like him—not sure if she wanted to hear what that answer might be.

"When it's over, I'll return," she said quietly.

"Of course. For your Fenran."

"Not only that. I'll return to—to say good-bye." She hesitated, then added with a self-deprecating laugh that faded before it could fully form, "For what little that may be worth to you."

The Benefactor didn't answer for a few moments and, looking up again, Indigo saw that his expression was closed, as though he was lost in some private reverie. Then abruptly he gave his secretive little smile once more.

"It's more of a compliment than you know, Indigo. But—if, as it seems, you have some misplaced wish to please me—there is one indulgence I would ask of you before the last game begins. You might think it an old man's eccentricity, and a trifling one at that, but it would please me greatly if you were to agree."

There was a strong element of self-mocking banter in his

tone, but Indigo sensed a more serious purpose underlying the apparent drollery. "Please," she said, "name whatever you will. If it's within my capacity I'll do it."

"Oh, it's within your capacity. A very simple matter; in fact my greatest fear is that you will think less of me for inflicting such tedium on you." Again the humor in his voice, again the sense that it masked something far deeper. "I simply ask, Indigo, that you will consent to hear a story. You might call it *my* story, though perhaps after all this time it is arrogant of me to make such a claim. I want to tell you of how the people of Joyful Travail came to be as they are."

Grimya whimpered softly. Indigo laid a soothing hand on her head, then slowly stood up. Before she could speak, though, the Benefactor continued.

"I hope I do not flatter myself unduly by presuming that you may remember our first meeting, at the place they call my House? I said to you then, I believe, that my words and my deeds have become the law of Joyful Travail, and that that is my burden and the nature of the curse I brought upon my people." Abruptly his dark eyes grew over-bright. "I long to shed that burden. I long to tell the story, to relieve my soul of the shame and dishonor it has carried for so many years, and to be shriven." He paused, then regarded her with renewed intensity. "Will you shrive me, Indigo? Will you grant me the relief of telling my tale, before the final game begins?"

Their gazes were locked, and for the first time Indigo believed that she saw into the soul of the being who was—or had once been—the Benefactor of Joyful Travail. Within her she felt a stirring, a presence that was part of her now but that also knew what it was to be an outcast and a bringer of evil.

Nemesis's voice said: *"We must hear him, Sister. After all, what right do we have to deny him what he has given to us?"*

"I will listen. Gladly." She smiled. "Perhaps then I'll understand you as well as you seem to understand me."

For a moment, then, she had a glimpse of the man the Benefactor had once been. No longer old, no longer burdened, but a man rejuvenated, invigorated. A prince, she thought, strange though that seemed for one whose name was revered among a people to whom such concepts were anathema. A true prince, a true ruler. And a good man. A *good* man . . .

"Indigo." The Benefactor held out a hand toward her in a courtly gesture redolent of something past and gone, yet still alive, she knew, in his heart. "If you have found it in you to forgive an old man's fancies, then grant me one more indulgence. Sit with me; sit here, and let us dine in the old way, the civilized way that you and I were born and bred to know. This one last time, let it be as it was in happier days for us both."

Indigo blinked as, with a miragelike shimmer, a circular table materialized on the grass before the tower. There was food on the table, and wine flagons, and plates and cups . . . The Benefactor reached out and took her hand; she let him lead her to the table, let him draw out one of the two low-backed chairs that were set ready. She looked at the food, at the strange aura that shimmered around it. She looked at the flagons of wine, glistening with an unnatural sheen . . .

"No, it is not real." The Benefactor smiled nostalgically. "But for a little while, I think, it might be pleasant to do as the children are so fond of doing, and pretend. It will make the telling so much the kinder."

Indigo hesitated. Old, old memories were unraveling in her mind; memories of her long-lost home, Carn Caille; memories of Khimiz, her mother's land. The old ways, the civilized ways . . .

She reached out and touched one of the shining flagons. It felt fragile in her hand and the wine that streamed from it into her cup and his was as insubstantial as mist. But it sealed the bond between them.

Indigo raised her cup. "A toast," she said. "To the old ways . . ."

"My family reigned over the land for three hundred years," the Benefactor said. "In those days our country had another name, as did Joyful Travail, but I imagine they must be long-forgotten now." He fingered the stem of his cup but made no move to drink. "I believe that, on the whole, we were beneficent rulers. My father himself was a good man, I think . . . But it was only when he died and the crown fell to me that I began to realize the true nature of what I had inherited."

All three, Indigo, Grimya, and the Benefactor himself, were sitting at the table, Grimya on a low stool that had appeared at the Benefactor's will. The rich array of food before them remained untouched; even the wolf, it seemed, had no appetite.

"My training and my inclination were those of a scholar," the Benefactor continued. "I studied history, philosophy, and the arts of magic—ah, yes, you may well be surprised. The concept of magic no longer exists in Joyful Travail, but in those days things were very different. The House that the Committee so proudly displays to visitors was not the home I was brought up in. In my childhood there was a palace where that house now stands; a wonderful building created by craftsmen of true vision and further augmented by each succeeding generation of my family. There was beauty there, and learning and music and laughter; all the pleasures and diversions that enhance human life. The House did not exist. Joyful Travail, as it is now with its mean dwellings and its drab, regimented streets, did not exist. But the seeds were there, and when I came to rule I saw how those seeds were taking root.

"I believe, Indigo, that richness is a condition of mind

and not of wealth. You might argue, as many did, that it was all too easy for a man who had all the wealth he could need to hold such a view. I would differ. I would say—and my words are borne out by my own bitter experience—that all the gold and possessions that the world can offer are worth nothing without the wisdom of a joyous heart."

Indigo gazed down at the wine cup between her hands and smiled bleakly. "I was wealthy, once," she said. "Had I known what my future held, I would gladly have traded all I had for a moment's wisdom."

The Benefactor looked keenly at her. "Perhaps, then, you understand better than most that human nature is a thing of complex perversity. My people lived well under our rulership. My ancestors had worked hard to improve all aspects of life, and they had achieved a great deal. The fertility of our soil and the success of our trade with other lands was bringing increasing prosperity to all, and people had the freedom to rise to greatness, if greatness was within them. When I succeeded to the throne it gladdened me to think that any child born in my country might one day be a revered scholar, or a famed adventurer, or a great musician, or a noble statesman. I was an idealist, Indigo. An idealist, and, as I soon discovered, a fool.

"My father had tried to open my eyes to reality, but he failed. I saw only the shining light of greater and greater progress, illuminating a long and happy road that would lead to a future of true contentment. My people saw that light, too ... But to them, progress had a very different meaning. Oh, they were willing to strive, to earn, to better themselves. But in doing so they had only one purpose— to accumulate wealth for wealth's own sake. Wealth could buy them more of everything; firstly more than they needed, then more than they even wanted or could use. But even if they could not use the trappings of wealth, to *have* them was all, and to gain them was beginning to eclipse all other considerations. We still had our musicians and our scholars.

But a rich musician was held in higher esteem than a musician of only modest means, though his talent might be far less. And a man without one redeeming quality to his soul needed only to be a wealthy man, and in the eyes of his peers he was a king."

The Benefactor sighed deeply. "When I came to rule, I saw that my fine ideals meant nothing to my subjects, and that all they wanted of me was that I should lead them to greater and greater prosperity. They wanted only riches in the form of possessions and status. For seven years I tried to make them understand; I strove to guide them toward a wider philosophy. But all my efforts, all my strivings, were in vain."

He fell silent suddenly, staring at the tower, his eyes introverted. Grimya shifted and whimpered softly, and Indigo said, very quietly,

"So you . . . withdrew from the world? Is that how you came to find this land?"

He turned his head and looked at her. "Oh, no. Oh, indeed no. I should have done so; I should have accepted that I could never hope to mold them to my vision, and bowed to the inevitable. Had I done that, perhaps some of my ideals might even have survived. But I did not withdraw. Instead, I resolved to take vengeance." He looked quickly, obliquely at her. "Yes, I did say vengeance, although I see from your expression that you find such an idea hard to credit. Vengeance on whom? you are asking yourself. And for what? I will tell you. I sought vengeance on my people, for betraying me."

"Dear Goddess . . ." Indigo said softly. Then: "But how can one man take vengeance on a land? You are—" A slip of the tongue; she corrected herself with a wry smile. "You were mortal. Sorcerer or no, you couldn't have had such power."

"You're right, of course. Rulers are not gods, however hard some rulers might try to convince the world otherwise;

and I was never *that* foolish. But if I didn't have the power to take the revenge that I wanted, I did have the power to set my people on a course that would, in time, bring that revenge about. So, like a sea captain steering his ship toward a deadly reef, that is what I did.

"My strategy was simple. I said: Very well, if material things are all that my greedy children want, then material things they shall have—to the exclusion of all else. Let there be no music, let there be no philosophy, let there be no spirituality. No more adornments, for adornments are not useful. No more games and pastimes, for they are not tangible; they produce nothing and earn nothing. No delight in idle pleasures, for delight is not an asset that may be sold or bartered for profit. And as for the things that lie in other worlds, other dimensions . . . well, if we cannot see them and touch them and grasp them, how can they exist? No ghosts, no spirits, no demons; no powers of good or ill. They shall have no place in this new, enlightened age, for that is what my people deserve.

"I brought all this about, Indigo, and even now, after so many centuries, it strikes a chill chord in me to think of how easily the thing was done. I ordered my own palace to be torn down, proclaiming that its beauty had no worthwhile function. I had its lovely gardens plowed up and turned into crop fields that depressed the eye but filled the purse, and I pronounced this deed an example to be followed by all diligent persons. I built the House on its hill, a place of strict function without one adornment, and I urged my people to do likewise with their own dwellings, so that they, too, might be rid of all things that had no clear value. Then I exhorted them to hold tightly to what they had and build upon it. To work and to earn and to amass the fruits of their labors; then to rise above their neighbors and be judged in those neighbors' eyes by dint of what they possessed and by no other standard. To be proud of their avarice, proud of their logic, proud of the narrow and joyless existence they were carving out for themselves."

He stopped speaking. Indigo picked up her cup and twirled it between finger and thumb, though she didn't drink. "And it took root," she said somberly.

"Yes, it took root. So easily and so swiftly that within a mere five years I realized that they had no more need of my guiding hand but would continue surely and unwaveringly along the road to perdition of their own accord. My work was done. Thus I decided to . . . well, to phrase it with accuracy, to withdraw from the world and leave them to their own devices."

Indigo recalled her first visit to the House and Aunt Nikku's impromptu speech about the changes the Benefactor had wrought. "And your parting gift to them," she said, "was to pull down the very last symbol of the old ways— your own throne?"

"It was. I saw it as a final and appropriate joke, and I was so filled with spite and vindictiveness in those days that I laughed aloud at the prospect. No more kings! Let them instead have Committees of little men and women, I said, and let them forever enjoy the petty pleasure of squabbling and strutting for precedence among their own kind. I would have no more of it. I would be *free*."

The last word was uttered with such venom that it took Indigo aback. She was well aware of the Benefactor's bitterness and remorse, which he'd made no attempt to hide. But this was something of another order altogether.

"You said . . ." She hesitated, choosing her words with care. "You said that you *found* this world. Was that how you . . . avoided dying?"

The Benefactor didn't reply immediately. For some moments he sat motionless, one knuckle pressed to his lips, his eyes unfocused and their expression closed. Then, abruptly, he answered her.

"Yes, I found this world, and I fled to it, as you say, to

escape the need to die." He looked up. "But I soon discovered that I was not alone here. Others also sought its solace." He regarded her steadily. "The sleeping man in his tower. Your own Nemesis. Others—there have been many others; some who have stayed and some who have not. Perhaps the fact that I alone in this world was a whole, living man endowed me with some especial insight; that is a question I cannot answer. But their stories and their plights were somehow an open book to me; I knew what they were and why each one had come. And then before long the children of Joyful Travail began to arrive, and I realized the enormity of my crime." He sighed deeply. "So here I have dwelt, among the lost souls who have been denied the right to true life. And generation follows generation, each one languishing here until the minds that they have left behind should open to them again, or until the bodies they have left behind should die."

Indigo's throat felt tight and her muscles worked as she sought to find her voice. "What happens to their spirits, when the bodies die?"

"They fade from this world and are lost," the Benefactor said simply. "Many have passed in that way. Where they go, what becomes of them, I do not know; that is not a matter for a mere man. But I suppose it is a kind of death."

"And . . . what of you? What *are* you?"

"I am a living man, after a fashion. My physical self and my spiritual self were not sundered, and so I entered this world as a being complete in my own right. Here my body does not age and so I cannot die. That is the way of things in this dimension." He smiled a little bleakly. "Despite my philosophical and sorcerous pretensions I do not claim to understand why it is so, but I accept the inevitable. My spirit self may return to Joyful Travail without harm, but I dare not go back in my entirety for more than minutes at a time, for if I did . . . well, that is something that we have already touched on and perhaps it does not bear repetition."

When he stopped speaking there was a long silence. Indigo was staring at the laden table, but with a blind stare, oblivious to its splendid array. She knew now what would become of the Benefactor if she should succeed in her mission. There could be no place for him in Joyful Travail, yet without the children he loved there would be nothing left for him here.

She looked up at last, and her eyes lost their faraway aura, focusing on his face.

"Is this what you truly want?" she asked.

"Yes," the Benefactor said softly. "Yes, it is what I want. It is the only hope for the children, and I think perhaps it is also the only true hope for me." He paused. "Can you understand that?"

Indigo nodded slowly. "I believe I can." She blinked. "You are a very courageous man."

"No, I am not. I am simply a fool who has finally learned enough to repent of his folly." He reached toward her and his hand closed over hers. "I cannot move freely between the world of the spirit and the world of the body. But you can, and now you have the power to carry the things that are of this world back to Joyful Travail. Lead my children home, Indigo. Return to my people the spirituality that I stole from them so long ago, and show them how they can be whole again."

His fingers were gripping hers tightly, almost desperately, and Indigo returned the clasp strongly. "I will lead them." She had the power; she knew it, she could feel it alive within her, complete, as she was ... "Only show me the way, tell me what I must do, and I'll do it."

The Benefactor hesitated, then abruptly his sad face blossomed into a radiant smile. "The way is quite simple. In fact, you have already experienced something of it for yourself." He clenched one fist, then uncurled it again, and a small, glittering sphere materialized in his hand. "Catch the ball, Physician Indigo!"

He tossed it toward her and, not pausing to think, she caught it by pure reflex. Instantly the scene before her seemed to distort, as though she had suddenly shrunk to half her actual size and was looking at the world from an utterly different perspective. For a moment she was six years old again—

Then the illusion vanished, and she sat staring at the Benefactor with the shining ball cupped in her hands. Slowly, her mouth curved in a wry smile.

"You told me before that you are a sorcerer. I didn't realize until this moment just what order of power you can command."

But the Benefactor shook his head. "Oh, no, you overestimate me. This bauble is nothing more than a device, and its abilities, like mine, are very limited. It is simply a focus—or a mirror, if you will—to awaken, briefly, the youthful memories and youthful imaginations of those who catch it in flight." He chuckled fondly. "Koru calls it my magic toy. But it is not truly a toy, and it is not truly magic." He paused, gazing reflectively at the little sphere. "Perhaps, when you were a child, you had a little treasure-box, where you kept all the small and secret things that were most precious to you? Not valuable things as others would see them, but simple souvenirs or curios, which kept the memories of happy times alive."

She had had such a box, Indigo remembered, and after all these years the recollection of what it had contained suddenly came back to her. A seashell, a bird's feather, a plaited strand of hair from the mane of her first pony ... dozens of little personal mementos that she had prized above more obvious riches.

"These pretty baubles are like your treasure-box," the Benefactor said gently, reading her expression and knowing the thoughts behind it. "In that box your memories were preserved and nurtured, and each time you lifted the lid you gazed into a mirror of your own life. That is what my baubles can do; that is their power. You caught the ball; you lifted the lid of the treasure-box and you remembered. And . . ." He held both hands up, palms outspread, "One bauble can be followed by another, and another, and another—"

Indigo and Grimya both caught a startled breath as suddenly the air seemed to be filled with a storm of glittering, fragile spheres. They danced on the breeze, spiraling, spinning, floating and bobbing, reflecting the light in dazzling rainbows. In their midst the Benefactor sat, as more and yet more of the "magic toys" streamed from his hands. Then, abruptly, he snapped his fingers—and the glittering storm vanished.

"I can create as many pretty toys as you may need," the Benefactor said, giving his strangely gentle smile once again. "One for each bereft soul in Joyful Travail. To be offered to them, perhaps, as a physician might offer a healing draught?"

Indigo understood his meaning and, unexpectedly, her memory cast back over years and miles to another land and other friends. The Brabazons, that cheerful, rascally, and rumbustious family of showmen, whose next generation were even now traveling the roads of the Western Continent to bring fun and laughter to the scattered farms and towns. Once they had put on the show of their lives, a show that had defeated a demon, and that recollection put an idea into Indigo's mind. She had served a good apprenticeship with Stead Brabazon. She had learned some valuable lessons, and now, as then, she had her cast of players about her. Grimya, Koru, the children. And Nemesis . . .

She saw Grimya's ears prick alertly as she caught her thoughts. The wolf's tongue lolled, and her telepathic voice was eager.

*Yes, Indigo, yes! That is how it can be done! And it will be such fun for the children—a game such as they have never played before!*

Indigo rose to her feet. "I'll need my pony. And a wagon, such as a—a traveling showman might use." She returned the Benefactor's smile with a broad grin. "Or a traveling physician."

The Benefactor laughed his delight. "Whatever you wish, I can and will provide."

"And the children. Where are the children?"

"They are only waiting for your word."

Indigo glanced toward the tower. Was Fenran there now; had his sleeping mind brought him back to this world, to wait? Soon, she thought, soon the waiting would be over. Soon she would return in triumph . . .

She turned back to the table and said, clearly: "Sister! Show yourself!"

The air around her shimmered, and the slender figure of Nemesis was standing at her side. But Nemesis's eyes were violet-blue, while silver sparkled behind Indigo's lashes. Laughing, she held out her hand to the being, then turned to the Benefactor.

"We were two but now we are one. Together we will open the eyes of Joyful Travail. Call the children, Benefactor. Tell them that the new and wonderful game is about to begin!"

# ·CHAPTER·XIX·

The moon had set in the west, and only a handful of winking stars lit the silent streets of Joyful Travail. The entire town was in darkness; at this hour all diligent citizens were asleep in their beds and would not stir until dawn made the frivolous waste of candles and lamp oil unnecessary, and so there was no one to witness the peculiar phenomenon waking to life in the market square.

The pump at the center of the square wasn't particularly well maintained, and for some while a steady drip of water had been forming a dull puddle on the ground around it. Suddenly, strangely, the puddle began to glow, growing brighter and brighter until a clear and vivid light shone from it. Then the light began to stream upward, forming a coruscating arch of brilliance. And within the arch, dim at first but growing stronger and surer, the reflection of green rolling hills became visible.

The Benefactor had needed nothing more than the reflection of the spilled pump water to create a new gateway between worlds. And out of the reflection, through the arch of light, an extraordinary vehicle came rumbling and jingling cheerfully into the physical dimensions of Joyful Travail. The little wagon was covered by a bright yellow canopy, and from every possible anchorage multicolored pennants and streamers flapped merrily in the night breeze. The wheels—bright red—were fitted with scores of tiny bells, tinkling musically as the axles turned, and the harness of the pony in the shafts was festooned with dozens more, while a feathered caparison of red, yellow, and blue swayed and nodded above the pony's ears.

Indigo sat on the driving-seat. She was dressed in an extraordinary motley: full blouse with wide, lace-hung sleeves, pantaloons in five contrasting colors, scarlet stockings with sequined patterns on them, and shoes with outsize silver buckles. A wide-brimmed hat weighed down with feathers and baubles sat at a rakish angle on her head, and her hair, loosed from its customary single braid, sparkled with the gold and silver thread that she had twined into it. Beside her, Grimya had been dressed in a foolish little coat adorned with more bells, and velvet caps on both ears from which ornate tassels hung. Beyond the wolf sat Koru, wearing an equally bizarre and colorful costume with a comic, bewhiskered half-mask on his face that gave him the air of a mischievous lion cub. The Benefactor had scrimped on nothing in the preparations he'd helped them make, and their entire entourage, Indigo thought with satisfaction, looked unutterably ridiculous. So ridiculous, in fact, that even the people of Joyful Travail would find it impossible to set eyes on them and pretend to notice nothing untoward.

The wagon moved a little way from the gateway, then halted. Despite the noise that their arrival had made, not a single light appeared in the square, not one door opened, and not one face loomed at any window. That was just as Indigo had anticipated, for if any of the townsfolk had chanced to wake and hear them they would instantly dismiss the disturbance as an impossible thing and bury their heads beneath their blankets once more to return to the contented oblivion of sleep. Well and good; with more than an hour to go before dawn broke there would be ample time to set their stage and prepare for the game.

Koru screwed round in his seat and lifted the flap of the wagon cover behind him. There was an immediate flurry of whispering in the wagon, then a girl's voice called eagerly, "Are we there? Are we there, Koru?"

"Shh!" Koru put a warning finger to his lips, though her voice was far quieter than the noise of hooves and wheels and bells had been. "Yes, we're there!"

Giggles broke out. "This is fun! Isn't it fun, Koru, isn't it?"

"Yes; oh, yes." Koru let the flap go again and looked at Indigo. Below the mask his tongue licked at his lower lip, and she smiled encouragingly.

"You're not nervous, are you?"

"No-o . . . ," uncertainly. "But I keep thinking about . . . about Ellani." Suddenly what he wanted to say came in a rush. "I *know* she didn't really mean all the horrible things she said, Indigo, I *know* she didn't! She used to be so different, and I know why she changed, and it isn't her fault. But I'm so afraid that the magic mightn't work, that she might not . . . might not . . ." The flow of words petered out and his eyes misted helplessly.

Indigo understood, and she reached across Grimya to take the little boy's hand and squeeze it reassuringly. "Don't worry, Koru. The magic *will* work, I promise it." Her face was shadowed in the starlight and so Koru couldn't see her smile. "Remember, it worked on me!"

"Well, yes . . ." His expression began to clear. Indigo laughed softly. "Come on. You and I have work to do." She leaned back to the wagon flap and called in a low whisper. "Children! Are you ready? It's time to begin."

Like a small tide of shadows they climbed out of the wagon, murmuring, giggling, breathing eager comments to one another.

"Look! Look at the dark!"

"It's so *dreary*, isn't it?"

"We'll make it bright. We will!"

"This is a new game, a wonderful game."

"Have you got all the things? Where are they?"

"Here they are, look! Aren't they pretty?"

"Oh yes, pretty, pretty . . ."

"This will be such *fun!*"

The children numbered no more than a dozen or so—all that the wagon could accommodate—but that was enough to carry out the first part of the game. Later, when the ground had been laid, the rest would follow, and Indigo glanced quickly at the bright arch of the gateway and the otherworld gleaming peacefully beyond. The Benefactor was there now, keeping the other children entertained with games and stories while Nemesis waited for the signal to lead them through into Joyful Travail. Indigo smiled a quick, private smile then turned back to the wagon, from where what looked like a mad river of gold and silver was now flowing under her passengers' enthusiastic hands. In less than a minute a gloriously shimmering haystack of brilliance was piled up at the wagon's side and the children rushed toward her, dancing excitedly.

"Singing lady, singing lady!"

"We're ready! Can we go, can we begin the game?"

Indigo held up her hands for quiet, stemming the flow of their chatter. "You've got the magic toys that the Benefactor gave you? You've not forgotten anything?"

"No, no, of course we haven't!"

"We've got the magic toys, we know what to do! We're clever!"

"So you are!" Laughing, Indigo clapped her hands together. "Well then, we can all begin! Come on, now—three to the wagon with me, the rest to go with Grimya, and she'll show you what to do." And silently she added to the wolf: *Look after them, love. And good luck!*

Grimya had caught the children's exhilaration and she jumped up to lick Indigo's face. Then as she regained her feet her eyes suddenly focused on a spot beyond Indigo, and she gave a yelp of alarm.

Indigo swung round and her eyes widened. A door had opened in one of the houses behind her, and a figure was emerging. For two or three seconds Indigo's mind was thrown into utter confusion—*what was this; who in Joyful Travail could possibly have heard them or seen them*? But even as she floundered, Grimya cried aloud,

"Mimino! It is Mimino!"

The old widow was hobbling across the square toward them, and as she came out of the deep shadows into the starlight Indigo saw that her face was lit by a huge smile.

"Physician Indigo, you have returned!" Mimino was clutching a wrapped bundle, and as she approached she held it toward Indigo in a triumphant gesture. "See, see, I have the instrument! I have kept it safe, and it has not been burned!"

"My harp!" Astounded, Indigo ran to meet Mimino, taking the bundle from her and sweeping her into a joyful embrace in the same movement. "Oh, Mimino!"

Mimino laughed delightedly. "The instrument is safe! You are safe and the gray dog that talks is safe, and ..." She gazed around her at the wagon and the children, and her expression grew rapt. "Ah, this is well. This is very well!"

*Indigo,* Grimya communicated, *she sees! She is not like the rest—she can see what we are about!*

Of course, of *course* ... Mimino had been their one friend, their one ally. Old and useless in the eyes of her peers, scorned and ignored by those who believed they knew better than she, Mimino's eyes and mind and heart were open to far more than the cold, narrow compass of

Joyful Travail. And Indigo owed her an enormous debt, for without her intervention the elders would have brought everything to ruins . . .

"Mimino!" Clutching her harp in one hand she caught hold of the old woman's fingers with the other, drawing her toward the wagon. "I have work to do here, physician's work. Will you ride with me and help me?"

"Me?" Mimino pointed at her own breastbone, then made a negating gesture. "No, no; these old bones are not worthy—"

"They are worthy! They are *more* than worthy! Please, Mimino. I *want* you to come!"

Mimino pulled her hand free. She turned full circle, seeming to drink in all she saw as one in the desert might drink water from an oasis. Then:

"Physician Indigo, you are my friend and you are most kind." She clasped her hands together. "I will come, then; yes, I will come. This shall be a most happy thing, I think!"

Indigo helped her up onto the wagon's driving-seat and the old woman settled herself, beaming at the pony, at Grimya, at the children, three of whom were now bouncing impatiently in the back of the wagon. Indigo called to Koru, and the little boy came running, scrambling up beside her. Mimino, chuckling, put an arm around his shoulders, and Indigo gathered up the reins.

"Ready?" She grinned at them both. "Then we're away!"

With a creak and jingle and a zealous shout from the children that produced not a stir of response in the town, the wagon rolled out of the square and away along the road that led to the Foreigners' Enclave.

Ellani couldn't fathom what had woken her at such an extraordinarily early hour. Her room was pitch-dark and the square of the window barely less so, and the cockerels that had their run just beyond the Enclave fence hadn't yet set up their predawn clamor.

She turned over in her bed, restless and irritated. Perhaps it was simply that she still missed the noise of Koru's breathing on the other side of the light wooden partition that separated her sleeping quarters from his. Well, she thought resignedly, if that was so then she'd just have to grow used to it, for like it or not there was little hope of Koru ever returning to them now. She had accepted that and only thought it a great shame that her parents—and her mother in particular—still clung to their hopes, seemingly unable to fully accept the rational conclusion that she herself had already reached.

Ellani firmly believed that Koru was dead and that, indirectly, Indigo had killed him. Filling his mind with her wild nonsense, turning him from the path of a sensible progress toward adulthood ... Clearly, Indigo was quite mad. And poor Koru, still young enough to be easily led and influenced, had proved an all too willing victim. Sometimes since her brother's disappearance Ellani had woken in the night in a cold sweat, thinking that had she been only a year or two younger she too might easily have been drawn into Indigo's crazed web of fanciful lies. She blamed herself for not realizing the truth sooner and, when she had realized it, for not alerting her father and mother to the danger in time.

But it was too late for such regrets. Koru was gone, lost. He had run away, lured by Indigo's madness into a madness of his own. Where he had fled Ellani didn't even try to guess, but she was certain that he couldn't have survived, or the search parties would have found him. Eaten by wild animals; that was her surmise. Eaten, and nothing left of him. And though she mourned, as a dutiful sister should, she knew that life must go on and work must continue if all that they had achieved was not to go to waste. Such a shame, then, that her parents couldn't yet accept their loss with quiet minds and look to the continuing future.

It was raining. She became aware of it gradually as she lay in bed and sleep refused to return. The faint patter of drops on the roof, the gurgle of water flowing along the gutters and down to the collecting-tank outside the kitchen below her room. That was a nuisance, for when her morning schooling was finished she was to work in the fields, and rain impeded the hoeing and made it less efficient. Still, the water itself would be useful, for a full tank would mean less carrying of buckets and churns from the well that supplied the Enclave's needs. Ellani settled more snugly under her blankets, determined to sleep another hour. The falling rain lulled her. It had a pattern, *pit-pat, pit-pat*, and as she listened the pattern seemed to take on a musical rhythm, like the sound of Indigo's harp—

She sat bolt upright, her eyes wide and appalled in the darkness. *Harp* music? No—her ears were deceiving her. It was the rain, only the noise of the rain. Not music. She *despised* music, it was just a crude noise without sense and without value. And she hadn't wanted the wretched harp for herself; she'd only wanted to ensure that it was destroyed! She wasn't hearing music out there in the dark, she told herself ferociously. No, no. *Never.*

Then suddenly from somewhere outside she heard a peal of laughter, hastily smothered.

Ellani frowned, her momentary fright forgotten. Who in their right mind would be out unnecessarily in this weather? And *laughing*? What was there to laugh about, when rain was falling? For a few moments she listened and was beginning to think that she must have misheard, that the sound had been nothing more than a gurgle of water in some pipe, when it came again. Stifled giggling, then a hissing whisper, as though one person hastily hushed another. And a scrabbling noise, like small feet scurrying furtively away.

Someone *was* outside, Ellani was sure of it now, and she felt a sudden indignant conviction that some of the Enclave children were playing a joke at their neighbors' expense. Her immediate thought was that the culprit must be Sessa Kishikul. Sessa had never been right in the head, stubbornly refusing to grow up and abandon her childish ways, and she was a constant nuisance to others, leading the younger children in silly and worthless escapades. Slipping out of bed, Ellani felt her way across the room. If she could catch one glimpse of Sessa and her cohorts, she thought, just enough to identify them beyond doubt, she would report them to the elders of the Foreigners' Committee for delinquent behavior. That would see an end to Sessa's irresponsibility, and would put Ellani herself in good stead with the elders.

She reached the window and pulled back the slatted paper privacy-curtain, looking out into the wet and dismal pre-dawn world.

For a brief instant it seemed that several small shadows flickered on the periphery of her vision before darting out of sight. Ellani drew in a sharp, eager breath and rubbed at the misty glass, screwing up her eyes in her efforts to distinguish any further movement in the dark. Then, seemingly from nowhere, came a voice that made her hands clench involuntarily on the window ledge.

"Elli! Down here, Elli!"

Ellani's entire body tingled as though she'd plunged into icy water. It was Koru's voice!

"Elli! Elli, it's me, I'm here! Look, Elli—by the out-house!"

Her teeth started to chatter and she couldn't make them stop. Slowly, fearfully, she turned her head, peering down to where a small lean-to abutted the dark bulk of the house.

Koru was standing by the lean-to wall. As Ellani's mouth opened in a round O of astonishment he put a finger quickly to his lips, then beckoned.

"Come down, Elli! Don't wake Mama, not yet."

Ellani flung a quick glance toward her bedroom door, torn between the instinct to ignore the plea and run for her parents and the fear that, if she did, Koru would run away again before they could catch him. In her agitation it didn't occur to her to wonder how she could see her brother so clearly despite the fact that it was still dark ...

"Elli! Come on, Elli, come down!"

Ellani made her decision. Snatching up her wooden-soled outdoor shoes and her hooded rain cloak she was across the room in seconds, opening the door and making her way precariously down the stairs to the ground floor. Through to the kitchen—the door bolt squeaked but that couldn't be helped—and pausing only to put on the shoes and cloak, she let herself out into the chilly early morning. Rain spattered in her face as she ran across the yard—then as she reached the outhouse she slithered to a halt, skidding on the wet cobbles and flailing her arms to regain balance. Koru was no longer there.

"Koru? Koru, where are you?" Ellani turned first one way and then the other. "It's all right, I haven't woken Mother." She paused, listening, then exasperation began to eclipse her initial glad relief and her voice took on a waspish edge. "Koru, stop playing games; come out *at once!*"

Still Koru didn't answer. Then, as Ellani stood wavering between anger and concern, the quiet was abruptly broken by a ripple of musical notes, rising and falling.

*That harp!* Ellani jammed a fist into her mouth, her eyes widening as for the second time her mind tried to reject what her ears were telling her. This time, though, it was impossible to pretend that the sound was nothing more than a trick of the rain. Rising and falling, rising and falling—

"Koru?" Bewildered and frightened now, Ellani began to make her way toward the source of the music. It seemed to be coming from somewhere between her home and the next-door house, where a paved path led toward the Enclave gates ... Heart thumping, she had almost reached the path when, so suddenly that she jumped as though scalded, the sound of the harp swelled and modulated into a lively tune and a chorus of voices began to sing.

*Canna mho ree, mho ree, mho ree,*
*Canna mho ree na tye;*
*Si inna mho hee etha narrina chee*
*Im alea corro in fhye.*

Fright hit Ellani like a blow, but her feet slipped again
and she couldn't stop herself before she reached the end of
the wall. She stumbled round the corner of the house—and
her eyes started wildly in their sockets.

On the path, blocking the way to the Enclave gates, a vividly painted covered wagon stood in the midst of what
looked like a snowstorm of colored streamers. Around the
wagon children were dancing—*but they moved far too fast
to be real, and she could see through them, she could see
right through them*—and a mad old woman danced with
them, hurling more handfuls of streamers into the air with
delighted abandon. A vivid, unnatural radiance lit the wagon, seeming to shine from within it—and on the driving-seat
stood two incredible figures. One, silver-eyed—*no, no; no
one could have silver eyes, such a thing was impossible*—
wore a near-psychotic motley of clothes and had hair that
glittered, and her hands flashed and flickered over the
strings of the harp she held. The other, as insanely dressed
and with a mask covering half his face, was grinning broadly at her.

"Hello, Elli!" Koru shouted above the music and the
song. "Aren't you pleased to see me?"

Ellani's mouth worked frenziedly, helplessly. For one moment, unprepared as she was, the substance of the otherworld had broken through her defenses, and the images
embedded themselves in her brain before she could reject
them. Then, violently, the mental shutters slammed down,
trying to blot the whole mad spectacle from consciousness.
*This couldn't be happening to her! It was impossible, it
couldn't be there, it couldn't exist!*

Responding to her mind's desperate denials, the wagon

and the dancing children lurched and wavered before her. But, to Ellani's horror, as they began to fade it seemed that Indigo and Koru stood smiling in midair, and the mad old woman still laughed and whirled, and the harp music and the eerie chorus, *Canna mho ree, mho ree, mho ree,* still rang in her ears. Logic had no solution for this. It could not be. *It could not be!*

Ellani staggered backward. Inside she was silently and frantically screaming, *Go away, go AWAY!* But on another level she knew that it wouldn't go, she couldn't make it go, she couldn't deny it or pretend that this wasn't really happening—

Then, shocking her anew, Koru called out:

"Catch the ball, Elli—catch the ball!"

Something was hurtling from his hands toward her. It glittered as it spun through the air, and for one reckless moment Ellani was swamped by an instinct to catch it and hold it. She wanted it, wanted it; she had to have it, no matter what the price—then reason smashed back into her mind and she leapt backward, evading the shining ball as it seemed to come directly at her.

The ball fell to the ground and lay glittering at her feet. Ellani stared at it for the time it took her to draw breath, and then her voice rose in a shriek of sheer uncontrollable terror. She turned, running, losing her shoes but not caring, flying back to the open kitchen door and falling through it into the sanctuary of the house as she screamed, with all the power in her lungs,

*"Mother, Father, help me! Come quickly—come QUICKLEEE!"*

# ·CHAPTER·XX·

It took Hollend and Calpurna nearly ten minutes to calm their daughter sufficiently to make any sense. Ellani was babbling and sobbing together, and Calpurna, who had lived on a permanent knife edge since Koru's disappearance, was in danger of becoming infected by her hysteria. At last, though, Ellani's sobs subsided enough for some coherence to return, and Hollend knelt down beside the chair in which she huddled, looking anxiously into her face.

"Ellani. Now come on, it's all right, you're safe home now and no one can hurt you. Tell us, sweet—tell us what happened."

Ellani stared at him for a moment as though he were a total stranger. Then, her voice quavering, she said: "Koru . . . I saw Koru!"

Calpurna's face turned dead white and Hollend's eyes widened with a mixture of shock, chagrin, and anger. "Ellani, what are you talking about? If this is some—"

"It isn't, it *isn't!*" Ellani pointed a shaking finger toward the kitchen door. "He was *there*, he *was*, I *saw* him! And *she* was with him, *she* was, and there was a horse, and a cart, and a mad old woman, and he threw this glittering thing at me and—and—" She burst into a fresh flood of tears.

"Ellani!" There was a wild look in Calpurna's eyes as she pushed past her husband and clutched at the girl's arms, shaking her violently. "Ellani, what are you saying, what are you telling us? Where was Koru? Where, *where*?"

Hollend intervened, slapping his wife's clutching hands forcibly aside. "Stop that, woman, you're hurting the child!"

He'd never spoken to her in such a way before, and Calpurna was startled into silence. Hollend glared at her, then at Ellani. "Calm down, both of you, *now*!" His own heart was thudding irregularly and painfully; he was striving not to grasp at what Ellani had said, not to allow himself to hope.

Ellani hiccuped and sniffed. "All right," Hollend said after a few more moments. "Now, daughter, quietly and slowly, tell me exactly what happened and what you saw." He glanced up as he heard Calpurna draw breath. "My dear, please—I'm sorry I spoke so harshly just now, but let Ellani say what she can uninterrupted."

Her shoulders sagged and she lowered herself into another chair. Hollend turned back to Ellani. "Now, daughter."

Ellani swallowed. The hiatus had given her time to collect her wits somewhat, and it had also enabled rationality to start reasserting itself once more. A part of her mind still wanted to scream again at the memory of what she had seen, but another part, growing stronger every moment, told her firmly that what she had seen was impossible and thus she had not seen it.

"I—I woke up, and I heard a noise outside," she said. "I thought it was some children misbehaving, I thought it must be Sessa Kishikul and her friends, so I looked out of my window to see if I could see them. Then ... then I heard

someone calling to me, and when I looked toward the out-
house I saw—I saw . . ." Her voice trailed off as she found
herself forced to face the question: just what *had* she seen?
And she realized that she didn't want to search for the answer, because to do so meant admitting to—admitting to—

She was floundering when suddenly a disturbance from
outside the house broke the tension. Noises—a man shouting, a woman's shrill voice upraised.

"What on Earth—" Hollend started to his feet in surprise.
"Who's that? What's going on out there?"

"It sounds like—" But Calpurna got no further, for he
was already heading for the door, pulling it open and stepping out onto the veranda.

"Hollend, be careful!" Alarmed, she started after him and
Ellani jumped up and followed. There were more voices
outside; Calpurna heard Hollend call to someone, and then
the answering tones of Nas Kishikul, the Scorvan ore-trader
and Sessa's father.

"Nas?" Divided between relief and renewed anxiety,
Calpurna ran outside in her husband's wake. The rain had
subsided to a drizzle and dawn was just breaking, showing
the other Enclave houses in smudgy detail against a sullen
sky. The first thing Calpurna saw was that lights were shining in several neighboring windows and at least half a
dozen people were out in the compound or at their open
front doors. Nas Kishikul was heading toward their own veranda, signaling to Hollend; she opened her mouth to call
out to them again—but the words died on her tongue as she
stepped out of the front door and saw the extraordinary
thing for herself.

The roof of every house in the Enclave was draped and
adorned with long streamers of silver and gold ribbon. The
streamers twined around chimneys, tangled in gutters and
pipes, fluttered and danced over tiles and shingles in a mad
riot of color. Some had torn loose and fallen to the ground,
where they sparkled like rivulets of bright water.

"Hollend!" Calpurna ran to the veranda's edge and clutched at her husband's arm as a terrible, formless feeling of dread caught hold of her. "What is it? *What is it?*"

He couldn't answer; he only shook his head mutely, staring at the crazy spectacle.

"Hollend! Calpurna!" Nas had reached them and was climbing the veranda steps. His face was flushed.

"You see this? You see?" Nas's voice was heavily accented and he wasn't entirely at home with the tongue of Joyful Travail, which was the only language he and the Agantians had in common. "What is it, I ask? Who does it, and for why?"

Hollend shook his head. "We know no more than you, Nas."

The inexplicable fear still had hold of Calpurna and she rushed out words without pausing to think. "Ellani thinks someone incited the younger children. She said that Sessa—"

"Calpurna, that's enough!" Hollend interrupted sharply. "Ellani's talking nonsense; of course the children couldn't have done this." He turned again to the Scorvan. "Who did, though? That's the question."

"I think to fetch the elders," Nas said grimly. "Someone be having a joke on us, and I am one that doesn't find it funny!"

The other spectators had begun to gather round them, and there were mutterings of agreement. Hollend frowned. "The good Uncles and Aunts won't appreciate being roused at this hour . . . but perhaps you're right; perhaps they should see this without any delay."

"Hollend, wait." Calpurna caught his arm again. "Ellani—what did she say about Koru? Could this be something—"

"Koru?" Nas caught the name and cut in. "What's about Koru? Something to do with this?"

Hollend shook his head. "We don't know, Nas. Something disturbed Ellani a little while ago, and she—"

Before he could say any more there was a small disturbance outside a nearby house and a woman's voice cried out
in exasperation or anger or both. Her tongue was foreign but
Hollend and Calpurna recognized one word: *"Sessa!"*

Nas's tall, gawky, fair-haired daughter broke from the
midst of a small group of people by the Scorvans' front
door and, barefoot and in her nightgown, ran down the steps
and out into the road. Darting toward one of the fallen
streamers she snatched it up and held it high, pulling and
twirling it between her fingers and dancing from one foot to
the other. Her voice, crowing with delight like a small
child's, carried clearly to them.

Nas swore and set off to intercept his daughter. She saw
him and ran to meet him, her hands full of streamers, which
she tried to throw over him like a garland. Nas caught her
by one arm and pulled her, protesting loudly, away from the
pile of shimmering stuff that was already building up at her
feet.

"Bring her over here, Nas!" Calpurna called, her natural
mothering instinct temporarily eclipsing all else. She turned
to look over her shoulder. "Ellani, go and—" She stopped
as she saw that Ellani wasn't there but had retreated back
inside the house. Calpurna frowned and would have gone
after her, but at that moment Nas and the still-protesting
Sessa arrived, together with Nas's wife, who had run across
from her own house and was scolding her daughter in a
loud, shrill voice.

"Bring her inside, quickly." Calpurna shepherded the
family through the door. Ellani was in the main room. She
stood near the stairs, one clenched fist pressed to her mouth
and her expression strangely distorted. Calpurna looked at
her in concern. "Ellani? Are you all right?"

At the sound of Ellani's name, Sessa suddenly stopped
fighting against her father's hold. She looked absurd and
faintly pathetic with her bedraggled hair and shift and
draped still with stray streamers that Nas hadn't managed to

dislodge, but her eyes were lighting up as though with a new and splendid revelation.

"Ellani!" She switched from Scorvan to the language of Joyful Travail. "Ellani, look what I've found!" Her free hand unfolded and something glittered on her palm; then abruptly she drew her arm back. "Catch the ball, Ellani! Catch the ball!"

It happened so quickly that Ellani had no time to think. Sessa threw the little sphere; reflexively the younger girl's hands jerked up as though to protect her face, and before she could stop herself she had caught the ball.

There was a moment's absolute silence. Then the ball seemed to explode in a dazzling burst of light. Calpurna shrieked and fainted dead away, dropping like a sack of flour into the arms of Nas, who just had the presence of mind to catch her as she fell. Nas's wife backed away, eyes and mouth wide open. And as the light-burst and its aftermath faded, Ellani and Sessa stared at each other across the width of the room.

Then, slowly, Sessa's lips curved in a beatific and blissful smile. "Elli ..." She held out her arms to the other girl. "Come on, Elli. Come and see. It's so pretty, and such fun. Come and *see*."

Ellani's gaze was fixed on Sessa's face, but she wasn't seeing Sessa. She looked, instead, into another country and another time, as her earliest memories of days in Agantia before her father's business had brought the family to Joyful Travail rose unbidden from the forgotten depths of her mind. Flowers and fountains, toys and games and stories and music, the sound of her mother's laughter as a tiny girl toddled her first determined steps; all the color and wonder of the huge and exciting world she had left behind and put away as having no sensible *use* ... Tears started to stream down Ellani's cheeks. *There had been a wagon, gaily painted; a pony in the shafts with bells on its harness that made such a sweet sound. There had been other children, laugh-*

*ing and dancing like Sessa. There had been a song, a happy
song; she could remember it, she could hear it again now.
And her brother had been there. Her lost brother, whom she
loved dearly. She didn't want to deny it anymore. It had
been real. And she wanted, oh, she wanted so much, for it
to be real again* . . .

"*Koru!*" Her voice cracked, but the cry was from the
heart, from the soul. "Koru, where are you? Wait for me!
*Wait for me!*"

Before anyone could summon the wits to stop her, Ellani
had flung herself across the room and out of the front door,
with Sessa at her heels. On the veranda the two girls can-
noned into Hollend, sending him reeling, and then they were
jumping down the steps and running, running across the
compound toward the Enclave gates.

"Ellani! *Ellani!*" Collecting himself, Hollend roared after
his daughter as shock and fear and confusion crashed in on
him. Slipping, scrambling, he started after the two fleeing
figures. "Stop them, someone! Stop them!" But no one was
quick enough. And no one, save for Ellani and Sessa, saw
the phantom figure that came racing from the gates to intercept them as a child of the ghost-world, Ellani's own
doppelgänger, met their headlong rush and, like a will-o'-
the-wisp, flickered briefly at Ellani's side before they
merged and became one.

"Someone's coming." Koru leapt to his feet on the driving-
seat, causing the wagon to rock so that the pony snorted and
laid its ears back nervously. "Indigo, someone's coming!"

Indigo could see his face in the rapidly growing morning
light, and she felt the surge of hope that flowed from him.
Unconsciously her hands clenched tightly on the reins and
she peered toward the street, still sunk in dawn gloom, that
led back to the Enclave.

They had returned to the market square, where Grimya
and the children had done their work well. The entire square

was festooned with streamers. Undaunted by the drizzle, gold and silver ribbons undulated across the ground, danced on rooftops, fluttered from window ledges and chimneys; thousands upon thousands of them, an impossible, glittering mass shot through here and there with jewellike streaks of red and green and blue. The roof of the Committee House sported what looked like a mad mop of shimmering hair, and the children—Mimino had joined them now—were still working tirelessly, pulling more and more streamers from the wagon, adorning every available crevice as they laughed with delight at their achievements.

And still not a single lamp had been lit in any of the surrounding windows . . .

By the pump, the door into the otherworld shone with a steady light. Indigo could sense Nemesis's presence beyond the gateway, could feel and share the being's eagerness as they both waited. *Soon*, she thought; *soon, Sister* . . . Then:

"It's Elli!" Koru's voice rose to a shriek of elation and he bounced on the seat, waving his arms wildly. "I can see her, I can see her!"

*Grimya!* Indigo sent the quick telepathic call, and the wolf came bounding across the square. Her mouth was full of streamers and one, caught round her hindquarters, trailed behind her like a new and exotic tail.

"They're coming, love. Ellani and Sessa." Indigo felt an excitement to match Koru's. "The gamble worked, Grimya, I think it worked—Sessa knew what to do, she sensed it . . ."

The two small figures came racing into the square, and slithered to a halt. Sessa gasped, gazing around her at the shining wonder. But Ellani had eyes only for the wagon.

"Elli . . . ?" Koru said hesitantly. And his sister's face grew radiant.

"Koru! It is you, it *is*!" She ran toward him and he leapt down to hug her, the two of them dancing a mad caper as they embraced. "Oh, Koru, Koru, I thought you were dead!"

"Elli ..." He stopped then, his eyes filled with wonder. "You're different. You're just the way you used to be, the way I remember! The magic worked! Everything's all right again!"

Ellani stared about her with the air of a blind child whose sight had suddenly and miraculously been restored. "Oh ...," she said softly. "It's all *beautiful* ..."

"We did it! Me and all my friends. Elli, we're going to make them all see, *all* of them—Mama and Papa, and the elders—"

"Papa!" For the first time in several years Ellani used the old, fond diminutive for her father, though she wasn't consciously aware of it. "He'll follow. He saw us run, Sessa and me; he'll come after us. They *all* will!"

Ellani didn't want them to come, Indigo realized as she heard these words. In the girl's mind, for the first time, her parents and the elders of Joyful Travail represented not the proper and desirable security of convention, but an unkind, unfeeling power that threatened to take away her newfound joy.

"Ellani!" She called out, at the same time reaching for something that lay at her feet. "Don't worry, Ellani. We can make them see, too. We have the power, all of us."

In a window behind her, unnoticed, a lamp glimmered into life. Joyful Travail was beginning to awake.

Ellani stared up at Indigo, at her motley garb, at the wagon. In another window, a second light appeared.

"We ... ?" Ellani whispered.

"Yes. Here—take them." Three more of the shining spheres flitted from Indigo's hand—one to Ellani, one to Koru, the third to Sessa. "The magic will work again."

In cupped hands Ellani held the ball she had caught, gazing at it with wonder as understanding dawned. "Oh ...," she said, bereft of all other expression. *"Oh ..."*

"Help us, Elli." Koru turned to his sister, his blue eyes alight and fervent. "The more we are, the more we'll be-

come!" Unconsciously he was echoing the Benefactor's
own words, almost the last thing he had said to Indigo before the wagon had left the ghost-world to begin the game.

Ellani's eyes lit in answer. "Yes," she breathed. "Yes, I
will. I *will*!"

At that moment the third light in the square came on. It
shone from a window in the top story of the Committee
House, where the senior elders had privileged quarters for
their duty hours, and seconds later the squeak of an unoiled
hinge echoed across the square as the window was flung
open.

"What is this?" The voice from the high aerie was thin
and querulous; in the new lamplight the violet sash of Joyful Travail's highest rank showed suddenly vivid. "Someone
is making a disturbance! What are you about, please?"

On roofs and in doorways the children with their armfuls
of streamers stopped still, and for a moment there wasn't a
sound to be heard in the square. Then, suddenly and shockingly, Indigo's voice cut through the tense silence.

"Children! A song!" She snatched her harp from its place
beside her on the seat, swinging it onto her lap and striking
a chord, a chord that they all now knew well. "Sing, little
ones! *Sing!*"

And, shattering the cheerless peace of Joyful Travail, like
a lilting, joyful hymn to welcome the new day, a chorus of
voices rose up:

> *Canna mho ree, mho ree, mho ree,*
> *Canna mho ree na tye!*

Koru caught Ellani's hands and began to dance her
around in a zestful circle. Sessa, laughing, twirled and
jumped, and the other children, with Mimino among them,
came running and leaping, joining in the merriment. From
the high window in the Committee House a cry rose, a
shriek of outrage, of disbelief, of horror. And Indigo in her

jester's clothes, her fingers flying on the harp strings, sent out a call to Nemesis, her twin, her own self—

*"Sister, it's time! Bring the children! Come to us—come to us!"*

The arch of light above the pump glowed suddenly with renewed energy, then flared into glorious brilliance. And through the gateway like a living flood the entire population of the ghost-world children, with Nemesis at their head, came laughing, shouting, jumping, and tumbling into Joyful Travail.

# ·CHAPTER·XXI·

Nas caught up with Hollend at the Enclave gates, but by the time the two of them reached the road Ellani and Sessa were nowhere in sight. They slithered to a halt and Nas muttered a string of Scorvan oaths. "Which way they go? Into town or out? I didn't see!"

"Neither did I." Hollend glanced quickly at the dark bulk of the Duty House a few yards away. "I'm going to rouse the Foreigners' Committee."

"I do that," Nas said instantly, grasping at the chance of useful action. "You run faster than me; you go to the square, might catch the girls if they gone that way. If not, shout up the elders at the Committee House." His brows knitted. "We going to need all the help we can get."

Voices hailed them from the Enclave and they saw three more men hurrying toward them. Nas's wife was following them with Calpurna, who had recovered from her faint. Hollend nodded.

"All right. Tell Calpurna where I've gone." And he set

off at a loping run toward the center of the town as Nas turned toward the Duty House.

Whoever had perpetrated the senseless joke in the Enclave apparently hadn't been content with their efforts there, for as Hollend raced toward the middle of the town he found himself running—at times almost wading—through more and yet more of the preposterous glittering streamers. They littered the ground underfoot, flapping and tangling round his ankles, and several times he was forced to stop and tear them from his feet lest they should trip him. Distracted and flustered, he didn't pay any heed to the noise ahead of him until he was only a few yards from the market square. But when it did finally impinge he halted in sudden consternation.

*Music?* Yes—yes, it was, there could be no mistaking it! And voices singing. And shouts, high-pitched with rage or fright or both. Utterly confused by now but with an increasing sense of alarm, Hollend ran the last few paces and emerged into the square.

What confronted him looked, to his reeling mind, like something from a mad nightmare. A veritable army of citizens and elders was striving like frantic ants to tear down the tangles of streamers that covered every crevice of the square. They swept them from doorways and windows and corners, gathering them by the armful and trampling them underfoot, while from the open doors of the Committee House the autocratic Aunt Osiku and other high-ranking elders exhorted them shrilly to greater endeavor. Yet no sooner were the streamers trampled than they flew into the air again, whirling and sparkling, and with a shock that coursed through to his bones Hollend saw children—dozens of children dressed in strange, bright garments, their bodies insubstantial but their laughter ringing across the square as they snatched and hurled the streamers round in a glittering storm. In the midst of the mayhem a crazily painted wagon rocked like a ship on a rough sea, and on the wagon's seat stood a woman in bizarre clothes—*Indigo*? Surely not, Hollend thought incredulously; surely it *couldn't* be?—playing a harp like one possessed, while beside her an impossible figure with silver hair and silver eyes laughed and applauded. And, beating against Hollend's ears through the shouts and cries of the melee, the words of the song that they and the children were singing swelled in a rising tide.

> *Everyone, everyone, play and sing!*
> *Dance with us in the merry ring!*

It was the calling-dance that Indigo had used to lure Koru from hiding in the ghost-world. Hollend didn't know that, had never heard it before, but as he took in the words he was assailed by a violent and entirely unexpected emotion. It was irrational, it was mad, but he wanted to shout out to the toiling citizens: *No, stop, what harm are they doing? Leave them alone—they are beautiful!* The image of Sessa Kishikul, her face radiant, dancing among the streamers in the Enclave and crying out in delight, rose in his inner vision; he uttered an inarticulate cry of protest—

And a voice called shrilly from the crowd: *"Papa!"*

Hollend jolted as though he'd been struck an enormous physical blow. *"Koru?"*

"Papa!" Blond hair flying, eyes alight with joy, a little boy in jester's motley came rushing at him out of the throng, arms outstretched. Hollend's mouth opened in denial, in disbelief, in hope—and another familiar voice, the voice of Ellani, shouted to him as she raced in her brother's wake.

"Catch the ball, Papa! Catch the ball!"

The dazzling sphere came straight at Hollend's head. He reeled back; then, just as Ellani had done when Sessa threw the magic ball to her, he instinctively raised his hands to ward it off and caught it.

Ellani shrieked with joy and hugged Koru, and together they jumped up and down before their father.

"Papa, Papa, play and sing, dance with us in the merry ring!"

*Play and sing ... play and sing ...* Suddenly Hollend started to laugh and he couldn't make it stop. *Play and sing ... Catch the ball ...*

"Children—" He thought his legs were going to give way under him, but they didn't and they wouldn't and another, older, deeper part of him knew it. Such happiness, such ridiculous, foolish happiness—it earned nothing, it achieved no goal, it had no tangible value; it made no *sense*! But his son had returned to him safe and well, and both his children were clutching at his hands and trying to pull him into the dance, and he was laughing and shouting like a child himself and he *wanted* to dance, he *wanted* to dance, like the old days, the days when something more than money and position had mattered!

Then from the unlit street behind him, another world away now it seemed, a woman cried out in shock and anguish.

"It's Mama!" Koru spun round, and Hollend spun, too, in time to see Calpurna come running into the square with Nas's wife panting behind her. As he looked at Calpurna's haggard face the spell almost broke, for in her stark expression was all the power that years under the influence of Joyful Travail had wrought, and for a moment Hollend's newfound world threatened to collapse.

But before he could move, before he could speak, Koru sprang forward.

"Mama!" He saw Calpurna's mouth contort with shock and his own lips widened in a huge smile. "Mama, look what I've brought home for you!" He ran to her, holding up a shining sphere, a perfect twin to the one with which Ellani had ensnared their father. "Here it is, Mama! Catch the ball!"

\* \* \*

So it began, and so each new link was forged, one following another and another and another as the great chain began to grow. The first barrier had been breached when the citizens and elders of Joyful Travail awoke to find their town aglitter with vast cascades of worthless and useless debris, for the sheer physical scale of the transformation was too great for even their rationality to withstand. They could not ignore the outrage, but though they strove not to see its perpetrators, not to hear their singing voices, not to believe in the hands that snatched the streamers from them even as they tried to clear them away, the breaching of the dam had paved the way for its complete collapse. The children were prancing like dervishes, weaving among the crowd, and people cried out in confusion and fright as they glimpsed the momentary whirl of spectral hair or the dazzle of a phantom skirt, or found themselves impulsively responding to a fleeting but lovely smile. Confusion spiraled as more and more bewildered newcomers arrived, drawn by the noise. Emerging from the houses in the square, hurrying from the surrounding streets or from the Foreigners' Enclave and Duty House, they were swept willy-nilly into the chaos. Indigo had abandoned her harp now, and she and her friends were in the thick of it, dancers in a rapidly growing circle that spread outward from the wagon; Mimino and Koru and Hollend and Calpurna and Ellani and Nemesis, all linking hands, calling others to join in their whirling celebration. Then a new cry began to rise, at first hard to distinguish amid the uproar but quickly becoming clearer and clearer.

*"Catch the ball! Catch the ball!"*

Soul to mind, ghost-form to living physical body, the children of the otherworld found the selves who had abandoned them, and worked the Benefactor's magic. A woman, her face rapt, broke into the circle at Indigo's side to join the dancers, and there was one less ghost-child in the square. Two youths came in on the other side and one kissed Calpurna while the other grabbed Koru's hand and whirled him round; a portly man, red-faced and wheezing with laughter and exertion, capered beside Mimino; and three more of the children were no longer to be seen.

On the steps of the Committee House Aunt Osiku and her companions ranted and shouted, unable to credit that they were powerless to stop the anarchy before them. What they saw, how the mad scene appeared to their still-shrouded eyes, no one could say and few cared. But suddenly a small girl so covered in streamers that she was barely visible ran from the crowd and up the Committee House steps, slowing to a halt in front of the elders' delegation. In one ebullient movement she flung off her adornments—and Aunt Osiku gave a horrified yell as for one instant, before her mind blotted it out, she saw her own youthful face grinning at her above a transparent body.

"Catch the ball, Osiku!"

And moments later the child was no longer there and Aunt Osiku stood wringing her hands on the steps with tears of nostalgia streaming from her eyes.

Like an inundation bringing life to a withered land, the intoxicating celebration of Joyful Travail's reawakening spread out from the market square. A joyfully shouting company of phantom children, with Aunt Osiku at their head, stormed the sacrosanct bastions of the Committee House, and in rooms throughout the building the cry echoed—*"Catch the ball, catch the ball!"*—before a stream of elders and secretaries and menials came dancing out through the great doors to join the spree. On the far side of the square someone had torn a wooden shutter from a window and was banging it with a stick in time to the calling-song, which now was being roared to the sky by a multitude of throats; others, grasping at the idea and delighted by it, snatched up anything they could find that would make a noise, and their impromptu band zestfully thumped out the rhythm of the hectic dance. People grabbed armfuls of streamers and hurled them at anyone and everyone within reach; a tug-o'-war began with a hastily plaited streamer rope, the participants laughing helplessly as they fell over each other's feet in their efforts to win. Everywhere there was noise and color and hilarity and undisguised zeal for life. And Grimya had one moment of sheer delight when, jumping and playing, snapping at the bright ribbons as they flickered through the air, she suddenly saw Thia among the crowd.

Thia was at present working at the Foreigners' Duty House and had been asleep in her small cubicle there when Nas Kishikul had arrived. With her keen nose for trouble she had attached herself to the party that set off after Hollend, and had arrived at the square to meet the full riotous flood of events head-on. Now she was pressed flat to a house wall at the corner of the street, and she was terrified. She couldn't deny what her senses were telling her, no matter how hard she struggled, and she was grasping desperately at the belief that she had fallen ill with a fever that had made her go quite mad. This was not happening. It was *not* happening. And when the gray dog that, once, had spoken to her in human tongue (but of course it hadn't, it *hadn't*; that, too, was part of the fever-dream) came rushing toward her with a ghostly child at its heels, and the child shouted, "Catch the ball, Thia! Catch the ball!" Thia didn't catch the ball but instead screamed at the top of her voice and ran like a hunted rabbit.

Her flight was doomed to failure. At a barked prompt from Grimya, the ghost-child—who was, of course, Thia's own doppelgänger—sprang onto the she-wolf's back and, riding her like a horse, gave chase. A group of young men and girls saw the fun and joined in, and Thia was trapped by the Committee House door. They caught hold of her, decked her with streamers, and then with a chorus of "*One!* and *two!* and *three!*" they lifted her between them and threw her kicking and shrieking into the air. Five times Thia flew up and came down to be safely caught, and when the game was done her captors covered her cheeks with kisses before the ghost-girl wriggled between them, pushed the magic ball into Thia's unresisting hands with a triumphant smile, then vanished.

Away across the square Indigo hadn't witnessed Thia's transformation and didn't so much as glimpse the juvenile as she went reeling dizzily away in the midst of her new friends. Indigo had other preoccupations: the dancing circle had become three concentric circles as yet more people joined in, and by this time almost all the participants were not phantom figures but the townsfolk of Joyful Travail. The children were rapidly becoming fewer and fewer in number as each glittering sphere found its mark, and the calling-song went faster and more avidly, *dance with us in the merry ring*, voices and rhythms and stamping, skipping feet in a glorious clamor together. So engrossed was Indigo, so caught up in the festive spirit of it all, that she didn't notice the change taking place at the heart of the square, and at first didn't hear the voice that shouted urgently to her both aloud and in her mind.

*"Anghara! Anghara, Sister!"*

At last, abruptly, it registered. Someone calling her name—not Indigo, but her real name, Anghara, which almost nobody knew. She broke step in confusion, looking over her shoulder, and saw Nemesis forging through the throng toward her. The being's eyes were wild and one slender hand gestured toward the pump where the wagon still stood. In her head, then, Indigo heard the distraught message.

*Anghara! The gateway!*

She stopped dead, and was barged out of the circle as the neighboring dancers, unable and unwilling to halt their own momentum, loosed her hands and went on without her. Regaining her balance Indigo looked toward the pump.

The bright arch, the doorway into the otherworld, was fading. Even now it had only a glimmer of its former brilliance, and the green hills on the far side had lost their color and turned to cloudy gray. Indigo stared at the gateway, not immediately comprehending. Then Nemesis had reached her and gripped her arm, swinging her around and looking into her face with desperation.

"Anghara, what of Fenran? *What of Fenran?*"

"Oh, no . . ." Understanding began to dawn, and with it horror. He was still there—Fenran was still there in the ghost-world, and the ghost-world was fading . . .

"Sweet Mother, no, *NO*!!" Startled heads turned as Indigo flung herself toward the arch. She and Nemesis reached it together; their hands went through, their arms, their heads, and suddenly Indigo felt an enormous force pushing her back, denying her, as the gateway began to disappear altogether.

*"DEAR GODDESS, HELP ME!"* She screamed the words with all her strength and, with Nemesis's hand gripped in hers, flung herself forward. It was as though a thousand tons of solid stone were pressing down on her, crushing the breath from her lungs, crushing flesh and bone—then with a yell she fell through the vanishing warp between dimensions and rolled onto the grass of the otherworld.

Gray grass. She saw it as she began shakily to rise to her knees, and she froze inwardly. Gray grass, its color gone, drained away. Swiftly she looked up, and before her she saw nothing but gray, stretching away to the horizon. Gray hills, smudged against gray sky. The gray trees of ghostly woodlands, dim and barely distinguishable. This world, the children's haven that they no longer needed, was dying.

A voice to her left said: "Sister . . ." Nemesis was rising, slowly and a little unsteadily, and Indigo felt a turbulent rush of relief at the knowledge that the being, her twin, herself, had come safely through the gateway with her. But the gateway itself . . .

It was gone. There was no shining arch, no reflection, not the smallest sign to show where moments ago the door between this world and Joyful Travail had been.

Indigo and Nemesis stared at it in silence. Neither knew whether this or any other door would—or could—open again to allow them to return to Joyful Travail. Beyond the barrier, Indigo realized, was Grimya—had the wolf seen what they had done and what had become of them? If she had she would be distraught, frantic yet helpless, even her telepathic abilities unable to penetrate the wall between dimensions. But at this moment even that didn't count to Indigo. One thing and one thing alone mattered, and when she looked at Nemesis again she knew that they were, truly and finally, one.

The indigo-eyed child pointed toward a faint and distant haze of what might, once, have been a forest.

"That way, Sister." A glance that said far more than any words seared Indigo momentarily. "And pray to the Great Mother that we're not too late!"

Their fingers twined, locked. Like ghosts in a world of empty memories, yet with a shared purpose that burned in them both like a furnace fire, they began to run.

Gray; nothing but gray. Grass and hills and trees and sky, a thin monochrome that depressed and sometimes deceived the eye. The warm, kindly light of the otherworld had dulled to a dismal overcast, and distances were hard to judge. Indigo and Nemesis seemed to have been running for hours without cease and without making any worthwhile progress. Indigo thought that a vague smudge between two indistinct hills ahead might be the woodland of the sleeping man's tower, but in this flat, colorless landscape it was no longer possible to be sure. The air had a stale taste, and the ghost-world no longer imbued them with energy; running was an effort, a strain, and Indigo's legs and lungs ached from exertion. And in all the land they neither heard nor saw any trace of another living presence.

But at last, though later it was hard to remember quite how it had happened, they reached the woodland and were racing down the last gentle slope toward the trees. No dark, rich green mass of foliage now, Indigo noticed with a new uneasy pang; the forest looked more like a bank of mist, the trees' outlines uncertain and bare of any detail. Entering the wood was an eerie experience, for it felt as insubstantial as it looked. Chill silence pervaded the atmosphere; not so much as a leaf stirred as they passed and once, unnervingly, Indigo touched the bole of a tree only to see her hand pass through it with no sensation, as though nothing was there.

"Hurry, Sister!" Nemesis's voice carried ominously in the stillness; a glimmer of fear laced the being's tone. "We have so little time!"

Indigo's thigh muscles felt as though they were on fire, but she forced herself to quicken her pace. *Faster, they must go faster . . . so little time . . .* The undergrowth beneath her feet was nothing more than a blur now, fading slowly into a blank and shapeless void, and she could no longer distinguish the forms of individual trees. Nemesis was a few paces ahead, and when the being suddenly uttered a cry and pointed forward, Indigo felt the warring clutches of relief and dread as she ran to join her twin.

They had reached the clearing. But the floor of the clearing was a featureless pool of nothingness, and the squat tower, though still visible, was a vague mirage floating at its center.

"Oh, Goddess . . ." Sickness welled from Indigo's stomach into her throat; she choked it back, staring at the tower and breathing hard and harshly. Could she reach it, or was that emptiness, that nothing, a deadly trap . . . ?

Her hand was caught suddenly and Nemesis stepped in front of her, gazing into her face.

"We must try. Whatever becomes of us, we must *try*."

Beyond Nemesis's slender figure the image of the tower quivered like a reflection in disturbed water. There was no time to consider, no time to think; within minutes it would be gone. Indigo nodded once, and together she and Nemesis stepped into the clearing.

Though they felt as if they trod on empty air, the ground beneath them was solid. Knowing that at any moment that might change, Indigo and Nemesis ran to the tower door. It was closed, but the substance had drained from it, and as they passed through it collapsed to nothing around them. The tower walls enfolded them, giving an illusion of substance; but it *was* only an illusion, for the shapes of the stone blocks were tenuous and unclear. And there, across the circular room, stood the high-backed chair where the sleeping man had his resting place.

And the chair had an occupant.

"Fenran . . . ?" Indigo hardly dared whisper his name for fear that even that small sound would shatter the tower's fragile and diminishing existence. Hand in hand still, she and Nemesis moved across the room—and looked down on the sleeping face and dark hair of her lost love.

"Fenran . . ." Hope leapt in Indigo, giddying and all-consuming. This time, *this* time, what she craved could come to pass; the power was within her, a part of her, flowing between her and the twin, the other Indigo, the other Anghara, who knelt at her side before the chair. As one their hands reached out, touched Fenran's face, and as their fingers made contact with his skin a flicker of movement passed like a breath across his closed eyelids.

"Fenran." Their voices were one as their hands were one. "My love, my dearest love. Awake. *Awake*."

The brown hands that rested so limply on the chair's arms moved. The fingers clenched as a spasm went through them. A sigh issued from Fenran's throat . . . then his gray eyes opened drowsily and, like one slowly emerging from a dream, he saw her.

"Anghara . . . Great Mother, great Goddess—*Anghara*!"

Indigo felt then as though every day, every hour of her existence had fused together into this one moment. No longer an illusion, no longer a dream, no longer a fleeting promise to be snatched away. This was true. This was real. Fenran had come back to her.

And from somewhere beyond them, deep in the wood, came a great, soughing sigh.

*"Sister!"* Nemesis sprang upright in alarm, and looked wildly around. *"The tower!"*

Shocked out of her newfound joy by the real terror in Nemesis's tone, Indigo looked up.

The tower was vanishing. Already its walls were becoming transparent, showing the blurred shadows of the wood as though through a murky window, and even as Indigo's eyes widened in horror the stones gave a last, dying shudder and faded from sight.

And from the chair, Fenran cried, "Ah, no, *no!*"

*"Fenran!"* Indigo's voice was a shriek of protest and terror. She spun back to the chair, Nemesis only an instant behind her—and was in time to see Fenran's figure turn to a gray ghost in a spectral gray chair that began to fade away into nothing.

*"NO! NO!!"* Frantically she grasped at his hand, but his hand had no substance; she couldn't hold him. She hurled herself forward, striving to catch hold of his body and pull him back from the grip of the dying world of phantoms, but her fingers closed on mist, on emptiness. He was shouting her name, his voice echoing as though from a huge and unreachable distance, and Indigo screamed back, fighting, struggling. The world seemed to invert into a sickening vortex, and for one instant she thought she'd succeeded, for suddenly she felt him, his clothes, his hair, solid and real in her clasp, and suddenly there were tangible walls around

them again, physical stone, slanting sunlight, a place she
knew—

*a single unfurnished chamber, naked earth and naked
stone; and a strange metal chest, not quite silver, not quite
bronze, not quite a steely blue-gray. And there was a time,
a time and a time, before we who live now under the sun
and the sky came to count time—*

Then out of the strengthening stone walls came a blast of
force, an enormous psychic punch that buffeted her violently backward. She lost her hold on Fenran, grabbed
wildly but found nothing; and then she was flung out of the
bare chamber, away and back to the ghost-world, to sprawl
empty-handed on the blank and featureless ground where
the tower and the woodland had been.

Indigo didn't move. Eyes tightly shut, breath held fast in
her throat, she was praying silently over and over again that
she was wrong, that it hadn't happened, that when at last
she mustered the courage to look she would find Fenran
awake and alive and by her side. It must be so. It must. It
*must*.

Something touched her hair. She tensed. And a voice that
was not Fenran's, but that was filled with a grief and sorrow
to match her own, said: "Anghara."

Nemesis was kneeling beside her. Indigo raised her head,
and the last vestige of hope seeped away. The clearing was
empty and the last shadows of the woodland slowly dissolv-
ing away. The sleeping man's tower was gone, and in the
last moments of its existence it had taken Fenran's awakening spirit and sent it back to become one again with his
physical form.

She could have done it. She could have brought him
through, spirit and body together, as she herself had come
through to this world. One minute, no more, would have
turned dismal failure to joyous success. One minute to
strengthen the link, to open the door between dimensions.
She had *seen* the door; she had looked through it, she had

touched and held Fenran briefly as his living body awoke in that other place, and had she just been granted a few seconds more she could have held him and brought him through. Instead . . .

She started to sob, a choking, ugly sound that the empty world threw back in a flat echo. Nemesis moved toward her, stood before her, and the being's arms went around her in a wordless attempt to comfort. Together they stood for some moments, their tears mingling. Then, slowly, the distinction between that which was Indigo and that which was Nemesis began to blur, until only one solitary figure, head bowed so that her auburn hair hid her face from view, and her silver-flecked indigo eyes filled with tears, stood alone and desolate in the gray emptiness of what had once been a forest clearing.

# ·CHAPTER·XXII·

The Benefactor found her there, as he had known he would. Though the woodland trees were by now no more than faint impressions, too slight to conceal him, she was unaware of his approach and only when he spoke her name, very softly, did she raise her head.

The Benefactor looked sadly at her and said: "Indigo, I am so very sorry."

Indigo gazed back at him. Somewhere in a remote corner of her mind she was struggling to find words with which to rail at him for what had surely been a monstrous deception and betrayal. But in truth she knew that he hadn't deceived or betrayed her. As fallible, as mortal, as human as she was, he had believed—as she had—that all would be well. And, aware now of the terrible mistake he had made, he felt her grief and his remorse, like a knife twisting in his soul.

She could offer him no solace; nor could she hate or even reproach him. When she did finally speak, her voice was sterile, lifeless.

"One more minute. That would have been enough."

"I know. I tried ... I tried to hold it back, but I did not have the strength. I think it would have been beyond the power of any mortal man."

Strangely she didn't doubt that he *had* done all he could; all anyone could. She nodded.

"What will you do now?" the Benefactor asked. She had the impression that the answer was important to him, but she didn't reply, only lifted her shoulders in the smallest of shrugs.

"Grimya is waiting for you," the Benefactor said gently. "And this world is waiting, too, for its last occupants to leave." He took three slow steps toward her. "Come with me, Indigo. There is nothing more for either of us to do here. Let us return home together."

Indigo said bleakly: "Home ... ?" And suddenly a memory stirred. *There was a time, a time and a time, before we who live now under the sun and the sky came to count time ...* She felt a clutching sensation within her chest as though something had taken physical hold of her heart and squeezed it as the memory clarified and brought revelation.

She knew where Fenran was. Not only his soul, not his sleeping mind, not his image—but Fenran, whole and alive. She knew. She *knew*.

Her head came up again, quickly, and in her mind a slow but hot fire began to ignite. Not the fire of faith, not yet; she didn't dare to give it rein yet. But the first spark of renewed hope. The Benefactor saw it in her eyes, and he smiled a sweet, sad, wistful smile as he reached out to her.

"Come, my dear friend. I will show you the way."

His fingers were as cool and dry as parchment, and frail to her touch, as though they might at any moment break and crumble like brittle leaves. With his other hand he traced a sigil before them and the outline of a tall mirror appeared, hanging in the air. Within the mirror's frame daylight

slanted down from high and dusty windows into a bare, neglected room.

"This is the last of the gateways," the Benefactor said
very quietly. "When it closes again it will be for the final
time, for this world is no longer needed."

He made a courtly gesture, and Indigo preceded him to
the glimmering glass. She looked back one last time at the
fading shadows of the ghost-world—truly a ghost-world
now—and then she stepped into the mirror. The tingling
sensation as she passed between dimensions was familiar
now and lasted only a moment before dark, muted colors
swirled where before there had been only gray, and she
stood in the empty hexagonal room on the top floor of the
Benefactor's House.

Behind her there was silence, and abruptly she realized
that the Benefactor had not followed her. Puzzled, she
turned around and saw his figure looking at her through the
glass. For a dismaying moment she saw doubt and fear in
his expression and was convinced that he had changed his
mind and intended to remain in the ghost-world. She
reached toward him in alarm—but before her hand could
touch the mirror the Benefactor seemed to give a great
though inaudible sigh, and the glass shimmered as he, too,
stepped through into the mortal world.

The Benefactor's gaze traveled slowly about. There was
little here to see, but his eyes drank in each small detail as
avidly as those of any pilgrim visiting the House and standing in its most venerated room for the very first time. Then,
softly, he laughed.

"A temple to the god of Reason," he said, and Indigo suspected that he was speaking to himself rather than to her. "It
is a very sad paradox. But then, I never wanted a shrine to
my name, and so perhaps this is appropriate." With mea-
sured steps he walked toward the roped-off plinth, where
the ancient crown sat in lonely splendor on its solitary cushion. "They will come here soon from the town, to unlock

the gates and dance in the garden. And that will be only the beginning, for they will carry their newfound joy wherever they go, and it will spread outward until every part of this land is imbued with it." He smiled. "One might say that it will be like a contagion, but I hardly think that is an appropriate simile, do you? Even for a physician?"

Indigo returned the smile. "No. Not even for a physician."

"What they will ultimately make of this House, and what they will do with it, I do not pretend to know. But there will be no more need of Aunt Nikku and her kind to keep it safe from unworthy hands." He paused, then turned to face Indigo. "How can I ever find adequate words to thank you, Indigo? Such words as would express it do not exist. And as for deeds . . ." He shook his head helplessly. "I thought I would be able to repay you, but instead I have failed you."

He looked old suddenly, Indigo thought, his hair grayer, his skin slack and pallid. Old, and forlorn, and lonely . . . She went to him and touched his hand. "If you did fail, it was not through any fault of your own."

"You offer me more kindness than I deserve."

"No, I don't think so. For you gave me . . ." She hesitated. How could she define what he had given to her? It was the gift of sight after fifty years of blindness; but that allegory alone could not even come close to the whole truth of it, for it was so much more than that. At last, simply, and believing he would understand, she touched her own heart lightly and looked up at him. Silver glimmered in her eyes and she said, "You gave me myself."

His hand closed over hers. "Ah, Indigo . . . if I can believe that that is true . . ."

"It is true." In chagrin then she saw that two tears were trickling down his cheeks, which now were deeply furrowed. And his hair . . . It was receding, it was white, thin, little more than a frail nimbus . . . With a terrible sense of foreboding Indigo began to realize what was happening to him.

"Benefactor—" Her fingers tightened on his and she felt the bones, so thin, almost fleshless. "Benefactor, you—"

"My dear friend, my dear friend." Gently he pulled his hand away. "It is nothing. It is only what has been inevitable."

His deep brown eyes were rheumy now, his full lips seamed and sunken, and his frame seemed to have shrunk inside the robe he wore so that its folds hung about him like a shroud. And Indigo knew that the Benefactor was dying. Years ago—centuries ago—he had found a kind of immortality in the ghost-world, and while he remained in that haven time had had no meaning for him. But now he had returned to the world of physical flesh, and in this world time could not be denied.

She remembered then what he had said to her, a long time ago it seemed now, at their second encounter in the woodland clearing. He had known from the beginning what would become of him if he should return to the mortal realm; he had spoken of it then, calmly and with certainty. Yet with the final departure of the children to work his last, triumphant magic in Joyful Travail, the ghost-world that had sheltered him for so long had no further reason to exist. There was no haven left for him. Only a choice between emptiness and death.

"Don't grieve for me, Indigo." His voice was no more than a dry whisper now, like the dust stirring in this empty room. "I am glad it is over at last; whatever lies ahead of me, oblivion or something else, I will welcome it, I think."

She could hardly bear to look at his face, for the changes were coming more swiftly, speeding him toward the end, and the ancient, shriveled man before her bore only a faint resemblance to the Benefactor she had known.

"I know your thoughts," he said, "and I thank you for them. But I am beyond the reach or need of any physician."

A painful chuckle; he was gently teasing her, she realized. "Yet if you would grant me one final boon, I will ask a service of you."

"Anything." Her voice caught on the last syllable. *"Anything."*

He nodded. He could barely stand upright now. "I have a last task that I wish to perform, but my strength is failing and it may be beyond me. Please, if you will, take my arm and help me to the plinth."

She did as he asked her, and with difficulty, leaning heavily on the support she gave him, he shuffled to where the crown lay. His hands were crabbed and shaking and he could barely lift the ancient thing, but he clutched it tightly to his chest and turned around until he was facing the mirror. Then:

"No. No, I cannot do it; I no longer have the strength. You must do it for me, Indigo."

He swayed; she held him. "What must I do?"

"Two birds with one arrow, my dear friend. Two birds with one arrow. Take the crown and throw it at the mirror."

Trembling, he pushed the crown toward her. She caught it as his fingers lost their grip, felt its chilly patina.

"Now," the Benefactor said, and there was elation in his voice. *"Now."*

She threw. Her aim was true; the crown struck the mirror almost at its center, and the glass shattered as the wooden frame collapsed. For one instant a blinding light filled the room—then it was gone, and all that remained of the mirror was a litter of glittering fragments strewn about the floor. And the crown . . .

The crown lay amid the wreckage. It had sheared in half, and even as Indigo looked at it the two pieces began to change. They darkened, twisted; she heard a faint, abrasive sound, like rust scraping, then the thin *snap* of old metal giving way. Before her gaze the ancient, broken crown of the Benefactor and his ancestors crumbled to dust and was gone.

A sound like the creaking of a tree branch issued from the Benefactor's throat. "It is over. At last it is over. My last wish is granted; I have seen the end of this unhappy epoch." He turned with difficulty to Indigo. "You have made me happy."

He collapsed suddenly, and, taken unawares, Indigo barely managed to catch him as he fell. She lowered him to the floor—there was nowhere else—and he lay gazing filmily up at her, his breath coming with great difficulty now. But despite his weakness he could still smile, and he could still speak.

"I think there shall be no more regretting," he whispered. "But, perhaps, for one thing." He tried to laugh but only achieved a thin wheeze. "I wish that I could recall . . ."

"Recall . . . ?" Indigo prompted softly when he did not continue.

"Recall . . . what it was, so long ago, so very long ago . . ." He faltered, struggled on. "To be kissed by a woman who . . . loved me . . ."

Indigo said nothing. But she leaned forward and, slowly and deliberately and with great gentleness, planted a kiss upon the withered lips that trembled in the shrunken face. She felt no repulsion, no distaste, no sense of the grotesque. It was simply her own answer and her own farewell to a cherished friend.

She saw him smile, saw his eyes close for the last time, and she rose to her feet and turned away, knowing that time was not done with him even in death, not wanting to see the final transformation. Glass splintered under her feet as she crossed the room, and she wished that she could have reached the high windows and flung them open to let in the day.

Then, distantly, she heard the sounds. Voices—many voices, raised in song, and behind them the thump and thud of gleefully improvised percussion: sticks and staves and cooking pots and field and kitchen implements in joyous, jumping rhythm. And in the midst of the din, faint but unmistakable, the sweet, silvery jingle of harness bells.

*They will come here soon from the town, to unlock the gates and dance in the garden . . .* She recalled the Benefactor's words, his belief that the new spirit of Joyful Travail would be carried and radiated abroad from the town to spread its light throughout the entire Nation of Prosperity. Listening now to the singing, the rhythms, the whole cheerful noise of the approaching procession, Indigo had no doubt of it. What human heart, no matter how sour and crabbed, could resist such a tide of happiness? They would succumb; they would *all* succumb. Joyful Travail's blithe citizens would give them no choice. It grieved her that the Benefactor had not lived to see his prophesy fulfilled, but she hoped—and, in a quiet and private level of her mind, believed—that, wherever his soul had gone, he would hear the merriment and rejoice with his people. And perhaps that was the most fitting epitaph of all.

The procession would be here within minutes and she wanted to see them arrive. Above all she wanted to see Grimya, who she knew would be riding on the wagon. Even now she could feel the wolf's mind eagerly seeking her—how had Grimya known? she wondered—but though she ached to reach out in response she forced herself to hold back. Just a few moments more and she would call out in return; then they would be reunited and she would greet her beloved friend and hold her and hug her and kiss her. There would be other friends to greet, too; Koru and Ellani, Hollend and Calpurna and Mimino; even Thia and Uncle Choai and Aunt Osiku. The rifts of the past were lost now and forgotten, for the Benefactor had brought back the magic he had stolen from Joyful Travail so long ago. Now the true healing, that which was beyond the power of any single physician, would begin.

And for herself . . . ah, yes. For herself there would be a new dawning, as significant in its own way as the dawn breaking over Joyful Travail. She, too, was healed, and though she had touched Fenran only to lose him again, this time—unlike the other times, which had ended in delusion and grief—there was not merely hope, but promise. For the first time Fenran was truly within her reach, for she knew where to find him. Not in a dimension of demons, not in an impossible limbo, but in this world, in a place separated from her only by a sea voyage. What the place was now after fifty years, what it signified to the people who once had been her own people, Indigo didn't know. But she could name it. The Tower of Regrets . . .

Within her, in a place so deep and so primal that she could not name it, a presence stirred. Her enemy, but an enemy no longer. Nemesis had a new name now, and they were one.

Silver gleamed anew in Indigo's eyes as she thought the words, felt the words. *"Sister, I am going home. We are going home."*

She turned from the window. It was hard to steel herself to look toward the plinth, for she didn't know what she might see there and, not knowing, she imagined the worst. But there was nothing. No decaying corpse, no brown bones, no ancient robes disintegrating in the dust. At the very last, time had been kind, and had granted the Benefactor's mortal remains the dignity—perhaps the ultimate dignity—of nonexistence.

Indigo smiled a bittersweet smile and whispered: "Goodbye, my dear friend."

The barren, empty room at the top of the House repeated her words in a soft echo that died slowly away into silence. For the space of five heartbeats Indigo stood motionless, looking at the place where the Benefactor had been, listening to the triumphant voices coming nearer and nearer to the House.

> *Everyone, everyone, play and sing!*
> *Dance with us in the merry ring!*

Pain and pleasure and glory together swelled in Indigo's heart, and she ran down the stairs and out into the morning.